WAR

Simon Hawke

WAR

Random House and its affiliate companies have worldwide distribution rights in the book trade for English language products of TSR, Inc.

Distributed to the book and hobby trade in the United Kingdom by TSR Ltd.

Distributed to the toy and hobby trade by regional distributors.

Cover art by Tony Szczudlo. Jacket Design by Dawn Murin.

BIRTHRIGHT and the TSR logo are trademarks owned by TSR, Inc.

All TSR characters, character names, and the distinctive likenesses thereof are trademarks owned by TSR, Inc.

First Printing: May 1996
Printed in the United States of America.
Library of Congress Catalog Card Number: 95-62205

9 8 7 6 5 4 3 2 1

ISBN: 0-7869-0495-X
3133XXX1501

TSR, Inc.
201 Sheridan Springs Road
Lake Geneva, WI 53147
U.S.A.

TSR Ltd.
120 Church End, Cherry Hinton
Cambridge CB1 3LB
United Kingdom

BIRTHRIGHT™ Books
by Simon Hawke

The Iron Throne

War

In Memory of Amanda

"...and flights of angels sing thee to thy rest."

Hamlet, Act V, Scene II
William Shakespeare

Acknowledgments

I would like to thank some special people who have provided immense support and encouragement throughout the writing of this novel, and through some very trying times that accompanied it. If a man's wealth is measured by his friends, then I am very rich indeed.

My very deepest gratitude to Robert M. Powers, Sandra West, Janis Gemetta, David Foster, Heather Bowman, James and Margie Kosky, Bruce and Peggy Wiley, Philip E. Fletcher, Brian Thomsen and all the good people at TSR, all my good friends in the ECS and SCA, and others I may have failed to mention due to terminal exhaustion. You know who you are and you know how I feel. Thank you one and all.

prologue

The stench of death on the evening breeze was overpowering. There was a thrumming in the air from the buzzing of the flies, thousands of them, swarming over the bloody corpses on the battle-field as the sun slowly sank behind the mountains. Katrina lifted her riding skirt as she walked among the broken bodies littering the churned up ground, looking to see if she could recognize any of them.

There was Cedric, the archer, who had taught her to shoot when she was a little girl and neither of her brothers would agree to show her how, because they said it wasn't ladylike. Dark blood matted his thick gray beard as he lay sprawled out on the ground, eyes and mouth open, flies clustered on his gaping wounds. One arm still held his crossbow, but the arm was no longer attached to his body. It lay beside him, hacked off, on a patch of bare ground dark with all the blood that had soaked in. And there, just a few yards beyond, was Gavilan, captain of the horse guard, who had helped her train her first colt. He would never ride again. Unhorsed by a spear that still transfixed him, the sharp angle giving testimony to how it had been thrust upward by a foot soldier. The spear had caught Gavilan in a vulnerable spot just beneath the arm, where he had no armor to protect him. He had probably raised his sword to bring it down on his antagonist, who had been lucky enough to strike first.

Katrina could almost picture it, how the spear had been thrust upward just as Gavilan had raised his blade and leaned down from the saddle, his momentum as he rode helping drive the iron tip right through his coat of mail as the spearman braced against the ground. A fluke. The spearman might easily have missed and struck the breastplate; the tip would have glanced off; the shaft might have been snapped. The odds of getting it just right, maintaining balance as the spear ripped through the mail and passed into the chest . . . Gavilan must have been dead before he hit the ground. His helm was open, with just the steel nasal jutting down between his eyes, which were open and staring blankly at the sky.

I should be horrified, thought Katrina. I should be in tears. My body should be racked with sobs, as Mother's was when they brought Father home. I should be feeling . . . something.

Instead, she just felt numb. She walked like a somnambulist among the carnage, the cool breeze ruffling her long red hair as the sun set slowly behind the mountains. It was as if she were somehow apart from herself, in the middle of it all, yet at the same time disconnected from it.

Katrina paused as she spotted Branmor's crest on a white tabard soaked with blood. Tall and handsome, blond and blue-eyed Branmor, who had danced with her not two weeks earlier at the feast held in honor of Lady Lydia's sixteenth birthday. Katrina had reveled in the jealous looks she got from the other young ladies of the court as she and Branmor led the promenade, his eyes never leaving her as they danced. His visored helm had been split by a powerful blow from a short battle-axe, and Katrina was grateful she could not see his face. The blade of the axe had cut through almost to the collarbone and was still embedded there grotesquely. Somehow, despite the graphic evidence, it did not look real.

None of it looked real. The scene was like a frozen image from some nightmare. Many of the bodies were draped over one another, as if they had been dumped there from a loaded charnel wagon. And too many had faces that she knew. Some had no faces left at all. She had to pick her footing carefully as she walked among them.

Had she wanted to, she could have crossed the battlefield without ever setting foot upon the ground, just by stepping from corpse to corpse to corpse.

Katrina had never seen a dead body before. She had always been sheltered from such things. Now, she was surrounded by hundreds of them, strewn across the battlefield like discarded dolls. Unnaturally stiff and already bloating from hours of lying in the open under the summer sun. The battle had taken place that morning between the forces of Derwyn of Boeruine and Kier of Avan, two of the most powerful dukes in the crumbling empire, and this was the grisly aftermath of their ambition. Nothing had been settled. Each wanted to sit upon the Iron Throne now that the emperor was dead, slain by the Gorgon with no heir to take his place. Each commanded armies that had met in battle after fighting a number of small skirmishes designed to test the other's borders. And each had retired with what forces they had left when it became apparent that if they continued, their armies would simply slaughter one another. No clear victory for either side was in the offing.

Neither of them could afford to sustain extremely heavy losses. A few hundred men here and there could be replaced eventually, but greater losses would leave them undermanned and vulnerable, at least in the short term, to attack by any of the dozen or more other aspirants to the Anuirean crown. So they had prudently withdrawn to fight another day. And all these men had died, essentially, for nothing.

So this was war, thought Katrina.

She tried to imagine what it must have been like in the heat of battle, with men sweltering in some sixty pounds of armor and grunting with exertion as they fought, while the morning sun rose higher and the choking dust raised by all the churning feet and hooves coated their parched throats, already raw from screaming. She could almost hear the din, the cacophonous clangor of the blades, the neighing of the horses, the shouts of the commanders, the cries of the wounded and dying, all blending together like the howling of some gigantic and terrifying beast.

Thank the gods that I am not a man, she thought.

Her father had been brought home on a stretcher, and if he managed to survive his wounds, the physic said he would be crippled.

3

Her brothers had not come home at all. Both of them were lying out here somewhere. She had come out to look for them, but now she didn't want to find them. She had thought, perhaps, if they were wounded . . . but there was no sound on the battlefield at all. No moans. No cries. Nothing. Just an eerie stillness.

And the buzzing of the flies.

"Terrible, is it not?" a low voice said from behind her. A woman's voice. Katrina turned.

Standing a short distance away was a figure dressed in a dark, woolen cloak with a hood covering her head. The cloak came down to her ankles and she carried a long wooden staff. The hood kept her features in shadow, so Katrina couldn't make them out. In the twilight, she saw only darkness where the face should be. A shiver passed through her. It was as if Death were standing there, looking out over its melancholy domain.

But this figure was flesh and blood, a woman like herself. Doubtless, Katrina thought, this woman had come out to the battlefield in search of fallen kin, just as Katrina had. As the woman approached, Katrina could make out strands of long blond hair escaping from under her hood. As she came closer still, Katrina could see how beautiful the woman truly was. Her features were fine and delicate; her skin, like porcelain. She looked young, but there was something about her gaze that did not speak at all of youth.

"Terrible," the woman repeated as she gazed out across the battlefield, "and yet, at the same time, magnificent."

"Magnificent?" said Katrina, astonished at the comment, so bizarre and inappropriate.

"Indeed," the woman said, her gaze sweeping the awful scene around them. Her voice was throaty and sensual. "Do you not find it so? Does it not overwhelm you? Does it not seize you with its terrible majesty? Is it not almost more than your senses can encompass?"

"Yes," said Katrina, following her gaze. "Yes, I suppose it is, when you put it that way."

"There are few things in this world that can be so magnificent and terrible as war," the woman said, still gazing at the battlefield as the shadows lengthened. "It represents man in his true element, enacting nature's endless drama, the survival of the fittest." She turned

4

to Katrina. "Have you ever seen two colonies of ants at war?"
Katrina shook her head.

The woman smiled. "Well, perhaps you have and simply didn't
pay attention. Boys are much more apt to notice such things. They
will stop and stare for hours, enraptured by the struggle. Two tiny
armies, each as organized as any that men could ever field, even
more so, if truth be told. Locked in their grim struggle, one force attacking, one defending, they will fight for hours, sometimes even
days, oblivious to any small boy who stops to watch them. And in-
evitably, when that boy grows tired of the spectacle, he will kick
over the anthill and stamp upon the ants . . . without even really
knowing why. Then he grows up to be a man, and joins an army,
and becomes caught up in the same struggle. And regardless of
whatever else he may have managed to accomplish in his life, war
reduces him to the same size as that ant. And the gods look down
and watch, just as that small boy once did. There is an irony in that,
and a clue to the mystery of life."

"I never thought of it that way before," said Katrina, turning to
look out across the darkening battlefield. "You make it sound so
bleak . . . so pointless."

"Life is pointless, if it is merely lived," the woman said. "There
are forces acting upon all of us. The point is in knowing what they
are and understanding them, then making the best use of that
knowledge, so that one lives in tune with those forces, rather than
in discord."

"How?" asked Katrina.

"Take hold of my staff," the woman told her.

Katrina looked puzzled, but did as the woman said. No sooner
had her fingers touched the staff than she felt them start to tingle.
The tingling sensation quickly passed up along her arm and spread
throughout her body. She trembled, but it was not from the evening
chill. Her fingers couldn't seem to let go of the staff.

"Now, look around and tell me what you see," the woman said.
Her voice sounded distant, even though they were standing right
beside each other.

"I see waste," said Katrina, slowly. "I see a battle that was fought
between two forces, evenly matched. A battle in which nothing was
resolved. So it is a battle which must be fought again. And there

shall be other battles just like this one, between other forces, all competing for the crown. Each trying to dominate the other. And it shall go on . . . and on . . . and on."

The woman nodded. "And is there no way to break the cycle?"

"Not until one is stronger than the other," Katrina said, trembling as she held the staff. It seemed as if some sort of energy were flowing through it and passing into her. "Strong enough to stand against all others who would stake their claim to rule the empire."

"And how might that be accomplished?" asked the woman.

"If the two strongest contenders were to unite," said Katrina, "then none of the others, individually, could stand against them. Not unless alliances were formed. And one alliance would lead to others as the weaker parties joined their forces to defend against the stronger. And those left out would seek to ally themselves with the contender they deemed to be the strongest, with the best chance of victory in the end. And in this way, the empire would one day be reunited."

She was amazed at how clearly she could see it. She understood now. The ebb and flow of power, alignments and realignments, the politics of struggle and survival. It would not happen overnight, but it was inevitable. It was the way of things. Such were the forces which controlled these men, who had died here on the battlefield, caught in an inexorable tide of events that none of them had been able to resist. And she, too, had been caught up in the flow, her father crippled, perhaps dead by now, her brothers slain. . . . Now there would be no one to care for her or for her mother.

The sudden realization came upon her with a shock. What was she to do? How would they live? Her mother was no longer young. If no man were to take them in, what would become of them? It shall be up to me, thought Katrina. She was young enough and pretty enough to attract any number of men of means and position. Branmor had not been the first to show an interest, and she knew how jealous many of the other girls had been when he had started to pay court to her. But where was Branmor now? A handsome and promising young knight, a favorite of Avan's, now he lay dead with all the others, rendered equal in standing at the last with the lowliest man-at-arms. And with the coming wars, the risk would be the same for any other man. Unless, perhaps . . .

" 'Allo, my lady!"

Katrina jerked, startled out of her reverie. She closed her fingers on empty air. The staff was gone. So was the woman in the hooded cloak, as if she had never been there at all. Katrina turned, disoriented and confused.

Several riders were approaching at a walk. She turned to run, then realized she would never be able to outdistance them. What had happened to the woman in the cloak? There was no sign of her on the open field. Katrina scanned the bodies around her on the ground, thinking perhaps her companion had seen the riders and was trying to conceal herself among the dead. . . . But no, she was nowhere to be seen. Katrina turned back to face the approaching riders.

"This is no place for a woman, my lady," one of them said, coming to a halt before her. He wore a dark tabard with a crest she was unfamiliar with over a suit of mail. Perhaps he wore a breastplate under the tabard, but he was not in full armor. Nor were any of his companions. "It grows dark," he said. "The dogrobbers will be coming out soon with their torches, to strip the bodies of the fallen and gather such booty as they may." He cast an appreciative gaze over her. "It is not safe for you to be here."

"No, I imagine not," she replied. "But do I have more to fear from the dogrobbers than from you?"

The knight smiled. "The dogrobbers are likely to be somewhat less chivalrous."

"Well, if I am to be raped and taken, then by all means, let it be done chivalrously," she replied.

The knight chuckled. "You hear that?" he said, glancing over his shoulder at his companions, who shared his amusement. "A riposte of wit, and in such surroundings as these, no less." He turned back to her and bowed from the saddle. "My compliments, my lady. But I know you not. Are you of Avan or Boeruine?"

Not Avanil, she thought, but Avan. The province of Boeruine bore the same name as the family which governed it, but the duke of Avan's holding was called Avanil. He was asking if she was for Kier of Avan or Derwyn of Boeruine. Such was the new way of things, she thought. Not where are you from, but to whom do you owe fealty?

"My father and my brothers fought for Kier of Avan," she replied.

"So?" the knight said. He glanced back at his companions. "It

7

seems we are confronted by the enemy." They grinned. He turned back to Katrina. "And how fared your kin on this day?"

"My two brothers lie here somewhere, slain," she replied flatly. "My father was still alive when last I saw him, but he was maimed, and the physic said that he may not survive."

The knight nodded. His companions looked grim. "I am sorry for your loss," he said sincerely. "It would seem that you have far more reason to despise Derwyn of Boeruine than ties of vassalage alone."

"If I were to despise Boeruine," she said, "then I would have just reason to despise the Duke of Avanil as well, for each played an equal part in this. Yet, did either really have a choice? Or were they merely playthings of the gods, pieces moved about in their never-ending game? Do I despise Boeruine? I think, if I were to despise anyone, it would be the emperor for getting himself killed in a lost and foolish cause, leaving the Iron Throne without an heir to sit upon it."

"What is your name, my lady?" asked the knight.

"Katrina of Tremayne."

"Lord Derek Tremayne's house?"

"My father," Katrina said.

The knight nodded. "I know of him. A goodly knight, by all accounts. I am Derwyn of Boeruine."

Katrina's eyes widened and she swallowed hard. She curtsied, as much to mask her reaction as out of courtesy. "Forgive me, my lord," she said. "Had I known who you were, I should not have addressed you in so familiar a manner."

"I did not take exception," Derwyn replied easily. "You shall enjoy the hospitality of my tent tonight. It would not be safe for a beautiful young woman to go riding back alone after dark."

"And if I were to refuse, my lord?"

"You need have no fear for your virtue," Derwyn assured her. "You have my knightly word on that. In the meantime, we shall send a messenger for word of your father. Bors, fetch the lady's horse."

In the distance, she could already see the flickering torches of the dogrobbers as they made their way onto the battlefield. Darkness cloaked the bodies lying all around her, rendering them as indistinct lumps upon the ground. Soon to be stripped bare by the dogrobbers, she thought, disgusted. But then they too were merely trying to survive.

Her thoughts turned back to that strange woman who had vanished as suddenly as she had appeared. Was she truly flesh and blood, as she had seemed, or had she been a spirit? Or was she a sorceress? That staff . . . She could still feel its power coursing through her. And Katrina knew that, somehow, she had changed.

As the knight named Bors brought up her horse, she allowed him to assist her into the saddle, then glanced at the duke. So you rode out from your camp tonight to see your handiwork, she thought. Does it satisfy your lordship? Are you proud?

He was regarding her curiously. She thought, do you like what you see? And how good is your knightly word to vouchsafe my virtue? Who is to say nay to you should you decide to break it? He raised his eyebrows at her scrutiny and she lowered her gaze demurely. "I thank you for your kindness and your chivalry, my lord," she said, softly. "You honor me."

"The honor is mine, my lady," Derwyn replied, bowing slightly from the saddle.

She recalled hearing that he was a widower. His late duchess, the Princess Laera, had given him a son, the Baron Aerin, who stood next in line to inherit not only his father's title, but quite possibly the throne as well, by dint of his descent from the Emperor Michael's bloodline. However, there were many who disputed his legitimacy. Michael Roele had six other sisters, all of whom had married various nobles and produced offspring of their own, and since Laera's death, dozens of men had come forward—from young noblemen to men-at-arms and stableboys—all claiming to have been her lovers. The treacherous part that she had played in the death of the Empress Faelina, to say nothing of her evil sorcery, had made Princess Laera the most hated and reviled woman in the empire. She had brought disgrace down on the House of Boeruine, and word had it that Lord Derwyn would not even permit her name to be mentioned in his presence.

Katrina wondered how Lord Derwyn managed to justify his son's claim to the throne if he could not even mention the name of Aerin's mother. And she wondered how Aerin felt about it all. Accusations against Princess Laera were countered by accusations from supporters of Lord Derwyn that her sisters—or their husbands—had bribed the men who had come forward to give testimony to Laera's numerous infidelities. Lord Derwyn was either the victim of vicious political intrigues or else he was the greatest cuckold in the empire. Quite possibly both, Katrina thought.

The Baron Aerin would not be at the camp, if the stories she had heard were true. It was said that Lord Derwyn was very protective of his son, through whom he laid his much-disputed claim to regency. Derwyn feared conspiracies and the possibility that harm might come to Aerin, thereby nullifying his claim. Baron Aerin was thirty-one years old and had never even seen a battlefield. It was said that he had never fought in tournament or, some said, even held a sword. He was kept cloistered within the walls of Seaharrow, Lord Derwyn's impregnable castle on a rocky bluff overlooking the Miere Rhuann, guarded like a rare and precious jewel. What must it be like, Katrina wondered, to live a life like that? And how must Aerin feel about a father who keeps him practically prisoner?

She glanced at Lord Derwyn as they rode back toward his camp. He was not a young man, perhaps in his midfifties, yet he still looked very fit and handsome. His face bore the lines of age and his hair was white, but his vitality was clearly evident in the brightness of his eyes and the alertness of his gaze. His voice was deep and rich, and he possessed all the courtly graces, but his chin was weak and there was a softness about his features. It was said that Laera, while she lived, had kept him firmly under her thumb. A man who could be controlled, by the right woman. And he had never remarried.

He sent Bors to Avanil to find out how her father fared. A chivalrous gesture, to be sure. And, under the circumstances, Lord Kier would be sure to give Sir Bors safe-conduct. But the physic's words came back to Katrina, as he had spoken them to her outside her father's chamber, where her mother waited, weeping, by his bedside. "I shall not lie to you, my lady. The truth is that I fear your father shall not see the dawn."

My two brothers dead in battle and my father dying, thought Katrina. And here am I, found wandering on the battlefield amid the corpses, angered, shocked, and numb with horror. . . . Who would blame a woman for succumbing to her grief in such deeply tragic circumstances? Who would blame her for turning to a strong man for comfort and solace?

How long has it been, she wondered, since Lord Derwyn had a woman?

BOOK I

THE MISTRESS AND
THE BREED

chapter one

It was hard, leaving the Aelvinnwode. The forest had always been his home. It was all he knew. "Well, Father, you got me into this," said Gannd, as he sat beside his campfire, "now it's up to you to set my feet on the right path. I would appreciate a little guidance, if it wouldn't be too much trouble."

No one was there to answer him. He knew that. His father had died long ago. At least, he thought his father had died long ago. Gannd wasn't really certain, because he'd never even known him. Aside from that, time flowed differently in the elven forests than in the human world. He knew that, too. He just didn't know why. It was something no one had ever been able to explain to his complete satisfaction, not even his uncle, Gylvain Aurealis, who served as wizard to Prince Fhileraene himself. Gylvain had been out among the humans, as had Gannd's mother, Sylvanna. That was how Gannd had been conceived. She had told him the story many times. When he was a child being put to bed, he had requested it over and over, and she had never grown weary of telling him the tale, no matter how many times he'd asked.

It began many years ago, when reports had reached the ebony

palace of Tuaranreigh that a raiding party had crossed over the border from the goblin realm of Thurazor and was moving through the Aelvinnwode. It was not known what the goblins had intended, but they had been the sworn enemies of all the elves since time began and their presence was not tolerated in the kingdom of Tuarhievel. Prince Fhileraene dispatched a force of elves under the command of Gannd's uncle, Gylvain, with orders to intercept them. But the goblins had moved quickly. It was a small war party of wolf riders and, mounted on their feral steeds, they quickly crossed the Aelvinnwode and reached the human province of Boeruine, where they had taken two young humans captive. They were returning to the snow-capped mountains of Thurazor with their prisoners when Gylvain's party came upon them.

The two young humans were resourceful and had contrived to escape their captors when they made camp for the night, but the boys were on foot and stood little chance against pursuing wolf riders. Their escape had been discovered, and the goblins had already caught up to them, when the elves arrived on the scene. They had slain the goblins and Gylvain brought the two young humans back with him to Tuaranreigh, where they had a formal audience with Prince Fhileraene, seated on his famed Thorn Throne.

It turned out that the two humans were none other than young Prince Michael Roele, heir to the Iron Throne of the Empire of Anuire, and his friend and future high chamberlain, Lord Aedan Dosiere. Through treacherous collusion with the goblins, Duke Arwyn of Boeruine had arranged to have the boys abducted, ostensibly for ransom, but he had planned to keep the ransom and allow the goblins to sell their captives into slavery—or kill them, he did not care which—so that when the ailing emperor died, Boeruine could claim the throne.

Lord Arwyn had not counted on the two boys being rescued, nor had he counted on Prince Fhileraene's desire to incur an obligation on the part of the young heir to the empire for the benefit of the elven kingdom of Tuarhievel. Fhileraene had word sent to Lord Tieran, Aedan's father and the High Chamberlain of Anuire, that his son and the young prince were well and safe in his care and would be escorted back to Anuire at the proper time.

When the old emperor died soon afterward, Lord Arwyn showed

his hand. Fhileraene waited until the Duke of Boeruine had committed himself, then sent a unit of elf warriors to escort Prince Michael and Lord Aedan safely back to the palace of Anuire. As a gesture of support to cement the alliance between them, Fhileraene decreed that the elven escort should remain with young Prince Michael and help him to secure his rightful place upon the Iron Throne. Among that escort were Gannd's uncle, Gylvain, who had become mentor to the boys, and Gannd's mother, Sylvanna.

Together, they had fought many battles to help Michael Roele reclaim his throne. It was after they had returned from a disastrous expedition on a failed campaign that Lord Aedan and Gannd's mother became lovers. In truth, Sylvanna told her son, they had loved each other long before, but they had never acted on that love, nor even spoke of it, because they came from different worlds. The days when elves and humans had warred with one another were not so distant that memories of those conflicts didn't still hold some power. The alliance between the elves of Tuarhievel and the humans of Anuire was, at best, an uneasy one. Aside from that, elves were immortal, while the span of a human life was short. Lord Aedan, as the emperor's high chamberlain, had to make a marriage that was politically suitable. It was unthinkable that he, a blooded noble of Anuire, should take an elf to wife.

But in the aftermath of a campaign during which many lives were lost, they had turned to one another for comfort. They had shared only one night of passion, but that one night had quickened Gannd within his mother's womb. And she had never told Lord Aedan, for to prevent any hint of scandal, he had taken the Lady Ariel in marriage. And Sylvanna left Anuire soon afterward, returning to her people.

Gannd grew up in the elven kingdom of Tuarhievel having never known his father. All he had were the stories that his mother told him of their days at the Imperial Cairn, the palace of Anuire, and the times they'd spent together in the field on campaigns. Of those, his favorite story was the tale of how they had fought the undead in the Shadow World and then escaped the deadly arachnids of the Spiderfell. Through these tales his mother told him, Gannd had built up a picture of his human father as a mighty warrior and a noble knight. But he could only imagine what his father had looked like.

Gannd had never even seen the likeness of Aedan Dosiere in either a portrait or cameo.

Gannd's mother had told him that he bore a strong resemblance to his father, except, of course, for his elven features. Humans did not have pointed ears; their eyebrows tended to be thicker and without so pronounced an arch; their hair was not as thick, and it came in light hues as well as dark, turning gray or white only with advancing age, whereas elven hair was always either black or silver, often a combination of the two. Humans also tended to be stockier, thicker in the waist and chest. Their voices, it was said, were so guttural and harsh upon the ears that elven voices could often leave a human spellbound. Gannd's mother had told him that his father's voice was not unpleasant, once she had grown used to it. It was deep and had good timbre, for a human.

As a child, Gannd had taken to having imaginary conversations with his father, one-sided dialogues in which only he would speak. At first, he would pretend his father answered him, but as he grew older these dialogues grew increasingly rhetorical and were no longer childhood imaginings, but merely an old habit that gave him occasional comfort. Occasions such as now, when having left all that he knew behind, he had embarked upon a quest to find that part of his life which he had always felt was missing: the human part.

His mother disapproved of his leaving and had tried to talk him out of it. "You have never been among the humans," she told him. "You do not know what they are like. Some, it is true, are good-hearted and fair in their dealings with both man and elf alike, but many still remember the old conflicts and they do not bear us any love. You shall always be an outsider among them. Often scorned, always distrusted, because you are not of their kind."

"But I am part human myself," Gannd had protested.

His mother sighed and shook her head. "No, my son," she said. "You are a half-elf. Here, in the Aelvinnwode, you will always be accepted, even though you are not full-blooded Sidhelien, and none will ever scorn you for the human blood running through your veins. But out there, in the human world, half-elves are called half-breeds, or 'breeds' for short, and those who use the word always speak it as an insult. To them, you shall always be something less than human and less than elf, for you represent to them a thing they cannot countenance—a love between our races and a union of the two."

And, his mother added, they would always know him for what he was, for he could pass for neither human nor elf. Humans did not have his elven features, and elves did not possess the thickness he had through the chest and shoulders or the human roundness of his face. The legacy of both races was clearly written there. He had his father's square chin and jawline and his mother's elven eyes, a striking, crystalline shade of silver-gray that did not occur in humans. And though his mother's hair was raven black, streaked with silver highlights, his own was auburn, like his father's, with elvish silver running through it in thick streaks. He would stand out in any crowd. The only difference was, among the elves, it would not be cause for comment. Among the humans, they would either comment derisively, straight to his face, or else there would be whispering behind his back, or even more violent reactions.

Still, Gannd had remained firm in his choice. There was another world out there, a world to which he felt at least in part connected, and of which he knew nothing. Until he found it, until he made connection with his father's world, he felt that he would never truly find himself.

Once she saw that he was firm in his decision, Sylvanna had resigned herself to it and sought not to make their parting difficult. Reluctantly, she gave him her support and her blessings, and there were no tears, for that was not Sylvanna's way. Elves were not given to emotional displays and Sylvanna was not only an elf, she was a warrior. "Do what you feel you must, my son," she told him, "and take with you my blessings and my love. I ask only that you comport yourself with honor in all things, and disgrace neither your Sidhelien nor your human lineage. But whatever happens, whether you achieve grace or fall from it, remember always that you have a home here, and that a mother always will forgive what others may condemn."

"Take this amulet," his uncle Gylvain told him on the night they parted, "and wear it always. Never take it off, and guard it with your life."

"What is it, Uncle?" Gannd had said as he held the amulet, a dark, smooth blood ruby polished to a brilliant sheen. The gem was the size of a small plover egg, oval-shaped and set in filigreed silver, attached to a stout, braided silver chain. It was beautiful, a masterpiece of the jewelers art, and worthy of a king.

"It is the most powerful magic that I own," replied the elven mage. "Unlike ordinary spells, which the adept must learn anew each time he uses them, this enchantment has no limit. It used to be my teacher's and he passed it down to me. It has served me well throughout my life, and now I hope it may serve you, if you learn to use it wisely."

"What sort of spell does it bear?" asked Gannd.

"The spell of time," said Gylvain somberly. "Should you close your fist around it, shut your eyes and think of a hawk in flight, it will grant you the small boon of a moment's respite, just an instant, a fraction of a space of time, but with that time, you may collect your thoughts. And sometimes the ability to do that can make all the difference in the world."

"A hawk in flight," said Gannd. "A special sort of hawk or any hawk at all?"

"Red-tailed or peregrine, sparrow hawk or kestrel, nighthawk, it is all the same," said Gylvain. "See the creature soaring in your mind's eye and your spirit shall fly with it to the Bridge of Sighs, where time stands ever still. If you think of me when you stand upon the bridge I shall come to you and offer what wisdom I possess, for with the years, the gem has forged a bond with me. But without the amulet in my possession, I can remain there only briefly. While you . . . you can stay indefinitely. And therein lies the danger."

"Danger?" Gannd said, puzzled. "What sort of danger?"

"The danger of fear and indecision," Gylvain had replied. "You may remain upon the Bridge of Sighs for however long you like, and yet, when you return back to your body, scarcely an instant will have passed. If what is about to happen in that next instant should prove more than you can face, then the seductive power of the bridge can make you want to stay there always."

"But if I could return at any time," said Gannd, "and no matter how long I stayed upon the bridge, I would always come back to the same moment that I left, then where would be the danger?"

"The danger would lie not in remaining on the bridge, but in yourself," Gylvain replied. "For if you fear what is about to happen in the moment you depart, the longer you might remain upon the bridge, and the more your fear will grow. And as it grows, it will only torture you. You will be outside of time, and that which you fear will always be waiting for you upon your return."

"But to return, I would need only make the choice, is that not so?" asked Gannd.

"Indeed," said Gylvain. "But choosing to face what you fear can be the hardest of all choices to make. Remember, the amulet does not stop time. It merely removes you from its flow to give you pause. And that pause may be a blessing . . . or a curse. It all depends on you."

"If this Bridge of Sighs is outside the flow of time," said Gannd, "then do you mean to say that it lies in the Shadow World?"

"The Bridge of Sighs is found within a misty region between the Shadow World and the world of light we know," Gylvain replied. "It was once a bridge between the two, a long, long time ago, before the death of the old gods, before the birth of the awnsheghlien, before the first humans ever set foot on Cerilia. Now, one can travel the length and breadth of this land and never find it. Even the halflings, who can move between the worlds, can no longer find their way there. The Bridge of Sighs can be found only by magic, and it now leads neither to the Shadow World nor back to this one. It is a span that leads from nowhere, to nowhere. And so it cannot be crossed. But once you stand upon the bridge, you can see everything . . . and nothing."

"I do not understand," said Gannd, shaking his head.

Gylvain had merely smiled. "Nor do I," he said. "It is beyond all understanding. It can only be experienced. Someday, you will see for yourself and then you will know."

Gannd fingered the amulet around his neck as he recalled his uncle's words. He had not yet tried to use the spell. Yet, he had felt its power from the moment he slipped the amulet around his neck. And he knew enough of magic to know that it was not something to be treated lightly.

Unlike his uncle, Gannd was no adept. Like his mother, he had been raised in the tradition of the warrior arts, rather than the ways of spellcraft. On the first anniversary of his birth, four items had been placed before him. One had been a rolled-up spell scroll, bound with a simple rawhide thong. The second was a dagger. Care had been taken to make sure the dagger was an old and simple one, with an unpolished blade, so that there would be no shiny metal surface to attract him. The third was a simple arrow whose head was dulled as was the dagger's blade, with fletching of unassuming gray and brown. The fourth had been a small lute, strung with gut and carved from oak. Had he reached for that first, he would have been trained in the tradition of the bard, learning the skills of the musician and the art of lyric composition. Had he reached for the scroll, he would have been taught magic, learning the arcane ways of the sorcerer. Choosing the arrow would have meant a life in the depths of the Aelvinnwode learning the ways of the ranger. But he had picked up the dagger, and so had been raised on the path of the warrior.

With an uncle who served as wizard to the elven court, it was inevitable that Gannd should learn at least a few relatively simple spells. However, to become a full-fledged adept required enormous discipline and many years of dedicated training. It was a life of almost constant study, requiring great concentration, for the nature of most spells was such that the energy required to conjure them depleted the adept, and each time a spell was cast, it was necessary to relearn it before it could be used again. Sometimes, with spells that were not especially demanding, this was a relatively simple matter of committing afresh to memory a few arcane words and gestures, but the more powerful spells often required lengthy preparation. As a result, most adepts kept a mental storehouse of ready spells, already prepared for casting, and were at the same time always learning new ones, or preparing anew those that had been cast before. Few people had the patience or the mental stamina for such a life, which was why there were far fewer adepts than non-adepts and even fewer true wizards. All elves were taught the ways of the woodsman and the hunter, but when it came to following their path in life, most trained as either bards or warriors, and of those few who first picked up the scroll, most did not persevere in the advanced study of the craft, instead becoming healers, scholars, or apothecaries.

Gannd had the ability to use a few elementary spells, but his true talents did not lie in that direction. From the start, it had been clear that the blood of warriors flowed through him. His mother was among the finest fighters Tuarhievel had ever produced and his human father had been a blooded noble of Anuire, who had inherited from his ancestors the blood powers they had acquired when the old gods died at the battle of Mount Deismaar.

What a day that must have been, thought Gannd. It had marked a turning point for all the races of Cerilia, for it had been a day that literally changed the world. Mount Deismaar had been levelled. The land bridge that had connected the continents of Aduria and Cerilia disappeared beneath the waves in the fearsome earthquakes that followed. And the cataclysm was remembered ever after as the Twilight of the Gods.

It had been the first and, until recently, the last time elves and humans had fought side by side to defeat a common foe, the Dark Lord known as Azrai. Initially, the elves had given Azrai their support, for the God of Evil had promised to rid them of the humans who were invading elven lands. But then the elves had learned that the Dark Lord intended to betray them after they had helped him win his victory, and the elven armies crossed over to the human side. When the tide turned against the human tribes, the old gods manifested themselves upon Mount Deismaar and joined in the battle with their champions. And as the human tribes of Cerilia, aided by the elves, did battle with the Dark Lord's host, the old gods confronted Azrai. The war of the gods had unleashed such power that the gods themselves were destroyed, taking with them the mountain on which they had stood. The earth trembled and deep fissures opened in the ground, belching smoke and flame.

The death of the old gods had released a storm of god-essence, a wash of divine energy that swept down the slopes of the disintegrating mountain with the force of a hundred hurricanes. Those whom it struck first, the champions of the old gods and the Dark Lord, ceased, in an instant, to be human as they absorbed the full brunt of the divine essence and were transformed into gods themselves. Thus were the new gods created from the old. And as the remains of the godstorm swept across the battlefield, it imbued all those who stood there with what became known as blood abilities, or blood powers, for they were passed on to succeeding generations in each bloodline. Those who had survived the battle and the cataclysm that followed became known as the "blooded." And in time, many of these blooded lines became much stronger, either through intermarriage or through bloodtheft, wherein one blooded individual killed another to take his victim's blood powers for his own. And thus were the abominations born, those once-human creatures who used the powers gained by bloodtheft to transform themselves into fearsome monstrosities as dangerous as they were hideous. The elves were the first to become aware of these new beings and they gave them a name: Awnsheghlien, "blood of darkness."

All this Gannd had learned as he grew up, for it was part of the new lore, added to the elvish lore in the years following the battle of Mount Deismaar. And it was unique in that it was the only part of elvish lore that was common to the lore of humans. But to the elves, the new lore had necessitated a rethinking of the old, for these events had shaken elvish traditional beliefs to their foundations.

Prior to the wars between the elves and humans, elves had never believed in the existence of the old gods. Priestly magic that called upon the powers of the gods was unknown to them. Elven wizards had always practiced magic that drew upon the powers of fire and water, earth and air. When the humans came, their adepts were able to call upon a form of magic that elves had never known, and so they had no defense against it. The priestly magic of the humans had given them a powerful advantage, and it was the primary reason why the fabulous elvish courts of old no longer existed. Little by little, the elves were inexorably driven from their lands until they now occupied only a few of the heavily forested regions of Cerilia, and a handful of small kingdoms were all that now remained of the glory that Gannd's people once knew, before the humans had arrived.

Yet, priestly magic had meant much more than defeat for the Sidhelien. It meant an entire restructuring of their beliefs. They had never worshiped gods, having instead a deep reverence for nature, for the moon, the sun and stars, and rituals were performed during the cycle of the seasons not to petition them as gods, but to become attuned with the natural flow of things. The Sidhelien saw themselves as being a part of nature, not something separate from it.

But the humans saw their gods differently, as beings apart from nature, and rulers of its various aspects. The Andu, from whom the modern Anuireans were descended, had worshiped Anduiras, their god of nobility and war. The Rjuven worshiped a god named Reynir, the deity of woods and streams. The Basarji had worshiped Basaïa, their goddess of the sun, and the Masetians, whose swift sloops had plied the waters of the coasts, had venerated Masela as the goddess of the seas. The human tribes had an entire pantheon of gods, with each tribe worshiping its own through priests who administered their rites in stone temples, some as elaborate and imposing as the finest castles of the empire. During the old conflicts, those priests had called upon their gods for magic to aid the human forces in their battles. And the magic had worked.

The elves had not believed in the existence of the human gods, yet the reality of priestly magic proved cruelly undeniable. And how could they continue to deny the existence of the human gods when they had seen with their own eyes how they had manifested at the battle of Mount Deismaar?

The scholars of the Sidhelien courts had met afterward in convocation in the Aelvinnwode to wrestle with this weighty problem. The result of their deliberations had been the new lore, which held that all systems of belief were valid to those who truly believed in them. The human gods were real for the humans, and were made manifest by the strength of their beliefs. This also meant that the beliefs of the Sidhelien were no less real, as demonstrated by the efficacy of the magic of fire and water, earth and air. Just as the beliefs of the Sidhelien gave reality to their lore, which humans could perceive, so did the beliefs of the humans give form to their gods, which the elves could see. And what governed all of this was the Cycle of Creation, which had no beginning and no end.

The forces of nature had resulted in the creation of the elves, because there had been a need for them in the natural cycle of all things, and the stewardship of nature practiced by the Sidhelien ensured its continuation. Likewise, the humans—in accordance with their lore—were created by the gods they worshiped, for those gods needed worshipers to ensure their own continuation. And when the old gods died at Deismaar, the new gods arose to take their place.

Haelyn, the champion of the Anuireans, had been transformed by the god-essence of Anduiras into the god of battle; Erik, the druid, took the place of Reynir, the Rjuven god of forests; Avani of the Basarji arose to become their new goddess of the sun, and so on, with all the human tribes. Champions in battle became deities in death . . . or in transformation, as the humans now believed. And their new gods were no less real to them than the old ones had been. Reality gave rise to belief, and belief gave form to reality. Thus, the new lore of the Sidhelien.

But even as he had learned the new lore as a child, Gannd had perceived that it left unanswered questions. And these questions troubled him. In the quiet moments of the night, moments such as now, when he was alone beside his campfire in the stillness of the forest, he would often find his thoughts turning to those troubling questions. If reality gave rise to belief, and belief could be made reality, then which came first? And how much belief was necessary to influence reality? If one ceased to believe in what was real, then would the reality in which belief was lost cease to exist?

"These are not questions for a warrior," Gannd's trainer, Ruslahn, had told him with disdain. "A warrior should be more concerned with the temper of his blade and the trueness of his arrow's flight. If you wish to devote yourself to pondering unanswerable questions which defy all search for meaning, then go become a mystic and do not waste my time."

Gannd was very young then and did not know what a mystic was, so he had asked his uncle. Gylvain raised an eyebrow at the question, but had not hesitated to reply.

"A mystic," he told him, "is one who devotes his life to contemplation and a search for meaning, what the humans call 'philosophy.' Among humans, soothsayers are often mystics, of a sort, as are their priests and scholars, on occasion. Rarely will a human warrior take the mystic path, but it has been known to happen. Among the Sidhelien, true mystics are rare and tend to lead solitary lives. The questions which concern them occupy their minds to the exclusion of all else and this leads them to withdraw from the community, which they come to find oppressive. They go off to live alone, deep in the forests, where they live quietly and humbly, seeking to find the truth in contemplation. Some are very spiritual in their lonely quest, while others grow cynical from frustration. Many are more than just a little mad. Why do you ask?"

Hesitantly, and a little nervously, considering the explanation he had just received, Gannd told his uncle about the questions he had asked Ruslahn and the reply his trainer gave him.

"Yes," Gylvain said with a wry smile, "that sounds very much like Ruslahn. He is one of our most honored and respected warriors, but he has little patience for intellectual pursuits."

"Does this mean that I have chosen the wrong path?" asked Gannd. "Was I meant to be a mystic, rather than a warrior?"

"You chose the dagger, did you not?" Gylvain replied.

"Yes," said Gannd, "but if I had chosen the arrow, I would have been meant to follow the path of the ranger, and choosing the scroll would have set my feet upon the path of the adept. There was no choice for mystics."

"Precisely," said his uncle.

Gannd had frowned. "But . . . I do not understand."

"Because mystics cannot choose," said Gylvain, with a smile. "They choose neither the arrow, the dagger, nor the scroll. That is how we know when a child is destined to become a mystic. When he cannot decide." He had seen the puzzled expression on Gannd's face and chuckled. "Do not concern yourself. You have chosen the right path. It is just that you seem destined to become a warrior with a touch of the mystic in your heart. No doubt, it is because you are part human. Humans can be complex creatures. They are plagued with more uncertainties. Your father was a warrior, but he was something of a mystic, too. Like you, he often questioned the path that he was meant to take, even though he was born to his destiny. Humans are often like that."

"Why?" asked Gannd.

Gylvain had smiled. "Well, because they are only human."

And that was when Gannd knew that someday he would have to leave Tuarhievel and go out among the humans, to learn more about that part of himself that was different from the other Sidhelien and questioned the destiny that he was born to, rather than accepting it.

"Well, Father, my mother gave me life," Gannd said, as he stared into the fire, "but you . . . you gave me doubts and questions. I hope that you will help me find some answers."

"Perhaps your father is not the proper one to ask," a low voice came from behind him, in the darkness.

Gannd sprang to his feet and drew his sword. "Who goes there?" he demanded.

Elves could see by starlight in a way that humans never could, but they could also hear sounds too faint for human ears. This stranger had approached so quietly that Gannd had not heard even the slightest sound. And for a moment, he could not see anyone, either. But then his sharp gaze picked out a shadowy figure standing by a tree, a figure dressed in a dark, hooded cloak and carrying a staff.

"Who are you?" he demanded.

The figure stepped forth into the firelight and pulled back the hood. Gannd saw it was a woman. A beautiful woman, with striking features and long, golden hair. "I am called the Wizard," she replied.

"You are human," Gannd said.

She raised her eyebrows. "Are you certain?"

Gannd snorted. "You seem young for an adept."

"I may be older than I look."

"Have you no name?"

"Wizard will suffice."

"There are many wizards."

"There is only one like me." She glanced at his blade. "If you mean to use that, Sidhelien, do so. If not, put it away."

"That would leave you with an advantage," Gannd replied.

"And what would that be?"

"Your wizard's staff," said Gannd. "To say nothing of your other skills as an adept, if that is what you are."

"You know something of the craft?"

"My uncle is a wizard. Gylvain Aurealis."

"Your uncle's reputation is well known and respected," said the woman. "Very well. I shall put aside my staff to do honor to his kin." She glanced at the long, gnarled staff. "Stay, Calamity."

The staff remained standing on its own as she stepped forward, releasing it, and came toward him. Gannd sheathed his blade.

"That is a handsome sword," the woman said, as he slid it back into its scabbard. "Folded from the finest elven steel. A warrior's blade."

"It was a gift from my mother," Gannd replied.

"Does it bear a name?"

"It is called Bloodthirst."

"Of course. Sylvanna's blade. I should have known."

"You know my mother?"

"I know of her, but we have never met. What is your name, Sidhelien?"

"I am called Gannd."

"You are part human, I perceive. Who was your father?"

"Lord Aedan Dosiere, late High Chamberlain of the Empire of Anuire," Gannd replied, proudly. Then, after a moment's hesitation, added, "But I never knew him and, in truth, have no right to his name."

"So. A love child, then."

"Others would use a less charitable appellation, Wizard," Gannd replied dryly.

She smiled. "Indeed, they might. May I warm myself a while by your fire?"

"You are welcome, my lady."

"Your mother taught you manners. That is good. They shall always serve you well." She crouched by the fire and Gannd watched the firelight reflected from her face. She was truly beautiful, but then he realized that it could only be an effect of wizard's glamour. For all he knew, she could be an old crone. With adepts, one could tell little by appearances.

"Wine?" he said.

"Thank you." She accepted the leather wineskin and squeezed a stream into her mouth. "Where are you bound?" she asked him.

"On a search," he replied. "To where, I do not know yet."

"And what is it that you seek?"

"Answers," he replied. "And do not ask me to what questions. I am not yet even certain what the questions are."

"Questions such as those you were asking of your father?"

"My father is dead," said Gannd. "As I said before, I never knew him. I just . . . speak to him sometimes," he added awkwardly. "To his spirit, if you will. I find it comforts me."

"There is nothing strange in that. What would be strange is if he would reply."

"You mock me."

"No," she answered with a smile, shaking her head. "Sometimes, if one longs to hear a certain voice badly enough, one can actually start to hear it. Or to believe one hears it. And if your belief is strong enough, it can become real. Some call that madness." She gave him a sidelong glance and raised her eyebrows. "Others call it the new lore."

"Now you mock our lore," Gannd said.

"Do I? There is a fine line between the madman and the mystic. And neither can perceive it very clearly. But it helps to be aware of its existence."

"That is something very like what a mystic might say," said Gannd, unable to resist a smile.

"There is a bit of the mystic in all of us," the Wizard replied. "Some just pay closer attention to his voice."

"And what does your mystic voice tell you?" asked Gannd.

"That you have an interesting path ahead of you," she replied. "It will be arduous, and it shall twist and turn more than a few times, and present you with many choices, some more difficult than others."

"And will I find the answers that I seek?"

"That depends on the questions you ask," she said. "And on what you are willing to trade for those answers. How badly do you want to know?"

"Why?"

"There are forces in this world which control us all," she replied. "Few perceive them; fewer still understand them. But they can be felt. Would you like to feel them?"

"How?"

She stretched forth her hand. "Come, Calamity!" she said. The staff, which stood like a young sapling perhaps a dozen feet away, suddenly came flying to her hand. She held it upright, with its tip upon the ground. "Take hold of my staff," she said.

Gannd stretched out his hand, but he stopped just short of touching the staff, hesitating.

"Go on," she said, gazing at him steadily. He met her gaze and held it for a moment.

"No," he said, withdrawing his hand. "I think not."

She cocked her head curiously. "I thought you wanted answers."

"I do," he replied, "but before I bargain for them, I want to know just what I'm trading. All magic bears a cost."

The Wizard smiled and pulled back her staff. "Your uncle taught you well. Give him my regards when next you see him."

"I shall."

"I think you will do well upon your quest, Sidhelien. I wish you luck finding the answers that you seek."

Gannd bowed his head to her. "Thank you, my lady."

When he looked up again, she was gone, as if she had vanished on the wind.

With his fingertips, he lightly touched the amulet around his neck. The gift of time, he thought. A pause in which to think. This time, he had needed no magic to take pause and collect his thoughts. Just a moment's pause, as his uncle said once, an instant, and sometimes it can make all the difference in the world. There was a lesson to be learned here.

"Thank you, Uncle," Gannd said softly. And he lay down beside the fire to sleep.

chapter two

Katrina decided she was going to like living at Seaharrow. The massive stone castle had been the seat of power for the House of Boeruine for generations and dwarfed the stone-towered keep of Avanil, which until she beheld Seaharrow, Katrina had always found impressive. The current duke's ancestors had built their castle high upon an imposing rocky bluff that overlooked the Sea of Storms and dominated the town of Seasedge and the entire surrounding countryside.

Its location, as well as its construction, made Seaharrow an impregnable fortress. The east wall of the castle was built flush with the high, sheer cliff that rose above the sea, making it impossible to approach from that direction. The outer, south-facing wall had been constructed close to the edge of the promontory that rose above the rock-strewn stretch of shore below. Those sharp and jagged rock formations at the base of the cliff made an approach en masse from the south untenable. Men would have to move individually among the treacherous terrain, all the while subject to the buffeting of the waves crashing into the rocky shore. Likewise, from the north, an approach by troops was stymied by the same conditions. The only possible way to approach the castle was from the west, along the winding road that led up to the summit of the gigantic rock promontory, and all along the way, advancing troops would be exposed to the archers and catapults upon the crenelated castle battlements. And even if an advancing force should succeed in reaching the castle, they would come upon a formidable defense that was unique to the barbican of Seaharrow.

Instead of a moat, which the location of the castle made impractical, the drawbridge spanned a ravine that had been carved out of solid rock to a depth of fifteen feet, at the bottom of which, firmly set in mortar, were rows of thick and sharpened stakes cut from the trunks of young trees taken from the surrounding pine forests. And as attackers struggled to surmount such a difficult obstacle, they would be subject to a rain of arrows and bombardment from the battlements above. If ever a castle was invulnerable to assault, thought Katrina, then Seaharrow was that castle.

Her seduction of Lord Derwyn had not proved difficult at all. Once they had returned to camp, his knights had gone to their own tents with knowing looks, and she had gone with Derwyn to his opulent pavilion. She knew he was attracted to her, but at the same time, he seemed guarded, so she did not try to force or hurry things. She could well understand his hesitance, considering what she knew of his late duchess.

The Princess Laera of Anuire, the Duchess of Boeruine, had been the eldest sister of the Emperor Michael and there had already been whispers about her questionable virtue when she had married Derwyn. Initially, she had been betrothed to Derwyn's father, the Archduke Arwyn, but Arwyn had been too canny to take such a vixen for his wife. Instead, he took advantage of the rebellion he had started based on his spurious claim to regency and married her off to Derwyn, thereby strengthening his claim to the Iron Throne with an additional tie by marriage to his bloodline. Unfortunately, Michael Roele stood in the way of his ascension.

Arwyn had declared him dead, killed by the goblins who had kidnapped him, but when the young emperor returned to Anuire from Tuarhievel, Arwyn had claimed that he was an imposter, part of an elvish plot to destroy the empire. Perhaps there were some who actually believed him, but most of the nobles who gave him their allegiance doubtless did so based on their belief that the young emperor, or pretender as Arwyn branded him, stood little chance against the empire's foremost warlord. They were wrong.

When Arwyn fell in battle, slain by Michael, the emperor had magnanimously forgiven Derwyn for the transgressions of his father and confirmed his succession to the title, thereby reuniting the war torn provinces. Thus, Lord Derwyn had become Archduke of Boeruine and the emperor's sister had become his duchess.

But Laera had been as blackhearted as she was beautiful, something Derwyn had known from the beginning, for she had been traitor to her own brother and had spied against him for Boeruine during the rebellion. Yet, despite his initial antagonism and firm resolutions to keep it a marriage in name only, Derwyn had fallen hopelessly in love with Laera, a testimony to her seductive powers and wily machinations. He had remained completely ignorant of how she had cuckolded him repeatedly throughout their marriage with a number of lovers that seemed legion, and he had never suspected that his wife was a pupil of the evil Calador, a sorcerer who had sold his services to none other than the Gorgon, and through whose magic Laera had caused the empress to give birth to an abomination. The poor young empress had not survived the horribly traumatic birth and the hideous offspring had been killed, after which the vengeful emperor had embarked upon a war against the Gorgon which had cost him his life. In the end, the Lady Ariel, wife to the High Chamberlain Aedan Dosiere, had killed the treacherous Laera when she tried to take her husband's life and ever since, Lord Derwyn had lived with the disgrace his wife had brought upon his house.

With the emperor dead, and no heir to the throne, Derwyn's claim was strongest. He was of the same bloodline as the Roeles and had he been his father, few would have contested his right to succeed. But Derwyn had never been the man his father was. Arwyn was a champion who had proved himself time and again, both in the lists and in combat, and until recently, the only combat Derwyn had seen was during the rebellion, where it was his father who had led the troops. And Derwyn, in addition to being perceived as weaker than his father, was saddled with the disgrace that Laera brought to him, not only as a traitorous adulteress, but as the most reviled murderess in the history of Anuire. Not a single duke or baron had granted him support.

In the years since, Derwyn had never remarried nor been known to keep any mistresses. And he had spent every waking hour consolidating his control over his own holding and building up his troops, intent on taking by force what he believed was rightfully his due. What would, in all probability, have doubtless been granted to him were it not for Laera. Small wonder, thought Katrina, that he was distrustful of women.

Yet, when word arrived the following day that her father had not survived his wounds and that she had become an orphan and her mother a widow, it had given Katrina the perfect opportunity to turn to Derwyn for solace. And it was not merely a ploy. Her grief was genuine. She had dearly loved her father, as she had loved her brothers, and her heart was broken. But at the same time, she had to think of herself and her mother now. They had no one to look after them. And Lord Derwyn was quite the potential prize.

Sir Bors had returned with the news of her father's death as they were striking camp the next day and preparing to march back to Seaharrow. Katrina had expected the worst and she took it bravely, but the news still hit her hard. She had managed to retain her composure, save for a few tears, until the next night, when they stopped to make camp. And then she finally broke down, unable to hold it in any longer as the waves of grief washed over her.

Derwyn had not come near her since she joined his camp and had acted like the perfect gentle knight, but when he heard her sobbing, he could not ignore her distress. He had started off merely trying to comfort her, but then things quickly took on their own momentum, fueled not only by Katrina's grief and need to be held and protected, but by Derwyn's own long-suppressed desire.

Afterwards, when they lay next to each other, Derwyn became distant. Even by the dim light of the candles, Katrina could see that the initial fires of passion had burned down to the embers of guilt and remorse. She had known that if she did not speak and ease his thoughts, whatever warmth toward her remained in him would grow completely cold by sunrise.

"What shall become of me?" she had asked softly.

In a flat voice, he replied, "That depends on what you want, my lady."

On instinct, she had said, "I want to be with you, my lord."

He turned to face her with a curious expression on his face. "Well, you are forthright, at least."

"And why should I not be? What have I to lose, having already lost everything? My mother is a widow and is well past the age when most men would find her comely. My brothers are both dead, as is the noble knight who was my suitor. I grieve for the loss of them, but I also worry for the future. Without you, my lord, what have I to look forward to?"

"I see," he had replied, and though he had not moved, she could feel him pull away. "So, what do you propose?"

"By rights, my lord, I am your captive of war and you may do with me what you please," she said. "As, indeed, you have already done."

"You think our congress has incurred an obligation on my part?" asked Derwyn, with an edge to his voice. "As I recall, you participated willingly and with enthusiasm."

"Say rather with desperation than with enthusiasm," she told him. "I was feeling lonely, grief stricken and afraid, and I longed for the comfort that you gave me. And the life-affirming passion, in the face of so much death. I freely do admit that I was willing. You are a kind and gentle lover, my lord, and despite what you may think, you did not take advantage of me. What I gave, I gave most willingly, because I wanted and I needed. As did you. It was a fair exchange, and so you owe me nothing."

"Indeed, then we agree," he said curtly, but she detected a softening in his tone. Though he was a grown man, there was still a boyishness in him, a tenderness he tried hard to suppress. She could see why he would have been no match for Laera.

She moistened her lips, took a deep breath, and plunged on. "It has been a long time since you have had a woman."

He tensed. "You have heard the gossip."

"I did not need to. Your own hunger spoke of it. But, yes, one hears things. I will not pretend to be able to discern the truth from falsehood in all the tales I heard, but if even half of what I've heard is true, then I can easily understand why you have avoided the company of women."

"Have a care, my lady. You tread on dangerous ground."

"Yet it is ground that must be crossed if you are ever to become free of your past."

"You presume too much upon too brief an intimacy," he replied, getting to his feet and pulling on his robe. "Before you say a certain name, I caution you to speak it at your peril."

She sat up. "Do not go, my lord. I shall not speak it. I have no wish to cause you pain. I seek, instead, to ease it."

"So what do you expect? You want me to take you as my consort? The daughter of an enemy I've slain in battle? You place too little worth upon your father's memory and too much upon your charms."

She fought down her anger. That was what he wanted, she realized. It would enable him to justify himself. Instead, she said, "My father's memory I will cherish till the day I die, but I must yet think of my mother, who is still alive. And of myself, as well. I place worth upon myself because it is worth that I possess. I only ask the opportunity to prove it to you. I do not pretend to love you, but I believe that I could grow to love a man like you, as indeed, you might grow to love me. And yet, I do not ask for that. I will take whatever you can give and repay it with my loyalty and my devotion. Take me for a mistress, if you will, and come to me as often or as rarely as you choose, and I should be content. Or else take me with you back to Seaharrow, where perhaps I may find another suitor to replace the one you slaughtered. Or take me into your service, as a kitchen maid if nothing else, so that I may earn my keep and my mother shan't go hungry. But if you send me back, my lord, then know that I have nothing to go back to. I am entirely at your pleasure and your mercy."

His expression softened as he gazed down at her. "You speak with uncommon honesty and frankness," he said. "For a woman."

"Not all women are the same," she replied.

"Perhaps not," he said, looking away briefly. "After certain events of the past, I had vowed celibacy. You may have heard that."

"In truth, my lord, I had not," she replied honestly. "It was never my intention to lead you to break your vow."

He shrugged. "It was my choice. I am not some stripling who acts entirely on impulse. The thought was in my mind from the first moment I saw you. I will not cry over milk I freely chose to spill. And I find your frankness has as much appeal as your beauty. They are two qualities that do not often come together. Especially in women."

"Some would say that they can both be found in harlots," she replied.

Derwyn chuckled. "Perhaps," he said. "But I would not consider taking a harlot for my mistress." He paused and his face took on a haunted look. "Even though I once took one for my wife."

"She used you more cruelly than any man deserves," Katrina said. "Even in death, she continues to torment you. Speak her name, my lord. Speak her name and let her go. Be free of her."

He swallowed hard, then took a deep breath and released it in a heavy sigh. "Laera," he said softly. And then he closed his eyes.

"There," Katrina said. "Now it is done."

"I once swore that I would never speak her name again," he said.

"And in doing so, ensured that she would be ever in your thoughts," Katrina said.

"That's two vows broken in one night," he said. "You are a bad influence upon me."

"I hope to be a better one, my lord."

"No promises," said Derwyn. "No sureties. I shall take you back to Seaharrow with me as my mistress. For the present. And you need have no fear of laboring in my kitchens. That would be unseemly. We shall send for your mother and have her domiciled in the castle. But mark you, you shall have no claim on me, nor upon my time. If the arrangement should not prove convenient, I shall make every effort to ensure your future welfare, but beyond that, I promise nothing."

"And I shall ask for nothing more," she said.

"Good. So be it."

"Shall we sleep on it, my lord?"

He smiled and came back to bed. And Katrina had smiled inwardly at the thought that though her father and her brothers may have met defeat in battle, she would win the war.

Now, as they approached the castle on the winding road that led up to the gates, she already saw how it would go. Derwyn had seen to it that Seaharrow was well maintained and fortified, and he had spared no energy in building up his troops and training them, but in all that time, Seaharrow had lacked a woman's civilizing touch.

She would proceed slowly, biding her time at first, then perhaps make a few helpful suggestions here and there concerning the castle's furnishing and upkeep, and then offer to free Derwyn of those concerns by taking them upon herself. Before long, she would be indispensable.

She would have to cultivate some friendships among the castle staff and find out as much as possible about the former duchess, so that she could demonstrate to Derwyn that, in every way, she was not at all like Laera. She knew that he desired her, and where desire was present, love could grow. She would be sure to nurture it.

She thought back once again to that strange woman she had met upon the battlefield. Who was she? A witch? A sorceress? A spirit? Or perhaps, a goddess? From the moment Katrina closed her hand around that woman's staff, everything had changed. She had become, somehow, imbued. In tune with the forces of the world. Yes, that was it. Find the power, and then follow its flow.

She had already begun. A mere day earlier, she had been an orphan with no prospects. Now, she was an archduke's mistress. It was not inconceivable that she might become a duchess. Though her father had not been descended from one of the bloodlines of Anuire, he had been a knight vassal to the Duke of Avanil, so she was not a commoner. Perhaps she occupied the lowest rung on the ladder of aristocracy, but nevertheless, she was not lowborn. And if it came to pass that Derwyn chose to marry her, and he succeeded in making good his claim upon the Iron Throne, then it was even possible that she might become the next Empress of Anuire.

I did not look for this, she thought. It was nothing that she could possibly have planned. She might have stayed at home, with her mother, and kept watch by her dying father's bedside. Yet some wild urge had driven her to ride out to the battlefield in the vain hope she might find her brothers. She had never found them. Once she saw what the aftermath of war was truly like, she hadn't wanted to find them. Perhaps she wasn't meant to. She had found something else instead, something very different.

Or perhaps, she thought, as she recalled that strange, mysterious woman, it had found her. Perhaps it was her destiny.

* * * * *

By the next midafternoon, Gannd had left the Aelvinnwode and crossed over into the land of Mhoried. There was no obvious demarcation of the border. The lands of Mhoried began where the forests of the Aelvinnwode thinned out and gave way to the highlands. He had never been so far from home before, but knowing that he would one day have to journey to the human lands, he had spent many hours studying maps of the empire and memorizing them, in addition to learning as much as he could from his fellow elves, especially those who dealt with traders, about the ways of humans.

He knew that Mhoried was one of the northernmost provinces of the part of the empire known as the Heartlands, which also included the provinces of Avanil, Alamie, Ghieste and Elinie. It was a region that covered the territory east of the Seamist Mountains and south of the Stonecrown range, west of the province of Coeranys and the elven kingdom of the Sielwode and north of the dreaded Spiderfell.

Of all these lands, Mhoried was the least stable. The elves of the Sielwode made no incursions into the human lands and tolerated none into their own, but Mhoried was vulnerable to invasion from the goblin realm of Markazor, which lay on its northwestern border. And any invasion from farther north by the forces of the Gorgon would surely come that way, though since the emperor's last campaign against that most feared of the awnsheghlien, the Gorgon had not ventured forth from his holding with his armies.

Nevertheless, the people of Mhoried were well aware of their precarious position, and it was said that Mhoried's highlands were home to some of the toughest and hardiest people of Anuire. The highlanders were woodsmen, for the most part, hunters, trappers, and fishermen, as well as freesteaders who raised sheep and crops. They were organized into clans, though these clans were not tied by blood relations so much as allegiance to the families for whom the clans were named, and the chieftains of these clans, in turn, gave their allegiance to the Mhor, who ruled the province from his forest fortress of Bevaldruor, or Shieldhaven in the Anuirean tongue. At one time, many of the human tribes spoke different languages, but ever since the formation of the empire when the first Roele took the Iron Throne, they all spoke Anuirean. In many of the human provinces, however, remnants of their old tribal speech still existed

in names, songs, and popular expressions. And that was about all
Gannd knew of Mhoried. Except one other thing.

The highlanders were not very fond of elves.

He stopped on a bluff overlooking a wide expanse of rolling hillside leading down to a grassy meadow liberally studded with rock
outcroppings. Ahead of him, to the east, a river flowed down from
the hills and meandered through the meadow, following a winding
course as it made its way down to the lowlands far to the south and
out of view beyond the mountains. To Gannd, who had grown up
in the thick, lush forests of the Aelvinnwode, the land looked rather
bleak, inhospitable, and lonely. Yet, at the same time, there was a
stark and simple beauty to it. He was not accustomed to such vistas
spreading out before him. The wind sweeping down from the
mountains ruffled the tall grass, causing it to undulate, giving the
impression of waves upon a vast green sea.

"Well, Father, what now?" he said, hitching up his pack. "You
have brought me this far. Now which way would you have me go?"

A sudden gust of wind came sweeping down the valley from the
north.

"South it is," said Gannd.

He was about halfway down the slope to the meadow, walking
with long and easy strides, when his sharp elven ears detected the
sounds of shouting and horses at the gallop, coming from the north.
A few moments later, a lone horseman came flying over the rise to
his left, his mount running at breakneck speed down the slope into
the meadow. He could see the rider lashing his steed with the reins,
urging it on to even greater speed. Even at this distance, Gannd
could see that the flanks of the horse were heavily flecked with
foam. If the rider kept up that pace for much longer, the animal
would surely give out and collapse.

The rider was about halfway down the slope, heading across
Gannd's direction of travel, when the reason for his haste appeared
over the rise. There were about a dozen riders in hard pursuit,
yelling and whipping up their mounts, and judging by the cross-
bows several of them brandished as they rode, their intentions
seemed decidedly unfriendly.

As they topped the rise, one of the pursuers loosed an arrow in
the direction of the lone rider, but at that distance, and from horse-

back, he had little hope of hitting his intended target. It was a wild shot, taken on a chance, and it predictably flew wide of its mark. But it was evidence of how anxious the pursuers were to bring their quarry down. Judging by the lather on their horses' flanks, the chase had lasted for some time. And the odds were certainly in the pursuers' favor. A dozen against one. Gannd had no idea why they were chasing the lone rider, but those odds hardly seemed fair.

As he watched, Gannd saw the lone rider's mount stumble on the lower slope and come crashing to the ground, rolling down the hillside with a high-pitched shriek that gave clear evidence the animal had been seriously injured. The rider was thrown to the ground. He landed hard, but rolled to the bottom of the slope and came up to his feet, a bit unsteadily, and drew his blade. He glanced at his injured mount, writhing on the ground, and put the poor beast out of its misery with one strong thrust. Then he faced his rapidly approaching pursuers.

Gannd started to run, moving easily through the high grass and heading down the hillside with long strides, his forward motion aided by the downward slope of the terrain. He was at least a couple of hundred yards away, but elves could run much faster than humans, even over difficult terrain, and Gannd was closing the distance rapidly as the pursuing riders closed with their quarry.

He was a big man, over six feet tall and powerfully built, with a massive chest and thick, muscular arms. His hair was light and cropped close to the skull and he wore no armor, only brown leather breeches, high boots, a dark green tunic belted at the waist and a black woolen cloak. They tried to ride him down, but the big man sidestepped the charge of the first horseman and swung his blade with both hands, slashing at his attacker. The man tumbled from the saddle with a cry and lay on the ground, motionless. One of the bowmen loosed an arrow and it struck the big man in the left shoulder, just below his collarbone and above his heart.

It didn't even slow him down. He ducked and weaved to avoid the slashing blades and charging horses, parrying two-handed as they tried to cut or run him down. Another of his attackers fell as the big man's blade struck home, but he was still outnumbered by ten to one, on foot against mounted men, and the outcome of the battle appeared to be a foregone conclusion.

Then someone shouted a command and the horsemen backed off, encircling the big man. Gannd realized what was about to happen. He stopped and quickly unslung his light, elven crossbow. With a smooth and well-practiced motion, he fitted a bolt from his quiver as several of the horsemen raised their bows.

The big man didn't want to wait to be shot down. He pulled a dagger and hurled it at one of the archers with deadly accuracy. It struck him in the chest, and he fell over backward even as he released his arrow, his shot going high and wild. At the same time, Gannd's arrow struck one of the other archers in the forehead, right between the eyes. He toppled to the ground as one of the other archers got off a shot that whizzed past the ear of the big man, who jerked aside with astonishingly swift reactions for a man his size, but by then the horsemen were aware that an attack was coming from an unexpected quarter. The leader spotted Gannd and waved his sword in the half-elf's direction, shouting out a command, and three of the riders broke off from the group and galloped toward him.

Meanwhile, the big man had not remained idle. Taking full advantage of the momentary diversion, he had produced a second dagger, thrown it at another of his assailants, with results as deadly as the first time, then charged the remaining horsemen. He leaped up onto one of the horses, knocking its rider from the saddle, and immediately engaged the others with his blade.

As the three riders thundered at him from about twenty or thirty yards away, Gannd brought up his bow and let fly another bolt. One of the riders cried out and tumbled from his saddle, shot straight through the heart. Gannd calmly stood and nocked another arrow as the two remaining riders quickly closed the distance. They were no more than ten or fifteen yards away and coming fast. He raised his bow, aimed quickly, and let fly. The arrow struck home, and the rider fell from his mount; then Gannd dropped the bow and leaped to one side as the last horseman came straight at him at full gallop. The flying hooves missed Gannd by mere inches as he hit the ground and rolled to his feet, drawing his blade as the horseman turned and came back at him.

Gannd could spare no time to see how the big man was faring against his remaining antagonists. As the last rider bore down on

Gannd, the highlander's face a mask of fury, and his blade held high, Gannd drew Bloodthirst from its well-worn leather scabbard. The blade of elven steel, once carried by his mother on the emperor's campaigns, felt like a natural extension of his arm. He sidestepped the horseman's rush, parrying his blow easily and turning it aside.

With an angry yell, the highlander turned again and came back at him. This time, Gannd waited until the last possible instant, then darted quickly across the horse's path, grabbing its reins near the bit and pulling down and to the side sharply. Jerked off-balance, the animal went down and its surprised rider was thrown. Gannd heard a sharp snap as the man landed and then moved no more, his neck broken in the fall. The horse got back up to its feet and shook itself with a neighing snort, uninjured. Gannd quickly retrieved his bow, slung it across his back, grabbed the animal's reins and swung up into the saddle.

The big man, now on horseback, was still engaging his antagonists, though there were fewer of them now. One lay either dead or unconscious on the ground, the one whose horse the big man had taken. Another was on his knees, clutching himself where he was wounded in the arm. Only the leader was left. A large and grizzled highlander, he seemed equal to the big man in his ferocity and swordsmanship.

Gannd sat astride the horse a short distance away and watched them fight. The big man was deceptively quick for his size, but he depended more on his strength than on technique. The older man was clearly not as strong, but he was no weakling, either, and he seemed to have more skill. Neither was an especially good swordsman, by Gannd's standards, but they were fairly evenly matched. The first to tire or make a mistake would lose. And a few moments later, the mistake was made by the older man. He misjudged a thrust, or else he was thrown off by the movements of the horses, and instead of going through the big man's chest, as it should have done, his blade merely passed in front of him. The big man immediately let go his reins and seized the older man's wrist, then kicked his mount in the flanks, dragging the older man right out of the saddle. For a moment, the older man hung there, squirming to break free, and then the big man struck him on the head with the pommel of his sword and let him fall to the ground, unconscious.

He turned his horse, saw Gannd watching, and saluted with his blade. Gannd nodded in acknowledgment.

"You'll pay for this, Reese, damn your soul!" shouted the wounded man from where he knelt a short distance away. "The clan will see you dead and hung out to feed the crows!"

"They'll be well sated with you lot, first," the big man replied. He rode over to the wounded man and dismounted.

"Come on then, you traitorous bastard!" the injured man shouted at him, as he struggled to his feet. "Let's finish it!" He reached with a bloody hand for the dagger in his belt.

Reese hauled off and punched him in the jaw. The man crumpled to the ground. "I'll not fight a man already beaten," Reese said. Then he sheathed his blade and knelt over the unconscious man.

"What are you doing?" Gannd asked.

"Binding his wound before he bleeds to death," said Reese, tearing a strip of cloth from the unconscious man's tunic.

"But he was going to kill you," Gannd said, puzzled.

"Aye, but he failed, didn't he?" Reese replied as he bandaged the deep cut on the man's arm. "I'll not hold that against him." He glanced up at Gannd. "I owe you my thanks, Sidhelien. And my life. But I must admit, I'm curious. Why did you choose to intervene?"

Gannd shrugged. "The odds did not seem very fair."

"And you are so concerned with fairness that you would have had me kill this man, even though he was well out of the fight?"

"It is what I expected, from a human," Gannd said. And then, realizing he had unintentionally given offense, he quickly added, "At least, from what I've heard."

The big man looked up at him again and grinned. "And an arrow in the back is what I might have expected from an elf. At least, from what I've heard."

"Half-elf," said Gannd.

The big man looked at him more closely. "Yes, so I see now, by your hair and features. Which of your parents was human?"

"My father. But I never knew him."

"Well, I never knew mine, either," Reese replied. He finished binding the man's wound and stood. "He'll live, I think, if the wound does not fester, but he'll not be wielding a blade with that arm again."

"Why were they chasing you?" asked Gannd. "Had you committed some crime?"

"To their way of thinking, I suppose I did," said Reese. "I was accused of stealing the virtue of the chieftain's eldest daughter. In truth, she surrendered it most willingly, but her father didn't quite see it that way." He pointed to the man he had pulled from his horse and knocked senseless. "That's him over there, the crusty old warhorse. Donal McMurtrie, chieftain of the Clan McMurtrie, and the Mhor's own right testicle, by fealty and honors won in battle. Damn near finished me off, the old buzzard. Would have, too, if not for your kind assistance." He came over to Gannd and held his hand out. "Duncan Reese, at your service."

"Gannd Aurealis."

"There was once a Sidhelien wizard who bore that surname," Reese replied.

"He still does," said Gannd. "Gylvain. My uncle. You know him?"

Reese's eyes widened slightly. "Not I. But I have heard of him. I try to have as little truck with sorcery as possible. No offense meant to your uncle, mind you. It is just that magic makes me rather nervous."

"I understand," said Gannd.

Reese was momentarily distracted by a moan coming from behind him. "Ah," he said, turning around. "The affronted sire awakes."

He went over to where McMurtrie lay, slowly coming to his senses, bent down, picked up the old man's sword, and hurled it as far out into the tall grass as he could. Then he prodded McMurtrie with his foot, rolling him over. "Are you awake then, McMurtrie?"

The chieftain stared up at him, fury in his eyes. "You'd do well to kill me, Reese, for if you don't, I'll hunt you down if it takes the rest of my days."

"Can't have all that many left, at your age," Reese replied.

McMurtrie reached for his dagger, but Reese had his swordpoint at the highlander's throat in an instant. "Now, now, let's not be rash. The fighting's over for this day."

47

"There'll be another," said the chieftain, scowling up at him. "You've despoiled my daughter, you lecherous pig. Don't you go thinking I'll forget."

"Look, you," Reese replied, his swordpoint never wavering from the older man's throat, "Maeve knew full well what she was doing. I was not her first, nor yet her second or her third, I'll warrant."

"Why, you filthy, lying, two-faced—"

Reese gently pressed home his point a bit and the older man fell silent. "Believe what you damn well please," he said. "But under the circumstances, I don't think I can continue in your service."

"Jest all you like," McMurtrie replied, "but you're a dead man, Duncan Reese. Kill me and my sons shall avenge me. And if I live, I'll come after you myself. You'll be marked for death by every clan in Mhoried."

"Then I suppose I'd best be leaving Mhoried," said Reese. "I was getting tired of this dreary country anyway. And you still owe me a month's back pay. I don't suppose you've got your purse on you."

He prodded around the chieftain's midsection with his swordpoint, looking for it. The old man slapped the blade away.

"Kill me and have done with it!" McMurtrie said. "But I'll not suffer any more indignities at your miserable mercenary hands!"

"Those hands were good enough to serve you when you needed men to help patrol your borders against goblins," Reese said. "And I might add that they were good enough to serve your daughter, too."

McMurtrie sputtered with rage and tried to get up, but Reese pushed him back down with his foot.

"Well, I suppose I'll have to content myself with mounts for myself and my friend here," Reese said. "And whatever coin these stalwarts might have about their bodies," he added, glancing at the dead men. "I don't think they'll be needing them. Oh, by the way, young Cullen over there has taken a rather nasty cut. I'd be getting him to a healer quick as you can manage it, else you'll have one less son to avenge Maeve's rather questionable virtue."

Reese leaned down and plucked McMurtrie's dagger from the old man's belt and stuck it in his own, then turned and walked away from the old chieftain. McMurtrie stared at Reese with pure loathing while the mercenary went to relieve the bodies of their purses and weapons.

"Aye, robbing the dead is about all a man like you is fit for!" said McMurtrie, getting to his feet. He glanced around and spotted a crossbow lying on the ground. A few yards away lay the body of one of the archers, with a quiver still slung over his back. Gannd could see the old man estimating how quickly he could snatch up the bow and reach the quiver, so he unslung his own bow and fitted an arrow to it, aiming it casually at the highlander and shaking his head slightly.

McMurtrie's frustrated rage was evident in the tension of his bearing. His eyes blazed. "I'll be remembering you too, breed!" he said.

He spoke the word as if it were an insult. Just as Sylvanna had predicted. For a moment, Gannd felt a strong temptation to shoot him down, but he resisted the urge. Reese returned with several swords and daggers, which he rolled up in a cloak he'd taken from one of the bodies and then lashed to the back of the saddle. The purses he'd recovered from the dead men he placed in his saddle pouch.

"Well, it won't quite make up for a month's pay lost," he said, "but it's better than nothing."

"You might want to take that crossbow, as well," said Gannd, indicating the weapon lying near McMurtrie, "or you may end up with an arrow in your back."

"Hmmm, good thinking," Reese said, glancing at the crossbow. He picked it up, retrieved the quiver from the dead man lying near it, and swung up into his saddle. McMurtrie stood, impotent, watching them with his jaw clenched. "Well, that should about do it, I think," Reese said.

"Aren't you forgetting something?" Gannd asked.

Reese frowned. "What?"

"That arrow in your shoulder."

"Oh, that," said Reese, glancing at the bloody shaft as if noticing it for the first time. "Best leave it where it is for now. It could be the only thing holding a blood vessel together."

"I hope it festers and poisons your damned blood!" McMurtrie shouted.

"Look to your son, McMurtrie," Reese replied. "I'll live just to spite you." He glanced at Gannd. "Which way were you headed?"

"South," said Gannd.

"South suits me just fine," said Reese.

They rode off together, leaving the chieftain shaking his fist and shouting imprecations in their wake.

chapter three

Katrina was given her own room in the castle, small by Seaharrow's standards and hardly opulent, but it was nevertheless a considerable step up from what she had been accustomed to at home. Her father's tiny holding, given by the good grace of Kier of Avan, had been a simple country keep, one small, three-story, round tower of roughly mortared, rough-cut stone with a square wall and a courtyard of hard-packed dirt that became as muddy as a hog wallow every time it rained. It stood watch over a handful of crofts scattered over the nearby countryside: tiny, thatch-roofed and dirt-floored one-room cottages in which families of peasants lived all crammed together, spending their days toiling in the fields for their lord, raising crops, tending sheep, chickens, pigs or cattle, and turning over most of their hard-earned produce to their lord and master, who in turn sent a good part of it to his own lord and master, the Duke of Avanil.

Katrina recalled how, as a child, she had believed her father was a powerful and important man until the first time she had been taken to Daulton, the capital of Avanil, where she had seen the duke's castle and the city over which he ruled. It had been a rude awakening. She had idolized her father, but on that day, when she first realized his true place in the scheme of things, he seemed diminished. It made her feel cruelly disappointed.

Seasedge was not as large a city as Daulton, nor as densely packed, but it nevertheless held an important place in the history of the empire. Ever since the days of the first Roele, it had been the summer capital of Anuire. During most of the year, especially in winter, it was lashed by fierce storms that swept in off the sea, but in the summers, the climate was more temperate, and each year, the emperor had come to Seaharrow to hold summer court. The population of the city had swelled from the arrival of not only the emperor's large retinue, but nobles and their families and retainers from all over the empire. The inns and hostels filled to overflowing, farmers from all over the surrounding countryside brought their produce to the city's markets to feed the burgeoning populace, skilled artisans set up their tents and booths to sell their wares, bards vied with one another for the attentions of the crowd in every tavern, and tournaments were held on the coastal plain below the castle.

Things were different now. No emperor sat on the Iron Throne, and so there was no summer court to be held. Seasedge was quiet and subdued, its people sullen and resigned. In the years since the emperor's death, the city's fortunes had declined. Derwyn still had to levy taxes to support his castle and his army, especially now that he had nearly doubled its size, but without the yearly bolstering effect of all the trade brought by summer court, the city's economy had suffered. And each year, it continued to grow worse. Derwyn had to make his move. He could afford to wait no longer. Hence, the attack on Avanil. He needed to make war on the neighboring provinces and conquer them, or else go broke.

In the years following the emperor's death, the lord high chamberlain, Aedan Dosiere, had acted as regent, doing everything he could to hold the empire together. However, as he had grown older, the enormity of the task weighed on him more and more. There was no shortage of claimants for the throne, and while all had strong support in their home provinces, none could claim overwhelming support throughout the empire. Lord Dosiere had been faced with an unenviable task: recognize one, and the others would rebel. Nor could he claim the throne himself, for he could boast no right to it by bloodline. He could but act as regent, trying as best he could to balance the power struggles within the aristocracy while calling repeated convocations in efforts to find a candidate for the throne whom all the nobles would support. No such man was ever found. It was not easy to fill the shoes of a Roele, though it seemed everybody wanted to.

As time dragged on and convocation after convocation ended in failure to resolve the situation, many of the nobles had started to resent the high chamberlain and accuse him of stalling and intriguing to retain power for himself. There were minor flare-ups in the outer provinces as various nobles jockeyed for position in the uncertain and highly volatile political climate. Finally, Aedan Dosiere died, and there was no one left to hold everything together.

The present high chamberlain, Aedan's son, Davan Dosiere, lacked his father's diplomatic skills and could not command the same respect his father had won upon the field of battle during the emperor's campaigns. He was regent in name only and held a precarious position as little more than the custodian of the crown. Outside the capital province of Anuire, he held no authority, and it was said that he held precious little in the capital itself. The empire had lost its heart and was fragmenting. There was going to be war, a civil war so long and fierce that it would make the recent battle between Boeruine and Avan look like little more than a skirmish, for all the death that had resulted.

Alliances were forming and solidifying. Armies were being reinforced with vigorous recruitment and mustered for the coming conflict. There was no telling where it would all end, or when, but it had already begun. Storm clouds hung over the empire, and it was still uncertain how the demihumans would react, or the awnsheghlien. But one thing was for certain—Katrina would be at the center of it all, the ebb and flow of power.

Her fortunes had improved significantly. Though she had only a small room in the east wing of the castle, just down the corridor from Derwyn's chambers, it was nevertheless twice the size of her little bedchamber in her father's keep. Her large, four-poster bed was the biggest and most comfortable she had ever slept in. She had been given an entire new wardrobe, better than anything she had ever worn before, and she now had jewels befitting the mistress of a duke.

She had not become a part of Derwyn's daily life, at least not yet, but that was no more than she'd expected. She was there merely to provide diversion, when and if he chose to avail himself of her company. They soon settled into a pattern.

He came to her several nights a week, not always on the same nights, but always after he had finished meeting with his commanders and advisors and everyone else had already retired. These meetings often lasted late into the night. Sometimes she had already fallen asleep, and his knock on her door awoke her. He never told her when he was going to visit her, nor did he ever send word if he wasn't coming. His behavior in this regard was a constant, unspoken reminder of their agreement. She was there for his convenience, only for so long as it remained convenient. She understood. He needed to feel that he was in control. It was his way of reasserting his authority. But only a man who was insecure in his authority would feel the need to assert it so often.

She soon learned to gauge his moods and know how the meetings went from how he acted when he came to her. If he was angry, he wanted to make love at once, forcefully and without preamble. It would go quickly, and he would lie spent beside her and stare up at the ceiling for a while, not wanting to talk, before he got up and returned to his own chambers. If he was frustrated, he felt the need to talk, to vent his feelings before he gave vent to passion. If he was anxious, then he needed to be held and comforted, though he did not like for her to speak at such times. It was as if allowing her to speak to him in a comforting manner would be an acknowledgment of weakness. And since Derwyn had always been eclipsed by his strong and overbearing father, he was determined to act strong and refrain from showing weakness or vulnerability of any sort. Katrina found it surprisingly easy to figure out the workings of his mind. He was a powerful noble, one of the most powerful in the empire, yet at heart, he still lived in his father's shadow. Just as his son, Aerin, lived in his.

Katrina was not yet quite certain what to make of the young Baron Boeruine. His father had brought home a mistress who was younger than his son. She had not expected Aerin to welcome her with open arms and he had not. When she was introduced to him, Aerin had greeted her with polite but sullen equanimity. She did not know his exact age, but he looked to be about thirty. He was dark and sharp-featured, and he must have favored his mother, for he did not strongly resemble Derwyn. Katrina wondered, given everything she'd heard about the Princess Laera, if Aerin was indeed Derwyn's son. Given the lack of resemblance between them, she wondered if the same thought had occurred to Derwyn.

The relationship between father and son was formal and somewhat distant. If Derwyn loved his son, he certainly didn't show it outwardly, and Aerin, in turn, behaved with his father as a vassal would to a liege lord. There was no sign of any warmth between them. When he glanced at his father, Aerin's expression was neutral, but there seemed to be a flicker of resentment in his eyes. His mother's eyes. And therein lay a clue to their relationship, Katrina realized. Every time Derwyn looked at his son, he could not help but see Laera. And he could not love him. When all was said and done, for all his power, Derwyn was just a man, with faults like any other man.

But if Derwyn did not quite fulfill all Katrina's dreams and fantasies, at least he was a good provider and did not abuse her. She had fine clothes to wear and good food to eat and friends to keep her company. She had been assigned a lady-in-waiting, a privilege and luxury she'd never had before, and they quickly became close. Lady Angharad was about the same age as Katrina, the daughter of Viscount Amante, one of Lord Derwyn's army commanders, and she was a font of social wisdom and local gossip. She seemed to know everything that was going on, and with Angharad's help, Katrina learned which of the wives and ladies of the duke's retinue could be trusted and which were spiteful and duplicitous, which of the servants could be relied upon and which were known to carry tales in exchange for a few coins, which of the men close to the duke were capable and honest and which were devious and ambitious opportunists. Angharad, Katrina thought, might have made a skillful minister. She had a natural talent for assimilating and evaluating information and for judging people, a skill Derwyn seemed to lack. In Angharad, Katrina had found not only a new friend, but a very useful ally.

The one dark cloud over Katrina's new life was her mother. Shortly after she had been installed in her chambers at Seaharrow, she had sent for her mother to come and join her. To her dismay, her mother had refused. She had not only refused, but she had sent back a scathing, hateful letter, condemning her daughter for being a traitor and becoming the whore of the man who had killed her father and brothers. She would sooner starve to death, her mother wrote, than come to Seaharrow and share in her daughter's degradation.

Katrina had been infuriated by the letter. How could her mother be so foolish as to fail to understand? After all, she had not been thinking only of herself, but of her mother, too. It was her welfare that she had been concerned with as much as her own. And what did treachery have to do with anything? Her father and her brothers were dead. Derwyn had killed them. Maybe not with his own hand, but even if he had, was it not only just that he now take care of her mother and herself? As to the matter of being a traitor to Avanil, had Kier of Avan offered to take them in and provide for them? Should she have overlooked such practical considerations in favor of misplaced idealism?

Katrina's mother wrote that she would take care of herself and wanted nothing more to do with her daughter. She had accepted a position as a seamstress. A seamstress! Well, Katrina thought, if her mother wanted to live like a peasant, then so be it. But she would not allow her life to be destroyed merely because her father and brothers had the misfortune to fight for the losing side. She had no intention of making the same mistake.

* * * * *

By nightfall, Gannd and Reese were approaching the eastern borders of Alamie. They stopped to camp by the banks of the Stonebyrn River in the shelter of a copse of willow trees, where Gannd removed the arrow from Reese's shoulder and then washed and dressed his wound. Pulling out the arrow had to be accomplished slowly and carefully, yet the mercenary didn't make a sound as it was done. He merely winced slightly and then sighed as it came out. They caught some fish and cooked them over a small fire. The night was cool, quiet and peaceful. After the drama of their initial meeting, the rest of the day's journey had proved uneventful and they encountered no one as they rode at a slow and easy pace, following the course of a stream that flowed down into the lowlands and emptied out into the Stonebyrn.

As they had ridden side by side, and occasionally walked a bit to rest their horses, they talked and got to know each other. Reese actually did most of the talking. The big man was loquacious and easygoing, unaffected and gregarious. Gannd found him very likable. He'd never met a mercenary before, though he had heard of these soldiers of fortune from his mother, who served with them in the emperor's campaigns. Her opinion of them had not been very high.

"There are soldiers who fight for a cause," she had told him, "and then there are those who fight for money. And when profit is a soldier's only motive, his heart is never truly in the fight. To be sure, there are those to whom the profession of arms is its own cause and they take as much pride in what they do as does the finest artisan, but among mercenaries, such men are rare. Mercenaries, or 'free companions' as they often call themselves—an ironic term, considering they charge dearly for their company—are unlikely to be willing to lay down their lives for any cause, because they do not believe in causes. They will fight for whomever offers the most pay. As such, their loyalties are generally governed by their purse strings. These days, no army can afford to do without at least some mercenaries, but most commanders regard them as a necessary evil, and they're rarely granted much respect or trust. It is not a profession that attracts the better sort of people, and frequently, it attracts only the dregs."

It was a description that did not quite seem to fit Duncan Reese, though he made no bones about the fact that he fought only for money. He had a roguish charm about him, an easy smile and an infectious laugh. And though he had made the profession of arms his life, he did not dwell on his heroic exploits. Instead, the stories he told as they rode together were concerned not so much with his feats in battle as with amusing anecdotes of situations he had witnessed or been part of. Often, Gannd noted, they seemed to involve women. Nor did Reese shy of telling stories where he came out looking less than heroic, such as the tale which involved the incident that led up to their meeting.

"Oh, I tell you, I knew that lass was trouble from the first moment I laid eyes on her," he said in a tone of wry resignation as he stretched out his legs and leaned back against the trunk of an old willow. "She had the knowing look about her."

"The knowing look?" Gannd asked as he sat beside the fire.

"Ah, you'll know it when you see it, lad," said Reese. "It's when a woman looks at you as if she owns you and can see right through you. The way a cat looks at a canary just before it pounces and leaves naught but a spray of feathers. It's the look a woman gets when she knows you find her comely and desirable, and it's a look that lets you know that she knows exactly what you're thinking and might just be of a similar frame of mind herself. Though, of course, that doesn't mean she won't make you jump through hoops like a trained dog to gain her favors."

"And the chieftain's daughter had this look?" asked Gannd.

"Oh, she had it, all right. And she knew that I knew exactly what that look meant, too. And I said to myself right then and there, look to yourself, Duncan. This one is trouble on the hoof. I'd seen her sort before a time or three."

"So, if you were thus forewarned by your experience, why then did you allow yourself to become . . . mixed up with her?" asked Gannd.

Reese chuckled. "Have you ever seen something that you want, lad, and you know you can't have it? It only makes you want it all the more. I knew full well I was playing with fire and that I might get burned, but you see, that only added spice to adventure. I said I was experienced, but mind you, I never said I was very smart."

Gannd merely smiled and said nothing.

"But here I've been talking your sharp ears off all day long, and you've said precious little about yourself," said Reese, producing a pipe from his pouch and filling it.

"What would you like to know?" asked Gannd.

"Well, your plans, for one thing. Elves don't often leave their lands to go wandering about in human country by themselves. For my own part, I could care less how large your ears are, but there's some who'd try to lop them off, you know."

"So I've been told," said Gannd. "They might find the task easier to contemplate than to execute."

"Perhaps," said Reese, "but why invite the trouble? Or is it that you've worn out your welcome in Tuarhievel?"

"No, Tuarhievel shall always be my home," said Gannd, "but there is another part of my life, my heritage, about which I know next to nothing. Firsthand, at any rate."

"The human part, eh?" said Reese, lighting his pipe.

"Yes. It is part of who I am, after all."

"So you're off to discover the truth about the father you never knew?" Reese shook his head. "If your mother never told you of him, then chances are she must have had good reason."

"Oh, she told me who he was," said Gannd. "And more, besides. But he died some time ago. I said I never knew him, not that I never knew his name. My father was Lord Aedan Dosiere."

Duncan raised his eyebrows. "You mean the late emperor's high chamberlain?" he said, surprised.

"The same. Did you know him?"

"Knew of him," Reese said. "There's few that didn't. He was a man much admired. He spent the last years of his life trying to hold the empire together. There are those who resented him for that, because he got in the way of their ambition, but after the Emperor Michael, there was no man who was respected more. And you say he was your father? You are certain of this? There can be no question?"

"None," said Gannd, shaking his head.

"Well, I'll be hanged," said Reese. "That means you're blooded!"

"In a manner of speaking, perhaps," said Gannd, with a shrug, "but as my parents never married, I can make no claim to the bloodline of the Dosieres."

"That wasn't what I meant, lad," Reese replied. "I was talking about your blood powers."

Gannd frowned. "My blood powers?"

"You mean to tell me that you do not even know your own blood abilities?"

Gannd shook his head. "I have heard of blood powers, of course," he said, "but then I am Sidhelien."

"You are also part human," Reese replied. "Besides, there are blooded Sidhelien, too."

"There are?" Gannd said, surprised.

"Of course. Any elf descended from those who fought at Deismaar may be blooded."

"Are you certain?" Gannd said, puzzled. "I have never heard of such a thing. And I was raised upon the lore."

"Perchance your elf lore fails to make mention of it," Reese replied. "Come to think of it, that would hardly be surprising. The Sidhelien did not believe in the old gods. Or at any rate, they never worshiped them. You know the story of the death of the old gods at the battle of Mount Deismaar?"

"Yes, of course," said Gannd. "That is part of the new lore. The god-essence released by the death of the old gods created the new gods from their human champions and bestowed blood powers upon all those it touched."

"Including the elves who fought at Deismaar," Reese said. "Strange you should not know that. What does your new lore tell you about the gods? The human gods, that is."

"That they sprang from the same Cycle of Creation that gave birth to the Sidhelien," Gannd replied.

Reese grunted. "Well, that certainly allows for the truth of both elven and human beliefs. And it leaves room for considerable freedom of interpretation. Be that as it may, I'll not dispute the question of belief with you, for I hold that each man has the right to follow his own path and worship as he chooses. However, what does your new lore say about elves being imbued with hereditary blood powers gained from the old gods of the humans?"

Gannd frowned. "Nothing."

Reese grunted. "Hmm. Strange. But then again, perhaps not so very strange after all. It fits our various conceits."

"What do you mean?" asked Gannd, confused.

"Well, when humans speak of bloodlines, they do not refer merely to the mundane matter of their ancestry, you understand. Among humans, it is a term used only to refer to those descended from the blooded of Mount Deismaar. I, for one, can claim no such descent, though for a while, when I was just a lad, I nursed the fantasy that my unknown father was descended from one of the heroes of Mount Deismaar. I looked forward to the day when my blood abilities would manifest. Alas, they never did, which gave me my answer. Whoever my father may have been, he was not of the blooded, else the blood powers would have manifested in me when I entered manhood."

"Then would that not have been so with me, as well?" asked Gannd.

"Perhaps not," said Reese. "It may work differently with elves, for all I know. And then of course, our lifespans are very brief compared to yours. A human of your age would be a full grown man, but for an elf, you are still a stripling. Perhaps your abilities have yet to manifest themselves. Either way, the Dosieres are among the blooded of Anuire. If their blood flows through your veins, then it's likely you have inherited some of their bloodline's powers."

"If that were true, then why would I have not been told of it?" asked Gannd.

Reese shrugged. "Your guess would be as good as mine. Blood powers are a source of great pride among the blooded humans of the empire. I imagine elves have their pride, too. At the risk of re-opening old wounds, we humans drove your people from their lands with the aid of priestly magic, called down from the gods by the clerics who traveled with the human armies. It was the one weapon that gave us superiority, for it was something elves could not really comprehend, having never encountered it before. I can only imagine how they must have felt, those elves who fought at Deismaar, having joined the battle on the side of the Dark Lord, so they could fight against their old human foes, only to find themselves betrayed and forced to cross over to the human side to ensure their own self-preservation. And then, as if that indignity were not enough, the gods whom they so long denied not only appeared in the flesh before their very eyes, to join the battle, but in their death imbued them with powers born of divine essence. What can you say about a god whom you neither worshiped nor believed in, who turns out not only to have been real, but whose death empowers you to be more than what you were?"

"It was for that purpose that our scholars brought forth the new lore," said Gannd, "to account for what happened and make sense of it. But the new lore says nothing about blooded elves."

"And yet there are more than a few," said Reese. "There must be, for there were many elves who fought at Deismaar."

"Do you know for a fact that there are elves with blood abilities?" asked Gannd.

"I have met at least two, that I can recall," said Reese. "It was quite some time ago, but there was no question they were blooded." He frowned, thinking for a moment. "Come to think of it, however, they never mentioned being blooded. They never spoke of it at all. Had I not witnessed them using their abilities, I would not have known they had them."

"What were the circumstances in which you witnessed this?" asked Gannd.

"Battle, both times," Reese replied.

"Indeed? You seem too young to have fought in the emperor's campaigns."

"Uh . . . no. That was before my time."

"So when did you fight with elves?" asked Gannd.

"Well . . . I didn't fight with them," Reese replied uneasily. He cleared his throat. "I . . . uh, fought against them."

"Oh," said Gannd. "I see."

"They were not your people," Reese added quickly. "That is, they were not the Sidhelien of Tuarhievel. They were from the Sielwode. And they were entirely in the right, I might add. We had knowingly trespassed on their land."

"We?" asked Gannd.

"Men of the Clan McMurtrie," Reese explained. "That fine old gentleman we left back there in the valley. I had advised them against entering the Sielwode, but they were rather anxious to avoid pursuit by members of the Clan Dunravie."

"Why were they pursuing you?"

"Because we stole some of their cattle."

Gannd raised his eyebrows. "McMurtrie hired your services so that you could be a cattle thief?"

"Well, at the time he hired me, he did not trouble to explain that stealing cattle would be among my duties," Reese replied dryly. "These highlanders regard that sort of thing as an unremarkable occurrence. They steal one another's livestock with monotonous regularity. When they're not occupied with chasing goblins who raid their lands, they're busy raiding and killing one another. They seem to believe that if it isn't nailed down, it belongs to whomever is quick enough or sneaky enough to take it."

"Are you not a highlander yourself?" asked Gannd.

"Me? I should say not! I am Dieman, born and bred."

"So what brought you to the highlands?"

Reese shrugged. "A man of arms goes where he can find work to suit his trade. And in recent years, the pickings have been lean. However, all that is changing now. The empire is crumbling and there will be war. I have heard it has already started in the southern regions. Before long, all the provinces will surely be caught up in it. And I intend to make the most of what opportunities may arise. A resourceful man can do quite well for himself in wartime. You could do worse."

"Are you suggesting I become a mercenary?" Gannd asked.

"Why not? You seem to handle yourself well. There is always work for good fighting men in wartime. And you will find that you need money to get along in human lands. If you want to discover the human side of your heritage, then I can think of no better way to do it. War brings out the best in men. And also the worst. War was what defined your father's life. As it will define your brother's."

Gannd stared at him. "My . . . brother?"

"Well, half-brother, anyway. Lord Davan, the present high chamberlain of Anuire. He is the son of Lord Aedan Dosiere and the Lady Ariel." Reese raised his eyebrows. "I had assumed you knew."

Gannd frowned and shook his head. "No. I did not. My mother never mentioned anything about him."

"Hmm. Well, no reason why she should have, I suppose," said Reese. "Perhaps your father was not yet married to Lady Ariel when he met your mother."

"I cannot believe my mother would have lain with him if he were married," Gannd replied.

"No doubt," said Reese quickly. "I did not mean to imply anything."

"I understand. She did say he was very young when they met. What is he like, my . . . brother?"

Reese shrugged. "Not having met the man, I can only repeat what I have heard. I do not move in such exalted circles, you know. But they say Lord Davan is not nearly the man his father was. He cannot hold the crown. Certainly not against Derwyn of Boeruine."

"You believe Boeruine will seize the crown by force?"

"Well, he certainly intends to try," said Reese. "He is said to have a formidable army, but he lacks support outside his province. Avanil will stand against him, as will Alamie, which will likely give their allegiance to Kier of Avan. The provinces of the Southern Coast have no compelling reason to support Avan, but even less to support Boeruine, so chances are a contender for the throne will eventually emerge from those provinces, as well. As for the Eastern Heartlands . . ." He shrugged. "It is anybody's guess which way they will go. They may form their own alliance behind someone like Torin of Ghieste or one of the guildlords of Bhalaene, or else they may wait to see how the balance of power plays out elsewhere. The Khinasi of Elinie will likely take as much advantage of the ensuing instability as possible, and the Mhor cares for nothing but his own highland domains and will stay well out of it, if he can. If not, he will support whoever promises him the most. Of the regions of the Western Coast, Brosengae, Taeghas, and Talinie have traditionally allied themselves with Boeruine. Beyond that, who knows? What are the elves likely to do if—or perhaps I should say when—the war breaks out?"

"I have no idea," Gannd replied.

Reese grunted. "Well, there you have it then. We live in uncertain times. And they are liable to grow even more uncertain in the not too distant future. I think it's going to be very interesting . . . and potentially quite profitable."

"Where do you think Lord Davan will stand?"

Reese snorted. "Squarely on both sides of the fence, for as long as he possibly can. The once mighty army of Anuire is no more. They disbanded after the emperor's last disastrous campaign and scattered to their various home provinces. Anuire still has the Imperial Guard, but they are too few to stand against Boeruine, and their loyalty was always to the emperor. Well, now there is no emperor, only a high chamberlain who rules as regent in name only. In reality, he controls the Imperial Cairn and the city of Anuire and little more than that. Davan Dosiere's position is precarious and he surely knows it. If Derwyn of Boeruine were to attack Anuire, Dosiere could not possibly defend it without aid. He would doubtless turn to Kier of Avan, whose army is probably the strongest in the region. But if Boeruine gains the support of the provinces of the Western Coast, then Avan would need to make alliances as well. What Boeruine can promise his allies is obvious: lands and titles when he becomes emperor. But what can Avan promise those whose support he hopes to gain? Nothing . . . unless he receives some guarantee from the high chamberlain that he will be in a position to reward his allies suitably if Lord Derwyn is defeated. Which means that Lord Davan would have to promise him the Iron Throne."

"And if he does not?" asked Gannd.

"Well, Lord Davan needs the Duke of Avanil to keep Boeruine at bay. Avan cannot do that on his own. At least, not if the nobles of the Western Coast throw their support behind Lord Derwyn. So Kier of Avan needs to make alliances. But with nothing to promise his allies if the high chamberlain does not name him successor to the throne, can Avan gain the support he needs? Either way, can he afford to allow Boeruine to take Anuire? If he does, then what is to prevent Boeruine from forcing the high chamberlain to acknowledge him as emperor? Davan will either confirm Boeruine to safeguard his own life, or else Boeruine will kill him and proclaim himself emperor anyway."

"So it would appear that the Duke of Avanil will have to help defend Anuire, whether my half-brother promises him anything or not," said Gannd.

Reese nodded. "I think I would agree with that. Which means that Davan doesn't have to promise the Duke of Avanil a thing unless he wants to. Militarily, the high chamberlain's position is quite poor. But politically, he has room to maneuver. If he's smart, he'll refrain from making any promises to Avan until he sees which way the wind blows. Suppose, for example, the guilds put forth their own contender for the throne? With the considerable influence they command throughout the empire, it is quite possible they can muster more support than either Avan or Boeruine. Then where does that leave Davan if he formally recognizes Avan's claim?"

"I begin to see what you mean about all the uncertainty," said Gannd. "So where does Duncan Reese stand in all of this?"

Reese smiled. The flickering flames of their campfire made shadows dance across his face, giving him a slightly demonic aspect as he grinned. "When it gets down to the short strokes, my friend, Duncan Reese stands for Duncan Reese. But then, no man profits who truly stands alone. A wise man knows how to choose his enemies as well as his friends. He knows how and when to pick his battles. Well, at the present time, we do not yet possess enough information to make such decisions intelligently. At this point, we may only theorize."

"Indeed? And what is your best theory?"

Reese pursed his lips thoughtfully as he leaned back against the tree trunk. "From what I've heard, Derwyn of Boeruine has the strongest army in the empire at present."

"So you mean to enlist with him?"

Reese held up his hand. "Not so fast, my friend. Let us consider our options carefully. Boeruine is said to have the strongest army at this time. Well, one might think that means his chances are the best. However, if he has spent time building up this army and training them, then doubtless he already has his full complement of officers. He may need able bodies, but he does not necessarily need men to lead them. There will be attrition, to be sure, as the war progresses, but a standing army in need of new officers to replace those who have fallen will promote from the enlisted ranks, not from among mercenaries who came late to the conflict and whose loyalty could be subject to some question. And in time of war, a man who looks to improve his lot seeks a place where he can rise the fastest. So . . . Boeruine is on the march. Or if not yet, then he soon will be. That means those who will oppose him need to build up their forces quickly. And it is there that we must look for our opportunities.

"After Boeruine, the next strongest seems to be Kier, the Duke of Avanil," Reese continued. "Those who oppose Boeruine will doubtless flock to him. Now, he too has a standing army, but it is not as large. Lord Derwyn has the advantage of numerical superiority in the forces left to him by his father, and they are more seasoned. Therefore, Avan needs to play catch-up in the race. He must also forge alliances, and quickly. All of which means he cannot afford to be particular about how he fills out his ranks . . . and his corps of officers. So it would seem we could serve our interests best by offering our services to Kier of Avan."

"You take for granted that I have decided to go with you," Gannd replied with a smile.

"Well, have you anything better to do?" asked Reese.

Gannd shook his head, still smiling.

"Good. Then it's settled. We shall ride together, soldiers of fortune off to war. We have nothing but good prospects before us, a fair sky full of stars above us, strong horses and strong blades, a warm fire, and bellies full of river trout. I tell you, what could possibly be better?"

Gannd smiled. "A wise man knows how to take pleasure in the simple things."

"And so he does," Reese agreed. "Is that a proverb from the elf lore?"

"No, it is a saying of my uncle Gylvain's."

"Well, here's to him, then," said Reese, making a toasting gesture with a small wineskin, squeezing a stream into his mouth, then tossing it to Gannd. "Are you a light sleeper?"

"Yes."

"Good. Then I'll take the first watch. Get some rest. I'll wake you around midnight."

"Are we in unsafe territory?" Gannd asked.

"No place in the empire is safe these days," Reese replied. "A wise man always has someone he can trust to watch his back. That's one of *my* sayings."

Gannd smiled. "Well, good night, then." He stretched out on the ground and covered himself with his cloak while Reese leaned back against the willow tree and smoked his pipe. Before long, Gannd was fast asleep.

* * * * *

He wasn't sure what woke him up at first, but then he heard Reese softly saying his name. "Gannd . . . are you awake?"

The horses were skittish, whinnying and pulling against their reins, trying to pull free from the tree to which they were tied.

"Don't move," said Reese softly. "Be quiet and listen."

Instantly, Gannd was alert, lying on the ground and listening intently. The fire had burned down low. For a moment, he heard nothing but the sounds of the frightened horses and the soft crackling of the wood burning, but then there was a faint rustling out in the darkness, just beyond their camp.

"Your ears are better than mine," said Reese in a voice little above a whisper. "How many are out there?"

Gannd lay still and listened for a moment. The sounds were very faint, though he could hear them clearly. They were being very quiet and stealthy. He was surprised Reese had been able to hear them at all. "At least four, maybe five or six," he said in a low voice. "They're moving to surround us."

"I thought as much," said Reese, reaching casually to put some more wood on the fire.

The breeze was blowing from the north. Gannd sniffed the air. "They are not human," he said.

"What are they then?" asked Reese.

Gannd shook his head, puzzled. "I cannot tell. I do not know the scent."

"What does it smell like?"

"Musky," Gannd said. "Strong and gamey. But from the sounds, they move like men."

Reese tensed. "Gnolls," he said. "Damn. Look to your blade, lad. We're in for a nasty fight."

Gannd had heard of gnolls, but he had never seen one. They were a race of feral humanoid creatures that resembled hyenas, only much larger. They walked erect, on two legs, with arms and hands much like a human's. They possessed a rudimentary intelligence, but it was savage and brutish. Though capable of making clothing, tools and weapons, they much preferred to steal them from their victims . . . whom they'd then consume. Their natural habitats were the mountains and high plains of the northern regions, but they were known to range far and wide in hunting packs, stalking their prey by night.

"If there are only five or six, then they are advance scouts for the main pack," said Reese. "With only two of us, they must think we're easy pickings. Let's hope the main pack isn't close at hand."

"And if it is?" Gannd asked.

"If it is, we're dead," said Reese. "When they make their move, they will rush us all at once, howling like a pack of hounds. They will try to separate us, the better to take us down. We must keep together. Stay by the fire. They can see well in the dark. If worse should come to worst, make for the river and swim for it. You can swim, I trust?"

Gannd nodded. He reached for his crossbow. He had barely closed his hand around it when the creatures rushed them. They came bursting out of the thicket surrounding the copse of trees, howling and yipping like banshees. Moving with swift and practiced precision, Gannd drew a bolt from his quiver and in one smooth motion fitted it to his bow, drew back, and let fly. One shot was all he had time for. The bolt took the first charging creature in the neck and it went down, and then the others were upon them.

Gannd swung his bow hard, like a club, smashing it into the snarling maw of one of the charging creatures. It yowled and went down to the ground, its jaw and several teeth broken, but the impact also broke the bow. Gannd dropped it and drew Bloodthirst. The curved blade of elven steel gleamed in the firelight as he side-stepped quickly and slashed at a gnoll that came leaping at him, brandishing a short battle-axe. The beast howled as Bloodthirst sliced cleanly through its flesh, severing bone and tendon, and the clawed hand holding the axe was chopped off at the wrist. With a human, the fight would have ended there, but even wounded as badly as it was, the creature kept attacking, snapping at Gannd with its jaws as it shrieked in pain. He kicked it away and brought his blade down in a chopping stroke at the juncture of neck and shoulder. The gnoll collapsed to the ground, thrashing and squealing as it spewed blood from its wounds. Another stroke finished it off.

Reese, standing back-to-back with Gannd, killed the first gnoll that came at him with a powerful, two-handed blow from his sword, splitting its skull, then ran another one through the stomach. As Gannd finished off the gnoll he had clubbed down with his bow, Reese was brought down by the last one as the creature leaped at him from the side, knocking him off balance. They fell to the ground, rolling, and Reese dropped his blade. He cried out with pain as the gnoll sank its fangs into his left bicep. He smashed it with his fist, but could not dislodge the beast. It bore him down, its jaws clamped firmly on his arm, its right hand holding a dagger poised to plunge into Reese's chest. He grabbed the creature's wrist and they struggled on the ground, then the gnoll released its hold on the human's left arm and started snapping at his throat. Gannd brought his blade down, just above the creature's waist, severing its spine. It died instantly and collapsed on top of Reese.

"That's twice you've saved my life," said Reese, breathing hard as he rolled the creature's body off him.

"You're bleeding," Gannd said. "We need to get that wound bandaged."

"Not now," said Reese. "We need to get out of here. The main pack cannot be far behind, and there will be at least fifteen or twenty of them."

Even as he spoke, Gannd could hear their high-pitched, yipping cries in the distance, rapidly approaching.

"Get the horses," Reese said. "Quickly."

There was only one. Gannd, unaccustomed to horses, had not tied his as securely as had Reese and the animal had pulled loose and bolted when the gnolls attacked. He untied Reese's frightened horse, which neighed and tried to pull away from him as he held its reins, its eyes rolling as it reared up on its hind legs. Gannd had to dig in his heels and hold on tight to keep the horse from wrenching loose. It took several moments for him to get the animal under control, during which time the gnolls' cries came much closer.

"Hurry!" Reese shouted as he finished gathering up their things.

Gannd helped him mount, then swung up behind him. The frightened animal needed no urging as Reese guided it into the river. The horse plunged in and started swimming, clearly terrified by the yipping cries of the gnolls. The companions had scarcely cleared the riverbank when the creatures burst into their campsite. Gannd could hear their drawn out, ululating howls as the gnolls found the bodies of their packmates. As they started to drift downstream, Reese guided the horse across to the opposite bank at an angle, so that it would not have to fight the current, while the gnolls paced them on the bank behind them, snarling and howling with rage. Gannd could not tell for sure how many gnolls there were, but there were well over a dozen. A moment or two more and the ugly creatures would have been upon them.

"Can they get across?" asked Gannd in a worried tone.

"Not unless there's a nearby bridge or ford," Reese said. "Gnolls are not good swimmers. They dislike the water."

"I could tell," said Gannd, wrinkling his nose at their powerful scent, wafting toward him on the night breeze. He glanced down at Reese's arm. "You are hurt. You have lost a lot of blood."

Reese shook his head. "That's of little consequence. A gnoll's bite is poisonous."

Gannd frowned. "My people have often encountered gnolls. We have never found them to be poisonous."

"In these parts, they carry a disease. A disease that may as well be poison. It can be fatal," Reese replied. "It depends on how much of the infection has entered the bloodstream, so the bleeding helps. We must avoid binding the wound so long as it bleeds freely."

"How long before the disease takes effect?" asked Gannd with concern.

"Not long. Within the hour, I shall weaken and succumb to fever. It will alternate with chills. Soon after that, I shall become delirious. Then, if enough of the poison has entered my bloodstream, I shall fall into a stupor."

"And then?"

"Then my heart will stop and I shall die."

"Is there nothing to be done?" asked Gannd.

Reese shook his head. "Not to my knowledge. The flow of blood may wash out some of the bad blood and give me a fighting chance, assuming I don't bleed to death."

Their horse reached the opposite bank and climbed up out of the water. Behind them, the pack of gnolls howled in anger and frustration.

"You shall have to take the reins," said Reese, slumping forward in the saddle. "Head southeast. There is nothing more to be done at present. With Haelyn's help, I may get through this. If I'm still alive come morning, then the worst will be over."

"Don't talk," said Gannd. "Save your strength."

Reese merely nodded. Now that the initial rush of energy from fighting off the gnolls had ebbed, his strength was fading fast. He had already been wounded once, earlier that day. Now, the gnoll's bite was quickly taking its toll. Duncan Reese was as strong as an ox, thought Gannd, but there was a limit to how much anyone could endure.

The moon was full as they rode across the plains of Alamie, heading in a southeasterly direction. There were no signs of any roads or nearby farms or settlements. The rolling grasslands stretched out for as far as the eye could see, the flatness occasionally interspersed with stands of willow or cottonwood trees. Before long, Reese had weakened to the point where Gannd had to keep his arms around the wounded man, holding him in the saddle, otherwise he would have slid off to the ground. His breathing grew more labored, and he was burning with fever. It was still a few hours til dawn when Gannd reined in and stopped beneath a stand of cottonwoods. They would have to stop here. Clearly, Reese could go no farther.

Gannd dismounted and helped Reese down to the ground. He laid him on his back and covered him with a cloak. The big man was breathing raggedly, struggling to draw air into his lungs. His massive chest rose and fell with the effort as his mouth tried to gulp down the air. He made Gannd think of an impossibly large fish out of water. His forehead was beaded with perspiration, and it rolled down his cheeks and matted his hair. Duncan's eyes were closed. He was flushed and barely conscious. The maddening thing was that Gannd couldn't think of anything he could do to help.

He moistened his lips and his hand went to his throat, feeling the enchanted amulet hanging beneath his tunic. Reese needed time. And Gannd desperately needed his uncle's advice. He pulled out the amulet and closed his fingers around it, shutting his eyes and thinking of a hawk in flight.

As he clutched the amulet, he pictured a red-tailed hawk with its wings spread wide, gliding high above them on the wind currents, and he seemed to hear its shrill, echoing cry upon the wind. . . . And suddenly, it felt as if he were rushing up out of himself, hurled into the air with such speed that there was only the sensation of wind whistling past and a dark blur all around him as even the stars became streaks of light shooting past. . . . The whooshing sound around him grew, then fell and rose, fell and rose repeatedly, like strange waves of wind crashing upon some distant, rocky shore.

It all happened so impossibly fast . . . the illusion of hearing the cry of the hawk, the strange sensation of leaving his own body and hurtling through space, and now . . . he found himself standing in a luminous gray mist that swirled around him, parting to reveal a gigantic archway of stone that spanned an impossibly wide chasm that appeared to have no bottom. There were no guard walls on either side, nothing to prevent a fall into the seemingly bottomless abyss. He could not see where the bridge began or where it ended. It simply seemed to go on forever, spanning a misty chasm that appeared to have no beginning and no end. He stood between two worlds, in a timeless zone between the World of Light and the dreaded Shadow World. Nothing moved here except the wind, which rose and fell in pitch, like the sound of the world breathing. He stood upon the Bridge of Sighs.

chapter four

It was an unsettling, desolate place, shrouded in mist and cold. Gannd felt as if he were suspended in eternity. And then he realized that was exactly where he was. He stood between two worlds in a timeless silence broken only by the sighing of the wind. Gannd swallowed hard and closed his eyes. Uncle, he thought, where in the Lady's name have you sent me? Help me, Uncle. Please. I need you.

"I wondered how long it would take before you chose to try the amulet's spell," his uncle's voice said. It seemed to echo all around him, as if borne upon the wind.

Gannd looked all around, but could see nothing except the swirling mists, which occasionally parted to reveal the gaping chasm on both sides. He estimated the bridge was about fifteen feet wide. No danger of falling so long as he kept close to the middle of the span and did not venture too close to the edge. There was enough room for several horses to cross abreast, or perhaps a small carriage, so long as the progress was slow. With the mist eddying around the bridge, covering its slippery surface with foggy tendrils, it would be all too easy to move a few feet in the wrong direction, slip, and go right off the side.

"Uncle?" he called out. "Uncle, where are you?"

"No need to shout," Gylvain replied. He came walking through the mist, dressed in his midnight-blue sorcerer's robes. Gannd stared at him. He seemed solid, as if he were actually standing there in front of him.

"Uncle? Is that really you?"

"Whom else were you expecting?"

"No one. It is just that you . . . you seem so real," Gannd said, staring at him. It seemed incongruous to see Gylvain in such strange surroundings. The whole thing had the aspect of a dream.

"Reach out and touch me," Gylvain replied.

Gannd stepped forward, reaching out to his uncle. His hand passed right through. Gannd, startled, quickly drew it back.

"No need for alarm. We are both real, but only our astral selves are present here, not our physical bodies," Gylvain said. "They remain where we have left them, fixed in time, while we now stand beyond it."

"Uncle, I need your help," said Gannd. "A friend, a human, has been bitten by a diseased gnoll and now lies nearly senseless. He is feverish, his breathing labored. I fear that he may die."

"Was there bleeding from the wound?" asked Gylvain.

"Much. He said that it would help wash out the poisoned blood, but it has also weakened him severely. And he was already wounded, shot with a crossbow. He is a large man, and a strong one, but I fear that he has reached the limits of his endurance."

"If he is strong, and the wound has bled, there is a chance he will survive," said Gylvain. "If a gnoll bites and does not tear the flesh greatly, the wound may not bleed much and the disease will spread more quickly. On the other hand, if the flesh is torn and the wound is ragged, it will bleed more, which reduces the amount of bad blood spreading through the bloodstream, but at the same time increases the chances of more mundane infection."

"What can I do?" asked Gannd.

"You must place him on his back, with his upper body slightly elevated, so that he may rest comfortably and breathe more freely. If his breathing has already become labored, and he is feverish, then he is now at the point of greatest danger. Cleanse the wound as best you can and dress it as I taught you. If your friend should succumb to delirium, watch to see that he does not swallow his tongue and choke himself. Try to keep him awake and talking. If he slips into unconsciousness, he may not revive. Beyond that, there is little you can do."

"But . . . what about magic? Is there no spell that could be employed to help him recover?"

"Magic used for healing is one of the most subtle and demanding aspects of the art," Gylvain replied. "It requires years of dedicated study. And it is certainly not something I could teach you here. If you wanted to learn magic, you should have picked up the scroll rather than the dagger."

"But . . . I was a mere infant then!"

Gylvain raised his eyebrows. "That is hardly my fault."

"Then . . . there is nothing I can do to help my friend?"

"There is, perhaps, one thing. . . ." Gylvain hesitated.

"What, Uncle? Tell me, please."

"You are descended from the bloodline of the Dosieres," the mage said. "And the power of healing was among their blood abilities."

Gannd shook his head helplessly. "But how am I to know if I have inherited that power? And even if I have, how would I use it?"

"That I cannot tell you," Gylvain said.

"Cannot? Or will not?"

"Don't be impertinent," Gylvain replied irritably. "Most Sidhelien would not even discuss the subject of blood powers with you, even though you are half human."

"Why? Because it is inconvenient to our beliefs? Because it admits the truth of the human gods in addition to our own? Or perhaps at the expense of them?"

Gylvain compressed his lips and regarded his nephew steadily, his gaze stern and disapproving. "You speak with the rash impetuosity of youth, Gannd," he said. "Though it is normal to have doubts about spiritual matters at your age, it is not seemly to impugn another's faith merely to settle the question of your own. Especially when it is the faith of your own people. You should know better. You were raised to revere the Lord and Lady. Now, after only a short time in the human world, you question them. Is your faith that weak?"

"If it fails to acknowledge truth, then it is our faith that is at fault and not the strength of my belief," Gannd countered.

"You speak nonsense. We do not deny the existence of the human gods. We merely do not worship them. They do not serve our needs. Aside from that, we still recall that it was their magic the human priests called down upon us in the wars. We can acknowledge the existence of the human gods, but we have little reason to revere them."

"Not even if they bestowed the boon of blood powers on the elves who fought at Deismaar and their descendants?"

"I count myself fortunate not to have been blooded," Gylvain replied. "If you have inherited the blood powers of the Dosieres, then you may find that they are less a boon than a curse."

"How can it be a curse to have the ability to heal?" Gannd asked.

"I shall leave you to discover that for yourself, if indeed, that is an ability that you possess. However, that is a question you must settle for yourself. From what I know of blood powers, based upon what I have observed, will plays a key part in bringing them forth. But know this: not all blood abilities can be controlled completely once they are manifested. And I do not know all the blood powers of the Dosieres. There are some, such as divine rage, which was one of the blood powers of the Roeles, which defy control altogether. I saw the Emperor Michael manifest this power during his campaigns. Once in the grip of it, he would slay whoever and whatever came within his reach, friend and foe alike, and there was no stopping him until the rage had run its course. Each blooded line has inherited abilities that are passed on from generation to generation, but there is never any telling which of the blooded line's abilities an individual may inherit. Nor is there any way to predict what effect a mixed blood-line, such as elf and human, may have upon the powers that may be passed on. The blood of the Dosieres runs in your veins. Their blood powers may be dormant within you, as well. But if you should awaken them, take care, for there is no telling what you might bring forth."

"I must do something to try to help my friend," said Gannd.

"The desire to help is laudable," said Gylvain. "But the act may have consequences for which you cannot be prepared."

Gannd frowned as he gazed at his uncle. The mage was slowly

becoming insubstantial, like a specter, gradually fading from sight. Gannd could now see through him.

"I cannot remain here any longer," Gylvain said. "The power of the amulet can summon me only for a short while. The longer you wear it, and the more you use it, the more it shall become attuned to you and lose its link with me. I have given you what advice I can. You must do what you think best, Gannd. Good luck."

As he spoke, Gylvain faded from sight and Gannd was left alone, standing on the windswept bridge. He took a deep breath and exhaled heavily. There was nothing to be gained from remaining any longer. Reese would still be in the same condition as he left him. If there was anything that he could do, he would have to seek the ability within himself, for better or for worse. And Reese couldn't get much worse.

Gannd reached up and grasped the amulet around his neck. He closed his eyes and once again pictured a hawk in flight. He imagined a nighthawk soaring high above the treetops of the Aelvinnwode, and he heard its screeching cry, which seemed to emanate from his mind to manifest in his surroundings, echoing through the chasm, over the sound of the sighing wind. He felt rushing wind and, for a moment, he became alarmed, thinking he had somehow slipped and fallen, but he was rising rapidly rather than falling. He kept his eyes shut to avoid the vision of that unsettling, blurring plunge through the ether until he finally felt the ground under him once more. He opened his eyes to find himself kneeling once again by Duncan's side. He glanced around, momentarily disoriented. It seemed as if no time had passed at all, as if that entire episode on the bridge had been nothing more than a brief reverie, a daydream that had lasted for the space of an eyeblink. And yet he knew it had been real.

Reese moaned softly. Gannd bent over him, propping him up slightly. "Duncan . . ."

Reese was breathing slowly and heavily. His eyes were shut. "Duncan . . ."

"Tired . . . let me sleep. . . ."

"No, Duncan, come on, wake up. Talk to me."

Reese swallowed hard and opened his eyes. "Gannd?"

"You have to talk to me, Duncan. Don't go to sleep. If you pass out, you may not revive again."

"Mmmph . . . hard to breathe."

"I know. But you must stay conscious."

"Dying . . ."

"Not if I have anything to say about it," Gannd replied. He slapped the mercenary lightly on the cheeks. "Come on, Reese, stay awake. Talk to me. Tell me one of your stories."

"Too tired. . . . Can't breathe. . . ." He closed his eyes.

"Duncan . . . Reese! Damn it, open your eyes! Stay awake!"

"Can't . . ."

His breathing was ragged. There was a rattle in his throat.

"Duncan, damn you, don't you die on me!"

The breath hissed out of Reese slowly, and his chest did not rise again.

"Reese!"

He had stopped breathing. Gannd shook him. No response. "Reese! Come on!" He shook him again, then slapped him, then pounded him on the chest. He bent over, putting his face close to the human's. There was the faintest trace of breath, so shallow as to be almost unnoticeable, and it was irregular. Reese was trying to stay alive, but was failing.

Gannd held him in his arms and looked helplessly up at the heavens. "In the name of the Lady, Uncle," he cried. "What do I do?"

His uncle's words upon the Bridge of Sighs came back to him. "From what I know of blood powers . . . will plays a key part in bringing them forth."

In desperation, Gannd tightened his grip on Reese, shut his eyes and concentrated fiercely, focusing his thoughts on one thing only.

Live, he thought, with all the intense fervor he could muster. Live. . . .

Gritting his teeth with concentration, he focused all his energies on that one thought, as if he could somehow will his own strength to pass from his body into Duncan's. He began to tremble. It felt as if a fever were coming over him. His chest began to ache, and heat seemed to be building up inside him, as if he were burning up. Then he felt it start to flow, moving from his chest and into his shoulders, down into his arms, growing warmer and passing through his wrists into his hands and fingertips. He continued concentrating, willing his strength into Reese. Gannd started to grow dizzy, but he kept his focus, fighting the vertiginous sensation while clutching Reese with all his might.

Reese shuddered suddenly and his chest rose as he gasped, sucking in a rasping, hoarse breath of air. He coughed, made a choking sound, then gulped in another breath, like a drowning man fighting to get air into his lungs. Moments later, he was sitting up, breathing normally, though he looked shaken.

"By Haelyn, I thought I was done for," he said.

Gannd was on his hands and knees, his head hanging down, his forehead damp with perspiration. He felt weak and dizzy.

"Here, take it easy, lad," Reese said. "Lie back and rest a bit. You'll need to get your strength back." He got up, a bit unsteadily, and took the waterskin from the saddle of their horse and held it for Gannd to drink. "Saving my life is getting to be a habit with you," Reese said. "I'm starting to accumulate a debt I may not be able to repay, though it won't be for lack of trying."

"I feared you were dead," said Gannd.

"Well, I'm not, thanks to you. I had no idea you were a healer."

"Neither did I," said Gannd weakly. "At least, not for certain."

"In that case, I'm right glad you found out," Reese replied with a grin. "So now you know you're blooded. You've inherited your father's blood abilities, if not his name and title. Which, considering the way things are these days, you're probably better off without. Either way, I owe you my life. Yet again."

"I'm pleased that I could help."

"And I promise you that while I live, I shall not forget."

Gannd smiled. "The way you're going, that might not be very long."

Reese chuckled. "Well, I'll try to do my best not to tax your energies in keeping me alive."

"I feel exhausted."

"That is no surprise. You drew upon your own strength to heal me. You need to get some sleep now. I will keep watch. It will be sunrise before long, but we can continue our journey around midday, after you have rested sufficiently. And at the first town we come to, we shall use some of that gold I took from those highlanders and secure lodgings and a fine meal at an inn, then see about purchasing another horse and a new crossbow to replace the one you broke. It will not be an elven bow, I fear, but I shall buy you the best one we can find. And perhaps some new clothes and a dagger or two, eh? What do you say to that?"

But Gannd had nothing to say. He had fallen fast asleep.

*   *   *   *   *

The town of Seasedge had become like an armed camp. Derwyn needed to replace his casualties and further build up his army, but he did not have very far to look for new recruits. Word of the indecisive battle between the warring dukes of Boeruine and Avanil had traveled fast throughout the crumbling empire, and it wasn't long before men from the surrounding countryside started arriving in Seasedge by the score. Some came from as far way as Ghieste and Elinie in hopes of joining Boeruine's army. Times were hard and work was scarce. Several seasons of poor harvests in the western provinces had left many people hungry and more than a few greedy and ambitious nobles, unchecked by an emperor's authority, had ruinously increased taxes on the people of their domains, augmenting their own wealth at the expense of the beleaguered commoners. The once-thriving trade between the provinces had become irregular and undependable as various local dukes and barons began to levy their own tariffs on imported goods within their domains and quarrelled with the powerful merchant guilds, who resisted by placing trade sanctions on their provinces, thereby unintentionally helping to create black markets which thrived on profiteering.

The common people suffered most from these developments, and many crofters and tradesmen throughout the empire found themselves unable to earn a livelihood and sustain their families. Not a few had their crops and livestock seized for inability to pay their increased taxes, and many found themselves reduced to homelessness and penury. There were more beggars on the streets in every town and city and more brigands on the roads between them. Lawlessness was on the increase everywhere.

In such times of desperation, there was no shortage of willing recruits for Derwyn's army, especially since the custom of plunder during wartime offered soldiers the opportunity to enrich themselves. Each day, new arrivals came to Seasedge in carts and wagons, bringing all of their possessions with them, many coming on foot, alone or with their families, carrying all they owned upon their backs. Innkeepers in Seasedge doubled, tripled, and quadrupled their rates, taking full advantage of the shortage of accommodations and gouging everyone. Many of the townspeople and farmers in the vicinity took in boarders, often cramming them into whatever space was available, even in barns, stables, and drafty storage sheds, or simply letting them pitch tents or erect crude shacks out in their fields in return for rents charged or labor performed. It was a new form of indentured servitude. Commoners at the very bottom of the social ladder who once worked the fields for their lords suddenly found themselves in a position where they could lord it over indigents who were willing to perform menial labor in return for a small room or a bed or even a little plot of ground on which to pitch a tent or build a lean-to. The town of Seasedge and its environs were seeing the birth of a new lower middle class

The army of Boeruine was encamped in the fields below the castle, while on the plains beyond the town, a tent city of transients had sprung up, stretching all the way to the borders of the Aelvinnwode. The army encampment was kept relatively clean and orderly, with discipline strictly maintained by the watch, but in the tent city on the outskirts of the town, conditions had grown filthy and squalid. And in the wake of all those who came to enlist in Derwyn's army came the camp followers and peddlers who sold everything from cheap sundries and dry goods to weapons of inferior quality and watered-down wine and ale. Then came the gamblers, the cutpurses and the pickpockets, alleymen and usurers, prostitutes and rogues of every description, as well as swaggering mercenaries who went everywhere armed to the teeth, adding a malevolent presence of intimidation to every inn, gaming house, and tavern. Brawls were a daily occurrence; murders were becoming commonplace; theft and robbery was rampant.

The sheriff's men-at-arms were simply unable to cope with it all and, within the confines of the tent city on the outskirts of the town, they didn't even bother trying. Those poor unfortunates were left to fend for themselves as best they could. Some banded together and hired ruffians, would-be mercenaries of evil disposition and limited ability, to guard their little sections of encampment, which led to competition between bands of thugs-for-hire and only made things worse.

The archduke was displeased with the state of affairs, but took some solace in the knowledge that things were just as bad in Avanil, as reported by his spies. Of course, if he had spies in Avanil, it was a foregone conclusion that Lord Kier had sent spies to Boeruine, as well. Neither was yet prepared for a return engagement, but it would not be long. The race now was to see who could build the larger army faster and whip them into shape for a campaign. And seeing to that was taking all of Derwyn's time and energy.

During the daytime, Katrina rarely saw him. He was always out in the fields with his knights and men-at-arms, seeing to the drilling of the new recruits and the organizing of supplies, sending foraging and hunting parties out to bring in game and produce from the forest and outlying farms to keep the growing army fed. This, needless to say, imposed a hardship on the local farmers, who were not paid for any of the crops or livestock that the archduke's men commandeered. Many of them, out of pure self-preservation, had started trying to conceal their dwindling assets, though the penalties were severe if they were caught. Between the economic hardships imposed on the populace by the necessity to maintain, supply, and feed the army, and the difficult conditions brought about by all the new arrivals, a great deal of resentment was building in the common people. If Derwyn was oblivious to this, either because he did not care or else was simply too preoccupied to notice, Katrina was well aware of what was happening. But it was not something she could come right out and say.

As mistress to the archduke, it was not her place to act as his advisor or offer unsolicited opinions. She was there for his convenience, as per their arrangement, and she knew that Derwyn's natural distrust of women, stemming from his disastrous marriage to the late, unlamented Princess Laera, would result in any advice that she might offer being either summarily dismissed or regarded with suspicion. So long as she kept within the boundaries of her clearly defined role, Katrina's position would remain secure . . . assuming she continued to please Derwyn. And she made it a point to become a subtle master in reading his moods and divining what it would take to please him.

However, she had much more in mind than simply being Derwyn's concubine. If she remained within the strict boundaries of that role, sooner or later he was bound to tire of her. And Katrina had not come so far nor sacrificed so much merely to be discarded at the archduke's whim when he grew bored with her. Derwyn was a powerful man, but at heart, he was still the weak son of a strong father. Deep down inside, that was what drove him in his obsession to win the Iron Throne, to succeed where his father had failed. And the insecurity that lay at the heart of Derwyn's personality was something Katrina was learning to exploit.

Lady Angharad was her chief tool in this regard, a valuable source of gossip and information who was becoming ever more adroit at gathering such intelligence. And the other key resource Katrina was starting to develop was the archduke's son.

She saw Aerin now a great deal more than she saw his father. While Derwyn's days were filled with the pursuits of war, Aerin's days were filled with boredom and ennui. He was a full-grown man, older than Katrina, and yet he was treated like a delicate child by his father, confined for the most part to the castle and schooled in such things as the history of the empire, political strategy, trade policies, theology, and philosophy, all in preparation for the day when—his father hoped—he would one day succeed him to the Iron Throne.

Aerin was not permitted to learn the art of swordsmanship, nor was he allowed even to ride, since Derwyn was concerned about the possibility of injury to his only heir. If he was going to be the future emperor, then it was fitting that he ride in carriages and have vassals do his fighting for him. Derwyn did not wish his son to become like the late Emperor Michael, irrepressibly leading troops into battle where he could be killed. As a result, Aerin was being trained more like a future minister than a future king. He was Derwyn's only heir and, as the son of Princess Laera, his only direct tie to the Imperial House of Roele. As such, Derwyn regarded him less as a son than a commodity. And, in doing so, he was treating Aerin much the same way his own father had treated him.

Initially, Aerin had been an enigma to Katrina. She could seem to get no real sense of him. He was always courteous to her, but he was distant and had struck her as sullen and introverted at first. However, there was more to Aerin of Boeruine than met the eye, as Katrina soon learned from Lady Angharad.

In a sense, there were two Aerins—the public Aerin and the private one. The public Aerin was the one Katrina saw, and the one his father knew. The private one was kept beneath the surface, but it was a side of Aerin that his father never saw. Once she had learned of it, however, that such a side of him existed did not surprise Katrina, considering the way Aerin was forced to live.

Everyone at Seaharrow, it seemed, knew about the "private Aerin" save his father. And though Aerin was more or less discreet in his private pursuits, it was hard to keep secrets within the confines of the castle. Angharad gave Katrina full and detailed reports of things that Aerin did, the knowledge of which would never reach his father, not because Aerin commanded so much loyalty, but because everybody knew how Derwyn would react if he was told. For Aerin, it seemed, was very much his mother's son. A sexual libertine of the first order.

He had long since plowed his way through all the young female servants of the castle and then had started on the young single ladies of his father's court. The possibility of marriage with an archduke's only son, especially when there was a chance he could become the emperor someday, meant that his advances were not often refused, and on those rare occasions when they were, Aerin's dogged persistence in pursuing his suits usually won out. He was dark and handsome and well-formed, schooled in all the courtly graces, and he had a natural facility with words aided by his bardic studies that enabled him to compose romantic poems and ballads. No one woman ever held his favor for any length of time. His appetites were simply too voracious. Denied any other physical outlets for his energies, Aerin had become a sexual monomaniac and it had not taken long for him to work his way through all the eligible single ladies of Seaharrow and start upon the married ones.

As Angharad explained it, there was actually less danger to this sort of wooing than Katrina might have thought. For one thing, married ladies of the aristocracy were often neglected by their husbands and starved for any kind of romance. Many of their marriages had been arranged for reasons of combining family wealth or making political connections. Passion rarely played a part in such aristocratic unions. In most cases, women of noble families were married young and if they did not fall in love with the husbands who were chosen for them, they learned at least to perform their wifely duties with a degree of equanimity. As time passed and their husbands grew increasingly bored with them, being the object of the affections of a handsome and lusty young lord often proved a temptation too difficult to resist. Of course, they had their positions to consider, so it was a foregone conclusion that they would be discreet and take special pains to conceal their affairs, nor would they be likely to complain if Aerin suddenly grew tired of them. And, Angharad had added, even if by some chance a husband should learn of the affair, it was unlikely that he would jeopardize his own position by challenging the son of the archduke. Aerin knew all this, of course, and took full advantage of the situation.

Rumor had it that Aerin had a special room somewhere within the castle where he pursued the more adventurous of his assignations, a room to which women were brought blindfolded, so that no one would know exactly where it was. When Katrina pressed her, Angharad admitted that she had been taken to that room herself on a number of occasions, before Aerin's tastes had wandered in new directions. Katrina insisted that Angharad describe the room, whereupon she was regaled with a curious tale that caused Angharad to blush nervously when she spoke of it, but it was clear that she had found the experience exciting.

"Did he hurt you?" Katrina asked.

"No, my lady," Angharad replied. "In truth, at first, I was afraid he might, but he swore to me upon his honor that nothing would be done that I would not first permit."

"And did he keep his promise?"

"Yes, my lady."

Katrina frowned. "Why, then, did he have those things?"

"I asked him that myself," Angharad replied. "And he explained that often one discovered things about oneself when one tried . . . new experiences."

"Indeed? And did you? Discover things about yourself, I mean."

"Yes, my lady. But he did not force me to do anything I did not wish to do."

"How interesting," Katrina said. "And how would you describe him as a lover?"

Angharad smiled slyly. "Potent and imaginative, my lady."

Apparently, Aerin had refined his tastes and skills in lovemaking to an unusual degree. It made Katrina wonder. How and where had he come by such knowledge? And if he was as obsessed with the passions of the flesh as his father was with the winning of the Iron Throne, then could not that obsession be turned to some advantage?

Katrina wondered where his secret room was. She knew that castles often had secret rooms and passages concealed behind their walls. These were designed as an added measure of security, in case the walls were breached in an attack and invaders stormed the castle. Usually, such hidden rooms were connected with secret passageways that led underground, to a point beyond the walls, so that an escape might be effected. Seaharrow was very old, however, and it had never fallen in a siege throughout its history, so it was entirely possible that there were rooms and passageways that had been forgotten over the years. Either Aerin had discovered such a room by accident, or else there was someone in the castle who knew about it and showed it to him. Katrina determined to find out.

Logic also dictated that someone had helped Aerin to obtain the things that he had hidden in his secret room. And taught him how to use them. Given the sheltered life that he had led, it seemed most probable that it must have been one of his tutors. But which of the graying scholars charged with Aerin's education had furthered it in such an unusual direction? Through Angharad, using the contacts she had developed, Katrina began to make discreet inquiries. And at the same time, she slowly started to develop a closer relationship with Aerin.

Now that she knew he had a weakness, she wanted to find out how it could be exploited. Slowly, she was beginning to formulate a plan.

chapter five

Two days of steady travel following their crossing of the Stonebyrn brought Gannd and Reese to the city of Lofton, the capital of Alamie. The journey was mostly uneventful, save for the night they stopped at a small roadhouse in a village roughly thirty miles from the city. The countryside they had been traveling through was mostly flat and fertile farmland, with acres and acres of corn and hayfields. They had purchased another horse from one of the farms they passed, paying much more than it was worth, but the farmer had been hesitant to sell. Reese made him a generous offer that he grudgingly accepted, as if angry at being paid more than he could refuse. The farmer had not spoken to Gannd at all, but his manner toward him had been sullen and hostile. The memory of the farmer's sour expression and cold resentment stayed with Gannd for a long time as they continued on their way.

When they reached a small village and stopped to spend the night, Gannd experienced similar reactions from the people they met there. No one spoke to them, and the looks they received were far from friendly. They had reined in at the roadhouse, tied their horses at the railing, and gone inside to inquire about a meal and a room for the night. That was when Gannd was once again reminded of his mother's warning.

"I don't rent rooms to breeds," the burly innkeeper had said, scowling as he looked at Gannd.

"You're renting it to me," said Reese. "And who I choose to share it with is none of your concern."

"You can stay, but I won't have no breed under this roof," the innkeeper replied in a surly tone. "He can sleep out in the barn with the horses if he likes, but I won't have him staying here."

"I want a room," said Reese, with an edge to his voice as he stared hard at the innkeeper, "and a good hot meal, for both of us. I'm willing to pay in gold. We have traveled a long way, and we are tired. But not too tired to burn this place down to the ground if we're not treated properly. Do I make my meaning clear?"

The man considered for a moment whether or not he wanted to make an issue of it, but after sizing up both Reese and Gannd, he sullenly backed down. They took their things up to the room, then came down for their meal, which the innkeeper served to them with thinly veiled disgust. There were a few other patrons in the roadhouse, and Gannd was uncomfortably aware of their cold looks as they sat as far away from the half-elf as possible.

"I fear my company may prove to be a disadvantage," Gannd said.

Reese raised his eyebrows. "So far, you've saved my life three times. Exactly how is that a disadvantage?"

"I meant that others may judge you unfavorably by the company you keep."

"I have better things to do than go through life being concerned with what other people think," said Reese. "I do not suffer the judgment of fools." He raised his voice considerably with his last statement, for the benefit of the other patrons in the roadhouse, and they all hastily averted their eyes. "I do not judge a man by his place of origin, the cut of his clothes, or the length of his ears," he added, lowering his voice to a normal level. "If we were in Tuarhievel, would you distance yourself from me because of who I am and what I do?"

"No," said Gannd. "Of course not."

"Well, there you have it, then. I am no stranger to such attitudes," he said, jerking his head in the direction of the other patrons. "Mercenaries are not held in very high esteem, especially by the so-called 'better class of people.' But it makes no difference who you are. Wherever you go, there will always be those who will look down upon you because of what you do or where you come from, your race, your faith, your manner of speech, your style of dress. Put a blooded aristocrat in with a gang of brigands and they will mock him for his manner and his fancy dress and disdain him for his lineage. There is good and ill in all groups. I have met simple peasant farmers who had more nobility about them than most aristocrats. And I have known noblemen who were more unprincipled than the commonest sort of thief." He shrugged. "I find it much too time consuming to detest entire groups of people. I prefer to dislike them individually."

Gannd smiled and they spoke no more about it. But at the same time, he noticed that the surly innkeeper was not upset to see them go when morning came.

In Lofton, he experienced more of the same. As they rode through the streets of the city, Gannd noticed many people staring at them—at him, in particular—with that same cold expression the innkeeper'd had. Elves were doubtless an uncommon sight in human cities. They probably did not see many half-elves, either.

In some respects, Gannd couldn't really blame them for their hostility. Though elves and humans had fought together at Mount Deismaar, and the elves had certainly made the crucial difference when they came over to the human side, the two races had a long history of enmity before that, and not even elven scholars would dispute the fact that the elves had changed sides only because they had discovered that the Shadow Lord planned to betray them. Since then, elves and humans had fought together only once, when warriors from Tuarhievel had joined the Emperor Michael's forces during his campaigns, but there were still places where tribes of elves pursued the *gheallie Sidhe*, their sworn war against the humans. The most notorious of these tribal leaders, Rhuobhe Manslayer, had vowed he would not rest until all humans were exterminated. Humans entered elven forests at their own peril. Even in Tuarhievel, where Prince Fhileraene welcomed human traders and sought to keep the peace, sporadic outbreaks of the *gheallie Sidhe* were not unknown.

There were, however, two sides to the story, one of which the humans usually chose not to see. They were the invaders. Cerilia had been a Sidhelien kingdom until the humans came in the Invasion of the Seven Tribes and declared war upon the elves, forcing them from their ancestral lands. And though there were many elves who sought to live in peace with humans, there were just as many who had vowed never to forget.

In Tuarhievel, Gannd had never experienced hostility from anyone because he was half human. He had always been accepted as Sidhelien, one of the people, and though he had known that he was different, he was never made to feel that that difference made him less than anybody else. Among the humans, however, it was another matter. He saw open hostility in many faces. In others, unconcealed disgust.

Reese proposed to sell their horses and book passage on a river sloop to Bhalaene, where the River Tuor met in confluence with the River Maesil. From there, he said, they could continue down the Maesil to Anuire, the imperial capital, where they could purchase new horses and resupply themselves, then continue overland to Daulton, the capital of Avanil, where they would apply for service with the Duke of Avan. Gannd had never traveled on a river sloop before and he was looking forward to the new experience.

There were several ways of traveling down the river, Reese explained. The cheapest, of course, was to build a raft or purchase a small boat that they could row, but that would also entail the least degree of comfort and the most amount of work. They would have to pole the raft or row the boat themselves, watching out for drifting logs or rocks beneath the surface, and they would have to make for shore each night to camp and fend for themselves to find their supper. Alternately, they could book passage with a packet barge and save themselves the trouble of navigating the river by themselves, but the accommodations would be crowded and uncomfortable, as packet barges were little more than large rafts with gunwales, used primarily for shipping goods downriver on a one-way trip and providing little or no shelter from the elements. They would have to sleep on the hard deck and eat whatever they could bring with them that did not require cooking.

Booking passage on a river sloop was more expensive, but much more comfortable. Like the packet barges, the sloops were constructed in the boatyards of Lofton from wood taken from the foothills of the nearby Five Peaks region. And like the packet barges, they only made a one-way trip, as it would present too many difficulties to bring them back upriver. Unlike the barges, however, which were broken up for lumber once they reached their destination at either Moerel or Anuire, the river sloops continued all the way down the Maesil to where it emptied out into the Arnienbae, where they would be fully fitted out in the shipyards of Anuire to sail the Straits of Aerele as merchant sloops north to the Tael Firth or east to the Gulf of Coeranys.

"The sloops do not sail in the winter," said Reese, "but at this time of year, the yards are busy and there is usually one leaving every week. They take on passengers and charge dearly for the fare, pure profit for the shipbuilders, of course, but you sail in comfort down the river, sleeping in the cabin bunks, and as an added inducement to help justify the fares they charge, your meals are provided by the crew."

"Have we enough to pay for such a luxury?" asked Gannd.

"More than enough, thanks to the Clan McMurtrie," Reese replied, hoisting his saddlebags with a grin. "It should leave us with just enough left over to buy horses once we reach Anuire and resupply ourselves for the journey to Daulton. Once there, we shall find employment soon enough."

"How can you be so sure?" asked Gannd.

"Because Kier of Avan prepares for war," said Reese. "And he knows that Derwyn of Boeruine will spare no expense in building his army. Rest assured, my friend, we shall find employment easily enough."

They made inquiries and learned that the next sloop would be leaving downriver in two days. That gave them some time to kill. The first thing Reese did was book passage for them; then they found a buyer for their horses at a local stable, where Reese received a fair price after some haggling. The next order of business was to find a place to stay. After their experience at the roadhouse, Gannd decided it would be more prudent to pull up the hood of his cloak when they went in search of rooms. His elven features were not unusually pronounced, but he thought it best to conceal his silver-streaked hair and pointed ears. He did not wish to cause Reese any more trouble.

The first two places they checked were full, but they found a room at the third inn they came to near the riverfront. Apparently, there were a lot of people traveling downriver, though most of them would either be booking passage on the packet barges or traveling overland, following the river's course to Bellamie. From Bellamie, they would either continue southward, to Anuire, or else head east to Ghieste, Osoerde, and Elinie, or west to Avanil or Brosengae. Some people were coming from the eastern provinces, heading west, anxious to avoid the coming conflict. They were commoners, tradesmen, and crofters traveling with their families, leaving behind everything they knew to make a new start somewhere else. For them, the future was uncertain, but they knew what to expect from war and so were fleeing from it. Others were heading toward it— mercenaries seeking to offer their services to one side or the other, most probably did not care which; commoners down on their luck, willing to brave the risks of warfare in return for new clothes on their backs and three square meals a day; peddlers, artisans, and laborers looking for the opportunities that wartime could present. And women, mostly young and poor, hoping either to find some soldier who would care for them or else seeking to sell their favors, bartering their self-respect for gold. They all brought an air of tense anticipation to the dusty city streets.

The inn Reese found was not one of the better establishments in Lofton, but it was cheap and the innkeeper scarcely even bothered to look up at them as Reese and Gannd paid for two nights of lodging in advance. The tiny room was up one creaking flight of stairs and contained only two straw pallets on the bare wood floor, a battered washbasin, a table with two rickety stools and a smelly, battered chamber pot. The walls were unpainted wooden planks and the window held no glass. Two rickety wooden shutters kept the breeze out, after a fashion, and there were several candle stubs provided for illumination.

"Well, it's not a palace," Reese said as he gazed around at the sparse accommodations, "but it'll do for a couple of days. Beats sleeping on the wharves, at any rate."

They had noticed that many travelers were doing precisely that, sleeping on the wharves amidst their piled possessions, with nothing to protect them from the elements. What struck Gannd most about the city was the crowding and the filth he saw everywhere. Refuse and waste was simply tossed into the alleys, and rats scurried among the garbage. It was such a contrast to the forest city of Tuarhievel, where even the dirt paths were swept and everything was kept clean and orderly, to ensure the least possible amount of impact on the natural surroundings. Humans seemed to lack an affinity for nature, and they lived more densely packed together, at least in the city. Gannd wondered if it was a matter of preference or necessity.

"A bit of both, I suppose," Reese said, when Gannd questioned him about it. "Some people prefer to have a little space around them, so they live in small villages or out in the country. Others prefer city life, because they see certain advantages in it. If you are a tradesman, for example, then business will be better in a city, where you can draw upon more customers. Or if you are looking for a job, a city will provide more opportunities. Some people enjoy the entertainments that a city has to offer. They prefer the increased pace of life in a city to the quiet of living in the country." He shrugged. "Elves have cities, too, don't they?"

"Not like this," Gannd said as he opened the shutters and stared out at the street below. "There are so many people in such close proximity, and yet they all seem strangers to one another. And there is a feeling of—" he searched for the right expression "—apartness from nature. There are no trees, no shrubs, no flowers or plants of any kind. . . . And there is filth and refuse everywhere. There is so much noise, and the atmosphere is malodorous and oppressive. Why do people tolerate such conditions?"

"Good question," Reese replied. "Regrettably, I don't have a good answer. It's just the way things are."

Gannd shook his head. He wanted to understand. In a way, this was all a part of him, of who he was. This was his father's world, and he had come here so that he could know and understand it. But it made no sense to him. Why would people want to surround themselves with an environment that was so unpleasant? He could understand the farmer who cut down trees so he could plant crops and make things grow, but he could not fathom why people would want to cut down trees merely to crowd their buildings close together.

"Well, if you want to find out what city life is like, then we should go out and sample it," said Reese. "Unless, of course, you're tired and want to sleep?"

Gannd frowned. "Have we not been out and sampling it already?"

Reese chuckled. "Hardly. I don't know about you, but I could do with something to eat. And then we can go out and find ourselves a little entertainment. What do you say?"

Gannd was curious to find out what sort of entertainment a human city had to offer, but the memory of their reception at the roadhouse was still unpleasantly fresh. "Perhaps you would be better off going by yourself," he said. "You will likely find a better welcome if I remain behind."

"Nonsense, I won't hear of it," said Reese. "There are places where your gold is as good as anybody else's."

"But I have no gold," said Gannd.

"*Our* gold," Reese replied, impatiently. "It would not be mine to spend if not for you. We are partners in this adventure, are we not? Besides, you left Tuarhievel to see what the human world was like. You won't learn that by staying in this room. It's bad enough we have to sleep here," he added, looking at the mattress pallets dubiously. "However, if we have a little luck tonight, we just might be able to secure more comfortable accommodations."

"How?" asked Gannd.

Reese grinned. "Come on, I'll show you."

They left the inn and headed to the riverfront. It was growing dark and traffic on the streets had thinned out considerably. Reese seemed to know where he was going, so apparently, he had been here before. They headed away from the warehouses by the wharves and the clusters of people camped there, cooking meager suppers in iron pots over tiny fires, past the boats and barges tied up at the docks, and down a winding street of two-story buildings built one against the other. Torches had been lit and set in sconces by most of the doorways. Scantily dressed women lounged against the sides of many of the buildings, beckoning and calling out to them as they passed. Some lifted their skirts to show their legs, some opened their blouses to display their bosoms, some revealed even more. It was not difficult for Gannd to figure out what they were selling. He had never seen a prostitute before, and he gazed with curiosity at the first few they passed, though he found their manner coarse and repellant.

"This is not the safest part of town," said Reese as they walked, "so watch yourself."

"Why have we come here then?" asked Gannd.

Reese chuckled. "To find some entertainment."

"With these women who display themselves so lewdly?" Gannd asked, finding it difficult to believe that any man could find such behavior attractive.

"Not unless you wish to catch the pox, or find tiny livestock grazing on various parts of your body afterward," said Reese.

"Tiny livestock?"

Reese glanced at Gannd and grinned. "You really are an innocent, aren't you? You mean to tell me you have never had a woman? No elf girls back in Tuarhievel?"

"No," said Gannd. "Elf girls do not sell themselves or behave in such a manner. And I do not think they have tiny livestock, either. Do all human females have them?"

Reese laughed. "No, not all. But one can never be too careful. It's best to stay away from these whores. Being with a woman is much more satisfying when she wants you and not just your money. Ah, here we are. I believe this is the place."

They had come to a two-story building made of mortared stone and wood with large, heavy double doors that had torches set into the walls at either side. There were several windows on the first floor, with shutters that opened inward, and black wrought iron grillwork covering the openings. A heavyset but muscular man with thick arms and a shaved head stood by the door, his arms folded, a sword and several knives at his waist. Above the double doors hung a red-painted wooden sign carved in the shape of a sloop with the words "The River Queen" emblazoned on the hull in gilt letters.

"Ever been to a gaming house before?" asked Reese.

Gannd shook his head.

"Well then, pay attention. Follow my lead and stick close. Don't wander off and don't let yourself be drawn into any games, no matter how simple they may look. Remember that the purpose of a gaming house is to separate foolish people from their money. The trick is not to be too foolish. That takes experience and skill. Now, this place will be full of cheats, pickpockets, fast-talkers, and con artists . . . and women who will cozy up to you and steal your underdrawers while they're smiling at you and batting their eyelashes. So be suspicious of everybody. They're all out after your money."

"But I still don't have any money," Gannd said.

"Well, I suppose that simplifies things, then," said Reese. "Just leave everything to me. Any questions?"

"Yes, I have two," said Gannd.

"Ask."

"Why is going to a place full of such dishonest people regarded as entertainment?"

Reese stared at him for a moment. "Because the entertainment is in the risk involved, in playing and winning, in coming out ahead."

"I see. It is the challenge you enjoy, then?"

"You might say that. What's your second question?"

"What are . . . underdrawers?"

Reese snorted and shook his head. "Never mind. I'll explain some other time. Come on, let's go inside."

The heavyset bald man greeted them with a sullen nod and opened the door for them. Gannd noticed that what he first took for a plain tunic with colorfully decorated sleeves was actually a vest, and the decorations were on the man's bare skin.

"Why did that man paint his arms?" Gannd asked as they walked inside.

"They're called tattoos," said Reese. "And it's not paint. The designs are permanent. It's done by injecting colored inks under the skin with needles."

"Is that not painful?"

"Yes, I understand it is."

"Why is it done?"

"For decoration."

Gannd frowned. "So . . . for entertainment, people go to places where they know there are thieves and try to avoid being robbed. And for decoration, they suffer pain to force ink under their skin with needles."

"Well, some of them do," said Reese with a shrug.

"Would it not be simpler and less painful for them just to paint themselves if they wished to decorate their bodies?"

"I suppose, but then the paint would eventually wear off."

"So they are willing to suffer pain because they are too lazy to paint new designs when the old ones have worn off?"

Reese glanced at him. "Can we discuss this another time?"

"You asked if I had any questions. . . ."

"I did say that, didn't I?" He shook his head and sighed. "Just remember what they are and ask me later."

Gannd nodded. "If you wish."

The interior of the gaming house was one large, open room with stained, planked wooden flooring and plastered walls. The plaster was cracked and chipped in many places. Several large, square wooden columns supported the beamed ceiling and had iron lamp sconces attached to them. There was a long, crowded bar at the back of the room, with flights of wooden stairs on either side leading to the upper floor, which had a gallery overlooking the main room. There were booths along the walls, where people sat talking and drinking, and gaming tables spread throughout the room. Most of the tables were small, where people sat and played at cards. At the larger tables, people stood around and threw dice or spun wheels. The place was noisy and crowded, hot and smoky from the lamps, the press of bodies, and pipe smoke. Gannd wrinkled his nose in distaste. So far, this did not seem very entertaining.

Reese led the way to one of the large tables, where people stood around, taking turns throwing dice onto its leather-covered surface. A man with a long stick stood at the head of the table, pulling in the dice after they were thrown and directing the play.

"Ante up for the next round, please," he called out. "The ante is four coppers. Players ante up, please."

Reese traded some gold coins for coppers, then tossed four onto the table. The game master used his stick to rake in all the other coppers and dropped them into a small black iron pot at the end of the table. Reese leaned close to Gannd.

"This game is called Hawke's Gambit," he explained. "The ante, or wager, is determined by the number of sides on the dice used for each pass. There are six passes in a round. You start with a four-

sided die. Each player throws, and the high roll takes the pot. If anyone ties for the high roll, they share the pot between them. The next
pass adds a six-sided die. You throw both the four and six together,
so the ante is ten. You add up the score and high roll wins, ties split
the pot. The third pass adds an eight-sided die. You now throw all
three. Four plus six plus eight equals eighteen, so you ante up eighteen coppers. Fourth pass adds a ten-sided die. You throw all four,
the ante is twenty-eight. Fifth pass, a twelve-sided die is added.
That makes the ante forty coppers. The sixth and final pass adds the
twenty-sided die. The ante is sixty. Players may drop out after any
pass, but cannot start again until after the last pass is completed and
a brand new round begins. And on the last pass, you may also elect
to play Hawke's Gambit, which is an additional, separate wager.
You decide how much you wish to wager, in addition to what is already in the pot for the sixth pass. On this separate wager for
Hawke's Gambit, however, other players have the option to raise. If
they do, then you must match their raises to stay in. When the wagering is completed, you then make the sixth and final pass. High
roll takes the pot. But in the separate wager for Hawke's Gambit,
you are betting on the final score, which is the total of all six passes.
Whoever has the highest total wins the wager for Hawke's Gambit.
Then play begins again."

"To what end?" asked Gannd.

"To see who wins the most money," Reese replied patiently.

"But the chances of losing seem significantly greater."

"The idea is to beat the odds."

"How?"

"Well, that's where luck comes in," said Reese.

"I thought you said it was a matter of experience and skill," said
Gannd, puzzled.

Reese rolled his eyes. "Yes, that too. Now be quiet and watch."

The players had all anted up and the first pass began. Reese rolled
a two and lost. On the second pass, he rolled a one and a three, for
a total of four, and lost again. On the third pass, he rolled a two, another two, and a four, for a total of eight, but three other players
rolled higher scores, so he lost again. He was now down thirty-two
coppers.

"You do not seem very skillful at this game," said Gannd.

"Just shut up," said Reese irritably. "My luck will turn."
Gannd wanted to ask how he knew that, but kept silent and just
watched instead. It was clear that his comments and questions were
getting on his friend's nerves. But it was more than that. It was the
game itself. It was having a curious effect not only on Reese, but on
the other players, too. Gannd watched their faces. They all had expressions of tense anticipation as each player made his or her pass.
When a player rolled a low score, it resulted in relief for the other
players, but for the player whose roll was low, the result was anger,
disappointment, or frustration. A high roll, on the other hand, and
the taking of the pot, brought about a momentary joy, with excla-
mations of delight, but these emotions were short-lived as the next
pass came around and the tense anticipation returned once again.
Overall, the amount of negative emotions brought about out-
weighed the positive. And as the gaming progressed, and more
money was lost, Gannd watched the players grow more tense. Their
intensity increased. Several had started to perspire. All in all, it did
not seem very enjoyable. Gannd wondered why this was considered entertainment.

On the fourth pass, Reese rolled a one, a three, a two, and a four,
resulting in a total of ten. Not high enough to beat several of the
others. He lost again. His loss of twenty-eight coppers on the fourth
pass, added to his previous losses, brought his total loss to sixty
coppers. On the fifth pass, however, he did better. He rolled four,
six, seven, eight, and eleven, for a total of thirty-six, which gave him
the high score. He won the pot. There were six players in the round,
and each had anted up forty coppers into the pot.

"Ha!" cried Reese. "You see? I told you my luck would turn!
That's a win of two hundred and forty coppers!"

"But you have lost sixty," Gannd pointed out, "so you have really
won only one hundred and eighty."

Reese glanced at him and grimaced. "I am still ahead of the
game," he said sourly.

"So far," said Gannd.

The players anted up for the sixth and final pass. Reese rubbed
his hands with anticipation.

Gannd watched as the other players anted up. There were three
hundred and sixty coppers in the pot. But then the game master

said, "Announce your wagers for Hawke's Gambit, please. Player Number One?"

Player Number One, a nervous-looking young woman who kept licking her lips, had not done well so far in the round. She passed on wagering for Hawke's Gambit.

"Player Number One passes," said the game master. "Player Number Two?"

Player Two, a swarthy man with a pock-marked face and long, greasy hair, wagered twenty coppers. Player Number Three, a heavyset older man with a red-veined nose, matched the wager of twenty. Player Number Four, who had won the most so far, saw the wager of twenty and raised it fifty. Players Two and Three matched it. Player Number Five pursed his lips anxiously. He was a merchant, judging by his clothes and the rings on his fingers. He glanced around at the other players briefly, then matched the wager of seventy coppers and raised it by one hundred. Player Two gave him a hard stare, then matched it. Player Three shook his head. "Too rich for my blood," he said, passing, thereby forfeiting the seventy coppers he had already put up. Player Four matched it. It came down to Reese.

"A hundred and seventy coppers to stay in, good sir," the game master told him.

Reese nodded. "I'll see your hundred and seventy," he said, pushing a gold piece and seven silvers toward the game master, "and I'll raise you another hundred." He tossed in another gold piece.

Player Two snorted. "He's trying to buy the pot."

"Another hundred to stay in, gentlemen," the game master announced.

"I'll call your bluff," said Player Two, tossing out a gold piece.

"I'll see it," said Player Four.

Player Five glanced at Reese with a scowl. "I'm in," he said.

The game master raked in the coins. "The wager for Hawke's Gambit is two hundred and seventy," he said. "Players Four, Two, Five, and Six are in. Total at stake, one thousand one hundred and fifty. Three hundred sixty in the pot for the sixth and final pass. The house takes ten percent of final wagers. That leaves three hundred twenty-four to the winner of the final pass, one thousand thirty-five to the winner of Hawke's Gambit. Final pass, please."

All six players had anted up for the final pass, so all six rolled. Player Number One, the nervous woman who had declined to wager on Hawke's Gambit, rolled the high score, throwing a four, a six, a seven, a nine, a twelve, and a twenty, for a total of fifty-eight. She won the pot for the sixth pass, but then did some quick calculations and groaned loudly when she realized she would have won Hawke's Gambit with her total score for all six passes had she wagered on it. Cursing to herself, she left the table.

The game master totaled the scores of the remaining players, announcing each total. Player Number Four came in with the highest cumulative score, winning the wager for Hawke's Gambit, having outscored Reese by only nine points.

"Damn," said Reese. "Well, it was close. I didn't do so bad. At least I won that one pass."

Gannd frowned. "But you ended up losing ninety coppers," he said.

"I'll make it back in the next round," said Reese.

"The likelihood of that seems slim," said Gannd.

"Is that so? Well, why don't you try it if you think you can do better?" Reese replied.

Gannd shook his head. "I have no wish to try. And I did not say I could do better. I fail to see where skill plays any part in this. It is all pure chance. The only real winner is the house. By taking ten percent of each final wager, they risk nothing, but make money with each round."

"That's how the game is played," said Reese.

"It is a good game, if you are the house," said Gannd.

"Or if you beat the odds and win," said Reese. "I did win that one pass."

"But you are still poorer by ninety coppers."

"Well, easy come, easy go."

"It seems to go much easier than it comes," said Gannd.

"You know the trouble with you?" said Reese. "You just haven't got the right attitude."

"Ante up for the next round, please," said the game master.

"So, do you want to try or don't you?" Reese asked.

"No," said Gannd. "Perhaps I do not understand, but I fail to see why you find losing money entertaining."

"All right, never mind," said Reese, impatiently. "We'll try a different game. Maybe if you play this time, you'll get the idea." He counted out some gold pieces and gave them to Gannd. "Let's try a couple of hands of Dragon."

Gannd shook his head. "I do not know this game."

"It's easy, look, I'll teach you. We'll get a deck of cards."

They sat down in an empty booth and ordered a couple of drinks. Reese asked the serving girl to bring them a deck of cards.

"Now," he said, spreading the cards out on the table, "the dealer deals out five cards to each player. All the cards come in suits. The suits are swords, pentacles, cups, and wands. Some cards have numbers, from two to ten, and some are court cards. The court cards are dragons, kings, queens, and knights, one to each suit." He identified the cards as he spoke, holding them up. "Dragons are the highest cards. Then come kings, queens, knights and then the numbered cards, ten, nine, eight, and so forth. You with me so far?"

Gannd nodded.

"Now, it's how the cards go together that matters. You can have a pair, which is two of any numbered card, such as two threes or two fours, or a pair of court cards, such as two kings or two knights. A pair of threes beats a pair of twos, fours beat threes and so on, up to dragons. Two pair, such as two threes and two fours, beats one pair, no matter how high, otherwise, the same rules apply. Three of a kind beats two pair. A straight, which is when you have them all in sequence, like this, beats three of a kind. A flush, or five cards of the same suit, beats a straight. A full court, that's three of a kind and a pair, beats a flush; four of a kind beats a full court; a straight flush, five cards of the same suit in sequence, beats a full court; and a dragon flush, which is a straight flush to the dragon, beats everything. You understand?"

"I think so," Gannd said. "It seems simple enough."

"Well, those are just the basics. The strategy involved is much more complicated. This is a game of judging odds and possibilities. That's where skill and experience come in."

Gannd listened carefully while Reese outlined some of the finer points of the game. After a while, Reese was satisfied that Gannd had the basics down, and they went looking for a game. They soon found one that broke up when two of the people playing left the table, considerably poorer than when they sat down.

"Mind if my friend and I sit in?" asked Reese.

The dealer looked up. He was lean and dark, with collar-length black hair and a trim goatee. He was dressed in a black leather vest and tunic with black breeches and well-polished black boots that came up to his knees. He wore a gold and silver medallion of Haelyn on a gold chain around his neck. He glanced at Gannd and raised his eyebrows. "Anyone have any objection?" he asked.

One of the other players, a balding man of middle age who had the look of a tradesman, barely gave Gannd a glance. "If the breed's got money, I'm not too proud to take it."

The third man, a burly mercenary with a patch over one eye, simply shrugged. He wore a sleeveless brown leather tunic over bare skin, a wide belt, and dark green breeches. His chest and arms were muscular, but he was thick around the midsection.

"Sit down," the man in black said.

"I have never played this game before," said Gannd.

The man in black smiled. "You have to learn somehow."

Reese sighed and shook his head. The mercenary with the patch merely grunted.

"The game is straight draw, pot limit ante, knights or better to open," the man in black said, shuffling the cards. He passed them to the tradesman to cut the deck. "Ante is one copper to start."

They each anted up one copper, and the man in black dealt the cards. A serving girl came up and took their drink orders. A limit of one copper didn't seem so bad, thought Gannd. It wasn't very much to lose. "Excuse me," he said, "may I ask a question?"

"Go ahead," the dealer said.

"What does it mean, knights or better to open?"

"It means that you have to have at least a pair of knights before you can open the betting," Reese explained.

"But does that not reveal what cards you hold?" said Gannd.

The tradesman snorted and shook his head.

"It means that whoever opens the betting has to hold at least a pair of knights," Reese explained patiently. "But it could also be a pair of queens or kings or better."

"Makes it more interesting," the man in black said with a smile.

"And if no one holds at least one pair of knights?" asked Gannd.

"We ante up and start again," said Reese.

Gannd frowned. "How is that more interesting?"

The man in black chuckled. "You'll get the idea." He glanced at the tradesman.

"Pass," the tradesman said. Obviously, he did not have at least a pair of knights.

"Pass," said Reese.

Gannd looked at his cards. He held no court cards, only a pair of twos. Not enough to open. "Pass," he said.

"Pass," said the mercenary with the patch.

"Dealer passes," said the man in black.

They all threw in their cards and the deal went to the tradesman. He shuffled, then passed the deck to be cut. "Ante up," he said.

Gannd tossed one copper onto the table.

"It's pot limit," said the man in black, raising his eyebrows.

"I thought the limit was one copper," Gannd replied.

"Pot limit ante means what's in the pot. We each anted one for the first hand. That makes five in the pot. You need to ante up four more."

"I see," said Gannd. He pushed out four more coins. He hadn't understood correctly, then. Reese had not explained about this pot limit variation.

"I pass," said Reese.

Gannd looked at his cards. A king, a dragon, a three, a four, a five. But no pair of knights. "I pass, as well," he said.

The man with the patch passed, as did the man in black.

"Dealer passes," said the tradesman. They all threw in their cards again and the deal went around to Reese, who started to shuffle the cards. This time, each player had to ante up thirty coppers to stay in. They had started with one each, for a total of five in the pot, which made the next ante five each. But this time, with the five from the first hand and the twenty-five from the second, there were thirty coppers in the pot, so that was the pot limit. Once again, no one had knights or better to open, so they threw in their cards and the deal came around to Gannd. As he shuffled carefully, not able to manipulate the cards as adroitly as the others, Gannd frowned, thinking.

There were thirty coppers in the pot after the second hand. That made the ante thirty for the third. Five times thirty was one hundred and fifty, added to the thirty already in the pot from the previous hand made for a total of one hundred and eighty. The ante had increased dramatically in only a few moments. Now, with the fourth hand, they had each anted up one hundred and eighty, for a total of nine hundred. Added to the one hundred and eighty already in the pot from the previous hand, it would make the ante for the next hand one thousand and eighty if no one had knights or better to open.

No one did.

The deal passed to the man with the patch. They each had to ante up one thousand and eighty coppers. Added to the one thousand and eighty already in the pot, it would make for a total of six thousand four hundred and eighty. Gannd could now see what the man in black had meant when he said that this would make things "more interesting." Everybody anted up, except Gannd.

"That's a thousand eighty to stay in," the man in black said, looking at him.

Gannd shook his head.

"You ran out, eh?" Reese said, glancing at him.

Gannd shrugged.

"Better luck next time," said the man in black. Which meant that Gannd forfeited everything he had put into the pot, losing it all without even having played a single hand.

He understood now how players could be sucked in by the low starting ante, never realizing how quickly it could mount up given the odds of not having knights or better to open. They could easily get in over their heads and lose everything before they realized what happened. Reese had warned him about the possibility of cheating. Well, with a game like this, there was no need to cheat. The man in black was obviously quite experienced at it. And at taking advantage of players who did not understand the odds.

With Gannd out, the remaining four players each anted up one thousand eighty, making for a total of fifty-four hundred in the pot. However, this time, the tradesman was able to open. That meant he had at least a pair of knights, maybe something better. He bet a hundred coppers, or one gold piece. With so much money in the pot already, it seemed like a small bet. The man in black smiled faintly. Reese matched it. Gannd glanced at his cards over his shoulder. He had two pair, a pair of fives and a pair of tens. The patch put in a gold piece, as did the man in black.

"How many?" the man with the patch asked.

"Two," the man in black said, casually discarding two cards. The patch dealt him two more.

"Three for me," said the tradesman. He discarded, then picked up his new cards and added them to his hand, pursing his lips slightly.

"I'll take one," said Reese, discarding one card. Revealing, Gannd realized, that he had at least two pair, possibly four of a kind, or was attempting to draw to a straight or a straight flush. A moment's thought told him that the odds were very much against that, however, so the man in black would probably be safe in assuming that Reese had at least two pair, with the possibility of filling out a full court on the draw, or four of a kind.

Reese picked up his card. A ten of pentacles. He had a full court.

"Dealer takes four," said the man with the patch. Which meant that the card he was keeping was undoubtedly a high court card and he was hoping to improve his hand by drawing to it. In other words, he had nothing, but was reluctant to throw in his cards because of all the money he had already put into the pot. So his gamble, at the moment, was greater than that of anyone else sitting at the table.

The tradesman had opened, which meant he had at least a pair of knights to begin with. He had discarded three, which meant that they were probably low cards. Gannd considered what his chances were of improving what he had. To get a full court, he would have to draw three of the same kind, and the odds were very much against that. It was somewhat less unlikely for him to draw two of the same kind, which would give him two pair, not enough to beat Reese. To get four a kind, assuming he held two knights, meant he would have to draw two more knights, and there were only four in the deck. Again, extremely unlikely, considering the possibility that one of the other players might already be holding at least one. And it was a safe bet that the man with the patch was holding a court card. The other possibility was that one of the three cards the tradesman drew might give him three of a kind, which meant he would have at least three knights or better. If he did not fold now, then he had at least two pair, one of which had to be knights or better, or three of a kind, all court cards. But still not enough to beat the full court Reese held.

The man in black had taken two, which meant he almost certainly had three of a kind. However, he had not opened, which meant that he couldn't be holding knights or better. Unless he had drawn two knights, which would give him a full court. But the chances of that seemed slim. It was possible that one of the cards he had drawn would give him four of a kind, however, lower than knights, but still enough to beat three of a kind or a full court.

The tradesman had opened, so it was his bet. "One hundred," he said, putting in another gold piece.

"I'll see your hundred," Reese said, "and raise you two." He tossed in three gold pieces.

"I'm out," the patch said with a grimace of disgust, putting down his cards.

The man in black tossed in three gold pieces. "I'll see the three," he said, "and raise a thousand." He casually tossed two shiny platinum pieces onto the pile in the center of the table. He had four of a kind, thought Gannd. There was no way Reese could win.

The tradesman sighed with resignation and shook his head. "Too rich for me. I fold," he said, putting down his cards.

"Looks like it's you and me," the man in black said to Reese.

Reese gave him a long look. Surely, Gannd thought, he must realize the man in black had the stronger hand.

"A thousand, eh?" he said.

The man in black regarded him steadily.

Reese smiled. "I think you're bluffing."

"It will cost you a thousand to find out," the man in black said.

Reese had only five gold pieces left in front of him on the table. He pushed them out into the center of the table, then took out his purse and shook out four more gold pieces, the equivalent of four hundred coppers. It was all he had left.

"It seems you're a little short," the man in black said.

Reese exhaled heavily.

Gannd tossed a gold piece onto the table.

Reese glanced at him with surprise, and then relief. Gannd merely shrugged.

The man in black gave Gannd a long look.

"Call," said Reese, laying his cards down face up. "Full court."

The man in black smiled faintly and laid down his cards. He had three nines.

"God's breath!" said the tradesman, with disbelief. "You raised a thousand on three nines?"

The man in black simply shrugged.

Gannd could not believe it either. He had been convinced the man in black had four of a kind.

Reese raked in his winnings and got up from the table. "Thank you for the game, gentlemen."

"Leaving so soon?" asked the man in black.

"It's past my bedtime," Reese said. He smiled. "Good night."

"Enjoy your winnings," said the man in black.

Reese headed for the bar. Gannd followed close behind, catching up to him. "Lucky thing you had that gold piece," Reese said. "When you folded, I thought you'd lost it all."

"I did not have enough to continue," Gannd replied, "and I thought it best to hold on to that one coin, in case you should lose everything."

Reese glanced at him, puzzled. "Then why did you give it back to me?"

Gannd shrugged. "I was curious to see how you would react when you lost it all."

Reese stared at him. "You thought I was going to lose?"

"I was convinced of it. I was certain the man in black had four of a kind."

"What made you think so?"

"Well, it seemed obvious," said Gannd. "He had kept three cards and discarded two. As you explained it to me, he could have been trying to draw to a straight or a straight flush, but his chances of getting the exact two cards he needed seemed extremely slim. It was more likely, since he was an experienced player, that he had three of a kind. Considering his wager after the draw, it seemed obvious that he must have drawn a fourth. And you could not have beat that with a full court." He shook his head. "I do not understand. My reasoning was based on your instruction, so it would seem you should have reached the same conclusion. Yet somehow you knew he was bluffing. How?"

Reese grinned. "I didn't know. Not for certain, anyway. But I was betting that he was. However, it really wasn't all that much of a gamble."

"Why?"

"Because the odds of getting four of a kind are about one in four thousand," Reese replied. He shrugged. "I was just betting on the odds."

"I see," said Gannd. He pursed his lips thoughtfully. "There is more skill involved in this game than I had thought."

Reese stopped a serving girl on her way past them. "Is there a back way out of this place, my dear?" he asked, slipping her a gold piece.

She smiled and said, "Down the corridor to the right of the bar and through the kitchen."

Reese gave her another gold piece. "If anyone should ask, lass, you haven't seen us."

She raised her eyebrows. "Seen who?"

"Good girl," said Reese with a grin. He headed past the bar, threading his way through the crowd, and turned down the corridor with Gannd following close behind.

"Why are we going out this way?" asked Gannd, puzzled.

"Because we are going to be ambushed on our way back to the inn," said Reese.

ANUIRE

chapter six

They went out the back of the gaming house and into an alley strewn with refuse. It was late and it had grown very dark. Gannd could hear scores of rodents scurrying in the garbage underfoot and all around them. His eyes became accustomed to the darkness in an instant, unlike Reese, whose human vision took a moment longer to adjust.

"This way," said Reese, turning to their left.

"What makes you think we'll be attacked?" asked Gannd.

Reese gave him a wry look. "We have just won a great deal of money. However, winning it was only half the challenge. The other half will be trying to get ourselves, and it, out of this part of town in one piece. In case you hadn't noticed, there were a number of people watching the game as it progressed."

"I thought they were merely interested observers," Gannd said.

"What they were interested in observing was the growing pile of money in the center of the table," Reese replied, as they moved quickly down the alleyway. "Our friend in black had not counted on losing so heavily. I have a feeling he may not be very graceful about it. He did not put up much of an argument about our leaving. After a loss like that, most people become rather insistent about having a chance to win at least some of their losses back."

"Perhaps you should have given him that chance," said Gannd.

"Not bloody likely," Reese said. "He underestimated me once; he would not do so again. Besides, chances are he's not the only one who'd like to get his hands on what's in this purse. And it's a wise man who doesn't buck the odds. Speaking of which—" He paused, stopping for a moment and reaching for his bulky purse. "You'd better take about half of this. Just in case."

They transferred about half the money into Gannd's belt pouch.

"Now," said Reese, "it won't take long before they realize that we've slipped out the back way. And I don't have a great deal of faith in that serving girl's discretion. A few gold coins would probably loosen her lips easily enough. So any moment now, someone will be hot on our trail."

"Then why not confront them?" Gannd asked.

"Always consider your ground before you choose to fight," said Reese. "And the odds. At least half the men back there would not hesitate to kill for a fraction of what we're carrying. This is their town, and so the ground will be more familiar to them. We may still prevail in a fight, but we must remain here two more days and I would prefer not to have to answer to the local authorities for any killings. They would be very tempted by our money, too. In this situation, it strikes me that discretion would be the better part of valor."

"Then we had best hurry back to the inn," said Gannd.

Reese shook his head. "No, they'll be expecting us to go back that way. They won't know which inn we're staying at, but they'll expect us to head back toward the docks, where most of the inns cater to travelers heading downriver. What we must do is go in a direction they will not expect."

"But we have left some of our belongings at the inn," said Gannd.

"Nothing we cannot easily replace," said Reese. "You have your mother's sword. I doubt you would have left anything else of special value back there unattended."

"No," said Gannd, feeling the weight of the amulet around his neck, "just my pack, which holds a few supplies."

"Then forget about it. We have more than enough money now to buy whatever we need when we reach Anuire. The trick will be in keeping it."

"So where shall we go?" asked Gannd.

"We have two days before the boat departs," Reese replied, as they reached the end of the alley and turned right, down a narrow, darkened street. "So we need to find a place that's somewhat safer than that nest of thieves and roughnecks by the docks, which is where they'll be expecting us to be."

"You have such a place in mind?" asked Gannd.

"It just so happens that I do," said Reese. He glanced behind them nervously. "The question is, can we make it there without getting felled by daggers in our backs?" He stopped and listened for a moment. "Can you hear anything? Running footsteps, maybe?"

Gannd listened, then shook his head.

"With any luck, we may have given them the slip," said Reese. "Come on."

They almost reached the riverfront, heading down a narrow side street. Though the docks were ahead of them, and to their left, Reese turned right, toward the center of town. Suddenly, their way was blocked by several slight figures that stepped out from the shadows into the center of the narrow street. Reese's hand instantly went to his sword hilt.

"You gentlemen look lost," one of the figures said. The voice was male—very young. Several of the others snickered.

"They are only boys," said Gannd.

"Maybe we can help you find what you're looking for," the boy said slyly. "But there will be a charge for directions. It'll cost you whatever's in your purses."

Something gleamed in the darkness. A blade.

"Step aside, son," Reese said. "You don't want to do this."

There was a soft sound behind them. Gannd turned and saw several more boys step out into the street. There were seven of them in all, three in front and four behind. Gannd was not very good at estimating the age of humans, but he guessed that they were all probably in their early teens, with the exception of the leader, who seemed a little older. And all of them were armed. Several carried blades, while others carried clubs.

"Duncan . . ." Gannd said.

"Yes, I know," said Reese. "All right, son, if that's the way you want it," he added, and he drew his sword with an abrupt motion. Taking his cue from Reese, Gannd drew Bloodthirst, as well.

The boys suddenly seemed less certain, but they did not back down. "There's seven of us," the leader said. "You're not going to get us all."

"Want to bet?" asked Reese.

Gannd saw a couple of them look to the leader for their cue. But the older boy was indecisive. They had hoped for easy victims, drunken tradesmen or simple day laborers out looking for whores. They had not counted on this.

As the street toughs hesitated, Gannd's acute elven hearing picked up the distant sound of running footsteps, coming at them from back the way they'd come. "We are being pursued," he said to Reese.

"Well, that does it," Reese said with a grimace.

"Just give us the money," the lead boy said, a bit nervously, unwilling to back down in front of his followers. "That's all we want. Nobody has to get hurt."

"We don't have time for this," said Reese. He lunged and smacked the boy hard on the side of the head with the flat of his blade. The impact made a sound like a mallet striking a wooden peg. The boy's head snapped to one side; he grunted and collapsed to the ground, senseless, bleeding from his scalp. It was only a superficial wound, but it bled a great deal. The others, not realizing Reese had struck with only the flat of his blade, thought he had killed their friend. With a cry, Reese sprang at them, brandishing his sword, and Gannd spun around to face the four behind them, making showy flourishes with Bloodthirst, which whistled through the air. The boys broke and ran, scattering in all directions and leaving their leader lying in the street.

"Come on," said Reese. "Let's move!"

They started running.

"They must have figured they missed us and doubled back," said Reese as they ran. "How close are they?"

"Not far," said Gannd. "A few hundred yards, perhaps."

"Far enough," said Reese. They turned down another street that curved around toward the center of town. "A few more blocks and we should be able to lose them in the artisan's quarter."

After a few moments they heard shouts in the distance, behind them.

"They found the boy," said Reese.

For a moment, Gannd wondered if they would hurt him, then realized it was the money they were after, which meant they wouldn't even slow down. The youth would represent nothing more than a trail marker to them, something to tell them they were on the right track. Strange that he should be concerned about the boy. After all, those boys had intended to rob them, and they would not have hesitated to kill. But he was unaccustomed to the idea of children acting as predators. Such things simply did not happen in Tuarhievel. There was a lot about the human world he had yet to understand.

After a few more blocks, they entered a more densely structured area of the city, the artisan's quarter. Here, the buildings were taller, three and four stories high, but narrower, and constructed even closer together, one right up against the other. The lower floors held shops with large, rectangular windows, now tightly shuttered and locked. Above the windows, hanging out over the street, were wooden signs identifying the shops. In the daytime, the shutters would be opened and the wares inside the shops would be visible from the street. Here, the streets were also cobblestoned, instead of dirt. This was obviously a much older section of the city. There was lamplight visible in some of the upper windows, but for the most part, the streets were dark, most of the residents asleep.

The street curved around and branched off into two other streets. Reese stopped running, paused a moment, glancing down one, then the other, then took the street branching off to the right. It, too, curved around, and after a while, they reached a small circular plaza with a well in the center of it. Four other narrow streets radiated from the plaza like curving spokes from a wheel. Reese stopped again, catching his breath, but also trying to get his bearings.

"Damn," he said. "It's been a while since I've been here. I'm not sure. . . . No, I remember now. It's this way. . . ."

He led the way down one of the narrow streets as it curved away from the plaza. This area of the city resembled a maze. Gannd had always felt at home in the forest. Here, he had lost all sense of direction while they ran. One street looked much like any other. He couldn't understand how Reese knew where he was going. Or did he?

The sounds of pursuit were no longer audible to Gannd. Either he and Reese had lost them, or else the men had given up. Reese wasn't taking any chances, however. He kept on trotting down the street at a quick pace, glancing at the buildings occasionally, until they came to one that looked, to Gannd, just like all the others. Reese stopped and reached for a cord that hung down by the door. He pulled it sharply several times. From inside, Gannd could hear a bell ringing.

They waited. There was no response. Reese glanced down the street uneasily, back the way they had come, and rang again. "Come on, Terrell!" he said tensely.

Gannd could hear someone coming down a flight of stairs. A moment later, a small shutter in the door was opened from the inside and someone looked out.

"By Haelyn! Duncan!"

There was a fumbling at a bolt, and then the door was opened. Reese led the way inside. "Shut the door," he said quickly. "And bolt it."

The man who had admitted them complied. "What is it?" he asked, an expression of concern on his face. "What's wrong?"

"Shhh," said Reese, holding up his hand. He looked at Gannd. "Can you hear anything?"

Gannd listened. There was silence in the street outside. He shook his head.

Reese exhaled heavily, relieved. "I think we lost them."

"Same old Duncan," the man said with a wry smile. "It seems every time I see you, someone is after you."

Gannd glanced at the man, taking a good look at him. He appeared to be in late middle age, about five feet nine inches tall, and slim to the point of frailty, but there was a sharp vitality in his blue eyes. His gray hair was thinning at the crown, but long everywhere else, hanging loosely down below his shoulders. He had a narrow nose, a high forehead, a long face, and sharply pronounced cheekbones. His thin lips were curved in a wry smile. There was something immediately likable about him. He had a presence that seemed very self-assured and somehow serene. He was wearing a plain black dressing gown with a shawl collar and light black velvet slippers. He held a candle in a small brass holder with a ring on it.

"Well, if we are in no immediate danger," he said to Reese, "perhaps you could introduce me to your friend."

"Sorry," Reese said. "Gannd, this is my old friend, Terrell. Terrell, this my new friend, Gannd. You two have something in common. You've both saved my life."

"Which means we both have questionable judgment," said Terrell, good-humoredly. "A pleasure to meet you, Gannd." He held out his hand. Gannd found the man's grip to be firm and strong.

"And you, sir," he said.

"Please, call me Terrell. You both seem a little out of breath. Come, let me offer you some tea."

He led the way back toward the stairs. Gannd looked around at the darkened room. It was lined with wooden shelves that held a profusion of ceramic and glass jars of various sizes. There was a long wooden counter that held scales and mixing bowls and various implements. Bundles of dried herbs and bulbs hung from the rafters overhead. The room was filled with a pleasant, heady odor that was a mixture of herbs and incense.

"You are an apothecary?" Gannd asked.

Terrell glanced back at him and smiled. "Of sorts," he replied.

"Terrell is a wizard," Reese replied as they climbed the stairs. "An alchemist, a scholar, a healer, and other things besides."

"I have never met a human wizard," Gannd said.

"Gannd's uncle is a mage," said Reese.

"Indeed?" said Terrell. "What is his name?"

"Gylvain Aurealis," Gannd replied.

"Court wizard to Prince Fhileraene, no less," Terrell said, nodding. "I have heard of him, of course. An adept of considerable repute. It is an honor to play host to his nephew."

"You are very kind," said Gannd. "But I am no adept, myself."

"No matter. I have great respect for your uncle, though I have never had the pleasure of making his acquaintance. Perhaps, someday, if the circumstances will allow, you could introduce me. I would very much like to meet him."

"I would be glad to," Gannd said.

They reached the second floor and entered a large, carpeted

room. Lining the walls were shelves holding hundreds of leather-bound books, rolled-up scrolls, and more ceramic jars and glass containers filled with dried herbs and powders and other things Gannd could not identify. There was a large wooden table in the center of the room, with several plain wooden chairs, a heavy desk piled high with parchments and various bits of wizardly parapher-nalia, a fireplace, several stools and smaller tables holding lamps, thick candles, censers, caldrons of various sizes, amulets, daggers, wands . . . Everywhere Gannd looked, there was clutter, but it all had an organized feel to it. He assumed the sleeping chambers were on the floor above.

"Please, make yourselves at home," Terrell said as he hung an iron teakettle on a hook in the fireplace. He made a pass with his hand and mumbled a brief incantation under his breath. The logs in the fireplace ignited and immediately started burning brightly.

"Father? I heard the bell, and then voices on the stairs. . . ." A young girl in a white cotton nightdress hesitantly entered the room. The first thing Gannd noticed about her was that she was strikingly pretty, with long, dark blond hair and delicate, almost elfin features, but she was definitely human. She looked to be about thirteen or fourteen years old, slim and coltish, with a birdlike alertness. She stopped and cocked her head, a gesture reinforcing the birdlike im-pression, and Gannd suddenly realized she was blind.

"Who is here?" she asked.

"Well, look at you," said Reese with a smile. "You've grown into a lovely young woman, Mariel."

Her face brightened immediately. "Duncan!" she said with de-light. She held out her arms and came forward, heading toward the sound of his voice.

Reese got up and moved to meet her, taking her into his arms and hugging her, lifting her off her feet. She threw her arms around him happily. "Oh, Duncan!" she said. "It's been so long!"

"Much too long," said Reese. "You came only to my knees last time I saw you."

"My daughter, Mariel," said Terrell to Gannd.

Reese put the girl down, took her hand and led her over to the table. "Mariel, I'd like you to meet a friend of mine. This is Gannd Aurealis, of Tuarhievel."

She stood before Gannd, not seeing him, and held out her hand. "A pleasure, good sir," she said.

Gannd stood politely, even though she could not see him do so, and took her hand. "The pleasure is mine, my lady," he said.

She blushed prettily at his formal address, but as her hand came in contact with his, she stiffened suddenly and, for a moment, Gannd thought she was about to swoon. She gasped and swayed slightly, and Gannd stepped forward to steady her.

"No, let her go," said Terrell.

Puzzled and concerned, Gannd did as he was asked.

Mariel stepped back a pace and took a deep breath. She was flushed and appeared disoriented.

"Are you well?" asked Gannd.

"My daughter has the Sight," Terrell explained. "It is a particularly strong gift. What is it, Mariel? What have you seen?"

She shook her head, cocking it once more in that curiously birdlike manner. She reached out. "Give me your hand once more," she said.

Reese took a chair and pushed it up behind her. "Here, sit down," he said, gently pushing the seat against the back of her legs so she could feel it there. She sat and Gannd pulled up his chair, so that he could sit facing her. He gave her his hand.

"I felt a presence," Mariel said. "A very strong, disturbing presence." She held his hand in both of hers, frowning with concentration.

Terrell and Reese watched silently.

"There is a woman," she said in a slightly distracted tone, her sightless eyes seeming to stare off into the distance, "a beautiful woman with blond hair and striking eyes, a woman of great power ... an adept who moves in shadow."

"I met such a woman," Gannd said. "She appeared in my campsite one night before I left the Aelvinnwode. She wanted me to take hold of her staff—"

"Calamity," interrupted Mariel.

"What?" said Terrell, intensely.

"There was something about her," Gannd said. "As you said, a disturbing presence. I could not put my finger on it, but it was just a sense I had."

"Did you touch her staff?" Terrell asked, holding his breath and gazing at the half-elf with concern.

"No," said Gannd, looking at him. "I refused. I am not sure why. But I felt I could not trust her. And then she vanished, as abruptly as she came."

Terrell exhaled heavily and looked relieved.

"She is not done with you," said Mariel, still holding tightly onto his hand.

"What do you mean?" asked Gannd.

The girl shook her head. "I am not sure. I cannot tell. But she has touched you with her presence. You will be seeing her again. I am quite certain of it."

Gannd glanced uncertainly at Reese.

"There is another," Mariel said. "A woman, also. But I cannot see her. I merely sense her, indistinctly. Her fate and yours are linked. And this adept's presence has touched her, as well, but much more strongly. It hovers over her, dominantly, as if obscuring her." Mariel shook her head several times. "You must beware of this woman. Great powers move within her, powers she does not fully understand, but she is in their grip."

"Who is she?" Gannd asked.

Mariel shook her head again. "I cannot tell. I sense no image of her, only a feeling. But the forces that move within her will make her rise to power . . . and all whose lives she touches will know tragedy and chaos."

"And you say my fate and hers are linked?" asked Gannd. "Then I shall know tragedy and chaos, too?"

"The presence of the first woman, the beautiful adept, is what links the two of you," Mariel replied. "But her link with the woman is stronger, because you refused her, while the woman accepted." Mariel frowned. "I am not sure what this means. But somehow, you have both been chosen. All I can see is that your destiny is linked with hers, and Duncan's fate is linked with yours."

She released his hand and her eyelids fluttered. "I must rest now," she said. She got up unsteadily. Reese took her arm and led her back to the stairs. "You will stay a while, won't you, Duncan?" she asked, before going back up.

"Another day or so," said Reese.

"So short a time?"

"We must sail on the next boat to Anuire," said Reese.

"Anuire," repeated Mariel, cocking her head slightly. "Do not linger long in Anuire, Duncan. It is not a good place for you to be."

"I will remember," Reese said. "Good night, Mariel. I will see you in the morning."

"Good night."

She went back upstairs.

"I always knew there was something different about her," Reese said, turning to Terrell. "When did she first manifest this Sight?"

"Shortly after the first onset of her cycle," Terrell replied. "And it is growing stronger rapidly, perhaps in compensation for her blindness."

"I wonder who this woman might be," said Gannd.

"I cannot tell you who the second woman was my daughter saw," Terrell replied, "but I recognize the first, the beautiful blond adept with the magic staff she calls Calamity. She is known only as the Wizard and she is a force for chaos. You have both seen her?"

Reese shook his head. "No, only Gannd."

"Then she has marked you," Terrell said, gazing at Gannd.

"For what reason?" Gannd asked.

Terrell shook his head. "I cannot say. But you say you did not touch her staff?"

Gannd shook his head. "No. She asked me to take hold of it, but something told me nothing good could come of it."

Terrell nodded. "Then you have good instincts," he replied. "Heed them. They will serve you well."

"Who is she?" Gannd asked.

"No one knows for certain," Terrell replied, going to the fireplace to remove the steaming teakettle. "No one knows where she came from, or where she resides. If, indeed, she has any place of permanent abode. At one time or another, she has been seen throughout the empire, and these sightings have been reported for centuries. Wherever she goes, chaos follows. She is a harbinger of war and death. It is said by some that she brings it all about, but others believe she somehow feeds upon the energies released by conflict. Like a vampire. It is where her power seems to lie."

"What would have happened if he had touched her staff?" asked Reese.

Terrell shook his head. "I cannot say for certain. But it is not for nothing that the Wizard's staff is called Calamity. Mariel sensed that this second woman, whose fate is somehow tied to yours, has a stronger link with the Wizard because she accepted her, while you refused. I suspect this means that this woman touched the Wizard's staff and that, through this, the Wizard's power now flows through her."

"So then she has become an adept, too?" asked Reese.

Terrell shook his head. "No, it takes years of training and study to master the arcane arts. One cannot gain these skills from another in such a manner. But one can become subject to the influence of an adept. I think this is what my daughter meant when she said that this woman would rise to power. It would be through the Wizard's influence, somehow. But I seriously doubt that any good can come of it."

"And somehow, our paths are destined to cross," said Gannd.

Terrell nodded. "It would seem so. My daughter's gift is unusually acute. Since it has manifested, I have not known her ever to be wrong. It appears that peril lies ahead of you." He glanced at Reese. "Where are you bound from here?"

"Downriver to Anuire, as I said," Reese replied. "And from there, to Avanil, where we intend to seek service with the duke."

Terrell pursed his lips. "As mercenaries?"

Reese shrugged. "That is my trade."

"You think there shall be war?"

"There can be no question of it," Reese replied. "It has already begun."

"Yes, I heard that Lord Kier's forces met in battle with Derwyn of Boeruine's. But I also heard the fight was inconclusive and that each withdrew to his own territory."

"Only to prepare to fight again," said Reese. "Mercenaries from all over the empire are heading to Boeruine and Avanil. The Iron Throne is up for grabs. Boeruine and Avan both want it. And the prize is far too rich for either of them to give up the quest. Those aristocrats who are ambitious and wish to improve their lot will throw in with whichever of them they believe is strongest."

Terrell nodded gravely. "It is as I feared, then. War is inevitable."

"That's what I'm counting on," Reese replied with a grin.

Terrell sighed. "A sensible man would seek to avoid the conflict. But then, I have never known you to be very sensible." He glanced at Gannd. "But why you?" he asked. "You are from Tuarhievel. This is not your fight. You have no stake in this. Or do you?"

"My father was human," Gannd replied. "He was Lord Aedan Dosiere, the emperor's high chamberlain. I need to learn something of his world, so that I can learn more about myself."

"So you are half-brother to Lord Davan Dosiere, the present high chamberlain," Terrell said. "Does he know about you?"

Gannd shook his head. "No. I do not see how he could. I was born after my mother left Anuire, and she never told my father about me. She did not wish for him to feel any obligation."

"And you plan to meet your brother when you reach Anuire?" Terrell said.

"I had hoped to," said Gannd.

Terrell grunted. "And what about you, Duncan? What is in Anuire for you?"

Reese shrugged. "Nothing in particular, so far as I know," he replied. "It is merely on our way to Avanil."

Terrell pursed his lips thoughtfully. "Then perhaps it would be best if you did not remain there long. Or better yet, avoid the imperial capital altogether if you can." He glanced at Gannd. "It may not be wise for you to make contact with Lord Davan."

Gannd shook his head, puzzled. "But . . . why? If he is my brother . . ."

"For that very reason," said Terrell. "Consider: your father was high chamberlain, a post now held by your half-brother. And held uneasily, at that, with no ruler on the throne. How do you think Davan would respond when he discovered that his father had a bastard son with some elf girl?"

Gannd started to reply angrily, but Terrell held up his hand. "Hear me out. I do not say this to offend you, merely to make you realize how it would be perceived. Your father was a man much venerated in the empire. It is largely due to the respect given to his memory that Davan maintains his present precarious position, given the temper of the times. He frequently invokes his father's name as if it were an edict, to remind people of his distinguished lineage. He would probably see you as a threat, something that would tarnish the revered image of his father."

"There is no shame in my father's having loved my mother," Gannd replied with an edge to his voice.

"Except that he was married, and the emperor's high chamberlain," said Terrell.

"But I was conceived before my father married the Lady Ariel," said Gannd.

"Indeed?" said Terrell, raising his eyebrows. "Even worse, then. That makes you his firstborn. And a bastard. And a half-elf, to compound the scandal. Do you know if you are blooded?"

"He has the ability to heal," said Reese. "He used it to save my life. But he has not yet discovered if he has inherited any other blood powers from his father."

Terrell glanced at Gannd and nodded. "Mmm. So then tangible proof exists that you are of the bloodline of Anduiras, from which the Dosieres are descended. And yet, you are a half-breed. How do you suppose that will make Lord Davan feel?"

Reese grimaced. "He will see Gannd as an example of his bloodline being polluted."

"Are my people so reviled?" asked Gannd.

"Not by all of us, lad," said Reese, clapping him on the shoulder. "There are still many of us who recall the part the elves played in the emperor's campaigns. Not to mention saving his life when he was abducted by goblins as a boy. But to many, the elves are still the enemy. If for no other reason than because they are different. However, in your case, other things come into play. The firstborn typically inherits stronger blood abilities. When Davan finds out you exist, he will realize that he was not his father's firstborn. He may have inherited the name and title by virtue of his legitimacy, but he will still feel cheated. You have inherited what should have been his by right. At least, that is almost certainly how he will see it."

"I was happy to learn that I had a half-brother," Gannd said. He shook his head. "I had thought that he might feel the same."

"Lord Davan is far from being the man his father was," said Reese. "And what's more, everyone knows it. He has a reputation for being intransigent, petty, and vindictive. All the traits of a man who is unsure of himself."

"And there are those who would not hesitate to use you if it would help them undermine Davan's position," Terrell added. "They would play up to the sentiments of all those who regard elves with prejudice. You stand as a living reminder to them that elves are not necessarily the enemy, that both races can find common ground. And those who choose not to believe that will always look upon you as a threat—to their own sensibilities, if nothing else. Even elves would fall into that category."

"Among my people, I have never been made to feel inferior or tainted because I am part human," Gannd protested.

"You may never have encountered such reactions in Tuarhievel, where your family is well known and respected," said Terrell, "but in the Sielwode, and in Rhuobhe, especially, the Sidhelien would look down on you for being half human. Sentiments against humans run strong in most of the elven kingdoms. Not without some justification, I might add. However, my point is that bigotry is not confined to just one race. Its pernicious influence transcends all cultures and boundaries."

"I would not wish to be a source of distress to my half-brother," Gannd said softly.

"Then we shall make our stay in Anuire as short as possible," said Reese. "Only long enough to resupply ourselves for the journey to Avanil."

"That is probably for the best," Terrell said. "When do you leave?"

"Our boat sails in two days," said Reese.

"Then you shall stay here until then," Terrell said.

"We wouldn't want to impose," said Reese. "We have more than enough money to take rooms at the finest inn in Lofton."

"And possibly those people who were after you tonight would expect you to do just that with all your winnings," Terrell said.

Reese frowned. "Mmmm. That is a point I had not considered."

"Then it's settled. You will remain here," Terrell said.

"In that case, I insist on paying for our stay," said Reese, reaching for his purse.

Terrell reached out and stayed his hand. "Do not insult me, Duncan. We are friends. I do not need your money."

"For Mariel?" said Reese.

"If you wish to buy her a gift, I shall not object, so long as it is not extravagant," Terrell said. "But the best gift you could give her would be your presence. She has always been, and still is, very fond of you."

"Well, there's no accounting for taste," Reese joked. "So be it. Thank you, my friend."

"And now, we shall have our tea," Terrell said, "and you can tell me about what new adventures you have had since I have seen you last."

* * * * *

Katrina knew she had to proceed with her plan with the utmost caution, and to prepare fallback positions and ways to cover herself if anything should go awry. She knew perfectly well she would be playing with fire, but where there was nothing ventured, there was nothing gained. Such was the way of power.

Her gamble, however, would be a calculated one. The trick would be in making sure that she would be the one with the least to lose. And with what she already knew of Derwyn's history and personality, coupled with the knowledge she had gained from Angharad's innate skill in finding out everything that was going on in Seaharrow, Katrina felt reasonably certain that she could maneuver Aerin into a position where crossing her would bring his father's vengeful wrath down upon his head. But it all had to be done slowly, subtly, without Aerin ever realizing that he was being manipulated. But then, Aerin was a man, and one who was a slave to his own baser instincts, which put him doubly at a disadvantage.

In the beginning, Katrina had kept her contact with him to a minimum, largely because she was unsure of her ground and first wished to take his measure. She was not sure how he would respond to his father's having brought home a mistress. She did not know what his relationship with his mother had been. If they had been close, it was almost a foregone conclusion that Aerin would resent her. Though, from everything that she had heard about the Princess Laera, it was hard to imagine her truly caring about anyone besides herself, even her own son. And he was no more than an infant when she died. He could not have many memories of her. Still, there was a chance that, not truly knowing her, he might have idealized the image of his mother, in which case, the effect of Katrina's presence in the castle would still be the same. He would not welcome it.

At first, Aerin had given her few clues as to how he felt about the situation. He had struck her as a sullen and brooding type, introverted and somewhat aloof. But she soon realized that there was more to him than met the eye. He was rather immature for his age, but he was not stupid. He behaved one way in his father's presence and a very different way in private.

It wasn't long before Katrina realized that Aerin's manner in his father's presence was a pose, a mask worn to conceal his true feelings. Either consciously, or perhaps instinctively, he understood that it was important for his father to play the "Iron Duke," as he was known in the province. It was an appellation which had been coined at some time or another by one of his sycophantic knights, and Derwyn was particularly fond of it. It made perfect sense, of course. It made him feel that he was every bit the man his father had been, and it seemed to link him with what he saw as his destiny—to sit upon the Iron Throne. So Aerin treated his father with the proper deference and always acted a bit intimidated in his presence—much the way Derwyn had felt with his own father.

However, Aerin's somewhat sullen and obeisant manner toward his father concealed a fierce resentment. In his efforts to protect his son and mold him in the image of a future emperor, Derwyn had severely curtailed Aerin's freedom and alienated his affections. And Aerin had grown to hate him as a result.

Derwyn was apparently oblivious to the way his son really felt about him. If he had not been so preoccupied with his ambition, he might have been somewhat more observant. Every now and then, in an unguarded moment, Aerin's mask would slip when his father wasn't looking and, for just an instant, Katrina would see a look of sheer loathing in his eyes. Then, just as quickly, the mask would slide back into place. Yes, she thought, he was his mother's son, all right. But with his father's weaknesses. A combination that would prove unfortunate for him.

Derwyn's preoccupation with his army kept him on the training fields from dawn to dusk. Most evenings he spent cloistered with his commanders, discussing training procedures and supplies, strategy and tactics, and intelligence reports. That left both his mistress and his son much to their own devices.

Katrina had started out by working to establish her presence in the castle in such a way as to ingratiate herself to everyone. She made a point of comporting herself in an outgoing, helpful, friendly manner, taking care not to offend even the servants' sensibilities. At no time did she ever make any attempt to take up the mantle of Mistress of Seaharrow. She was the duke's mistress, nothing more. And she acted as if she were perfectly aware of her proper place. However, at the same time, by pitching in a little here, making a hesitant suggestion or two there, and professing a simple concern about being helpful and wanting to take part in the daily routine of the castle's maintenance and upkeep, she gave the impression of a woman who was anxious not to take advantage of her position as the duke's mistress and wanting to fit in and pull her own weight. It wasn't long before she had completely charmed everybody in the castle and, by unspoken agreement, was more or less unanimously accepted as the lady of the house. The first phase was complete. The second was a bit more complicated, but she went about it with the same degree of subtle manipulation and steadfast resolve.

The next step was winning over Aerin. But in a very particular way. It would not do to ingratiate herself with him as she had with everybody else at Seaharrow. She wanted him to perceive her in the same way, but at the same time, she maintained a somewhat more formal attitude with him. He was the duke's son and Derwyn was her lord and master. Consequently, it was not her place to be Aerin's friend. And she knew, instinctively, that if she tried to be, it would only cause him to resent her. She wanted some of that resentment, but only a very small amount of it. Merely a taste, just enough to motivate him. She wanted to be the woman whom everybody else was fond of, who had a smile and a kind word for everyone—but who still kept Aerin at arm's length. The unspoken implication clearly being, "I belong to your father."

She was polite to Aerin and always spoke to him in a warmly respectful manner, but still maintained that certain distance, an edge of courtly formality that made a wall between them. She did it in such a way that there wouldn't be anything specific he could put his finger on, but he was nevertheless aware of it. It was never anything she said. It was in her manner and it was not overt at all. In time, as their acquaintanceship developed, it began to frustrate him. Without quite knowing why, he soon started making efforts to break down the distanced reserve she manifested in his presence. He wanted to have more of an effect and not just be perceived and treated as his father's son. He couldn't help but notice that she treated him a little differently from everybody else. In a sense, that was only his due as the duke's son and heir. However, at the same time, his immaturity defined very narrow limitations in the way he looked at women—either as potential conquests, or as those who lacked enough attraction to fall into that category. Katrina was attractive. But Katrina was off limits. And, in a subtle manner, all her actions toward him underscored that point and constantly reminded him of it. Eventually, it was inevitable that Aerin would be tempted.

It took less time than she expected. And he was so transparent, it made her want to laugh. She was like a magnet and he the iron filing. He set out to produce an effect on her. And Aerin knew only one way to do that. Angharad had made it clear that he'd been tempted by forbidden fruit before. It added extra spice to his otherwise unremarkable existence. And Katrina was the most forbidden fruit of all. What better way for him to act out his resentment of his father than to seduce the duke's own mistress?

Aerin's tragic flaw was he thought that if he succeeded, it would allow him to control her. Instead, Katrina thought with smug self-satisfaction, it would be the other way around. And it was only fitting that what he did to other women would now be done to him. The sly manipulator was about to learn what it was like to be manipulated. That was not, however, Katrina's primary motive.

As Derwyn's mistress, the life she led now depended entirely on him. Katrina was well aware of this and took pains to ensure he would not tire of her. But at the same time, she did not want to keep her eggs all in one basket. Derwyn was getting ready to go off to war again. Katrina's life had already experienced one massive upheaval when her father, her suitor, and her brothers died in battle. If anything should happen to Derwyn, she would once more be left with nothing. She had no intention of allowing that to happen. If

Derwyn died, Aerin would inherit the dukedom. She wanted to make sure she would inherit Aerin.

She had no intention of giving herself to him. That, she realized, would be foolhardy and counterproductive to what she intended to accomplish. Her plan was merely to make Aerin want her, want her so badly that he couldn't even think straight. And the way to do that was to deny him—but at the same time, give him some subtle encouragement, feed the hope that he might be able to succeed in pulling off his most ambitious and dangerous seduction.

And it was so easy. All she had to do was play up slightly to his natural desires. He fancied himself quite the man with the ladies. But she acted as if she were completely immune to his charm, didn't even notice it. And whenever he would turn the conversation to himself—as his insecurity and immaturity often led him to do in an attempt to impress her—she would casually turn it back to the subject of his father and speak of him in glowing terms. It only served to infuriate and frustrate Aerin and made him redouble his efforts to get her to notice him as an individual and not just his father's son.

All it took was a little bit of time. And not much time, at that. After a while, Katrina began to act as if she found him interesting, but she kept him off balance. Just when he thought he was starting to get somewhere, she'd pull the rug out from under him and once more casually turn the conversation to the subject of his father. She played him like a fish, getting the hook implanted, allowing him to run with the line a bit, then reeling him in. A little closer each time.

After a while, she began to escalate the game. She began to act just slightly awkward in his presence, as if she were uncomfortable being alone with him. And from time to time, when others were around, such as at dinner in the great hall, she would occasionally allow him to catch her gazing in his direction, and then, the moment he noticed, she would quickly look away, as if guilty that he had caught her looking at him. Almost at once, she could see the effect it had on him. And again, it was so obvious it made her want to laugh.

Angharad kept her up to date on all the gossip reported by her spies. Aerin had started going back to some of the women he'd seduced before and then abandoned when he grew bored with them.

His libido had been primed. He could not get what he wanted, so he settled . . . but that would only serve to whet his appetite still further.

Soon, he became so bold as to start flirting with her. At first, she pretended not to notice, though he knew she did, because she wanted him to know. The game had changed now. He knew that he was not only having an effect, but that she might even be entertaining similar thoughts herself. Could she also be tempted by forbidden fruit? Was the boring routine of daily life at Seaharrow, coupled with Derwyn's excessive preoccupation with his army and his plans, making her feel neglected and possibly causing her to contemplate the spice of a dangerous liaison?

Every thought going through his mind was clearly written on his features, so much so that Katrina began to worry that others might notice. But no one did. Occasional glances in his direction, quickly averted when he noticed, were soon held a moment or two longer before she looked down, guiltily. Sometimes, at dinner, when their eyes met, she would give the added subtle touch of allowing her hand to shake a little as she held her goblet. Gradually, their exchanged looks across the table became more significant, impregnated with sexual tension. Then came more added touches on Katrina's part: biting her lower lip nervously, or allowing her breathing to become a little deeper, so that her bosom would rise. It was starting to drive Aerin to distraction. She could almost feel his hunger emanating toward her from across the table.

He soon began to sit directly across from her, under the pretext of making conversation about mundane matters, often just talking to somebody else while his foot sought contact with hers beneath the table. In the beginning, she avoided it, but after a while, she stopped moving her foot away when she felt his, as if pretending not to notice. Before long, when his foot rubbed up against hers, she would rub back. And his eyes would light up and his breathing would quicken.

Finally, he could restrain himself no longer.

She was doing some embroidery in her private chambers when she heard a scraping sound and noticed a secret panel opening in the wall. And there he was. She hadn't known about that secret passageway, though she had assumed that there were hidden rooms and passages within the castle. What she had not known was that there was one that led to her own chambers. How many times, she wondered, had he hidden there, watching her secretly? And had he observed her when she was with his father?

She gasped, pretending to be startled, which she was, but she played up her shock. "Aerin!" she said, dropping her embroidery and jumping to her feet.

"We need to talk, Katrina," he said, coming into the room.

She acted flustered. "What are you doing here? How did you . . ." She shook her head. "I never suspected. How long have you been watching me?"

"Long enough," he said, approaching her. "I have especially enjoyed watching you as you bathe and get ready for bed."

She blushed. "How dare you? Is that how a gentleman behaves?"

"It is how a man behaves when he is caught in the grip of an obsession," Aerin replied, staring at her intensely. "As I have been obsessed with you."

"You must be mad," she said. "I am your father's mistress."

"His possession, you mean," Aerin said with contempt. "For that is how he treats you."

"How he treats me is no concern of yours."

"You are wrong," said Aerin. "It is very much a concern of mine. He spends more time with his horses than he does with you. And probably lavishes more love on them—if, indeed, he knows anything of love."

"And you do?" she countered.

"I may have led a sheltered life here in the castle," he replied, "not by choice, I might add, but I am far from inexperienced."

She smirked at him. "Yes, I have heard about some of your experiences. And your little secret playroom."

He raised his eyebrows, surprised, but not thrown. "I do not know what you may have heard, but I have done nothing to be ashamed of and I have nothing to apologize for."

"Indeed? The husbands of some of the women you've . . . 'experienced' . . . might disagree with that."

"My, my," he said. "Someone has been gossiping, haven't they? I think I can guess who, but never mind. The fact is that if a man treats his woman properly, and knows how to fulfill her needs, she will not be tempted to look elsewhere for her satisfaction."

"I see," Katrina said. "And is that your goal? To see that every woman in Seaharrow is fully satisfied?"

"Is there something wrong in satisfying a woman's desires?"

"Perhaps not. But what makes you think that I am in need of your particular expertise in that regard?"

"You do," he replied.

"I do? Really? You may think too highly of yourself."

"Do not try to pretend that there has been nothing going on between us," Aerin said. "We are neither of us fools. I have seen you look at me with fire in your eyes, and you have not been completely unresponsive. The question is, are you going to continue playing at these childish games to titillate yourself or are you woman enough to act on your desires?"

"You presume too much," Katrina said. "What do you suppose your father would do if he knew you were here and if he heard you speak like this?"

"I imagine he would fly into a rage and punish me," said Aerin, "but he would not be too harsh. After all, I am his only heir, and his ambition to see a line of Boeruines ruling the empire would preclude his doing anything very drastic. More likely, he would get rid of you. Something he will probably do before too long, in any case. In the event you hadn't noticed, women do not play a significant part in my father's life. To my knowledge, since my mother died, you are the first to share his bed. Which is probably all you share with him, through no fault of your own. If you think you have any great claim on his affections, then you are only deluding yourself. My father does not know how to love. Trust me. I know from long experience."

"And you resent him so much that you seek to strike back at him through me, is that it?" she said.

"If that is truly what you think, then why have you encouraged me?" he countered.

"I? Encouraged you?"

"Oh, please. Spare me the innocent, outraged protestations. You know very well that you have not been unreceptive."

"So, because I have not totally spurned you, you have decided to pay court to me," she said. "By spying on me and stealing into my chambers through a secret passage like a thief. What's next? The gallant act of rape?"

"If that was what I wanted, I could have done it any time I wished," said Aerin. "And perhaps some part of you would like it if I did. That way, you could feel secure that you could not be held responsible. But I am not a rapist, my lady. I take only what is given freely."

"And you have had, by all reports, no shortage of those willing to give," Katrina said. "So why me?"

"Because you are different," Aerin said. "None of the others meant anything to me. And in truth, I meant nothing to them. The pleasure I took in them was just that and nothing more."

"So you merely used them."

"No more than they used me," Aerin replied. "I was a dangerous, romantic episode in their otherwise dreary lives with men who took them for granted. Perhaps some of the unmarried ones saw a possibility of effecting a more permanent attachment, one that might lead to their making an advantageous match. If so, then I did not hold that against them. But neither did I promise anything that I could not deliver."

"Well, at least you are forthright in that," Katrina said. "A woman likes to know what to expect."

"Spare me your sarcasm. Is your situation with my father any different?"

"That is between your father and myself."

"Quite so. But just the same, I will venture to guess at the arrangement, and you can tell me if I'm wrong. He promised you nothing, except to provide for your well-being while you were his mistress and perhaps to help you find another 'situation' when the arrangement ceased to suit his needs. And you knew that when you accepted. Or did you convince yourself that somehow, against all odds and evidence, you could make him love you and make you his duchess?"

"If he did, then I would be your mother," she replied, archly.

"Stepmother," he corrected her. "The difference is significant. And the odds against that, I would wager, would be greater than the odds of the Emperor Michael coming back to life to reclaim his empty throne. My father would no more marry you than he would wed his horse. He cares nothing for you. He is incapable of those kinds of feelings."

"And you are?"

"I could give you more than he ever could."

"Is that what you said to all those other women who became nothing more than notches on your bedpost?"

"I told you, I never made them any promises."

"And so you offer none to me."

"I am not as innocent as you may think," said Aerin. "I know precisely under what circumstances you arrived at Seaharrow. Your family was butchered by my father, yet you willingly became his concubine, for which your mother, your sole surviving relative, disowned you, calling you a traitor. But you did not come here with my father out of love. Or even lust. You came because you wanted to survive, because you had lost everything and sought to make a better life not only for yourself, but for your widowed mother, too. For which unselfish gesture she turned her back on you out of grief and misplaced pride, and because she understood nothing of the ways of the world. But you do, Katrina. I think you labor under no illusions, as I think you know precisely how insecure and ephemeral your position is at present. My father is more than twice your age. He may be healthy now, but even if he does not tire of you, if anything should happen to him on the battlefield where he so longs to prove himself, you shall be left with nothing. Unless I choose differently."

"And what does that mean?"

"It means that as duke, I shall need a duchess. And there shall be no shortage of women from good families who would seek to strengthen their positions and improve their bloodlines. But they would all be unknown quantities to me. At least, in certain matters that are not normally discussed in courtship and wedding arrangements."

"By that, I take it, you refer to your private liaisons."

"You and I, Katrina, we understand each other. And as I said, we labor under no illusions. You would not begrudge me my little pleasures and I would not begrudge you your past. It might raise a few eyebrows here and there, but if it were handled properly, it would be easily enough accepted. And we would both have what we wanted."

She stared at him. "I must be imagining things. Is it possible that you are actually proposing marriage to me? Your father's mistress?"

"When the time comes, you shall no longer be my father's mistress. My father will be dead and I shall be master of Seaharrow and Archduke of Boeruine."

"Ah, I see," Katrina replied with a smirk. "And against that eventuality, which might not occur for years, you expect me to surrender to you now?"

"It seems to me that would not be a prospect you would find entirely unwelcome. And I should think it an arrangement infinitely preferable to the one that you have now, which offers no security, no possibility of advancement, and no guarantees."

"You bargain with me like a merchant," said Katrina, her voice laced with sarcasm. "How could any woman resist such a romantic proposition?"

"We have already played the prelude to romance in the coy flirtation in which you have engaged me," replied Aerin. "And there shall be time for passion and romance in earnest after we have reached an understanding. But I came here tonight to put forth my proposition honestly and with forthrightness, out of respect for you."

"Well, I must admit, the approach is certainly original," Katrina said.

"It is a better offer than my father made you," Aerin said, stepping forward and taking her by the shoulders. "He gave you nothing but a bed and a roof over your head, which he could take away at any time. I offer you my name and rank. Value given, for value received."

She stared into his eyes. His face came closer as he bent to kiss her. But at the last moment, she turned her head. "I will not say I do not find your proposition tempting," she said in a low voice. "But as I said, I am your father's woman. And your father is still very much alive. You are a long way from inheriting his title. And other things, besides."

He drew her to him roughly and kissed her hard. She felt his tongue probe between her lips, resisted for a moment, then allowed the kiss, responding passionately, but only briefly. She broke the contact, pulling away sharply when his grip on her relaxed, and stepped back a pace.

"I would not wish your visit here to have been for nothing," she said. "You wanted to find out what it was like to kiss me. Well, now you know. But that is all you will find out, unless you choose to force yourself upon me. I made a bargain with your father. If he should choose to end it, then so be it. But until then, I intend to keep it."

Aerin smiled. "My father should show you more appreciation. It is a pity he does not."

"He has not promised me anything that he could not deliver, either," said Katrina. "I understood that and accepted it."

"Things change," said Aerin. "Many things can happen to a man when he goes off to war. We shall speak of this again. And perhaps sooner than you think. Until then, my lady, I bid you good night."

He bowed slightly and went back through the secret passageway, leaving Katrina to wonder exactly what he meant by his last remarks. She may have succeeded better than she thought. She smiled to herself, wondering if he was still back there, watching from concealment. Knowing Aerin, it was almost certain that he was.

Slowly, she started to remove her clothes as she prepared for bed.

chapter seven

Their time with Terrell and his daughter, Mariel, went by quickly, and Gannd found himself wishing they could stay longer. He understood why Reese had such a fondness for the wizard. He was unassuming and forthright, a simple man who had chosen a complex profession. But even so, he chose a simple way to follow it and approached his art with a quiet precision completely lacking in flamboyance. Though Reese had earlier professed that magic made him nervous, Terrell's magic seemed to be a singular exception. Perhaps it was because what spells he used while they were there were small ones, such as the lighting of the fire, merely things that made his day-to-day existence slightly more convenient.

Gannd could see by the way he went about it that Terrell was an adept of considerable skill, for though the spells he cast were simple, he executed them as if they required almost no thought at all. When he "cooked" dinner for them, for example, he would have all of the utensils in the kitchen working simultaneously, as if several pairs of unseen hands were busily manipulating them, and yet he was able to converse with Gannd and Reese at the same time. Gannd knew from having grown up around his uncle that even the

Gannd remarked upon it at the end of the next day, when they sat having some tea together while Reese was upstairs, telling Mariel a bedtime story—with himself as the protagonist, of course. Terrell was modest in discussing his abilities and explained why he chose to live the way he did.

"I have no wish to enter the service of some noble," he said. "I am comfortable living as I do. True, I could be wealthier and have a higher style of life if I were a court adept to some duke or baron, but then I would not really enjoy it. I am a man of simple tastes and needs and I like to call my time my own. And I prefer to decide which spells I cast, and how I cast them, and for whom. Nor would I wish to subject my daughter to life among the aristocracy. Theirs are not the values I would want her to adopt. With her blindness, they would never accept her as an equal, but would treat her as a cripple and look upon her as an object of pity. Mariel does not need pity. She needs acceptance, and to be treated like anybody else. Despite her blindness, there is little that she cannot do. Little that truly counts, at any rate."

"So then you live simply for your daughter's sake?" asked Gannd.

"No more than any devoted father does," Terrell replied, "even though she is not really my daughter. I adopted her when she was an infant. I found her on my doorstep, abandoned by her parents, whoever they may be, doubtless because she was born blind. I decided it was fate that brought her to me, and she has brightened my solitary life. I am happy with the way things are. I would change nothing. The sovereign remedy for a long life, my friend, is to fall in love with what you do. And take pride and satisfaction in the way you do it. I have my emporium downstairs, and it is open to aristocrat and commoner alike. Whether it is a noblewoman who comes through my door, seeking a love charm to make her more attractive to the object of her affections, or a simple washerwoman who seeks some physic for her aching knees, I serve all alike and take my satisfaction in having made some small difference in their lives. There are some whose plans are grander in scope, who hope to change the

142

world in some way that is significant. But for my part, I have learned that having a positive effect on the lives of those who cross my path is significant enough. And it seems to me that if everyone behaved that way, why then, the world would change."

When it came time for them to leave, Gannd felt that he had made two good friends in Terrell and young Mariel. As they parted, Mariel gave him a warm hug, then stiffened and almost swooned once more as she hugged Reese and the Sight came upon her again.

"Beware a man in black," she told him, with an expression of intense concern. "You have met before, and he bears you ill will."

"I think I know who you mean," said Reese, nodding. "But I believe we've given him and his friends the slip."

Mariel shook her head. "No, your path and his will cross again . . . and soon. He is very angry with you. Somehow his anger seems out of proportion to some small wrong done him."

"Yes, I imagine he would be angry," Reese replied, apparently unconcerned. "Don't worry, Mariel. I don't think he's any real danger."

"Do not underestimate him, Duncan," Mariel said earnestly. "Be careful. Please."

"I shall be. I promise."

They took their leave and walked to the square, where they hired a small carriage to drive them to the wharf where they would board the sloop. "Might as well arrive in style," Reese said with a grin. "We can afford it."

Their drive through the streets of Lofton to the docks was much more pleasant than their flight to Terrell's home a couple of days earlier. It was very early, and the streets of the city were just beginning to come to life as Lofton prepared for another day. The morning air was cool and brisk when the carriage dropped them off at the slip where the riverboat was moored. They checked in with the steward, who confirmed their passage, and boarded. The boat rocked gently at its mooring as the crew prepared to cast off. They went to their cabin to check the accommodations. It was small, but extremely comfortable, with two bunks mounted on the bulkhead, one over the other, and blankets and thick bedding, a lamp, a small table, and two chairs. The quarters were a bit cramped by landlubber standards, and the ceiling was low, but overall, the cabin was quite cozy.

Reese stretched out on the lower bunk and sighed with contentment. "Ah, this is the way to travel," he said. "Out of the weather, no need to pitch camp each night, no horses to worry about, nothing to do but laze around, lie back and float downstream. With a decent wind, we should be in Anuire in three or four days."

Gannd closed his eyes a moment, trying to visualize the maps he'd studied. "And about a day's ride from there to Daulton?"

"Oh, half a day, if we make good time and get good weather," said Reese.

"It's strange to think that I will be so close to a half-brother I have never seen," said Gannd, "and not stop to meet him."

"I can imagine how you must feel," said Reese sympathetically, "but it would probably be for the best if we simply stayed out of Davan's way."

Gannd nodded. "Yes, I understand. Still, it is a pity things could not have been different."

"Well, buck up," said Reese. "You wanted to explore the human world. You'll see a good stretch of it in the next few days. Come on, let's go up on deck and watch as we get under way."

As the sun was starting to rise in the sky, the crew cast off the mooring ropes and poled the boat away from the dock. They drifted downstream slowly as the sail was unfurled and raised. It luffed with the breeze until the boom was swung out to catch it and the sail filled with a cracking sound. Gannd found the whole procedure fascinating. He had never been on a boat before and knew nothing of sailing. The boat started to make headway downstream as the wind filled the sail and the pilot steered toward the center of the river. Gannd felt a huge smile on his face as he enjoyed the feeling of the wind in his hair and the sound of the water lapping against the hull. Then his smile died suddenly as he turned around.

"Reese," he said.

Reese turned in the direction Gannd was looking. Behind them, standing by the rail near the bow, was the man in black from the gaming house. He was still dressed the same way he was when they'd last seen him, only he had added a black cloak and black slouch hat to his apparel. And he wore a sword belted at his waist. He was looking straight at them.

"I'll be a son of a . . ." Reese's voice trailed off.

The man in black smiled and bowed his head toward them slightly, touching the brim of his hat.

"Mariel was right," said Gannd.

"I'm going to find out what this is all about right now," Reese said with determination. They started toward the man in black, who calmly waited for them to approach. He had a bemused expression on his face.

"Well, this is a surprise," he said.

"Is it?" Reese countered, his hand on the hilt of his sword.

The man in black appeared not to notice. "It seems we are going to be traveling downriver together," he said. "Where are you bound? Moerel or Anuire?"

"Where are you bound?" Reese asked.

"Oh, I only go as far as Bellamie," the man in black replied, casually.

"Interesting coincidence, how we just happen to be traveling on the same boat," said Reese.

"Yes, isn't it? Who knows, perhaps we can get up a friendly game or two to pass the time while en route."

"I wouldn't count on it," Reese replied. "I'm not much in the mood for playing cards lately."

"Really? That's too bad. A sporting gentleman would give me the chance to win some of my money back."

"I won it fair and square," said Reese. "And I intend to hang on to it."

"Well, that is your choice, certainly," said the man in black. "You know, we were never properly introduced. My name is D'kar. Juslan D'kar." He pronounced the "J" softly, with a "zh" sound.

"You are Khinasi?" Reese said.

D'kar inclined his head slightly. "On my father's side. But now you have the advantage of me." He raised his eyebrows, prompting Reese to give his name.

"Somehow, I don't think people often have the advantage of you," Reese replied. "Duncan Reese. And this is my friend, Gannd Aurealis."

"A pleasure to meet you both," said D'kar. Then, with a smile, he added, "Again."

"I thought we almost met again the night we left the gaming

house," said Reese.

D'kar raised his eyebrows once more. "Indeed? Perhaps you mistook someone else for me. I stayed rather late that night. I had to try to make good some of my rather considerable losses."

"And did you?" Reese asked flatly.

D'kar shrugged. "Oh, I won a few hands. But I fear it was not a good night, overall. Perhaps I shall have better luck in Bellamie."

"Yes, perhaps," said Reese. "You play well."

"So do you. Few would have had the nerve to call my bluff in such a situation."

"Nothing ventured, nothing gained," said Reese.

"So true. Well, I was up rather late last night and I did not get much sleep. So if you will excuse me, I think I shall retire to my cabin. I am sure we shall have the opportunity to speak again. After all, we are all in the same boat, so to speak." He smiled and tipped his hat, then went below.

"Nervy bastard," Reese said as they watched him go.

"He acted as if nothing happened," Gannd said. "Perhaps we were wrong about him."

"Oh, we weren't wrong."

"But if he stayed late at the gaming house that night . . ."

"He was lying through his teeth. He wasn't about to let us walk off with all that money. You don't think it's a coincidence he's on the same boat with us, do you?"

"Well . . . I suppose it's possible," said Gannd.

"Possible, perhaps, but not bloody likely," Reese replied.

"How could he have known we would be on this boat?" asked Gannd.

"It wouldn't have been too difficult for him to make inquiries," said Reese. "He had two days to do it in. All he had to do was ask around and see if a big blond man and a half-elf had booked passage on any of the craft heading downriver. And if we hadn't, you could be sure he would have been following us on the road leading out of town."

"What do you think he plans to do?"

"Get his money back, obviously. The question is, how many of the other passengers are in his pay? Or perhaps he's bribed some of the crew. It wouldn't take much. Jump us in our cabin in the middle of the night, then over the side with our bodies. And nobody would really care, one way or the other."

"Why not confront him now then, and get it over with?" asked Gannd.

"Because he hasn't done anything," said Reese. "We have no proof that he was the one who pursued us from the gaming house. And if we tried anything, then we'd be the aggressors and we'd have the whole crew down on us. No, we'll just have to watch our backs and sleep in shifts. So much for a nice, lazy voyage down the river."

"Well, all we have to do is be on the watch until we reach Bellamie," Gannd said. "He said that he was getting off there."

"I wouldn't believe anything he says. He might well get off at Bellamie, just to make us drop our guard. And then his confederates aboard the boat, whoever they may be, will make their move." He sighed and grimaced. "We might have been better off facing them in the streets, but I was hoping to avoid trouble. It doesn't look as if that's going to happen."

"At least we know when he will make his move," said Gannd. "If he goes to sleep during the day—"

"That's no guarantee of anything," Reese interrupted. "As I said, we don't know who else on board may be in league with him. He would never be this obvious if he were on his own. Take care not to turn your back on anyone. We shall just have to watch everyone for the remainder of this trip."

They did not see D'kar again that day. He remained in his cabin, though whether he was asleep or not was anybody's guess. But neither Reese nor Gannd were able to enjoy the voyage. Instead of taking in the sights as they sailed downriver, they watched everybody carefully while they were on deck, and made sure to cover one another's backs. Gannd kept wondering which of the crew or the other passengers might be in league with D'kar. When the steward brought them their meal in their cabin, Gannd watched him carefully. Did he look about the cabin to see where the money might be hidden? Or did he assume they had it on them? Or was he even involved? Gannd could not tell. The uncertainty made for a tense journey.

That night, when they went back to their cabin, they took turns staying awake. The cabin doors had bolts on them, but they were small and flimsy, and the doors were very light, meant really to provide privacy and nothing more. One good kick or a strong blow with the hand would easily suffice to break in. But the first night passed uneventfully, though while he was awake, Gannd tensed at every sound. And there were many sounds. The boat creaked and groaned, and each creak sounded as if it might be a footstep just outside the door.

It was difficult to tell how far they had traveled by the next morning. The ship sailed all through the night, and Gannd would have had no way of telling where they were even if he had been able to watch the countryside they passed. Reese had no way of knowing, either. He had not sailed downriver before, and though he knew the countryside to some degree, he was too busy remaining alert to any possible attack to pay very much attention to the scenery.

It was midafternoon of the second day of their voyage before they saw D'kar again. He had remained inside his cabin and came up after noon to stand by the railing and watch the scenery. When he saw them, he smiled and nodded politely, but did not attempt to engage them in conversation.

"I'd like to wipe that smile right off his face," said Reese tensely.

"Perhaps he really does not intend to do anything, after all," said Gannd.

"I wouldn't bet on that if I were you," replied Reese. "He's toying with us. He knows exactly what we're thinking. He's not a fool. He knows we're just waiting for him to make his move. He's hoping the tension will get to us and we'll make a mistake."

"I keep watching the crew and the other passengers," said Gannd, "wondering which of them might be waiting to stick a dagger in my back."

"It could be any of them," Reese said. "Times are hard, and some men will do anything for only a few gold coins."

That evening, D'kar managed to get up a small game on the aft deck near the wheelhouse. Gannd and Reese watched him play for a short while. Once, at the beginning, he raised his eyebrows at them and indicated that they might join him. Reese simply shook his head. After that, he more or less ignored them, playing with several of the other passengers and a couple of the crew. But it was impossible to tell if any of the players were in his pay. It could have been all of them or none of them. No one gave anything away. The stakes were small, unlike that night at the gaming house, but D'kar won steadily. He seemed completely unconcerned with them. Finally, they went below.

Nothing happened on the second night, either, though as before, Gannd imagined menace in every creak and groan of the wood and rigging. The constant tension of waiting for something to happen was getting to him. He was feeling jumpy. Reese was no better. When Gannd reached out to wake him, he bolted upright immediately, a dagger in his hand, and Gannd struck his head on the upper bunk as he jumped back, thinking Reese might take a swipe at him before he was fully awake.

"I'm sorry, lad. Damn it all, I've a mind to go down to D'kar's cabin right now and toss him overboard," said Reese apologetically, as Gannd rubbed at his sore head.

"That may not be such a bad idea," Gannd replied. "Why don't we do it?"

Reese grimaced. "Don't think I'm not sorely tempted. But I'm not a bloody murderer, and neither are you. We can't just kill a man for what we think he's going to do. Certain as we may be. That will take you down a road you do not want to travel. We have to wait until he actually tries to do it."

"Then I just wish he'd hurry up about it," Gannd said sourly. "This is getting on my nerves."

On the morning of the third day of their voyage, the boat arrived at Bellamie. They stood on deck and watched as several of the passengers disembarked. D'kar was not among them. They spotted him standing at the railing near the gangplank, watching as new passengers bound for Anuire came aboard.

"Well, so much for his getting off at Bellamie," Reese said wryly.

"Perhaps we should get off, then," Gannd suggested.

Reese shook his head. "That's just what he's waiting for. If we head down that gangplank, he will be right behind us. After all, he said he would be getting off at Bellamie, didn't he? But if we remain, then so will he, claiming that he's changed his mind and decided there would be better opportunities in the imperial capital. And we could hardly argue the point. No, we shall have to play this game out to the end. Have you been marking the new passengers who've come on board?"

Gannd glanced at him. "You think confederates of his are boarding here?"

"I shouldn't be at all surprised," said Reese, watching the people coming up the gangplank to see if any of them showed any sign of recognition when they saw D'kar.

"How would he have been able to arrange it?" Gannd asked.

"It would have been a simple matter for him to send word ahead by carrier pigeon before the ship departed," Reese said. "Especially if he already had connections here, which is quite likely. A professional gambler needs to keep on the move, otherwise his opportunities will soon dry up. Chances are he's been up and down this river many times."

"You sound as if you've met his sort before."

"Many times," said Reese. "Though I must admit, this one is more persistent than the others. Usually, they know enough to cut their losses and make it up with the next sucker. Our friend, D'kar, is going to unusual lengths to get his money back. Of course, he lost quite a bit of it. He may be broke. If that's the case he's desperate, and therefore willing to take chances."

"If he is broke, how could he afford to hire men to help him?"

"By promising them a cut of the loot," said Reese. "However, that has its own risks. They could just decide to keep it all and cut him out of it, in which case he'd probably wind up going overboard right behind us. There!" He grabbed Gannd by the arm. "That man in the dark green cloak . . . Did you see? He glanced straight at D'kar."

"I noticed," Gannd said, nodding.

"He has the look of a mercenary," Reese said. "But he's no longer young. A soldier down on his luck, a bit too old to command much of a price . . . just the right sort for D'kar. Mark him well and keep an eye on him."

Gannd had a good chance to do just that as the man came past them, heading to the cabins below. He was just shy of six feet tall, with a stocky, husky build and muscular arms. His hair was iron gray, worn loose down below the shoulders, and his sunken eyes were a shade of blue so light they resembled ice. He had a square jaw and a nose that looked as if it had been broken several times.

Gannd guessed he was in his sixties, which made him old for a soldier of fortune, well past his prime. His face was weather-beaten and he had a permanent squint from years spent out of doors, staring through a helm visor in bright sunlight. He wore a dark green woolen cloak over a black tunic and well-worn brown leather breeches, rough side of the leather out, tucked into knee-high brown boots. He wore a sword in a tooled leather scabbard and two sheath knives and carried a staff, though he walked with a spry energy that belied his years. He was grim-looking, and he passed them without a word or glance.

D'kar glanced at them and smiled, tipping his hat.

"I've about had it with this character," said Reese irritably. He moved bruskly toward the gambler.

"Good day," D'kar said innocently.

"I'm not so sure about that," Reese replied. "I thought you were getting off at Bellamie."

"Well, I had planned to," D'kar said, "but I've changed my mind. It strikes me that there would probably be better opportunities for me in the imperial capital. So it seems we shall be shipmates a while longer."

Almost word for word what Reese predicted he would say, thought Gannd.

"I hope you have a chance to take advantage of those opportunities," said Reese, gazing straight into the gambler's eyes. "It would be a shame if something happened to upset your plans."

"Why, what could happen?" asked D'kar, raising his eyebrows. "The river is calm, the weather is mild, and the pilot seems to know what he's about. I expect it will be an uneventful voyage to Anuire."

"If you're smart, it will be," Reese said with a hard edge to his voice.

D'kar frowned. "I fear I do not get your meaning."

"I think you do," said Reese. He poked the other man in the chest, hard. "Stay out of my way, D'kar. Whatever you're planning, give it up. It'll cost you much more than you think."

D'kar gave him a level stare. "You have already cost me plenty," he replied. "And it was most unsporting of you not to offer me a chance to even things up a bit. Now you threaten me." He glanced at a passenger standing nearby. "Did you hear this man threaten me?"

The man glanced at them briefly, then simply looked away, apparently not wanting to get involved.

"You heard," D'kar told him. "Just be sure to remember what you heard. Later."

"I'm warning you, D'kar," threatened Reese. "You try anything and you won't live to regret it."

"Well now, if that was not a threat, I don't know what one is," D'kar replied. "And here I have done absolutely nothing to provoke it. You know, I have seen many sore losers in my time, but a sore winner? That's a new one on me."

Reese grimaced with disgust and turned away. As the boat finished taking on passengers and made ready to get under way once more, they went back down to their cabin. As they came in, Reese kicked over one of the chairs in frustration.

"I shouldn't have done that," he said.

"You gave the man a warning," Gannd replied. "It seems fair enough."

"The trouble is that he's the only one who understood it was a warning. I should have kept my voice under control, but I was angry and I spoke too loudly. I'm sure at least a few people overheard. And it sounded like a threat, completely unprovoked. I played right into his hands."

"So what do you plan to do?"

"Absolutely nothing. In fact, I suggest we remain right here in this cabin for the remainder of the voyage. Make him come right through that door. It will only admit one man at a time. That makes it more difficult for them than if they caught us up on deck."

"I would agree with that," said Gannd. "But I am not looking forward to spending several more days in the close confines of this cabin."

"We should reach Anuire tomorrow morning," Reese said. "If D'kar is going to make his move, it will have to be tonight. Otherwise, he'll have to try to catch us in Anuire. Which is also a possibility."

That night, Reese took the first watch, saying he was too wound up to sleep. Gannd stretched out on the upper bunk, but sleep didn't come any easier to him. He kept his sword beside him on the bed, unsheathed.

"What happens if he doesn't make his move tonight?" asked Gannd.

"He'll follow us, or have us followed, more likely, when we reach Anuire and disembark," said Reese, nervously tapping his boot with the tip of his sword. "But then he'd have to find out where we were headed, and decide upon a good place and time to jump us. Depending on how persistent he is—and he does seem to be that— he could gather his men and follow us to Daulton. There would be any number of places on the road where he could hit us. If I were him, I think that's probably what I would do. But I'm not sure he's that patient. And he'd be taking the chance of losing us again when we reached the capital. No, I think it's going to be tonight. But he's going to have to work for it. Try to get some sleep."

Gannd shook his head as he lay back on the bunk. "I don't think I can. With all the noise this boat makes, the creaking of the wood, the stretching of the rigging, it all makes it seem as if someone is sneaking up on us just outside the door. And if it's going to be tonight, I'd just as soon remain awake. Remember, I see better in the darkness than you do. And I can hear better, as well."

"I don't dispute that," Reese replied. "But it won't help us if we're both tired when it happens. And if D'kar doesn't make his move tonight, then we'll arrive at Anuire without having had any sleep and we shall not be alert. That may be what he's hoping for, in fact."

"I thought you said he would make his move tonight."

"I think he will, but damn it, I don't know for sure. It would be handy to have Mariel's gift right now. That way we'd know what to expect."

"None of this sits well with me," said Gannd. "I was raised in the way of the warrior, and a warrior does not run from a fight or wait placidly when he knows an enemy is going to attack. If we had confronted D'kar on the streets back in Lofton, the night this all started, we would not be in this position now."

"You have a point," said Reese. "But I still think we made the right decision. I would much sooner deal with D'kar here on the river than risk being thrown in jail by the sheriff back in Lofton. His deputies are not exactly known for their evenhandedness. And they hang people for murder."

"How would it be murder if we were only defending ourselves?"

"It wouldn't be," said Reese. "But I don't think the sheriff would care much, one way or the other. Especially once he saw the contents of our purses."

"There are certain disadvantages to being rich, aren't there?"

Reese chuckled. "Not if you're rich enough to pay someone else to worry about it. Regrettably, we're not quite that rich."

Gannd swung his legs off the bunk and dropped to the floor lightly. "This waiting for something to happen is intolerable! If I have to stay in here all night, lying beside my sword and listening for every slightest sound, I shall go mad. I'm for going up on deck."

"That may be just what they're waiting for," said Reese.

"Then I say let's do it and get it over with!" said Gannd.

"There's something to be said for that," said Reese, "but I don't much like not knowing what we're going up against. We don't know how many of them there are."

"On the other hand, if we have to fight in here, we'd only get in one another's way," Gannd countered. "We might get the first ones through the door, but if they stormed us in strength in such close confines, they might easily overwhelm us. I'd rather be up on deck, where I'd have some room to move."

Reese thought about it for a moment, then sighed and nodded. "Very well. Your argument has merit, and this waiting is getting on my nerves, as well. Let's go."

Gannd listened for a moment at the door, then, satisfied that no one was lurking outside, they left the cabin and went up on deck. The moon was out and it was a cool night on the river. Everything was quiet, save for the soft creaking of the rigging as the boat sailed smoothly with the current. There was a mild breeze and the sails weren't filling evenly. They kept luffing with a flapping sound and then filling once again as the breeze picked up and then died down once more. The steersman stood at the wheel in the aft section of the boat, smoking a pipe as he sat on the box and held one hand on the wheel.

Gannd glanced toward the bow. He reached out and took Reese by the arm. "Look there," he said.

The man in the green cloak stood leaning on the railing, looking out at the water and the dark countryside as it rolled by. He glanced at them briefly, then looked away.

"It seems we're not the only ones awake," said Gannd. "I don't see anyone else except the steersman, though."

"We'll find out soon enough," said Reese.

No sooner had he spoken than someone else came up on deck.

"D'kar," said Gannd, recognizing him.

Behind him came others. Gannd recognized several members of the crew and a couple of the passengers.

"Well, it looks as if the waiting's over," Reese said.

"That suits me just fine," said Gannd, resting his hand on the hilt of Bloodthirst.

"Good evening, gentlemen," D'kar said. He stood a short distance away. He tipped his hat to them. The others started to spread out to either side. The man in the green cloak had turned to look in their direction.

"Having trouble sleeping, D'kar?" said Reese.

"You know, I just can't seem to get any rest," D'kar replied. "I keep thinking about all that money I lost. I'd spent the better part of the month winning it all. Quite a lot of work, really. All building up to a big game and a nice score. And you just come along and take it. It really has been preying on my mind."

Gannd glanced at the others. They had moved to flank them, getting them with their backs against the railing. The passengers were carrying swords. The crewmen had daggers and cutlasses. He hadn't noticed any of them carrying arms before. There were eight of them in all, not counting D'kar.

"Here's something else to occupy your mind," said Reese. "What makes you think these roughnecks won't simply toss you over the side once they've got the money? A lot more for them that way."

Gannd saw several of them exchange glances. Apparently, they'd been thinking along similar lines. But D'kar seemed unconcerned.

"Call it a calculated risk," he said. "They could, of course, try to double-cross me, but then it would only be a one-time proposition. Whereas if they live up to their part of the bargain, there will be other opportunities. It would take a lot of the gamble out of gambling if we did something like this every time I got into a game with a big pot. There would be more profit all around that way. Wouldn't you say so, boys?"

"Let's just get on with it," one of the passengers said in a surly tone.

"Well, we can do this the hard way or the easy way," D'kar said. "The easy way, of course, would be for you to simply hand over your purses and then go over the side and swim for shore. A bit inconvenient, perhaps, but at least you will survive none the worse for wear. Assuming you can swim, of course. The hard way . . . well, we know what that would be, don't we? So . . . which shall it be?"

"Nine against two," said Reese. "Not exactly sporting odds for one who calls himself a gentleman."

D'kar simply shrugged. "I tried dealing with you from a position of weakness once before and found you did not bluff easily. This time, I thought it would be more effective to play from a position of strength. Nine against two sound like very good odds to me."

"Nine against three," said a gruff voice.

Gannd glanced with surprise at the man in the green cloak. He stood behind the others, not having moved from his previous position. The way the others glanced at him sharply, Gannd realized they had been so intent on him and Reese that they hadn't even seen the other man. Now, he reached up and unfastened the clasp on his cloak. It dropped to the deck, and he drew his sword from its tooled leather scabbard. The moonlight gleamed off a highly polished, extremely fine-looking blade.

"I thought he was with them," Gannd said softly.

"So did I," Reese replied.

"I'd stay out of this if I were you, stranger," said D'kar. "This is no concern of yours."

"I'm making it my concern," the man replied. "Nine against two don't sound like very sporting odds to me, either."

"You think nine against three is much better?" asked D'kar, scornfully.

"I figure that makes the odds better than even. So, you going to fight or you going to talk all night?"

"Get them!" D'kar shouted.

The men immediately moved in, two of them hanging back to face the stranger. Gannd drew his blade and had no more time for keeping track of what was going on around him, his attention focused on the men immediately in front of him. They were confident in their superior numbers. And that was their mistake. Reese was an experienced mercenary, and Gannd had been raised with a sword in his hand. The first two men to move in on him were both crewmen armed with cutlasses. As the first man lunged, Gannd smoothly parried his blade to the outside, stepping into his thrust and bringing his sword up to block the downward slash of his second opponent. As he did so, he drew a dagger with his left hand and drove it deep into the first man's stomach, then let go of it and drove his left fist into the second man's midsection, stepping into the blow, then quickly backing up. It was all done so quickly and smoothly that he had stepped back even before the first man collapsed to the deck, clutching at the dagger protruding from his stomach. The second man, stunned by the blow that drove all the wind out of him, doubled over involuntarily, and Gannd brought Bloodthirst down in a powerful, two-handed blow, decapitating him. His head struck the deck and bounced, then rolled while his body, spouting blood like a fountain, fell to the deck.

Without pausing, Gannd immediately went for his next antagonist, whose jaw dropped when he saw how quickly his two companions had been disposed of. Gannd recognized him as another member of the crew and he, too, was armed with a dagger and a cutlass. With a cry, he unleashed a flurry of wild slashes with both weapons, trying to keep Gannd at bay. Gannd parried the first two blows, stepped back from the slashing knife, turned a third blow with the cutlass, bringing his blade down and around as he did so, making the man turn and throwing him off balance momentarily. That moment was all he needed, however, to reach out and snag the crewman by his tunic, continuing his momentum and swinging him around and shoving him forward. With a cry, the man went right over the railing and into the river.

Given a momentary respite, Gannd immediately looked to see how Reese was doing. He had disposed of one of his attackers, who lay dead on the deck, blood pooling around him from a wound in his chest. As Gannd watched, Reese was engaging two others, both passengers armed with swords. He blocked one blow, sidestepped another from his second antagonist, twisting to one side, and brought his blade around in a two-handed slash that took the man right in the side. He screamed and fell to his knees, dropping his blade and clutching at the wound, but in the same instant, the first man raised his blade and brought it down in a vicious cut at Reese's head. All this took no more than an instant, but even as Gannd moved to help his friend, the lethal blow was blocked by a blade that caught it on its downward sweep and stopped it as surely as if it had struck stone.

It was the stranger who had taken their part in the conflict. The two men who had faced him lay dead behind him on the deck and Gannd realized it couldn't have taken him longer than a moment to kill them both. Now, as he blocked the blow that would surely have killed Reese, he stepped in and grabbed his antagonist by the belt and, with one hand, hoisted him right off his feet and up into the air, throwing him overboard. The man's cry was cut off by a loud splash. That left only D'kar, who had stood back from the fight.

"Thanks, stranger," Reese said to the man who saved his life. The man merely grunted and started to move toward D'kar, but Reese reached out and took him by the arm, stopping him. "If you don't mind," he said, "this one's mine."

"Be my guest," the stranger said gruffly, stepping aside.

D'kar started to back away, looking for an avenue of escape.

"Not many places to run on a boat in the middle of a river," said Reese, advancing on him slowly. "That was the one flaw in your plan, D'kar. You were so sure you were going to win, you never prepared for the possibility of losing. Bad trait in a gambler. A fatal one."

The noise of the fight had awakened the sleeping passengers and the other members of the crew. They came up on deck to see what was happening and stopped short behind D'kar, staring at the bodies on the deck and at Reese, advancing on the gambler.

"What in Haelyn's name . . . ?" the captain said as he came up on deck just behind D'kar.

Moving quickly, D'kar spun around and seized the surprised captain before he could react and in an instant had a dagger at his throat. "Drop your blade, Reese, or I'll slit his throat," he said.

"Go ahead," said Reese. "Why should I care? What is he to me? For all I know, you bribed him to look the other way, just as you bribed those crewmen."

"You won't let an innocent man die," D'kar said, pressing his blade against the captain's throat and drawing a thin line of blood.

"You're bluffing."

"Very well, then. Call my bluff and see."

"Are you mad?" the captain said, his eyes wide with fear. "He'll kill me!"

"Tell your crew to disarm him," said D'kar. "Tell them to disarm all three of them, or else you die."

"Under the circumstances, I don't think they'd be too anxious to obey that order," Reese said. "So . . . it's your call. How are you going to play it?"

D'kar hesitated for a moment, then suddenly jerked the dagger away from the captain's throat and shoved him hard at Reese. As Reese quickly swung his blade aside, so the captain wouldn't be impaled on it, the captain staggered into him, knocking him off balance. D'kar raised his arm to throw the dagger. But before he could release it, Gannd's dagger came whistling over Reese's shoulder and plunged into D'kar's throat, right through the larynx. The gambler jerked and dropped his dagger. He made a hideous, choking, gargling sound, staggered backward, and went over the railing behind him, hitting the water with a splash.

"Nice toss," the stranger said.

Reese turned. "Thanks again," he said to Gannd. "That makes four. Or is it five now? I'm losing count."

Gannd shrugged. "No matter. But I was rather fond of that dagger."

"I'll get you a dozen new ones when we reach Anuire," Reese replied. "The best money can buy."

"I thought I was a dead man," said the shaken captain, bringing his hand up to his throat. His fingers came away wet with blood from the shallow cut. He stared at them, then looked up at Reese. "Would you really have let him kill me?"

"I guess we'll never know, will we?" Reese replied. "He didn't have the nerve to call my bluff."

"We owe you our thanks, good sir," Gannd said to the stranger, holding out his hand.

The stranger took his hand in a firm grip. "No need."

"I beg to differ," said Reese. "I don't know many men who'd do what you did. Considering the odds, it took courage for you to lend us a hand."

The stranger grunted and glanced at the bodies. "Seems to me you didn't really need the help."

"I'm not so sure, but it was much appreciated, all the same," said Gannd. "Might I ask your name, sir, so I shall know to whom we are indebted?"

"I am called Bran Dulcain," the stranger replied.

"Haelyn's beard!" said an astonished Reese. "You're Bran the Blade?"

"I have been called that, too."

"Do you know this man?" asked Gannd.

"Know him? I have been raised on tales of Bran the Blade since I was a boy!" said Reese.

Dulcain grimaced at this pointed, though unintentional reminder of his age.

"Do you know who this man is?" said Reese, his eyes filled with awe. "He is a living legend among free companions, the most famed mercenary who ever lived! He is a warrior of unparalleled repute, who has served with armies on campaigns from Coeranys to the Tarvan Waste. He has been hailed as the greatest bladesman in the empire and is said to have single-handedly killed over a thousand men!" He turned back to Dulcain. "I have dreamed of meeting you from before I was old enough to reach my father's knee," he said, offering his hand. "Duncan Reese, a landsman from your home province of Diemed. It is both an honor and a privilege to shake your hand."

Dulcain grunted, took his hand and shook it briefly, then turned to Gannd. "Does he always talk this much?"

Gannd grinned. "No, he's usually not this quiet."

Reese gave him a sour look.

"Did you really kill over a thousand men?" asked Gannd.

Dulcain gave a small snort. "A gross exaggeration, to be sure," he replied. "It was probably closer to two hundred. Of course, that is only a rough estimate. I have never bothered counting. I was trying to stay alive, not run up a tally."

"Imagine it!" said Reese. "I actually fought side by side with Bran the Blade!"

The name was clearly familiar to some of the crew and passengers who had gathered on the deck. They started talking excitedly among themselves and pointing.

"Have you nothing better to do than stand around and gabble like a bunch of geese?" the captain said irately. "Dump those bodies overboard, then scrub and holystone the decks. I'll not be delivering a bloodstained ship! Now stir yourselves!"

The crowd broke up, the passengers returning to their cabins below decks and the crew hustling to comply with their captain's orders. He turned to Gannd, Reese, and Dulcain. "First of all, allow me to thank you for saving my life," he said. "And second, please accept my most profound apologies." He glanced at the bodies the crewmen were already dumping overboard. "Several of those scum were men under my command. They signed on at the last moment in Lofton and, being shorthanded, I could not afford to be too particular. I have never had a passenger assaulted on any of my vessels. It is unpardonable. I shall see to it, gentlemen, that the price of your passage is refunded in full."

"That is very generous of you, Captain," Reese said. "Thank you."

"It is the very least I can do. I have some Anuirean ale in my cabin. Would you care to join me for a drink?"

"We'd be delighted, Captain," said Dulcain.

"Splendid. Give me a few moments to see to it that my men finish cleaning up this mess and then please join me in my cabin at your convenience." He bowed and took his leave, immediately barking out commands to his crewmen.

"I did not get your name, Sidhelien," Dulcain said to Gannd.

"Gannd Aurealis, at your service, sir."

"There was a Sidhelien mage named Aurealis who served with the late emperor on his campaigns," Dulcain said.

"My uncle," Gannd replied.

Dulcain nodded. "I knew him. I was with the Emperor Michael's army. If not for your uncle, we might never have returned alive from the Shadow World. There was also a Sidhelien warrior maid with us . . . Sylvanna, I believe her name was."

"My mother," Gannd replied. "I carry her blade."

Dulcain nodded. "A first-rate fighter," he said. "I trust they are both well?"

"Yes. They are back in Tuarhievel."

"And your father?"

"Dead," said Gannd.

"But he was human." It wasn't a question. It was obvious by Gannd's appearance that he was a half-elf.

"His father was Lord Aedan Dosiere," said Reese. "If you were on the emperor's campaigns, you must have known him, too."

Dulcain raised his eyebrows slightly, then grunted. "Yes, but only to a slight degree. I was merely a common young mercenary, and he was the emperor's standard-bearer. We did not sit around the campfire swapping lies, but I knew him well enough to respect him."

"I would like to hear you tell me something of the time you spent with him," said Gannd. "If you do not mind, that is. You see, I never knew him."

"No, I don't suppose you would have," Dulcain replied. "Your mother left Anuire the day after the emperor announced your father's betrothal to the Lady Ariel. She came back briefly to help in the fight against the Gorgon. She must have already been pregnant with you at the time. Or perhaps she had already given birth to you. I no longer recall clearly how much time had passed. But after the emperor was slain, she was not seen in the empire again. And no, I would not mind telling you what I know of your father. He was a good man. I was proud to serve with him. But that can wait for another time. Right now, we need to join the captain for that drink. This was, in truth, no fault of his, but he takes his duties seriously and feels responsible. We should try to lighten the burden of his responsibility somewhat."

It was late when they retired to their respective cabins and, between the drinks, the exertions of the fighting, and the easing of the tension, they were able to fall asleep almost at once. When they awoke, it was already well into morning and the boat had reached Anuire. The other passengers had already disembarked, but the captain had left orders that they were not to be disturbed. By the time they came up on deck, he had already seen to it that the representative of the shipbuilder in Anuire had refunded the money for their passage, and he insisted that they take it. They did, not so much because they were in need of it, but because they knew that it would help the man feel better. Then, as they waited for the dory that would take them ashore, Gannd got his first look at the imperial capital and at the emperor's palace, known as the Imperial Cairn, where his father had once lived.

The palace stood on an island at the entrance to the bay, its crenelated towers and parapets dominating the view. The rest of the city was constructed on a series of islands that dotted the harbor and were interconnected by low causeways, and on the gently sloping hills that rose above the bay. It was a much larger city than Lofton and had many taller buildings. As with Lofton, however, they were all clustered together, almost as if they were built one on top of the other, and there were many more structures that were built almost entirely of stone.

As they boarded the dory that would take them ashore, Gannd watched the gulls spiraling overhead and diving down to retrieve some bits of garbage tossed from the boats and ships moored in the harbor. The sharp, tangy smell of the sea was strong on the brisk wind that raised whitecaps on the bay. From here on, the rest of their trip would be on land. As the rowers pulled toward the docks, he turned and looked back at the Imperial Cairn, receding in the distance behind them.

"You're thinking about your brother?" Reese said.

Gannd nodded. "Do you think he's there now?"

"Not likely," Dulcain said, as he sat beside them in the dory. "Lord Davan maintains a residence on shore. He does not go out to the palace except on occasions of state, of which there are few these days. He prefers the comforts of city life." He stared toward shore and pointed. "That's his manor there, the one with the wall around it on the hill to our left. You see, it flies the imperial flag of the Roeles . . . although there are no more Roeles, and never will be."

"Why does he fly their flag, then?" asked Gannd. "Why not his own?"

"Because he is only regent and not emperor," said Dulcain. "And because that flag is about the only authority he truly has. If he were to replace it with his own, it would amount to his declaring himself emperor, and he has no right to do so. There are many who would rightly dispute any such claim on his part, on the grounds of greater rank and rule of succession."

"Derwyn of Boeruine, for one," said Reese. "And Kier of Avan, for another."

"And behind them there would be others," Dulcain added. "But those two probably have the strongest claims." He glanced at Reese. "Which do you support?"

"I plan to throw in my lot with Kier of Avan," Reese replied. And then it occurred to him that Dulcain might have different sympathies. "You're not for Boeruine, are you?"

"I never had much use for Arwyn of Boeruine," Dulcain replied. "I have still less for his son, who is not half the man his father was. I am for Avan. In fact, I am on my way to Daulton to join up with him."

"So are we!" said Reese. "We intend to offer our services to the duke. I have heard that he is building up his army for the coming war and is employing mercenaries. We hope to secure positions in his regiments."

"I shouldn't think you would have any trouble," said Dulcain. "You are both very able fighters."

"And you may count on us to vouch for you," said Reese. "Not that, with your reputation, you'll need it," he added hastily, "but . . . well . . . the commander of the free companions might have certain reservations concerning your, uh . . . well, your age."

Dulcain raised his eyebrows.

"Not that I think you're too old myself, you understand," said Reese awkwardly, "but . . . well . . . commanders are often hesitant to recruit soldiers past a certain age."

"I see," Dulcain said flatly.

"You don't have to worry, though," said Reese. "I'll put in a good word for you. We both will."

"I appreciate the thought," Dulcain replied. "However, I don't think I really have to worry about that."

"Ah, you know the commander, then?" said Reese.

"Intimately," said Dulcain. "I am the commander of the duke's mercenary regiment."

Reese looked as if he'd swallowed his tongue. He swallowed hard, cleared his throat, and the best he could manage in reply was a feeble, "Oh."

"But it was kind of you to offer to put in a good word for an old man," Dulcain said.

Reese remained silent until the dory reached the docks. They got out and climbed the steps up to the boardwalk. Dulcain went first, Reese followed, looking very ill at ease, and Gannd came up behind them. All around, there were dockworkers busily loading and unloading cargo from the boats, peddlers hawking drinks and foodstuffs, passengers preparing to board ships bound for various points throughout the empire, merchants checking manifests, wagon drivers piling up their loads, all contributing to a seemingly chaotic atmosphere of ceaseless noise and activity.

"You're being very quiet," Gannd said to Reese as they followed Dulcain at a slight distance.

Reese grimaced. "I think I have spoken quite enough for one day," he replied.

"You could not have known Dulcain was the commander of the duke's mercenary regiment," Gannd replied.

"No, but I might have taken the trouble to find out before I shot my mouth off," Reese said dryly. He snorted with disgust. "What an idiot I am! Offering to vouch for Bran the Blade! What in Haelyn's name was I thinking?"

"You were concerned that his age might be held against him," Gannd said. "You meant well."

"Then that makes me a well-meaning fool who has just insulted the very man to whom we must apply for service," Reese replied in a tone of self-recrimination. "What do you think that does to our chances?"

There was a carriage with the Duke of Avanil's crest emblazoned on it waiting for Dulcain. They stopped and watched as he handed his pack up to the coachman, then got in. He turned to them.

"Well? Are you coming or not?" he said.

Reese glanced at Gannd.

"Move it, soldier!" Dulcain said. "I haven't got all day. I intend to reach Daulton in time for supper."

They hurried to the carriage and got in.

"We are going to make one stop before we leave the city, coachman," said Dulcain. "Drive us to the Avenue of Armorers in the artisan's quarter. The shop of Herrick the Swordsmith."

"Very well, Commander," said the coachman.

Dulcain turned to Reese. "Herrick is the finest swordsmith in the empire," he said. "And you promised your friend here that you would buy him a dozen new daggers. The best money could buy, if my old memory serves me correctly."

"It does, indeed, Commander," Reese said lamely. "It does, indeed."

* * * * *

She lounged in the wooden bathtub, lying back and raising first one long, lovely leg and then the other, running the washcloth over each of them in turn, not so much scrubbing as caressing. He could not see the full curves of her breasts, for they were obscured by the tub's rim, but he could see her gently rounded shoulders and her bare back. Her skin was exquisite, like cream. The way she moved in the tub . . . She was like a cat stretching. Aerin could not take his eye away from the peephole. He moistened his lips. His mouth was dry.

The serving girls brought the buckets of water to rinse her off, testing it first with their elbows to make sure it was warmed to the proper temperature and had not chilled while they were carrying it up. They stood, waiting with the buckets, as she slowly rose to her feet in the tub, her back to him, and Aerin held his breath as he stared at her perfectly shaped buttocks. Her body was absolutely flawless. He breathed heavily as he watched the serving girls pour the warm water over her, one bucket at a time. The water sheeted down her body, making it glisten. Her long hair was plastered down against her flesh. Aerin shut his eyes, but just for an instant. He was breathing hard as he waited for her to turn.

But he was doomed to disappointment, for the serving girls wrapped their towels around her, gently patting her dry and helping her slip into her robe before she turned and stepped out of the tub.

"Leave me," she said.

They curtsied and departed.

Katrina walked over to the fire and stood before it for a moment, warming herself. He saw her in profile as she stood there before the blazing hearth, the firelight gently illuminating her face. Aerin could not believe how beautiful she looked. She made all the women he had known look plain by comparison. He resisted the temptation to open the secret panel and walk in on her, strong though it was. She would see him and once more adopt her proud, haughty demeanor. She was his father's concubine, and yet she treated Aerin as if she were a queen and he a commoner. It was infuriating.

What was it about her? There was not one woman who had ever failed to respond to him. Oh, they made their little token displays of resistance, but that was just a self-deluding game they played, a transparent ploy to maintain some self-respect and give themselves the illusion later that they had been overwhelmed by a powerful and forceful man whose desire for them was just too strong.

And he had learned early on that if he played up to that little game, overriding their small murmurs of protest with whispered endearments and passionate kisses, it would allow them to give themselves the license to become completely uninhibited, as if they couldn't help themselves, because they were too weak to resist him.

But Katrina was different. Katrina did not play those games. Katrina had no difficulty in resisting him. She stopped him in his tracks as surely as if there were a stone wall between them, like the one behind which he concealed himself as he watched her through the hidden peephole.

"I am your father's woman," she had said. Mere words. But words that, coming from her, were like a slap in the face.

What could an old man like his father do with such a woman? He could easily have watched them to find out, but he could not bear the thought of seeing his father naked and on on top of her. The very idea of it made his stomach turn.

His father knew about the secret passageways that honeycombed the castle, but he did not suspect that Aerin knew about them. He had found them on his own, years earlier and, over a period of time, had explored them thoroughly, especially the ones that afforded him a view from concealment of the chambers of various ladies of the court. He had learned a lot that way. He had learned that they moved and acted differently when they thought no man was watching. And that had taught him how conscious they were of the effects they produced when men were present.

But in his explorations, he had discovered an unexpected bonus. A hidden passageway that had clearly not been used for many years, judging by the thick layer of dust on the floor and the large cobwebs that stretched from wall to wall; a passageway that led to a hidden chamber, one that contained a fascinating collection of items that had baffled him for a long time until he eventually discovered their purpose.

He had made some sketches of them, hoping to find some evidence of what they were from the books in the library, but his researches proved fruitless. He had just about given up in frustration when his tutor found the sketches and asked him about the drawings.

Aerin had told him they were sketches of some items he had found, and his tutor wanted to know where they were. Though he was young, even then, Aerin had recognized a glint of excitement in his tutor's eyes and had known that the older man knew what those items were.

Knowledge was power. And in this case, it gave him power over his tutor. Aerin exploited the man's desire to find out what he wanted. He insisted to be told what the items were and what their purpose was before he would reveal where he had found them. At first, the man resisted, but it was a resistance that was easily overcome. His own desire and curiosity overcame it. And that had been the real beginning of Aerin's education.

He had promised his tutor he would show him where he found those things, but he did not say how he would show him. And when he was satisfied with his tutor's explanations, he insisted that the man put on a blindfold before he would show him where the items were. Once again, resistance. Once more, easily overcome.

He had tied the blindfold himself, and checked it several times, then insisted that the tutor's hands be tied behind his back as well, so that he could not remove the blindfold or lift it slightly to peek out from behind it. Strangely enough, his tutor had acquiesced to that request more readily. In time, Aerin came to understand why.

He had spun the man around several times, so that he would have no sense of direction, and then he led the tutor in a roundabout way, so that he would have no true sense of the distance, either. And he had not taken off the man's blindfold or untied his hands until they were in the secret room. The reaction of his tutor had been fascinating. The man trembled with excitement as he examined all the items and they spoke about them. The leather was old and cracked and needed replacement, but most of the other items just needed to be cleaned or oiled.

Over the next few months, when they were supposed to be doing their lessons, they had painstakingly refurbished all the items in the secret room and cleaned the room itself until it was immaculate. And, at his tutor's suggestions, some new items were added to the collection. By this time, they shared a guilty secret and were partners in crime. And once the work was finished, they had to test it out.

That, too, had been interesting and educational. And Aerin saw a side of his tutor that he had never suspected existed. It made him wonder how others would respond.

The first woman they brought into the secret room was one of the servants in the castle. She, too, had been blindfolded and her hands tied, so she would have no idea where she was or how to find the place again, even if she discovered the hidden entrance to the passageway. She had been frightened, at first. And then terrified. Aerin had been afraid her screams would be heard behind the walls, so they gagged her, but he later discovered that the thickness of walls completely muffled any sounds made within the room. And it was interesting to see how different women responded to the different items in there. Some even surprised themselves.

That had all started a long time ago. Since then, Aerin had used that room many, many times, with many different women. And he had learned that he could easily get his tutor to perform many services for him, merely by threatening to withhold his special privileges. The man had essentially become his slave. Anything that Aerin wanted, he would get or do for him. Just to be allowed to use the room again.

Aerin longed to get Katrina in the room. Her proud demeanor would not last long in there. But she knew about it. She knew more than he had given her credit for. She was clever. She was calculating. And she was absolutely intoxicating.

As Aerin watched her stand before the fire, his eye glued to the peephole, she untied the belt of her robe and let it fall open. From the side, the angle from which he viewed her, he could not see much, but then she moved slightly and the robe fell open even more and he could see her bare breast softly gleaming in the firelight. He caught his breath as she brought up her hand to touch it lightly, her fingers trailing over it.

Aerin found it hard to swallow. His breathing quickened as she caressed herself absently, staring into the fire, and then her hand trailed slowly down between her breasts and to her stomach, moving lower. She put her foot up on the stone step just before the hearth, revealing the full length of her leg, which seemed to glow in the flickering firelight.

Aerin's breath shuddered in his throat as he watched her close her eyes and lean her head back. He felt moisture forming on his forehead, and then the sweat trickled down his face like tears. He couldn't move. He stood, mesmerized. On fire.

Time stood still. And then, it was over. With a sigh, she pulled her robe back together and reached for the belt to tie it. And as she did so, she turned . . . and looked directly at him, as if the wall weren't even there.

Her lips curved up gently in a mocking little smile.

Aerin jerked back from the peephole as if stung. When he looked again, she had covered it with something from her side. He took his eye away from it and leaned back heavily against the opposite wall of the passageway. He licked his lips and took a deep breath, exhaling slowly.

And he decided that somehow, one way or another, he was going to kill his father.

BOOK II

THE DUCHESS AND THE KNIGHT

chapter one

The shop of Herrick the Swordsmith was an unassuming little
place from the outside, located on a narrow, curving side street just
off the square in the artisan's quarter of the imperial capital. It was
a narrow, three-story building made of mortared stone and wood,
similar to all the other buildings around it save for the fact that there
was no display window. Most of the other buildings in the quarter
had wide display windows in the front to attract passersby. In the
mornings, the shopkeepers would open the heavy wooden shutters,
then fold down or extend a wooden counter that would stick out a
yard or so into the street. On these, they could display their wares
and do business from inside their shops with customers on the
street. Passersby could stop to purchase something without even
entering the shops, which made things convenient for both patrons
and proprietors, as the interiors of most of the shops were small and
cramped.

Of course, this did slightly increase the risk of pilfering, which
was the main reason why most shopkeepers did not display their
finest products. A butcher, for example, would display only older or
cheaper cuts of meat, so that if some urchin ran by and snagged one,

he would not be out a fresh or expensive cut. Otherwise, people walking by would see the meat on display, know it was a butcher shop, and stop to ask about the better cuts inside. With Herrick, things were different.

The only thing to identify his shop was the sign outside, a simple wooden plank painted light blue with a sword on it. Not even his name. And instead of a display window, with a board shelf extending out into the street, Herrick had an ordinary window that was barred and shuttered. When the shutters were opened, they simply gave passersby a view through the iron-barred window of the shop's interior, which had no counters or shelving, but looked like a small and comfortable sitting room—with a profusion of swords and daggers hanging on the walls.

Dulcain explained the reason for such an apparently low-key approach. Herrick had no reason to advertise his name or business. He was, quite simply, the best swordsmith in the empire. His blades were priced well out of the reach of most people, but were esteemed as status symbols by wealthy aristocrats who, regardless of rank, had to put their names on a waiting list just like anybody else and were given no preference. And if they didn't like it, Herrick simply suggested, politely, that they could always take their business elsewhere. They never did.

Reese had heard of Herrick, of course, though he had only seen three or four of his blades in all his years as a mercenary. Few soldiers of fortune could afford them, except those with the finest reputations who could, obviously, command the highest salaries. But those who had the weapons often saved for years to get them and seemed duly convinced that their quality was well worth any price. Herrick made each one personally, and used apprentices only for small tasks. He never took on more than two, was extremely selective in those apprentices he did accept, and insisted that they serve a minimum of ten years apprenticeship before he would consider certifying them as swordsmiths in their own right and only after they passed one final test, which consisted of making a blade entirely by themselves and submitting it for his approval. The handful of apprentices Herrick had trained and certified as swordsmiths had all won the right to place a half-sized version of his simple "H" alongside their own device on the ricasso of their blades. Their work was prized almost as highly as their teacher's, but a blade made by Herrick himself was the ultimate accoutrement for any fighting man, who would not part with it for anything. When Gannd entered the shop and saw the blades hanging on the wall, he understood why. Sidhelien swordsmiths were justifiably proud of the blades they crafted. Nothing was finer than elven steel, the manufacture of which was a closely guarded secret. Elven blades were esteemed by human fighters, though few carried them. They were shaped for a different style of fighting than most humans were accustomed to, with the blades being lighter and narrower, though immensely strong, and slightly curved, having an edge on only one side of the blade. However, that edge was capable of being honed to a sharpness no human blade could match. Herrick's blades came close. Extremely close. They were not made of elven steel, but it was clear that at some point, Herrick studied the craftsmanship of elven blades with a fine eye and incorporated what he learned into his own designs.

Many human swordsmiths went to elaborate lengths to add ornamentation to their blades, such as engraving, wrapping with gold and silver wire, setting the hilts and pommels with precious and semiprecious stones, and making matching scabbards, twisting the crossguards into unusual shapes, and so forth. Herrick eschewed such practices. Every single blade displayed in his shop was plain and utilitarian, lacking any sort of adornment at all. He might use different materials for the crossguards and hilts, slightly different styles for the pommels, but that was all. They were simple, supremely functional, and beautifully made.

Herrick did not make scabbards or sheaths, Dulcain explained. That was up to the buyer to obtain. The reason for this was that Herrick had discovered, long ago, that wealthy aristocrats had a tendency to discard the simple, yet functional sheaths he'd made, replacing them with fancy, jeweled versions. They knew better than to ornament the blade, which would have destroyed its value, aside from which, no self-respecting swordsmith would undertake the task. One did not meddle with perfection. So aristocrats had sought to ornament their sheaths and scabbards to make up for the plainness of the blade. And rather than have anyone think that he might have made such a tasteless thing, Herrick had decided not to make sheaths or scabbards at all, so that everyone would know he had no hand in it.

"Mine is merely tooled leather," said Dulcain, "and it was my father's, so it has sentimental value to me. Still, Herrick sniffs disdainfully every time he sees it."

An apprentice entered when the small bell above the door rang, but left after Bran spoke only briefly to him. Herrick himself came into the shop from a back room a moment or so later. He was a small man, stocky and powerful-looking, with a close-cropped white stubble on his head that matched the stubble on his lined face. He wore brown leather breeches, short brown boots, a sleeveless brown tunic, and a leather apron.

"Bran," he said. "How nice to see you again. It's been a long time. I trust the blade still gives good service?"

"Of course, Master Herrick," Dulcain replied respectfully. "It is a privilege to carry it."

Herrick merely nodded, though he was obviously pleased by the compliment. "How may I serve you today?" he asked.

"I have brought two friends," said Dulcain, "who are going to be serving under my command in Avanil. And Duncan here promised his friend Gannd a dozen daggers, the very best money could buy, as a gesture of appreciation for the saving of his life. Since his purse weighs heavily upon him, I naturally brought him to see you."

Reese was obviously impressed to meet the master swordsmith, but at the same time, Gannd could see he was distressed at the prospect of paying for a dozen Herrick blades. Even if they were only daggers and not swords, they would still come very dearly. "One simple dagger would more than suffice," the half-elf said, "especially if it were steel of such exquisite quality."

Herrick smiled. "High praise, indeed, coming from a Sidhelien," he said. "Thank you."

Reese looked distinctly ill at ease. Nevertheless, he said, "No, no, a promise is a promise. I said a dozen daggers, and a dozen it shall be. So make your choice. I insist. And I will hear no arguments."

Gannd sighed. "You place me in an awkward position, my friend. I could not possibly take such advantage of your generosity. I would treasure even one such dagger."

"Nonsense," Reese replied. "I said, no arguments. I would have been dead four or five times over if not for you. And I could not spend my winnings if I were a corpse, now could I?"

"Perhaps I may be of some assistance in settling this matter," Herrick said. "It just so happens that I have a dozen daggers, made to order for a viscount of Avanil who, regrettably, was slain during the recent unpleasantness. If you would allow me. . . ."

He disappeared into the back and returned a moment later, carrying a wooden case. He set it on a small table and opened it. Inside, resting on a bed of red velvet, were two rows of matching daggers: six each, staggered, pointing one up, one down, with six-inch blades, short bronze crossguards, and rosewood hilts flared slightly at the middle, with cone-shaped bronze pommels. Gannd picked one up. It was balanced perfectly for throwing.

Herrick gestured to a simple, round wooden target on the opposite wall, unpainted except for a small red circle about the size of a gold piece in the exact center. "Please," he said, "feel free to try it out."

Gannd threw the blade. It struck in the exact center of the small red circle.

Herrick smiled. "I thought you were trained in the way of the warrior," he said, going to retrieve the blade.

"You know something of our ways?" said Gannd.

"A little," the swordsmith replied modestly, with a glance at Gannd's sword. He was too polite to ask.

"Would you care to see it?" Gannd asked.

"I would like that very much indeed."

Gannd unsheathed his blade and handed it to the swordsmith, who accepted it respectfully, holding it by the hilt and laying the blade across his forearm on his sleeve. He stared at it for several moments in silence, shaking his head slowly. "I have seen Sidhelien steel before," he said, "but never such as this. If only once I could make a blade like this, I would die a happy man." He looked up at Gannd. "I hope you will pardon my arrogance, it is truly inexcusable, but I cannot resist. If you would be willing to part with this, I would give you the daggers and a dozen of any of my swords, your choice."

Dulcain simply stared in astonishment, but Reese actually gasped.

"It was my mother's blade," said Gannd softly.

"Of course, I understand completely," Herrick said, returning the sword to him. "There can be no question of your selling it. I hope you did not take offense. I assure you, none was intended."

"Quite the contrary," Gannd said. "From an artisan such as yourself, it was the highest compliment. And if it were not a matter of sentimental value, I would leap at such a generous offer."

"A sword like this must surely have a name," said Herrick.

"Bloodthirst," Gannd replied.

Herrick raised his eyebrows. "Your mother was Sylvanna?"

"Why, yes," said a surprised Gannd. "You knew her?"

"No, I cannot say I did, but I had the pleasure of making a dagger for her, on commission from the Emperor Michael himself. He told me she carried an extremely fine elven sword named Bloodthirst, and he wanted to present her with a dagger that would be a worthy mate to it. I regret to say I never learned if she was pleased with my effort."

"She was, indeed," said Gannd. "She passed it on to me and I carried it for years. Regrettably, I lost it recently when the man I killed with it fell overboard."

"That was a Herrick blade?" said Reese, chagrined.

"In that case, perhaps you will allow me to do something to help ameliorate the loss," said Herrick. "These dozen daggers are a matched set that I would not like to break up, and as they were a special order, it is unlikely I would sell them anytime soon. It would take a particular sort of buyer. I will let your friend purchase them for you for a price of seventy-five gold pieces."

"Done!" said Reese immediately, taking the equivalent, fifteen platinum pieces, from his purse. The blades were worth twice that.

"And I will throw in something extra," Herrick said. "I do not make sheaths." He glanced briefly at Dulcain's tooled leather scabbard and sniffed. "However, when I accepted the commission for these daggers, one of my apprentices thought the customer might enjoy being able to display them all at once on certain occasions, so . . . Well, I'll show you what he made."

He went in the back and returned a moment later with a set of brown leather bandoliers, designed to be worn crossed, each with six plain leather sheaths sewn into them.

"These should go with the knives," said Herrick. "Perhaps you may find them useful."

Gannd put them on and slipped the daggers into the sheaths. Then he quickly drew one with each hand and threw them at the target. Both struck the center.

"If it is not disrespectful to speak so of the dead," said Herrick, "I think you will do those blades more justice than the man for whom I made them."

"You once told me you thought you were incurring a debt you feared you would be unable to repay," Gannd said to Reese. "Consider it repaid in full. Thank you, Duncan. It is a fabulous gift."

"I'm pleased," said Reese with a smile. He turned to the wall and took down one of the swords. "Master Herrick . . . how much would you charge for this?"

"For a friend of Bran's?" Herrick considered for a moment. "I could let you have it for two thousand."

Reese gulped. "In gold, of course," he said.

"Or four in platinum."

"He'll take it," said Dulcain. "Put it on my account."

"Certainly," said Herrick, with a nod.

Reese stared at Dulcain, stunned speechless. "I . . . I cannot—"

"Yes, you can," said Dulcain. "The Duke of Avan is paying me a king's ransom to command his mercenary regiment. And he has promised me a knighthood in the bargain. I intend to forge the finest mercenary regiment the empire has ever seen to justify his confidence in me. To do that, I am going to need an able drillmaster and a second-in-command I can trust. No mercenary worth his salt will fail to recognize a Herrick blade—or respect the man who carries one. You shall have to see to it that you live up to that respect. Consider it an incentive to perform up to my expectations."

Reese was so taken aback, he could think of no reply. They took their leave of Herrick, after being entered on his rolls as customers, which entitled them both to free service on the blades for life. Herrick took pride in his work. If a blade should break, he would replace it, free, no questions asked. And if any sharpening or other maintenance was ever needed, that too came with the price of purchase, for as long as the original owner had the blade. Gannd put on the bandoliers and sheathed the knives in them, to get used to the rig. They stopped briefly at a leather worker's for Reese to pick up a scabbard for his new sword. He chose a plain one that he felt the swordsmith would approve of; then they got back into the carriage and proceeded on the road north, leaving the city.

They drove through the outlying areas of the imperial capital, past farms and villages and country estates belonging to the city's aristocrats, then turned northwest when they came to a fork in the road and headed toward Daulton, the capital of Avanil. It had not rained recently, so the roads were in good shape, the dirt packed down firmly. Their passage raised some dust, but it was not oppressive. At certain times of the year, during the early winter and spring when the rains came, the roads became impassable. The hard-packed surface quickly turned into a muddy soup that would mire carriage and wagon wheels up to the axles and make horses sink in to their knees. At such times, it was impossible for armies to march. The prime season for war started in late spring and ran through the summer into early fall.

"I have done your friend Reese no great favor by appointing him my drillmaster and second-in-command," Dulcain explained to Gannd as they drove out of the city. The half-elf and Reese sat together, facing the old mercenary, who sat leaning comfortably against the cushions, his back to the coachman. "Lord Kier did not promise me a knighthood merely to tempt me to his service. The salary he offered alone would have been more than enough for that. The knighthood offers a generous retirement, but it is not without certain strings attached."

"As a knight, you could not so easily retire to live life as you please," Reese said. "You would gain rank and lands, but remain in vassalage to your duke for the remainder of your days."

"Precisely," said Dulcain. "I would become an aristocrat and enjoy a standard of life I could not otherwise have dreamed of, but it does not come without its price. Avan knows that, and he knows I know it, too."

"So he has done more than pay you handsomely to command his mercenary regiment," said Gannd. "By giving you a knighthood, he ties your fate to his. On one hand, he elevates you, and on the other, he ensures you share his risk of losing."

Dulcain nodded. "I see you understand."

"Is it worth it?" Reese asked.

"Obviously I think so, else I would never have accepted. It entails risk, of course, but men in our profession are accustomed to that. Still, I thought long and hard about it. I had retired to a simple, quiet life in Alamie, but it was a rather lonely one and, of necessity, quite frugal."

"But . . . you were always the best," said Reese. "I would have thought you a wealthy man by now."

"Reports of what I have been paid have always been exaggerated," Dulcain replied dryly. "And when I was your age, and at the top of my profession, I did not consider growing old. I lived fast and I lived well."

"It's the only way," said Reese, with a grin.

"It's a very foolish way," Dulcain replied. "But in all likelihood, no matter what I say, you will not appreciate that until you reach my age. I do not often feel loquacious, so I hope you will indulge me if I tell you a story.

"When I was a young man in my teens and early twenties, the most famous mercenary was a man named Ardran, from Osoerde. I held him in the same high esteem in which you now hold me. He was the best, and I wanted to be just like him. While others my age enjoyed their youth to the fullest, indulging themselves with pretty girls and boon companionship in alehouses, I lived with all the rigorous discipline and self-denial of a monastic cleric, training endlessly from dawn to dusk, honing my body, skills, and instincts in preparation for the day when I would be the next Ardran. I assumed the recreation and the women would come later, when I had reached my goal and fame would bring me everything I ever wanted. And it did. And for all the years I had denied myself, when the time came, I indulged my appetites to the fullest."

"You worked hard," Reese said. "You deserved it."

"That was how I felt," Dulcain replied. "But I had forgotten one thing. I had forgotten that one should always have a goal. One should always have something to prepare for, something to instill a sense of discipline and moderation. I had accomplished what I set out to do and thought all that remained was to maintain my status and enjoy the rewards of all my efforts. And, as I said, I did. I was paid well, but I spent freely. And I loved many women, but never chose one with whom to make a life. And then, one day, soon after I turned fifty, I met Ardran.

"Our paths had crossed before, when I was younger," Dulcain continued, "and the first time, he saw in me a promising young warrior. The second time, a few years later, when we both served together, he realized that I was a potential rival for the position he held, but still he treated me with kindness. This was the third time that we met, and things had greatly changed for him. For both of us. I had achieved my goal and become known as the best in my profession. I had fame, respect, money, women . . . everything I ever wanted. And Ardran had nothing."

"What do you mean, nothing?" Reese asked.

"Just that. Nothing," Dulcain said, taking a drink from a wineskin and passing it to them. "He had become a pauper. A sad and ailing old man. The reputation he had once enjoyed had become mine; no one spoke about him anymore. Every now and then, he would encounter someone who remembered hearing of him, but rarely would they credit that he was the man they'd heard about. He had never married, because he had never taken the time to settle down and make a home with a good woman. So he never had children, either. There was no one to care for him in his old age. His health was failing him; the ache had come upon his bones, and he needed to walk with the aid of a staff. And in his misery, he had become a drunkard. I could scarcely believe it was the same man I had known. And as I looked at him, a chill ran through my bones as I saw what could become of me."

"What became of him?" asked Gannd.

"He drank himself to death," Dulcain replied. "And I sped him along."

Reese frowned. "How?"

"I found a place for him at a comfortable inn and paid his room and board, hiring a serving girl at the tavern to see that he was fed and looked after. And if he wanted drink, I saw to it that he was given all he needed. At that point, he could no longer live without it. It was killing him. I knew it and he knew it. But he no longer had a life that was worth living and he welcomed the possibility of death. And so he died. And I helped him along. But at least he died in a warm room and in a comfortable bed."

Gannd and Reese sat silent and somber.

Dulcain took a deep breath and exhaled heavily. "I decided that what happened to Ardran would not happen to me. And so I had my new goal. I would save what money I could, putting it aside for my old age, and I would buy myself a little place where I could retire one day. And perhaps find a good woman to marry and have children with. Well, I found my place, and built my cottage, and retired thinking to find myself a wife. But then along came Lord Kier with his tempting offer, and I realized that it was everything I wanted. A knighthood and the land that would go with it would allow me to live out my days in comfort and security. And it would give me something more to offer to a woman than just a little cottage on a tiny plot of land and my good company. So my new goal is now within my reach." He pointed at Reese. "And you are going to help me to achieve it."

"I shall do my utmost to justify your confidence in me," said Reese.

"See that you do, for just as my fate is now linked to Avan's, yours is linked with mine. If I achieve success, then I shall see to it that those who helped me achieve it are rewarded." He turned to Gannd. "And that means you, as well, though in your case, the situation will be somewhat different."

"In what way?" asked Gannd curiously.

"I cannot offer you a position of command, which is not to say I do not find you capable. I do. Eminently so. But . . . let us speak frankly. You are a breed. While that is not something I would hold against you, there are those who will. Mercenaries are a rough and surly lot, often undisciplined, sometimes little better than criminals. They would not suffer having a half-elf placed in any position superior to theirs. And as a commander, it would be both imprudent and unfair of me to place you in any such position, however well suited for it you may be. It will be difficult enough for you to gain acceptance. Their respect is something you shall have to earn. I am confident you will. Once you have done that, then things shall be different. But until you reach that point, you can expect to have a rough time of it. If you wish to reconsider, I shall not hold it against you."

"I do not wish to reconsider," Gannd replied.

Dulcain nodded. "Good. I didn't think you would. And now, I've talked quite enough for one day. I'm going to take a nap. For some reason, I didn't get much sleep last night." He smiled. "I recommend you rest, as well. We shall have much to do when we reach Daulton."

He leaned back against the cushions and closed his eyes. Reese glanced at Gannd and shrugged, as if to say, "Might as well." Gannd nodded, and they leaned back against opposite corners of the carriage, wedging themselves in as comfortably as possible. The interior of the carriage was well finished and appointed, as befitted a high-ranking aristocrat, but it was still far from a smooth ride. The carriage bounced and swayed as it rolled on leather-cushioned wooden wheels down the uneven dirt road, every little bump and rut transmitting its presence to them through the frame. Still, it was a much more comfortable ride than they would have had in an ordinary carriage, which would not have been so luxuriously cushioned and upholstered, and it was preferable to riding on horseback.

As he leaned back and shut his eyes, Gannd thought about all the different modes of transportation he had sampled since he'd left the Aelvinnwode. He had started out on foot, then proceeded on horseback to Lofton, sailed on a river sloop to Anuire and now traveled to Daulton by nobleman's carriage. And all these experiences had come about as a result of meeting Duncan Reese.

It was strange how quickly the two of them had grown close. They had only known each other for about a week, and yet it felt much longer, somehow. In that short space of time, they had experienced a lot together. A fight with highlanders, an attack by gnolls, a midnight chase through the streets of Lofton, an assault aboard a ship . . . and all this was only the beginning. They were going off to join an army, in which they had now been enlisted by Dulcain, and would soon be marching off to war.

Gannd wondered what it would be like. He had heard stories from his mother, but despite that, he could only imagine what the reality was like. His mother told him that repeatedly when, as a boy, he had asked her to tell him stories of her days campaigning with his father and the emperor.

"When you're young," she'd told him, "the idea of war seems glamorous and fascinating. The stories you hear all sound like grand adventures full of guts and glory. But no matter how hard I try to convey the unvarnished reality of the experience to you, there is no way you will ever truly understand until you've been in battle. There is no way to prepare for it. It is the most intense experience you can have."

"More intense than giving birth?" asked Gannd.

His mother smiled. "Much more. That is something most women would never understand. But that is only because most women never go to war. They say men speak of war the way they do because they could never know the pain of giving birth, or the wonder of it, or the powerful emotions it engenders. But I have experienced both, and so I know. Yes, there is nothing to compare with giving birth. Truly, that is something men will never fully understand. But the intensity of the experience is different. It is the experience of creation, and after the pain comes relief, and the wonder and the joy of having brought forth life. But the intensity of battle is the experience of destruction, and afterward—if you survive—there comes only the relief of survival, and there is no joy in it. There is only sheer exhaustion, so profound it must be felt to be fully appreciated. And there is the horror . . . a horror one is not really aware of while the battle is taking place, because every fiber of your being is focused on the task at hand, and on trying to stay alive. It is only afterward that you experience the horror of it, when you look out across the battlefield and gaze upon a sea of dead and mutilated bodies, and hear the groans and screams of the wounded and the dying, and smell the stench of death itself—the odor of spilled blood, the stink of bowels that have released and bodies that have already started rotting in the sun. . . .

"There is nothing quite so terrible as war. Perhaps that is why men seem to love it so, because it reduces them to their essentials, as giving birth does to a woman. Both take up all your attention. While in a battle or while giving birth, there is no time to think of anything else. Your focus becomes sharp and clear; your entire being is concentrated on just one thing. The irony is that one creates while the other destroys. I understand why some men come to love war, just as some women come to love the pain of giving birth. It is not really the thing itself they love; it is how the experience affects them."

Gannd had not really understood then. He had a better idea of what she meant now that he was older and had experienced some combat, but it was not the same. He had fought, even killed men, but he had not been at war.

It was peculiar how he felt about it. It was not as if he wanted to experience it so much as that he felt he needed to, so that he could truly understand what his mother and his father had experienced, and how it had drawn them closer together. And he wanted to find out how it would affect him, what he would learn about himself when he was, as his mother had put it, reduced to his essentials.

He thought back to the first time he had killed a man. It was one of the highlanders who were pursuing Reese. There had been no time then to gauge how it had affected him, for he immediately had to kill again to stay alive. He understood now what his mother meant by that. He was not really able to feel anything at the time. He had been too busy defending himself. In the space of one week, he had killed a number of men and several gnolls. But, strangely enough, he didn't feel any different. He wondered why. It was no small thing to take a life. So why didn't it make him feel anything?

Regret? No, he did not feel that. He had done what he had to do. If he had not killed them, they would have killed him. He was not sorry for having stayed alive. Horror? Pity? Remorse? He did not feel any of those things, either. Not the way his mother spoke about them, certainly. Nor did Reese seem to feel anything like that, at least, not so far as Gannd could see. Dulcain had killed three of the men who had attacked them on the sloop. Well, two, if the one he had thrown overboard had not drowned. But that did not seem to affect him, either. Of course, Dulcain had killed many times before. Some two hundred men had died at his hands, by his own rough estimate. Perhaps he no longer even thought about it. But if so, then why not? To have killed so many men, to be known as an accomplished killer, surely that was something extraordinary. How could that possibly fail to be a defining characteristic of one's life? How could it be something that one merely . . . accepted?

Gannd thought back to the first time he had killed something on purpose. He had been just a boy, out in the forest practicing his archery. Even at a young age, he had uncanny hand-eye coordination and excellent aim. The squirrel represented a challenge, nothing more. Could he hit a moving target? A living one? After all, that was the entire focus of the way of the warrior. One did not shoot at target butts on the battlefield. He had nocked, drawn, aimed, and let fly. The squirrel fell from the branch without making a sound. When he picked it up, it was already dead. The crossbow bolt had torn a large hole through its flanks and the grayish red fur was matted with blood. The squirrel looked dead. Obviously. But he recalled that as his first significant impression. It *looked* dead. As if it had never even been alive. Its mouth was open, frozen in that attitude, and its eyes were utterly empty. It did not even really look like a squirrel anymore. That spark of vitality and animation, its . . . squirrelness . . . had departed. And Gannd felt sorry that he had killed it.

He did not feel sorry for any of the men he killed. Of course, he reminded himself, the squirrel had not been trying to kill him. It was just an inoffensive forest creature, felled by his crossbow bolt for no other reason than his curiosity to see if he could do it. He had not even killed for food, just for the experience. Maybe that was why he had felt sorry then and not now. Because back then, there hadn't really been a reason. What he had done had been unjustified. But still . . . it bothered him that he did not feel anything about the men he'd killed.

At some time, he must have drifted off, because he was suddenly awakened by a rude jolting of the carriage that threw him from his seat. In the next few moments, everything happened very quickly. He discovered later that the coachman had been killed, shot through the chest with an arrow, and had fallen from his seat. The horses bolted, and the carriage had slewed around a curve, struck a rut or a large rock by the side of the road, and overturned. The three men were tumbled around inside as the weight of the carriage slowed, then stopped the horses. In the ensuing quiet they could hear shouting and the sound of rapidly approaching horses.

Dulcain was the first out of the carriage. It lay on its side, and Dulcain threw open the door and hoisted himself up and out, dropping to the road with Reese right behind him. By the time he pulled himself out, Dulcain and Reese had already drawn their weapons and stood facing the horsemen barreling down on them. There were about nine or ten of them. As they rode down upon Reese and Dulcain, one of them dropped his reins, stood up in his stirrups, and raised a crossbow.

Crouching atop the overturned carriage, Gannd drew one of Herrick's daggers from its sheath on the crossed bandoliers and hurled it. It struck the bowman in the chest, and he tumbled from his mount before he could loose his bolt. In rapid succession, Gannd drew one blade after another, with both hands, and threw them. A second man tumbled from the saddle, then a third, and then a fourth, a fifth, a sixth—the others reined in sharply—a seventh fell to one of Gannd's new knives, and the remaining three quickly turned their mounts and spurred away, bending down low in their saddles to present the smallest possible targets as they retreated back down the road.

Gannd stood up, atop the carriage, watching as the remaining horsemen disappeared around a bend. He looked down at Dulcain and Reese.

Dulcain sheathed his sword and glanced at Reese. "I'd say your recent purchase has just paid for itself, wouldn't you?"

"I've never seen anything like that," Reese said. "I knew you were a good hand with a knife, but . . . Damn, that was fast!"

"Well, since Gannd's done all the work for us," Dulcain said, "the very least we can do is retrieve his knives for him."

One of the men was still alive, moaning as he lay in the road, clutching the knife embedded in his shoulder. Dulcain went down to one knee beside him, placed his right hand on the hilt of the protruding dagger, and leaned on it. The man screamed.

"Oh, I beg your pardon," said Dulcain apologetically. The man closed his eyes and gasped with relief as the pressure was removed. "You don't have the look of brigands," said Dulcain. "Your horses are too fine, and your weapons are better than average. So, who sent you?"

The man did not respond. Dulcain leaned on the hilt of the dagger again, putting more weight on it. The man screamed, even louder than before.

"Sorry, clumsy of me," said Dulcain. "Now . . . you were saying?"

The man reached for a dagger in his belt. Dulcain caught his hand by the wrist and, holding it in a strong grip, snatched the dagger from the man's belt and drove it through his palm. A hoarse, throat-rending scream erupted from the wounded man. Dulcain, still holding the man's hand by the wrist, twisted the dagger. The man screamed even louder.

"Now then," said Dulcain, when the man's screams died down to whimpers, "where were we?"

"No more . . . no more . . . I'll talk," the man said.

"I'm listening," said Dulcain.

"We were hired by the Archduke of Boeruine," the man said.

"Not by Lord Derwyn himself, surely?"

The man gasped with pain and shook his head. "N-no . . . a representative of his . . . in Daulton."

"Who?"

The man shook his head. Derwyn grasped the hilt of the knife protruding through the man's palm.

"No! Please! I swear by all the gods, I do not know his name!"

"Describe him, then."

"About his size," the man said, looking at Reese, "but dark . . . bearded . . . dark eyes."

"That could be anyone. What else? Be more specific."

The man moistened his lips, breathing hard. "He had a scar . . . from his right ear down to his chin . . . a sword cut, I think. He said a man would be coming on the road to Daulton . . . in the duke's carriage. We were to make sure he did not reach Daulton alive." The man swallowed hard. "We did not expect three of you . . . and we were given no name or description, so. . . ." His voice trailed off.

"So you decided to kill all three, just to make sure," Dulcain said.

The man nodded and shut his eyes. "I have told you all I know." He swallowed hard. "It was the truth, so . . . make it quick."

Dulcain stared at him for a moment, then said, "Get up."

The man opened his eyes and stared at him. Dulcain stood.

"You'll live," Dulcain said. "But if I see you again, I'll kill you. And you can tell your friends the same goes for them, as well. Tell them they have Bran Dulcain's word on it."

The man's eyes grew wide. "You're Bran the Blade?"

"I am."

The man shook his head. "We were never told. Had I known that—"

"You would have demanded more money," Dulcain said dryly. He glanced at Reese. "Take his weapons. We'll leave him for his friends to find, if they bother coming back. And let's unhitch those horses. We'll have to ride bareback into Daulton, and I don't want to waste any more time. We have a spy to catch."

* * * * *

"What are you doing here, Alain?" asked Derwyn. "I told you if you had news to report, to send it by the usual courier. By coming back here, you may have compromised yourself. If I have spies in Avan's camp, he undoubtedly has spies in mine."

"I am already compromised," the man named Alain replied. "The assassination failed. Bran Dulcain arrived in Daulton and immediately began asking about a dark man with a scar. I barely managed to get away in time. My usefulness to you in Avan's camp has ended."

"What happened?" Derwyn asked. "How did it fail? Or did you even bother staying long enough to find out?"

"I knew that you would want a full accounting, so I stayed in Daulton—at considerable risk to myself, I might add—long enough to contact the men I hired for the job. Only three of them made it back. Three out of ten. The others were all killed. But one of them must have survived long enough to talk. The three who came back didn't know for sure. They never bothered going back to check. In any case, Dulcain had my description, so whether he killed the man who gave it to him or let him live is anybody's guess."

"He killed all seven?" Derwyn asked. "He must be as good as they say, despite his age."

"He didn't kill any of them," Alain replied.

"Then who did?"

"A breed," Alain replied. "I don't know his name, but the men say he was traveling with Dulcain. And there was another man with them, but the breed did all the killing, with throwing knives as my men were riding up. If their report is to be believed, he dropped seven of them before they even realized what was happening."

"He was carrying seven knives?"

"At least, or so I'm told. He apparently had them sheathed in cross-belts on his chest. They said they never saw anyone so fast . . . or so deadly."

"Elf warriors are raised from childhood with blades in their hands," said Derwyn. "I can still recall how they fought us when my father tried to take the throne. Michael had a number of elf warriors from Tuarhievel with him. They were the equal of a battalion of our men."

"What would an elf warrior be doing riding with Bran the Blade?"

"How in Haelyn's name should I know?" Derwyn impatiently replied. "But you said he was a breed?"

"That's what I was told."

"How could they tell if they never got that close?"

"By the way he was dressed. And he had reddish hair with thick silver streaks running through it. Full-blooded elves do not have red hair."

Derwyn grunted. "The question is, was he just another mercenary or has Avan negotiated an alliance with Prince Fhileraene?"

Alain shook his head. "I do not know, my lord."

"You are supposed to know. Why do you think I had you there?"

"If Lord Kier has arranged an alliance with Tuarhievel, then it has been a closely guarded secret. I have heard nothing of any such negotiation."

"You have not heard much at all, it seems."

"They were coming from Anuire," Alain said. "That's in the opposite direction from Tuarhievel."

"By way of Lofton, you fool," said Derwyn. "And Lofton is but a few days' ride from the eastern borders of the Aelvinnwode. And this third man . . . You have no idea who he was?"

"None, my lord."

"You are worse than useless," Derwyn said. "I entrusted you with a simple task—which you failed—and as a result, Bran the Blade now leads Avan's mercenaries. He's a living legend to that motley lot, the closest thing they have to their own god. Every mercenary in the empire out to make a reputation for himself will now enlist with Avan, thanks to you."

"My lord, I feel I must point out that this was not my fault. I was given no information about the breed, or this other man. Had I known, I might have hired more men—"

"Might have hired? I sent you more than enough to get the job done. So what do you do? You hire ten thugs so inept that one breed takes out seven of them, with no help from Dulcain or this other man. How much of what I sent you did you pocket for yourself?"

"My lord, that is an unjust accusation. With all due respect, I had expenses and—"

"Expenses! And what of the money you were being paid by Avan? Where did all that go?"

"I was taking great risks on your behalf, my lord. Under the circumstances, I felt some compensation was justified. That is not unfair."

"You have the nerve to tell me what is fair and what is not?" Derwyn shouted. "Get out of my sight, you miserable wretch! And you can surrender your spurs to my chamberlain on your way out."

Alain stiffened. "I have always served the dukedom faithfully. And my knighthood was bestowed upon me by your father in recognition of that service."

"And I am stripping you of it! Now get out, before I have you thrown in the dungeons for your damnable impertinence!"

Aerin leaned back from the peephole in the secret passageway and smiled. A knight stripped of his rank would have little reason to feel any loyalty to the man who had reduced him. His temperamental father had just made an enemy for life. But what one duke could take away, another could return. And Sir Alain—now merely Alain—would doubtless do a great deal to get his spurs back. And for a baron's coronet, he would probably do anything.

Anything at all.

chapter two

Dulcain was disappointed to discover that the spy had managed to escape, but Lord Kier was furious when he found out who it was. Alain had been one of his best mercenary recruits, and he had hoped to appoint him as second-in-command when the famous Bran the Blade arrived, subject, of course, to the new commander's approval. Needless to say, Bran thought the choice was questionable and was not shy about saying so. Gannd thought Lord Kier was more angry at himself than anything else, for having had his judgment proven so disastrously wrong.

Kier of Avan was not a young man. He looked older than Dulcain by at least twenty years, which placed him somewhere in his eighties. But though he looked his age, he was in excellent condition, and his dark eyes still glinted with alertness and vitality. His hair was white, worn loose to his shoulders, and though his face was lined with age and his hands were liver-spotted, his chest was thick with muscle and his arms looked strong and firm. He had a considerable girth, but he carried it well. He eschewed the finery affected by many aristocrats of superior rank and instead dressed simply in a belted indigo tunic that hung well below his knees, light brown hose, and well-polished black boots. His only ornamentation was the chain of office he wore around his neck.

"I had considered Alain the best man in the mercenary regiment," Lord Kier said bitterly. "And he turns out to have been a bloody spy. To think of the confidence I placed in him . . ." He smashed his fist on the table, upsetting two wine goblets. A servant hurriedly moved in to wipe up the spill. "And I have always taken pride in my ability to judge men!"

"I would not say you were necessarily wrong, my lord," Dulcain said placatingly. "He must have been good to have gained your confidence as he did. If you judged the man for his abilities,then your confidence in him was surely not misplaced."

Kier grimaced ruefully. "I should have known he was too good to be true. He was undoubtedly one of Boeruine's knights. And who knows how many other spies Derwyn has managed to have infiltrate my forces?"

"At least as many as you have in his, no doubt," Dulcain replied. "Unless, of course, you have been derelict in your responsibilities."

Kier smiled at that. "They told me that you spoke your mind. I like that in a man. I am surrounded by sycophants anxious to ingratiate themselves with me in the hopes of future advancement when I sit upon the Iron Throne. It's nice to know that at least one of my men says what he thinks."

"I shall consider that license to speak plainly, my lord," Dulcain replied.

"Then do so, by all means."

"Very well. For one thing, your ascension to the throne is by no means assured. Derwyn is not the man his father was, everyone knows that, but on the other hand, Arwyn left his son one of the strongest and most seasoned fighting forces in the empire. An army is only as able as its generals, of course, but Derwyn has some good ones, and unless he is an utter fool and dismisses all of their advice—which I would certainly not count on—he's liable to learn a thing or two about being a general himself."

"He's been doing that, all right," said Kier glumly. "My agents report that he spends all his days out in the field, drilling his men, and sits up half the night planning and discussing strategy with his commanders. He may not have his father's experience, but he's been working hard to compensate for it. We fought each other to a standstill the last time we met, and I could find no fault with his generalship. Or that of whoever was commanding on the field that day, if it was not Derwyn himself.

"Go on. You rode through the camp on your way here. I imagine you must have formed some first impression."

"I did," said Dulcain. "The disposition of the troops, the layout of the camp, the sanitation and supply all seem, from a brief examination, adequate. However, the discipline of the troops is wanting. They have far too much time on their hands."

"I see to it that they are drilled every day," said Kier.

"It is not enough," Dulcain replied. "This evening, when we rode through the camp, we were challenged in only the most cursory manner. If we'd been spies, we would have easily bluffed our way past the pickets. They sit bored and listless at their posts, standing only when somebody approaches. In the camp itself, I saw a great deal of drinking and gaming. I saw women in the camp. Prostitutes or camp followers, it makes no difference. They have no place there. I saw vendors selling ale and wine. In the camp itself. Inexcusable. And I did not see a single officer. If there were any knights there, I could not tell them from the men-at-arms, which in itself is damning."

"The knights all return to their homes, or their quarters in the castle or in town, when the day's drill is done," said Kier. "I could not expect aristocrats to live quartered with the soldiers in the camp."

"Then do not expect to win this war, my lord," Dulcain replied.

Kier stared at him for a moment. Reese glanced nervously at Gannd. For a knight to speak in such a manner to a duke was nearly unthinkable. For a commoner to do it was unheard of, whether given license to speak his mind or not.

"I would likely have a mutiny on my hands if I were to order noblemen to live in the camp along with common soldiers," Kier replied. "On the battlefield, it is one thing, but while the army is encamped at home, in training. . . ."

"Is the perfect time to do it," said Dulcain. "You will not forge a strong and unified fighting force if the men-at-arms see their officers living apart in a privileged manner."

"You speak of commoners and nobles as if they were the same," Kier replied, raising his eyebrows.

"No, my lord, I speak of soldiers," said Dulcain. "Believe me," he added dryly, "no commoner will ever think he is the same as an aristocrat. They are painfully aware of the difference. But there is a difference in how commoners can perceive the nobles whose aristocracy they cannot fail to acknowledge. On his campaigns, the Emperor Michael marched along with his troops, often on foot, leading his horse, when he could easily have ridden. No one would have questioned it, of course, it was only to be expected. But when the soldiers saw him marching on foot, alongside them, with them, it had a profound effect. He eschewed luxurious pavilions and lived in an ordinary tent, as they did. He ate what they ate, endured all the hardships they endured, and insisted that his officers do likewise. He never rested until they all rested, never slept until they slept. And every man-at-arms under his command would have followed him straight into the jaws of death, as indeed, they did when Michael had the folly to march against the Gorgon. If you want your troops to win for you, my lord, then they must be willing to die for you. Gladly, unhesitatingly, and without question. And to do that, my lord, they must place you on a pedestal—not because of your rank, but because you command their love and their respect."

Kier raised his eyebrows. "Well, that was quite a speech, Dulcain. As it happens, I took part in the emperor's campaigns as well, if you'll recall."

Dulcain grimaced. "I'm becoming a blabbermouth in my old age. Somehow, as I advance in years, it seems that I have more to say."

"Indeed," said Kier. "I have often thought that if a man had nothing to say, the very least he could do was shut up. But your words have weight to them. And wisdom. Very well, then . . ." He stood. "Kneel."

Dulcain frowned slightly, but did as he was bid. Kier drew his sword. "You do not strike me as a man who stands on ceremony," he said, "so we shall dispense with the usual solemnities." He tapped Dulcain once on the right shoulder, once on the left, and again on the right. "I promised you a knighthood. Now you have it. Rise, Sir Bran."

Dulcain stared at the duke with incomprehension. "My lord . . . I

... I understood that the promise of the knighthood was contingent upon my performance in the coming conflict."

"Yes, yes, indeed, it was," said Kier impatiently, "but I cannot very well have a commoner commanding my troops and issuing orders to titled aristocrats. Which, come to think of it, means that a knighthood alone will not quite do. We shall have to make you a viscount, at least, or a baron of something or other. Fortunately, the last battle created a number of vacancies in the rolls. I shall have my chamberlain come up with something suitable."

Dulcain stared at him with disbelief. Reese stood slack-jawed. To go from common mercenary to titled nobleman in one fell swoop was mind-boggling.

"My lord," Dulcain said, dismayed, "I am honored beyond all my meager ability to express, but surely . . . surely such an unprecedented elevation will incur resentment among the nobles."

"Mmmm, I imagine it will," said Kier, as if he couldn't care less. "I suppose you shall simply have to deal with that as best you can. But I'm quite sure you'll manage. After all, if you're capable of lecturing a duke, you should be able to handle a few disgruntled knights."

Dulcain swallowed hard. "But, my lord . . . you appointed me to command your mercenaries. If I am to command your army, which I hasten to add is something I have never done before, then who shall fill the post for which I was originally hired?"

"Pick someone," said the duke. "Pick anyone you like. Not the breed, though, that simply wouldn't do. The men would kill him. Perhaps this strapping fellow here . . . What was your name again?"

"Duncan Reese, my lord. But—"

"He'll do, if you have confidence in his abilities," said Kier. "My judgment in these matters seems to have been somewhat lacking, since I was ready to appoint one of Derwyn's spies to be your deputy. I was not strong enough to beat Boeruine the first time. We came close to slaughtering each other to no good purpose. I need a better army, Dulcain. I expect you to give me one, and I don't much care how."

The duke crossed to a window and stared out, looking west, toward the province of Boeruine. He stood silent for a moment. Finally, he spoke again.

"Despite what you may think or what you may have heard," said Kier, "I have no wish to sit upon the Iron Throne and rule the empire. I am an old man, and the task requires the energies of a younger one. Especially with the empire disintegrating all around us. But I cannot bear the thought of Derwyn succeeding to the throne. That would be disaster. In Michael Roele, we had an emperor. In Derwyn of Boeruine, we would have a tyrant, subject to manipulation by whoever gains his ear and flatters him the most. I would much sooner have someone else put a stop to his towering and preposterous ambition. I have been to war many times before, and I do not relish the thought of going to war again. But someone has to stop him and, for the present, it seems I am the only one who can."

He turned away from the window. "I can still take the field with my troops, but I am too old to act as my own general. That is a job for a younger man, but one seasoned with maturity and not blinded by ambition. One who will do what must be done and politics be damned. One who is capable of leading by example, and who can accomplish the very things of which you speak—winning the respect, love and admiration of the common soldiers under his command. That eliminates every noble who has sworn fealty to me, because they have done so out of ambition, or fear, or greed.

"In the entire history of the empire, so far as I know it, no commoner has ever been elevated as I have elevated you. I have not done so because I am an old man who has lost all sense of perspective. I know precisely what I'm doing, just as you know that I have placed you in a very difficult position. I don't care what the nobles think. I care what the common soldiers think. It is they who shall win or lose this war. And it is they who shall suffer most for it. I want to give them a commander who can inspire them, who can give them hope. I want to give them a man they can look upon as one of their own. I want to give them Bran the Blade, the legendary mercenary, the simple commoner who became a noble knight and led them to a victory that saved the empire.

"It is the sort of thing that bards will sing about for years to come." He grunted. "For my own part, I do not care what they sing about. I only care about one thing. I need an army that can stop Derwyn of Boeruine. Give me that army, Dulcain. Let an old warrior die in peace."

* * * * *

Aerin was planning something; she could tell. The very air around him simmered with intrigue. Katrina had reached the point where she could almost tell what he was thinking. He was like a stubborn oyster she had tempted into opening its shell, not quite all the way, but just enough to see the pearl inside . . . surrounded by soft, vulnerable flesh.

Even the way he looked at her had changed. It was a subtle thing, not so much that anyone else would notice, unless perhaps they had been observing them both very closely all along. But it was there. She had seen his hunger and amused herself by feeding it and watching it grow. That hunger was still there, as powerful as ever, but now there was also something else. A sense of the hunger being tempered somewhat by a smug anticipation. He wanted her. She made him want her. But now, whenever he looked at her, she had the sense that he knew he was going to get her. In his mind, it had become a certain thing. It was merely a matter of time.

He had a plan.

Aerin had no hold on her. She had been very careful about that. She exposed no vulnerabilities to him, nothing he could use to pressure her so that he could get his way. So it could be only one thing. He must have decided to remove the one obstacle to his desires— his father. And if she had any doubts, they were soon dispelled as she paid close attention to the way he acted whenever Derwyn was around. Outwardly, Aerin played the same role he always had, that of the dutiful, respectful son, scholarly and somewhat timid, retiring and distant, as if preoccupied with things beyond the world of the mundane. But when the mask slipped, as it did more often now when his father wasn't looking, he gazed at Derwyn in a very different way. There wasn't any loathing anymore. There was just a coldness, a flat and knowing gaze, as if he were looking at a dead man.

When she first saw it, Katrina felt a sense of power unlike anything she had ever experienced before, except for that one time when that strange, mysterious woman had appeared to her on the battlefield. It was as if a jolt of energy ran through her, revitalizing her, bringing everything into a sharp focus with a crystal clarity. She had done that to him. She had taken a resentful son and turned him into a calculating parricide. In his mind, he had already accomplished the act. Now, it was just a matter of waiting for the execution . . . so to speak.

She wondered how he planned to do it. She did not believe him capable of actually doing the deed himself. He lacked the fortitude. Besides, that was not Aerin's way. The devious seducer would not do such a thing directly. Especially since he was still so intimidated by his father. He would have someone do it for him. That meant it had to be someone he could trust, or at least trust so far as to accomplish the deed. And it had to be someone Aerin would be able to control. He was adept at controlling women. Well, some women, at any rate, Katrina wryly thought. But this would not be a task he would entrust to a woman. It had to be a man over whom Aerin held some power. Or to whom he could grant something worth killing for.

Katrina went for a walk in the castle garden to mull the matter over. Who could it be? If Derwyn were dead, then Aerin would become archduke, and that would naturally place him in a position to grant special favors. Money? That alone could be sufficient motive for many people. But to set out to kill an archduke . . . It would have to be a great deal of money indeed to make it worth the risk of failure. No, she thought, money wasn't quite enough. It must be something else. Something more than money. Or in addition to it. What then? Rank? Position? That was certainly something Aerin would be able to grant as the archduke. But to whom would he be granting it? It could be anyone. And how would he approach someone with such a bold and daunting proposition? How could he be sure it would not be rejected out of hand or reported to his father? And he would have to be absolutely certain. Sure of his man beyond any doubt.

Katrina sat down on a bench beside a bed of roses in a little arched, trellised nook sheltered from view from the garden path. It was a quiet, serene, peaceful place for contemplation . . . even of something so sinister as murder.

To minimize the risk, Aerin would have to be certain that whoever he approached would not only benefit from Derwyn's death, but would want to see him dead for reasons of his own. Derwyn was not especially well loved. But was there anyone who hated him enough to want to kill him? Obviously, if Aerin had already set the plan in motion, as she felt certain he had, he must have found someone who did. But just wanting to see Derwyn dead and benefitting from that death was not enough to qualify a potential assassin for the role. It had to be someone who had a good chance of accomplishing the task.

Offhand, Katrina did not know who that might be. But she knew enough to work at finding out. It was time once again to have Angharad update her on all the recent doings and gossip in the castle. She could not tell Angharad specifically what she wanted to know, of course. That would be too risky. She trusted Angharad, but only so far. She had learned to value circumspection. She would have to listen patiently as Angharad went through everything that had happened at Seaharrow recently: Who was intriguing against whom, who was carrying on affairs, who had taken a recent trip to town to see the physic and buy a potion to abort an illicit and unwanted child . . . whose husbands were on the outs, and whose were in . . . and somewhere in all the gossip there might be something that would alert her as to who the candidate might be. The men were often closemouthed, but the women told each other everything, swearing to secrecy friends who in turn told their friends and swore them to secrecy, and so on, and so on, and so on. Only the men thought secrets could be kept in Seaharrow.

"So . . . how flows the power?"

Katrina started at the sound of the voice. She had thought she was alone. And a moment earlier, she had been. But no longer. The strange woman from the battlefield stood before Katrina, not three feet away, looking down at her with a bemused smile as she sat on the stone bench. As before, the woman wore a black hooded cloak that covered her from head to toe, save for her strikingly lovely and youthful face, framed by ash blond hair. And as before, she carried her staff. The staff. . .

"It's you!" Katrina said, glancing up at her with surprise. And then, involuntarily, her gaze drifted to the staff, as if drawn to it like a magnet.

"You have come a long way since last we met," the woman said. Even her voice was lovely. Low, throaty, and seductive. "And you will go farther still."

Katrina could not tear her gaze away from that staff. It looked so ordinary, merely a six-foot staff made from the bough of an ash tree, polished smooth, but somehow she knew that it did not get that way from being finished by some woodcarver, but from years of being handled. Untold years.

"Who are you?" asked Katrina. "How did you come here? What do you want of me?"

"The question is, what do you want, Katrina?" she replied, with a knowing smile. "That is the real question, the only one which truly has any significance for you. What does Katrina want?"

Katrina moistened her lips and her gaze went to the staff once more. She could not help it. It was as if she could feel the power vibrating through it, emanating from it like an aura.

"Yes, I know what you want. You want to taste the flow once more, feel it, commune with it, be one with it."

The staff moved toward Katrina as the woman held it out. Katrina licked her lips and swallowed hard.

"Go on. You know you want to."

With a convulsive movement, like a starving man grabbing at a piece of food, Katrina reached out for the staff and her fingers closed around it. The woman let go and Katrina jerked, arching her back as she felt the power surge through her with even more force than she remembered. It almost lifted her right off the bench. For a moment, she felt as if her spine would snap.

For the briefest instant, the world stood still, and everything became as silent as a tomb. The sound of the birds' singing ceased abruptly, and Katrina could no longer hear the wind blowing in off the Sea of Storms. It was as if she had suddenly gone deaf. And then she heard a soft buzzing in her ears that at first reminded her of the sound made by the flies on the battlefield that day, only it grew steadily, louder and louder, until a roaring filled her ears. It was a sound not unlike that of a storm lashing in off the sea, only much louder, so loud it threatened to make her head burst. She wanted to scream, but she could not. Her mouth opened, but no sound came forth. Yet, in her mind, it felt as if she were screaming. She jerked convulsively, again and again . . . and again, the flow coming in powerful waves that completely overwhelmed her and filled her with a surging heat that rose up from her groin and flooded her entire body. She put her head back, her eyes half closed, unfocused, glazed, her lips parted as she gasped, and then a low laugh rose up in her throat and rolled out of her, rising and then falling, becoming a long, low, sustained moan of pleasure and fulfillment.

"Milady? Milady?"

Katrina opened her eyes and blinked. Angharad stood before her, looking down at her with concern. "Milady, are you well?"

Katrina blinked several more times. The woman with the staff was gone, as if she had never even been there. But she had been. Katrina knew. She knew so much more now. . . .

"Milady? I heard you moan. What is the matter?"

Katrina smiled. "Nothing, Angharad," she said. "Nothing at all."

chapter three

They spent their first night in the castle as Lord Kier's guests, and the next day, he called together his knights and introduced them to their new commander. Their reactions were mixed. Some looked puzzled; some looked surprised; others were stunned and outraged. Up until that point, Lord Kier himself had been their commander in the field, but he had delegated many tasks to his subordinates, and apparently it was not entirely unexpected that he would appoint a general. But the knight commanders had naturally assumed that the appointment would come from their ranks. Instead, the coveted position had gone to an outsider, and a mercenary, at that. The strongest reaction came, predictably, from the ranking noble, Baron Dravan of Caulnor, who apparently had expectations that the position would go to him.

"My lord," he said, "this is outrageous! This man is not one of us! He is an outsider—a mercenary and a commoner to boot! For him to be appointed lord commander of the army is a slap in the face to every blooded noble in Avanil!"

"He may not be blooded, Dravan," Kier replied calmly, "but he is a noble. I have knighted Bran Dulcain and elevated him to the rank of baron. The formal investiture of Sir Bran as Baron of Daulton will be held at the beginning of the month, but until then, he is entitled to all the honors and privileges associated with his rank."

Dravan's jaw dropped, nor was his the only one. They were all struck speechless, though Dravan was the first to recover. "But Daulton is the capital city," he protested. "It is not a barony!"

"It is now," Lord Kier replied.

"Only the emperor can create a new barony!"

"Except there is no emperor," said Kier. "And imperial court protocol specifically prohibits an acting regent from creating new baronies when there is no heir and the succession is in doubt. However, my chamberlain advises me that no such prohibition applies to dukes or archdukes, as rulers of their provinces. Therefore, I interpret that to mean that I am completely within my authority to designate the capital city and its immediate environs as a barony if it suits my needs and purposes."

"My lord, this is an insult to all those present here," Dravan replied. "To elevate a commoner to knighthood, without his ever having served an apprenticeship as squire, is unprecedented in itself. But to install him as a baron . . ." His voice trailed off in indignation and outrage.

"Do you question my authority, Lord Dravan?" asked Kier, staring at the man.

"No, my lord, I do not, but I question your interpretation of imperial protocol and the rules of chivalry," said Dravan, speaking a bit too hastily, not realizing that the last part of his statement could easily be taken as an insult to the duke's honor. However, Dulcain was quick to step into the breach and point that out.

"My lord Baron," he said, in a level tone, "before this goes any further, I urge you to take back that last statement. It is an insult to the honor of the duke."

Dravan stared at him with astonishment, amazed that Dulcain would have the temerity to address him as an equal, much less accuse him of so grave an offense. "You dare presume to speak to me in such a manner, when I have been his lordship's faithful vassal these past twenty years and you are but lately come and bespurred from the humblest of stations?"

"Be that as it may, my lord," Dulcain persisted in an even tone, "I nevertheless have a duty to serve his lordship and protect his honor, so once again, I urge you to retract your statement. And apologize."

Dravan's eyes grew wide with shock and disbelief. "Apologize? You arrogant bastard! You want me to give an apology? I give you my gage instead!"

And with that, he threw down his gauntlet, before Kier or anyone else could stop him. Dulcain's lips twitched in a slight smile, and Gannd realized it was exactly what he wanted. He had subtly goaded Dravan into issuing a challenge to him, to take the onus off the duke and divert it to himself. He bent to pick up the glove as silence fell.

Kier reached out to take Dulcain by the shoulder. "I pray you, do not pick up the gage, Dulcain."

"I fear I must, your lordship. I have no choice. You have knighted me and chivalry demands it. Does it not?"

Kier grimaced. Dulcain was right. Nevertheless, he made one more attempt to defuse the situation. "Dravan," he said, "I most earnestly request that you retract your challenge."

He could not, under the code, demand it. And Dravan knew it.

"I cannot, my lord," he said stiffly.

"As the challenged party, I believe I have the choice of time and mode of combat," Dulcain said. It was a statement, not a question.

"Choose what you will," said Dravan. "Sword, mace, axe, or lance, it is all the same to me. I shall meet you at your pleasure."

"Very well," said Dulcain. "The time I choose is now. On the drill field. And the mode of combat . . . full armor and wooden practice swords."

The choice provoked an undertone of startled murmuring among those present. Dravan flushed and looked as if he were about to burst a blood vessel. "You seek to make a mockery of this?" he said.

"Not at all," Dulcain replied. "In time of war, I would not wish to deprive his lordship of even one man-at-arms, much less an able knight." He did not, in so many words, say that by challenging him, that was precisely what Baron Dravan had intended, but the implication was clear to all those present. "With his lordship's approval, we shall fight to first blood," he said, "or until one man cries hold. And if you should win, I shall step down in your favor . . . or that of any man his lordship may choose to take my place."

Dravan practically quivered with fury at the implication that he might not be the logical choice. "And in the unlikely event that you should win?" he said in a sneering tone.

"In that event, I shall trust to your chivalry to guide you in knowing your proper course," Dulcain replied.

"Suit up," said Dravan, through his teeth. "I am going to hammer you right into the ground." He turned on his heel and went to put on his armor.

"An interesting choice," Lord Kier said to Dulcain. "However, even in full armor, a man may still be killed with a strong enough blow to the head from a practice sword."

"Never fear, your lordship," said Dulcain. "I shall take special care not to injure Baron Dravan too severely."

"I was talking about you," said Kier, raising his eyebrows slightly. "Dravan is the finest swordsman in Avanil."

"In that case, I shall take even more care to ensure that I am not injured too severely," Dulcain replied.

Word of the duel spread through the camp like wildfire. It did not take Dravan longer than an hour to get his armor and suit up, but by the time the combatants met upon the drill field, practically the entire army had turned out to watch. Lord Kier appointed one of the knights marshal to oversee the combat and, armed with a staff, but wearing no armor himself, the marshal stood between them as each man faced the other, separated by a distance of about ten feet. Each wore full armor and carried a wooden sword and shield. The practice swords were the same length as real blades, but round and blunt, like fighting staves, about two and a half to three inches in diameter, with discs of stiff saddle leather serving as guards and leather strips wound around the hilts. Silence fell over the field as the marshal raised his staff.

"Combat shall be fought to first blood," he announced, "or when one of the combatants cries, 'hold, enough'. As marshal of the list, I shall reserve the right to cry 'hold' and stop the combat briefly after any telling blow, for the purpose of having the helm removed to check for flow of blood. If no blood is present, and both antagonists are willing to continue, then helms shall be donned once more and combat shall resume. Any failure to obey the instructions of the marshal will result in forfeiture. Do both combatants understand and agree with these conditions?"

Both men simply nodded. The marshal lowered his staff, holding it out before him at waist level, horizontal to the ground, between Dulcain and Dravan. He glanced at Dravan. "Are you ready, my lord?"

"Ready," said Dravan.

The marshal turned to Dulcain. "And are you ready, my lord?"

Dulcain simply nodded.

The marshal raised his staff. "Lay on!"

Dravan didn't waste a moment. With a cry, he came charging in like a juggernaut, straight at Dulcain, his wooden sword raised high and his shield before him. Dulcain calmly stood his ground and took his blow on the shield, answering with one of his own, whipping it around with a deft turn of his wrist as he brought his arm forward and caught Dravan in the side. The blow struck his breastplate where it curved around his flank, making a solid sound like a heavy wooden mallet striking metal. If it were a real blade and not a practice sword, it might have breached the armor and given him a wound in the side. At the very least, it would have severely dented the metal, weakening it.

Angered, Dravan struck again, and once more Dulcain took the blow on his shield and returned one of his own. Dravan raised his shield in time. They continued bashing away at each other, standing toe-to-toe and slugging it out relentlessly as the onlookers watched. The only sounds were those of the practice swords striking metal or their wooden shields. It had almost a rhythmic counterpoint as they smashed away at one another, neither man giving ground.

Gannd watched the combat with interest. It was a different style of fighting from what he was accustomed to. Elves did not wear full armor. In battle, they wore helms and breastplates, half plate to cover arms and forearms, gorgets to protect their necks and throats, and greaves to guard the lower legs and knees, but their helms were open-faced, sometimes with nose-guards, not full-faced, with visors, like the two combatants wore. Elven armor was lighter, not giving as much coverage, but allowing for greater mobility and speed. Dulcain and Dravan each wore at least sixty to eighty pounds of armor, though the wooden swords and shields were considerably lighter than their real counterparts. The men would tire, but not quite as quickly. The object of the practice swords, of course, was to allow for safer combat drills, and to enable the participants to fight longer, without tiring as quickly, the better to hone their skills and instincts. They did not really need to wear full armor with the practice swords, and during most drills, the men didn't. Partial armor would have easily sufficed. When they wore full armor, it was not so much for protection as to develop strength and practice moving in it.

"Under ordinary circumstances, in a duel of this sort," said Reese, as he stood next to Gannd, "the fight would be either to the death or to first cut—first blood. Or until one of the opponents cried, 'hold,' if that was agreed upon, as it was in this event. I've never seen anyone fight a duel with practice swords before, though."

"It seems much safer," Gannd said. "A far less violent way to settle a dispute."

"True," said Reese, "but under these circumstances, it is more difficult to draw first blood. A wooden sword does not cut. It would take a strong blow to the head, most likely. And with two skilled fighters, that could take a while."

"It should provide the troops with quite a show," said Gannd.

"Mmm, yes," said Reese. "But it's liable to last all day if both men are strong-winded and in good shape. Which is probably just what Bran intended."

Gannd frowned. "Why? I should think it would be in his interest to get it over with quickly."

Reese shook his head. "No, if he beat Dravan too easily, especially in front of all the troops, it would humiliate the man. Bran's too smart for that. I see his method now. He wants to make it a good fight, wear Dravan down, so that when he wins, it will appear to one and all that he really worked for it, that both were evenly matched, and that it could easily have gone one way or the other. In this way, Dravan gets to keep a larger measure of his self-respect and, at the same time, it will impress the troops right at the outset with Dulcain's abilities and perseverance."

"Very clever," Gannd replied. "But are you so sure that he will win? Baron Dravan seems quite the expert swordsman."

"Formal expertise," said Reese. "The kind one gets from years of training with a swordmaster and experience in the lists at tournaments. Dulcain got his in mercenary taverns, back-street brawls, and open melees upon the field of battle. I'll put my money on Bran."

Gannd smiled. "I do not think I'll take that wager."

"Smart man," said Reese.

"Half-man," said Gannd.

Reese grinned. "Twenty gold pieces on Sir Bran!" he cried out.

"I'll take that wager," one of the knights replied, and in moments, a dozen others made their bets, as well.

"This just may wind up paying for those daggers," Reese said when the wagering was through.

"Just remember what happened the last time you gambled," Gannd replied dryly.

"This is no gamble, my friend," Reese said. "It is a sure thing."

While they spoke, Dulcain and Dravan continued their combat at full pace, moving back and forth a little, but basically standing firm and slugging it out relentlessly, neither scoring any telling blows. The troops were all now shouting at the top of their lungs, the knights and nobles all exhorting Dravan to victory, the men-at-arms and mercenaries cheering for Dulcain. It was less a duel than it was a war. Dravan seemed truly devoted to his stated intent of hammering Dulcain into the ground. He did not give him even a moment's respite.

Gannd had seen duels fought before, though never in full armor. Or with wooden swords, for that matter. Elves practiced with steel. This was not a case of two opponents circling, feinting, thrusting and parrying, looking for an opening, lunging, then backing off. This was a contest of endurance. Whose arms would grow tired first? Who would weary of taking blows to his shield, succumb to numbness, and drop his guard? Whose reactions would slow just enough to let through a telling blow? The sounds coming from the field were not those of a duel or battle, with steel ringing against steel; they were the sounds of demolition. The repeated strokes were causing the shields to crack and the wooden swords to splinter as the two armored antagonists seemed intent on clubbing each other to death. On and on it went while the observers cheered themselves hoarse, raising such a din that people from the city came out to the field to see what was going on, swelling the size of the audience until it had at least doubled.

Afternoon passed into early evening and still the fight went on, considerably slower now as the exertion began to tell on both men, fit as they were. Dravan had the advantage of youth, being younger than Dulcain by at least fifteen years, but Dulcain had the advantage of experience. Both men were strong, but now their movements had grown sluggish and each was staggering under the weight of all their armor, within which they had to be completely bathed in sweat. The blows were coming farther apart now as both men gasped with the effort of their exertions. Some of Dravan's blows were missing by a wide margin as Dulcain twisted away from them, but failed to follow up as quickly as he had before. Even with the comparative lightness of the wooden swords, it was taking each man a considerable effort to raise them for each successive stroke. The rapid tattoo of blows which had marked the beginning of the combat had now slowed to a not-so-steady beat, not unlike that of the slow drumming of a death march. The movements of both men had grown spasmodic, uncoordinated. They looked like a pair of drunks flailing away at one another.

Blows were getting through regularly now, and several times the marshal called a halt as one or the other's helm was removed to check for blood. However, though the blows were getting through because the defenses had grown weaker as the fight progressed, so did the blows themselves weaken, and where in the beginning of the long fight they would have been powerful enough to cause a concussion if they had connected, now they merely stunned momentarily.

During those moments when the marshal called a halt, both men gasped for air as their faces were revealed, streaming with sweat, their hair plastered down to their foreheads, their eyes barely able to focus. Both men stood apart, slumped over, breathing like spent racehorses, and when the marshal had the helms put back on and stood with his staff between them, about to order the combat resumed, they somehow managed to straighten up, nod their assent, and start bashing away at one another once again with the command, "Lay on!"

"If Bran doesn't draw blood soon, they'll both collapse from sheer exhaustion," Gannd said. He was growing tired of just standing there and watching.

"He knows what he's about," said Reese, though he no longer sounded quite so certain.

The combat had now taken on the aspect of a clumsy ballet in slow motion. One man would advance, staggering, and strike a blow. The other would block it with his shield, attempt a counterblow, and then a full second would pass before the next exchange. Indeed, it appeared as if they were both about to drop. Then Dravan raised his sword, stumbled at Dulcain, and aimed a blow at his head—the target both men were now concentrating on with dogged determination. Dulcain raised his shield to take the blow, but instead of planting himself as he had done before, he summoned up his last reserves and moved into the blow, cutting down on the arc and preventing Dravan from putting all his strength into it. And as he took it on his shield, he continued his forward momentum and smashed bodily into his opponent. Dravan staggered back, and as he did so, his shield dropped momentarily, and Dulcain's wooden sword moved with a snap, flashing forward with a whipping motion and connecting squarely with the lower part of Dravan's helm, right over the jaw. Dravan staggered backward, lost his balance, and went down with a clatter. The crowd went absolutely still.

"Hold!" the marshal cried, lowering his staff between them.

Dulcain did not pursue the attack. He knew he had struck a strong and telling blow. The marshal had Dravan helped up to a sitting position and ordered his helm removed. Two men came forward to remove it, revealing blood pouring liberally from Dravan's mouth. His eyes were glazed, not focusing, and though he was conscious, he was just barely so.

The marshal went down to one knee and examined Dravan's jaw to see if it was broken. After turning the injured man's face gently and probing with his fingers, then manipulating the jaw to see how it worked, the marshal was satisfied that it was sound. He nodded to himself, stood, and declared Dulcain the winner.

The declaration was, of course, anticlimactic, because most of those gathered in the front ranks of the audience could easily see the blood coming from Dravan's mouth. The marshal made his declaration to a crowd that had already started cheering. Except some of the knights, of course, especially those who had bet on Dravan. Reese gleefully collected his winnings, but Gannd was more interested in watching Dravan's reaction. As Dulcain's helm was removed and Dravan was helped up to his feet, supported by several men, the blood was wiped from his jaw and he was given water to drink. Dulcain, too, drank from another bucket, which he then emptied over his head. Dravan rinsed and spat several times, then shrugged off the men supporting him and moved toward Dulcain. Gannd tensed.

Dravan stopped before Dulcain and stood gazing at him for a moment, then reached out and took him by the shoulders, smiled, revealing bloodstained teeth, and shook him gently, in a friendly manner.

"Well fought, Sir Knight," he said.

The men embraced, as warmly as full armor would allow, and then the troops came streaming out onto the field and hid them from view. A moment later, Dulcain was hoisted up onto the shoulders of the mercenaries who, of course, knew him, and they carried him off the field. Not to be outdone, the knights hoisted up Dravan and followed in their wake.

In one day, and with one duel that harmed no one, Dulcain had not only announced his presence, but won the respect of both knights and men-at-arms alike. And the admiration of his opponent, who thereafter became his second-in-command and staunch supporter. Reese was not disappointed that Dulcain had not given him the post, as Lord Kier had suggested. Instead, Dulcain appointed Reese as commander of the mercenary regiment, a position much more to the free companion's liking and one he felt he was infinitely more suited for. Among the mercenaries were some men he knew, having spent years in the profession of arms, and those who did not know him, and who wanted to test their new commander's mettle, discovered over the next few weeks that Duncan Reese was no pushover and would not back down from a fight. He soon had their respect.

For Gannd, it was a different matter. As his mother had warned him before he left the Aelvinnwode, he encountered prejudice and bigotry among the troops of Avanil. To some, it made no difference that he was a half-elf. To others, he was a lowly breed, unworthy of their company and a figure of contempt. That too would change, and Gannd would win their respect, but it did not happen overnight. Reese and Dulcain had gained acceptance far more readily, and being friends with both of them helped Gannd in finding a place for himself among the men, but not all of them were ready to grant him acceptance by virtue of association. That was something he would have to earn.

As the new lord commander, Dulcain's first order was that all knights live in the camp among the troops, specifically among the men whom they commanded. There was some displeasure at this, but Dravan backed him up, setting an example by being the first to comply. He had his pavilion set up in the camp and moved in with his squires and servants, and before long all the other nobles followed. Seeing the knights living among them in the camp bolstered the morale of the troops, even if the knights did have large and colorful pavilions and servants to attend them. That was, after all, only to be expected. But having their commanders living with them created a stronger bond between the knights and their men-at-arms than had existed previously, one which was only reinforced when Dulcain ordered that they all drill together every day.

Once again, resentment was curtailed by Baron Dravan setting the example. Early each morning, he was the first to turn out for weapons practice, throwing himself into the training sessions with an energy and an enthusiasm that proved contagious. And Dulcain was out there each day, drilling with them, doing himself everything he asked his men to do. He was older than most of them, and no young man with a healthy sense of pride and self-respect, whether commoner or aristocrat, would admit that an older man had more endurance than they did. But at the same time, they had all seen Dulcain's endurance demonstrated in the duel with Dravan and did not underestimate him. He gave them something to strive for and challenged their egos at the same time.

They would start each day with drills, then break for their first meal of the day, followed by a period of cleaning up the camp and seeing to the maintenance of their equipment, which in turn was followed by a daily inspection. Dulcain held them all to the highest standards, nobles and commoners alike. It soon became a challenge to the troops to pass his muster without revealing any flaws, something Dulcain made almost impossible to do. Still, before long, they were measuring up admirably, on occasion even forcing him into beneficial deceptions.

"I was walking my rounds of the camp the other afternoon and found a group of squires sitting around together playing at dice," he told Gannd and Reese one evening in his tent, smiling at the memory of the incident. "I decided they were being lax in their duties, so I called them to their feet and gave them all a proper tongue-lashing. 'What?' I demanded, 'Have you no more profitable a way to occupy your time? Have your lords had all their weapons and equipment seen to? Has everything been done that needed doing? Hop to it, let's see your masters' swords and armor, and there had better be no speck of dirt or a dull edge in sight!'

"Well," he continued with a chuckle, "they scattered to their respective tents and lugged back all the gear, which I then proceeded to inspect with a fine eye. And damn me if it wasn't all honed to a perfect edge and absolutely gleaming! I could not find fault with any of it. However, I could hardly let them know that. So I found a small, nonexistent nick in a blade edge here, a speck of invisible dirt lodged between some chain mail there, an imaginary squeaky joint in some piece of armor that could benefit from oiling . . . all perfect nonsense, of course. There wasn't a thing wrong with any of it. I dressed them down for wasting time lollygagging about when they had work to do and left them, thinking that not even I could have done a better job than they did, but better they should be kept on their toes.

"A short while later, I passed them on my return trip and saw them all sitting together in a circle as before, only this time cleaning and polishing and oiling with a vengeance. They were so intent upon their work they didn't see me. As I passed, one of them held up a perfectly honed blade that I'd found imaginary fault with, peered intently at the edge, shook his head and said, 'One thing's for sure . . . the bastard may be old, but he damn well sure can see!' "

To add a more competitive edge to the troops and build their spirit, Dulcain devised games for the regiments to play against each other, the prizes being such things as time off to go visit the town some evening or being excused from an occasional drill. Needless to say, this added considerable incentive for them to win, and the troops threw themselves into the games with as much intensity as if they were on their way to battle.

One of the more popular games Dulcain devised was called the "Bowl War," which took place in a slight declivity just beyond the camp where the ground dropped off to form a gently rounded depression with slopes rising on both sides, making a sort of natural stadium. Two teams would be selected, comprised of up to twenty men each, and they would outfit themselves with helms, greaves, gauntlets, and codpieces, wooden practice swords or polearms. No shields were carried. The players would all carry two practice swords each, save for one player on one side or the other who would be appointed as the "runner." The runner would carry only one wooden practice sword, and in the other hand he would hold an oblong leather ball stitched up from leather, about the size of a small melon. The field would be divided into two equal halves, with a zone at each end to be defended by each team, stretching the entire width of the marked-out field.

It was the runner's goal to carry the ball from his side of the field to the end zone of the opposite team, thereby scoring a point. He could not throw or pass the ball off to anybody else, but members of his team could defend him as he moved. The goal of the defending team would be to "kill" the runner, using their practice swords. If they succeeded, the possession of the ball would then pass to the defending team, who would then appoint their own runner and go on the offensive. Play would begin at the midpoint of the field, with three marshals appointed—one to govern the actual play on the field and two to monitor the flank boundaries. If any player stepped over the sidelines, he was deemed "dead" for the duration of that play.

The two teams would form lines at the midpoint of the field, facing one another, with the runner behind his own line, defended by one or two players. The marshal would give the commands of "Ready!" and "Lay on!" The two teams would then engage in a melee, with the defending team attempting to break through the line to "kill" the runner, while the offensive team would try to stop them and create a hole through which the runner could bolt for the opposing team's end zone.

The runner could, of course, defend himself with his practice sword, but he was at a disadvantage in carrying only one, since he also had to hold and retain possession of the ball. It was in the interest of the defending team to "kill" as many of the opposing team as possible, since that would weaken the line and allow them to break through to the runner. Likewise, the offensive team tried to "kill" as many of the defenders as possible, since that would increase the chances for the runner to break through unopposed.

Although the marshals observed the combat to look for "killing" or "crippling" blows, they could not possibly see everything in a general melee, so it was up to the honor of the players to acknowledge received blows that killed or crippled. Any blow upon the helm was considered to be a killing blow, as was any blow upon the torso. A blow to the arm was crippling, rendering that arm useless. The player could then continue the combat, but he had to drop one of his swords and place the crippled arm behind him, unable to use it for the duration of that play. It was possible to lose both arms, at which point that player could obviously not continue fighting, but he could attempt to interpose his body between the defender and the runner. Since he was unable to defend himself, it resulted in his being killed immediately, but it could buy a delaying moment. A blow upon a leg was also considered crippling. The player receiving the blow would then have to go down to one knee, but he could continue fighting. If both legs were crippled, then the player had to go down to both knees, but he could still continue fighting and hopping around.

If the runner happened to drop the ball while confronted by a defender, it was considered a "fumble," at which point the marshal would cry, "Hold!" and play would stop, all players freezing where they stood and going down to their knees. At that point, the runner who had fumbled and the closest defender would square off against each other, on their knees, and fight one-on-one, upon the marshal's signal, for possession of the ball. If the runner was killed at any time, the possession of the ball would pass to the opposing team, at the point on the field on which the runner had expired. The only other rule was that no thrusting was allowed. It made for a spirited competition and all the troops turned out to watch each Bowl War and cheer on their side. Regiments were pitted against other regiments, knights' squires against other knights' squires, and even, on one memorable occasion, two teams of peddlers that sold their wares outside the camp were pitted against one another, much to the amusement of the troops, as a ploy by Dulcain to cut down on the number of vendors clogging the outskirts of the camp. There were standings and playoffs and finally a championship, all hotly contested. The result was not only the increased benefits of training, but a marked rise in spirit and morale among the troops.

Little by little, Dulcain was forging the army of Avanil into a disciplined, crack fighting unit. The one area where success eluded him was in attempting to enlist the aid of the priests in the cause. Lord Kier had been entirely unsuccessful in this regard, and Dulcain fared no better. Dravan, Reese, and Gannd accompanied him to the temple of Haelyn in the heart of the city, an imposing structure of polished stone that rose above all the surrounding buildings. Its domed roof and fluted columns were among the most ornate examples of architecture in the city, rivaling the castle in opulence and grandeur. They climbed the long flight of marble steps—constructed of polished blocks quarried in Markazor and hauled all the way to Daulton— and entered the massive edifice through arched, heavy double doors made of cast bronze. Engraved into the bronze was a great mural depicting the cataclysm at the climax of the battle of Mount Deismaar, and the ascension to godhood of Haelyn the Champion.

Gannd had never before seen a human temple. In the Aelvinnwode, the Sidhelien temples were not enclosed structures, but standing stones and altars erected in open glades that were carefully and lovingly tended. The "roof" was the forest canopy and the "walls" were the surrounding trees and shrubs. The "floor" was the earth, strewn with pine needles and carpeted with moss. The feeling evoked was one of unity with nature, not separation from it, which was the impression Gannd received inside this temple. The intricately tiled mosaic floors, elaborate and exquisite as they were, were the very opposite of natural design, symbolic of order imposed externally and artificially. The paintings on the walls, giant murals depicting the life and times of Haelyn, from his exploits in the early wars of the six tribes to the climactic confrontation with the armies of the Shadow Lord at the battle of Mount Deismaar, were all highly idealized and unrealistic, lurid in their detail and in the impact of the colors used. The dome, high overhead, had a window in it that would allow the sun to shine through at high noon, surrounded by murals depicting the sun's rays touching the painted crests of the House of Anduiras, the line from which Haelyn was descended, the House of Roele, the House of Avan, and all the major aristocratic lines of the blooded nobility—including, ironically, the House of Boeruine—interconnecting them in the webwork of the sun's rays painted on the ceiling. Large bronze braziers were placed around the perimeter of the open temple chamber, as well as censers and heavy candle stands, all intricately wrought.

At the far end of the temple stood the altar, a massive edifice comprised of a sacrificial altar stone surmounted by gleaming crystals that reached up to the ceiling. The ritual tools of the priests stood upon the altar: candles, ritual daggers, chalices, scourges, caldrons and other items that Gannd did not recognize. Whenever he entered a Sidhelien temple in a forest clearing, he had always felt a sense of lightness and peace, of tranquility and union with the beauty of the natural surroundings. Here, in Haelyn's temple, he felt a sense of grim authority and foreboding.

The high priest of the temple came out to meet them, flanked by his acolytes. All three had shaved heads and wore long robes, though the robes of the acolytes were gray while the robes of the high priest were white, decorated with sun symbols and strange, geometric signs. The acolytes wore cords of white for girdles; the high priest wore a thicker cord of scarlet and carried an intricately carved and highly polished staff. Again, Gannd couldn't help but notice the contrast between the human priest and elven priests and priestesses. In the tradition of the Sidhelien, priests and priestesses looked much like anybody else, except when they were involved in rituals. They did not alter their appearance or dress differently. And during rituals, they were dressed simply, in loose white robes with garlands of herbs or flowers, or—depending on the ritual—

not dressed at all. There was nothing melodramatic about their appearance, dress or manner, quite the opposite. They sought simplicity in their appearance and lightness in their being. In contrast, the human priests wore robes that were emblazoned with mysterious symbols and affected colors of rank, such as in their corded belts. They dressed in a way to set themselves apart from others and affected a superiority of manner. Theirs, thought Gannd, was not a religion that embraced its followers so much as dominated them.

The priest glanced at Gannd and frowned with disapproval. "It is not every day we see a Sidhelien in our temple," he said. "To what do we owe this singular occurrence?"

It occurred to Gannd that he was standing face-to-face with the personification of the power that had driven his people from their homelands. His people. And yet, in a sense, the humans were his people, too, though he felt no real connection to them. He was of both worlds, one foot in either, and not really belonging to one or the other. At that moment, more than ever before, the priest somehow made him feel the extent of his isolation.

"My friend has never seen a human temple, Your Reverence," Dulcain replied. "He expressed the desire to come along and, as he is half human, I could think of no reason to deny him."

The priest fixed his gaze on Dulcain. "I know who you are," he said. "I cannot help you."

"But I have not yet asked—"

"I know what you seek," the priest replied, interrupting him. "It is impossible, as I have already told Lord Kier."

"But why?" Dulcain persisted. "When we go into battle, it is your people, your worshipers who will be dying. The magic of your priests could make all the difference in the world. They will be fighting to defend your city and your temple."

"My city, but Haelyn's temple," the priest replied. "And therein lies the problem. The province of Boeruine has temples dedicated to the great god Haelyn, also. In the old days, when we fought the Sidhelien," he glanced briefly at Gannd, "we fought unbelievers. Infidels. Yet if we were to take the side of Kier of Avan against Derwyn of Boeruine, it would be a very different matter. If I were to sanction and give aid to your cause, then the priests of the temples in Boeruine would likewise have to take the field with Derwyn's troops. Priests of Haelyn would be fighting priests of Haelyn. And that would be unthinkable. It would destroy the unity of the priesthood and the faith might not survive it."

"If a faith is true and strong enough, it should survive anything," Dulcain replied. "Worshipers of Haelyn will be fighting one another. Both sides will pray to the same god for victory. One shall win and one shall lose, as is inevitable in all conflicts, but the faith will not come out the loser, either way. It will survive. Though many of its adherents shall not."

"What is your point, Commander?" asked the priest.

"My point is that you seem less concerned about your worshipers than you are about the priests," Dulcain replied. "Specifically, the power of the priesthood. It must remain unified, no matter what the cost, because the priesthood of Haelyn is above such mundane matters as imperial politics. Or is it?"

"What are you suggesting?"

"I am just reminded of the jackals that gather while two stags fight for territory," said Dulcain. "They sit back on their haunches and merely watch the struggle. Then, when one stag loses and the other is exhausted, they move in for the kill."

The priest stared at Dulcain with eyes of anthracite. "You are not a believer, are you, Commander? Otherwise, you would not blaspheme so."

"Since when does questioning the motives of a priest impugn the existence of a god? Or is it blasphemy to ascribe political motives to your actions?"

"Bran, for Haelyn's sake!" said Reese, alarmed.

"No, I do not think so, Duncan," Dulcain replied dryly. "I do not think His Reverence does anything for Haelyn's sake so much as for his own."

"I shall ascribe your unconscionable arrogance and blasphemy to your pathetic ignorance and your frustration in not being able to get your way for the sake of your troops," the priest said in a tone of icy contempt. "Lord Kier may have elevated you in rank, Commander, but your rapid rise has done nothing for your humility or intellect. I shall pray for your enlightenment. This audience is over."

As they left the temple, Reese stared at Dulcain and shook his head. "That was a high priest of Haelyn you were speaking to!" he said. "You can't talk to somebody like that as you would to a recruit! Do you realize what he could do to you?"

"Strike me down with his priestly magic, you mean?" said Dulcain. He grimaced. "I think he would find that politically inconvenient at the moment."

"I'm not sure I'd want to take that chance," said Reese nervously. "I thought we went there to ask his help. Insulting him like that is not the way I would have gone about it."

"He had already refused Kier," said Dulcain. "I did not really expect to succeed where the duke failed. It was worth a try, but I assumed the outcome was a foregone conclusion."

"So then what was the point of it?" asked Gannd.

"If he was going to refuse, I wanted him to state that refusal and his reasons for it clearly, before witnesses," Dulcain replied. "And I wanted to make certain he would not get in the way."

"Of doing what?" asked Reese.

"If I cannot get priestly magic to support the troops," Dulcain replied, "then I will seek out magic of another sort."

"Adepts?" Reese said uneasily.

"Adepts, wizards, witches, mages, I don't much care what they call themselves," Dulcain replied. "I am only interested in the results they can produce. And now that the high priest has so pointedly refused me, he can hardly blame me for looking elsewhere. After all, I asked him first."

"Using priestly magic to support a war is one thing," Reese said as they walked through the streets, "but employing adepts is quite another. Priestly magic is called down from the gods. Wizards . . . there is no telling where they draw their powers from. No offense meant to your uncle," he quickly added, with a glance towards Gannd.

"Magic is magic," said Dulcain impatiently. "Ask your friend here. He grew up around it. One faith will perform rituals and say they are appealing to a god. Another will claim their power comes from some extraplanar fiend. Still another will maintain it is a power inherent in all things, in nature, and they are but finding ways of tapping it. All are still performing rituals meant to effect some change in conformance with the will. Power is power.

Whether it is used for good or evil depends not on where it comes from but on who uses it and for what purpose. For my part, I would sooner trust an adept whom I was paying and whose profit depended on his efficacy than I would trust some priest who had his own agenda."

"You meant to offend the priest!" said Reese, with sudden comprehension.

"As a general, I need to be able to command," Dulcain replied. "I can command a wizard who has accepted my commission. I cannot command a priest. And I could hardly discipline him if he failed to carry out my orders."

"So you meant to use wizards all along," said Reese. "Have you discussed this with Lord Kier?"

"Before I discuss any plan with him, I must first have a plan to present," Dulcain replied. "And that shall be our next step. We need to find ourselves a wizard to consult. Preferably someone with a reputation for being scrupulously honest, so that he may be trusted. And that, I suspect, will be more easily said than done." He glanced at Gannd. "You don't suppose your uncle would be willing to advise us?"

Gannd shook his head. "I do not know. But I could ask."

"The question is, will there be enough time?" Dulcain said dubiously.

Gannd felt the comforting weight of the amulet beneath his tunic. "I do not think time will be a problem," he replied.

* * * * *

The hawk screeched as it rode the air currents and the echo of its cry drowned out the mundane sounds of the city, which faded into the rising howling of the wind as time stood still. Gannd felt the Bridge of Sighs beneath his feet. Thick mists obscured the depths of the immeasurable gorge below him, undulating with the sighing of the wind. There was no sky, no sun, no earth anywhere in sight. It was as if he stood within a cloud that shifted constantly, offering him only momentary glimpses of his immediate surroundings . . . the bridge and the abyss below him.

"Uncle," Gannd said, "I need you."

"You called?" Gylvain said from behind him. Gannd turned around. His uncle came walking out of the swirling mist, approaching him, though he seemed not to walk so much as glide as the fog eddied around his legs.

"I have joined the army of Avanil," said Gannd. "They are preparing for a war with Derwyn of Boeruine, who plans to seize the Iron Throne."

"Like father, like son," Gylvain replied. "The humans never seem to tire of making war on one another. A most aggressive species. It is one of their more irritating qualities."

"The Lord Commander of the army seeks to enlist adepts to aid his cause," said Gannd. "He knows of your reputation. He says he served with you on the emperor's campaigns. Perhaps you know him. His name is Bran Dulcain."

"Bran the Blade?" Gylvain said. "I remember him. A mercenary and a very brave and able fighter. He must be an old man by now. How does it happen that he commands Kier of Avan's army?"

"He has been knighted by Lord Kier and elevated to the rank of baron," Gannd replied. "And he has also become my friend."

"I see. And through his friendship with you, he hopes to enlist my aid?"

"It is not quite as it sounds," said Gannd. "He came to my aid before he was made commander, and before he knew of my relationship to you. I believe him to be a good man and I believe his cause is just."

"And you want me to help?"

"I promised I would ask."

Gylvain remained silent for a moment. "It is one thing for you to take part in the conflict. You are half human. But for me to take part would be a different matter. I am not sure it would serve the interests of the Sidhelien."

"You and my mother took part in the emperor's campaigns," said Gannd.

"That was not the same thing," Gylvain replied. "The political situation was different, as Prince Fhileraene fully understood. Michael was the rightful emperor and Tuarhievel stood to benefit from the alliance. Now the succession is in question and a weak regent holds the throne."

"My brother."

"Yes."

"You never told me about him. Why?"

"It was your mother's wish. She felt that if you knew you had a brother—or half-brother, to be exact—you might want to meet him and she hoped to keep you with her in Tuarhievel. Even when you left, she hoped your curiosity about the human world would prove short-lived and you would soon return. She still has that hope."

"I cannot say when I will return," said Gannd. "There is still much I have to learn. Events have set my feet upon a path that I must follow to the end, wherever that may lead."

Gylvain nodded. "I understand. But it is a path that you will have to walk alone. I cannot help you. My first allegiance is to Fhileraene, and he would not approve of my leaving Tuarhievel at this time. If I were to join you, it would be perceived as Prince Fhileraene making an alliance with the Duke of Avanil. And it is by no means certain that Lord Kier shall win. If I took part, and Avan was defeated, it could have serious repercussions for our people."

"I understand," said Gannd. "Bran shall simply have to find another wizard."

"Why not seek among his own?" asked Gylvain.

"He is concerned that the adept he finds be honest and trustworthy," Gannd said. "I expect that he hopes to enlist a number of adepts, and he wants to find one of high repute who can advise him accordingly."

"I know of one such man," Gylvain replied. "We have never met, but I am familiar with his reputation. He is Terrell of Lofton."

Gannd smiled. "Yes, I know him. He holds you in high esteem, as well. He told me that he hopes to meet you someday."

"Perhaps that could be arranged." Gylvain began to fade away. "I must return now," he said. "Take care of yourself, Gannd."

"I shall. And give Mother my love."

"I will. Good luck."

His voice died away on an echo and Gannd stood alone upon the bridge. "Farewell, Uncle," he said. And as if in answer, the wind rose with a sighing sound and, for an instant—an instant without time—the mists parted and he could see the bridge stretching out before him. And he suddenly realized that he was not alone.

Before the swirling mists once more obscured his view, Gannd caught a brief glimpse of something, a vague and seemingly insubstantial form that stood upon the bridge some distance away, as if rising from the mists. It was a dark form, so dark that it seemed to absorb light. It stood motionless, but there seemed to be motion within it, a roiling blackness that was like the darkest night, only shaped in the vague form of a horse and rider, a form that seemed to be one unified shape, not quite resolved, but shifting, like a shadow with substance. And he recalled the stories that his mother told him of the Shadow World, to which this bridge had led once . . . perhaps still did.

For a moment, he beheld the frightening form of the mysterious Cold Rider.

And as he tried to banish the rising anxiety in his mind and concentrate upon the image of the hawk, he had the distinct impression somehow the Cold Rider would follow him if he could, that he wanted to cross the bridge—which his uncle said could no longer be crossed—into the World of Light. He did not know how he knew that, but he felt it, sensed it somehow, as a certainty.

The mists had rolled back in and he could no longer see the Cold Rider, but he had a strong feeling that he—it?—was still there. The presence was almost palpable, vibrating with malevolence. What sort of creature was it? He had asked his mother that when she told him the story of how she had seen the Cold Rider, and she had no answer for him. It happened when the magic of a halfling had opened a portal to the Shadow World for the Emperor Michael, so that he could march his army through it and travel through the timeless Shadow World across territory that corresponded spatially with territory in the World of Light, then return through another portal, thus effectively negating the concept of time in travel by leaving one point in the World of Light at one moment and, in the very next, emerging at another, far away, as if the entire army had been magically teleported—which, in a sense, they had been.

No one had ever done such a thing before. Though it was well known that halflings could create portals to the Shadow World, for it was where they came from, and they sometimes used this ability to travel from one point in the World of Light to another in the space of an eyeblink, no sane man had ever before considered voluntarily entering the Shadow World. It meant risking almost certain death.

At one time, the Shadow World had been much like the World of Light, only on a different plane of existence. That was when the halflings lived there, and their folklore—what little of it was known to humans and elves—spoke of blue skies and green pastures, of flower-covered meadows and lush forests that went on for miles and miles. Birds filled the air with song and strange, delightful creatures unknown to the World of Light filled the woods and fields with their vibrant presence. But then, one day, some terrible thing occurred that forced the halflings to flee their homeworld through portals they created, escaping to the World of Light, where they established communities of their own and sometimes lived among the humans, taking on their ways. No one seemed to know exactly what had happened, and the halflings never spoke of it—at least not to humans or elves—but whatever terror they were fleeing changed their world like a creeping plague and made it into what it had become: The Shadow World, a blighted landscape of dead forests and blasted fields, grass withered away, flowering plants obliterated and replaced with twisted, spiny, grotesque growths, gnarled trees that resembled twisted limbs with thorns instead of leaves. Everywhere a cold and damp, mist-shrouded miasma of malevolence seemed to kill or stunt everything it touched. The Shadow World was a place where time stood still, where the undead walked, where unquiet spirits lived in torment, and where the Cold Rider roamed upon his ghostly steed that was as black and featureless as he was, so much a part of him that it was impossible to tell where the rider ended and the mount began. Perhaps both were one—all the same mysterious entity.

On occasion, at certain points throughout the empire, at different times, but especially, it was said, on the Eve of the Dead, the borders between the worlds grew permeable and it was possible to pass from one into the other, in the same manner as halflings did when they conjured up their portals. There were many stories of both humans and elves who had somehow stumbled across one of these interstices and vanished, never to be seen again. There were unsubstantiated stories of creatures or entities that had briefly crossed over at these junctures and dragged some screaming victim back to a horrible fate. And of those who had heard the tales of the Cold Rider, no one had ever actually seen him—until that day when the emperor's troops crossed over to the Shadow World and witnessed the Cold Rider pacing them along a ridge as they marched. And a short while later, they were brutally attacked by an army of undead.

After being told that story, Gannd recalled how he had suffered nightmares in which the Cold Rider had pursued him. And now he had seen it with his own eyes. And it was a nightmare . . . but it was no dream.

With an involuntary shudder, Gannd shut his eyes and focused all his concentration on picturing a hawk in flight, so that his astral self could take wing with it and fly back to the World of Light, where it was safe, where there was only the danger of a war approaching and not the creeping malevolence of some black entity that filled him with a sense of overwhelming dread. He bit his lip and concentrated and he saw the bird take wing, floating high above him through the mists, crying out upon the wind. . . .

* * * * *

"It will be if Derwyn makes his move before we can—Gannd!"

Dulcain stumbled as Gannd fell heavily against him. The baron caught him as he collapsed, easing him gently to the ground.

"Gannd!" said Reese, kneeling beside him. "Are you all right? What happened?"

For them, no more than an instant had passed. What they had seen and experienced was the three of them walking down the street together, heading back to the encampment and talking about the possibility of finding a wizard to advise them when Gannd suddenly staggered for no apparent reason and fell against Dulcain as if collapsing in a swoon.

"Gannd," said Reese, gazing at him with concern, "what is it?"

Gannd stared up at Reese, still dazed, and blinked, unable to respond. He was breathing heavily. Dulcain started to loosen the laces of his leather tunic to give him more freedom to breathe, then stopped abruptly when he saw the amulet.

"By Haelyn!" Reese exclaimed. "Is that a ruby?"

"It's not colored glass," Dulcain replied.

"Look at the size of it!" said Reese. "It must be worth a bloody fortune!"

"Priceless, I would say," Dulcain replied. "It is a talisman."

"You mean . . . it's magic?"

"No," said Dulcain sarcastically, "it could be one of those unmagical talismans we're always hearing about."

Reese looked glum. "Well, you don't have to treat me like a fool."

"Then don't act like one. Gannd . . . Can you speak?"

Gannd nodded. "Yes, I can . . . now." He sat up with Dulcain's help. Several passersby glanced at them curiously, then hurried on their way. Whatever it was, they preferred not to get involved.

"Can you tell me what just happened?" Dulcain asked. "Did it have anything to do with the ruby amulet you're wearing?"

Gannd nodded. "Yes. My uncle gave it to me."

"You . . . went somewhere just now, didn't you?" Dulcain said.

"What are you talking about?" asked Reese. "He was right here with us!"

Dulcain sighed. "Duncan . . . shut up a moment, will you?"

"I went to see my uncle," Gannd replied.

"What?" said Reese, but Dulcain fixed him with a look and he fell silent.

"I have heard of this sort of thing before," Dulcain said, "but I have never actually seen it. Come to think of it, I haven't even seen it now. You left your body for a time, did you not?"

Gannd nodded.

"How long?"

"That is not a question I can answer," Gannd replied. "Where I was, time has no meaning."

Dulcain frowned. "Not the Shadow World?"

Gannd shook his head. "No, but not this world, either. A place between the two."

"I did not know such a place existed," said Dulcain. "Does it always affect you in this way?"

"No," said Gannd. "But while I was there . . . after my uncle had departed . . . I saw something. . . ." He moistened his lips. "The Cold Rider."

"I thought the Cold Rider was only a legend," Reese said.

"No," Dulcain said. "I saw the Rider once myself. A long time ago, in the Shadow World. And I almost didn't make it back. But I thought you said this place where you had gone was not the Shadow World?"

Gannd nodded. "No, it is not. It is a place between, but somehow, the Rider found it. I think he is trying to find a way to cross over."

"Could he have followed you?" Dulcain asked.

Gannd shook his head. "No, I do not believe so."

"Let us sincerely hope not," said Dulcain grimly.

"I am all right now," Gannd said, getting to his feet. "Forgive me."

"There is nothing to forgive," Dulcain replied. "What did your uncle say?"

"I regret to say he cannot help us," Gannd replied. "But he says he knows of an adept who can." He glanced at Reese. "Terrell."

"Terrell?" said Reese.

"You know this man?" Dulcain asked.

"He is an old friend," said Reese. "He lives in Lofton."

"Then why did you not mention him before?"

"Because Terrell would never get involved in anything like this," said Reese.

"Why not?"

"You'd have to know him," Reese said. "He is one of the most talented adepts in the empire and could easily find patrons among the wealthiest aristocrats. He could probably have served the emperor himself, but he has no interest in that sort of thing. He lives simply, quietly and frugally, and avoids the intrigues of politics. He likes to help people. Ordinary people. He would not want anything to do with making war."

"Few people do," Dulcain replied. "I cannot hold that against him. But suppose war was inevitable and he could help to make it shorter instead of being a long and drawn out conflict? Would not the lives spared in such an instance be an argument to sway him?"

Reese shook his head. "I cannot believe Terrell would be a party to anything that involved the taking of life."

"You are sure of this?"

"Dead sure," said Reese, "no pun intended."

"Suppose we did not ask him to do anything that would involve killing?" Dulcain said. "Might he consider a request for aid in such a light?"

Reese frowned. "How could he aid a war effort without being involved in the taking of life?"

"There are ways," Dulcain replied. "In any case, since he comes so highly recommended, and since you both know him, I think he should be approached. And if he cannot, or will not help us, then perhaps he can direct us to some adept who can."

"You want us to go to Lofton, then?" Reese asked.

"No, I cannot spare either of you for such a journey. I shall go to the duke's wizard and ask him to contact Terrell. He is old and too weak to undertake assisting us on a campaign, but wizards have ways of contacting one another, much like Gannd here spoke to his uncle just now, and that is something I am sure he can manage. I shall put my case to Terrell through him. But I would like you both to be there when I do, to effect an introduction and provide a reference."

Reese looked uncomfortable. "Magic always makes me nervous," he said. "If the duke's wizard is old and weak, as you say, what happens if he errs in his spellcasting and instead of contacting Terrell, conjures up some entity he cannot control?"

"I don't know," Dulcain replied flatly. "We shall simply have to see, won't we?"

"That is not what I would call an encouraging response," said Reese wryly. "Relying on the questionable skills of a wizard who is well past his prime strikes me as being rather unsafe."

Dulcain raised his eyebrows. "If you desire safety and security, my friend, you chose the wrong profession."

"I've had that thought a time or two myself," said Reese.

"So then what made you choose the rather precarious life of a mercenary?"

"Oh, just some foolish boyhood notions about growing up to be a hero like a man named Bran the Blade. Silly, wasn't it?"

"Quite," Dulcain replied. "Come on, Duncan, don't be afraid. I'll hold your hand. And if any nasty entities materialize, we shall simply tell them to mind their manners, for they are in the presence of the dreaded Reese the Reiver."

"Say, I like the sound of that," said Reese.

Dulcain sighed and rolled his eyes. "You would."

chapter four

She knew it was coming even before Derwyn told her. The army was going on the march. Derwyn had been neglecting her for a long time, coming to her chambers only once every so often, especially if he was frustrated with something or simply felt the need to talk. But one night, he came to her full of the nervous energy of anticipation and made love to her with a passion he had not demonstrated since the beginning of their relationship. It was, however, a distanced passion, self-contained and exclusive. He did not make love to her quite so much as he simply took her. He was not brutal or forceful, he never was, but he was focused purely and intensely on the act itself, rather than on her, as if he were using her as a vessel for his lust and nothing more. And after he had spent himself, which had not taken long, he quickly went to sleep, wanting to be cradled in her arms. He didn't want to talk at all. And when the same performance was repeated the very next night, she knew. He had set a date, and as it was approaching, he was driven by the need to vent his anxiety over the coming campaign.

Before long, the impending departure of the army had affected everyone and everything at Seaharrow and the town of Seasedge, where there was a palpable air of tense anticipation. Wagonloads of provisions kept arriving at the camp, which seemed to vibrate with activity. Blacksmiths, farriers, and armorers were kept busy round the clock, shoeing horses and repairing weapons, putting new edges on blades, replacing damaged plate or relinking chain mail. Leather workers refurbished saddle tack and relined helms, repaired leather tunics and breeches, fashioned new shield straps and rewrapped dozens upon dozens of sword and axe hilts. There was a new intensity about the drills, a sense of nervous excitement among the troops. They were going to war.

Soon they would find out if all the work they had been doing over the recent months would pay off. Would Avanil's army be more prepared? Would they be stronger? Or would they fall like chaff before the mighty blades of the army of Boeruine? Each night, as the day of departure approached, the campfires burned late into the night as soldiers sat around together, drinking and dicing and discussing their immediate future. Those who had families in town or in nearby villages took time to say their good-byes and make sure certain arrangements had been made—inasmuch as it was possible to prepare for such things—for what would happen in the event that they did not return.

Aerin's demeanor had undergone a subtle change as well. With the imminent departure of the army, he had grown more and more withdrawn, especially in his father's presence. Although, except for mealtimes—and when Derwyn came to her at night—Katrina rarely even saw the archduke anymore. He had become totally preoccupied with preparing for the war, and when he was in their company, it was as if she and Aerin weren't even there.

Derwyn had taken to inviting his knight commanders to dine with them, and while the meal progressed, he discussed the preparations for the march with his men, ignoring Katrina and Aerin completely. The little games they had played with one another under the table had stopped as well. Aerin was very careful not even to meet her gaze except in the most casual way, and only briefly. Katrina might have wondered what was going on behind those dark, hooded eyes of his, but she soon discovered that she had known exactly what he was thinking all along.

When she first realized it, she was so taken aback that it required great effort to keep her attention fixed on her meal and go on as if nothing out of the ordinary had occurred, when indeed, something quite extraordinary had happened. The realization did not come all at once. It dawned on her in a subtle way, during the course of the meal. Derwyn was sitting at one end of the table, flanked by his knights, discussing battle strategy and supply problems, and other final preparations for the march. He was oblivious to their presence as Katrina and Aerin sat across from each other at the other end of the long table.

As they ate quietly, barely looking at each other, Katrina was aware of the forced calm that Aerin was maintaining. She had grown to know him so well by now that most of the time she could tell, more or less, what he was thinking. Whatever it is he's planned, she thought, it's coming. He's trying to maintain his composure, overdoing it a bit, so as not to reveal the eagerness with which he's looking forward to the army's departure. That's when it will happen, on the march, or perhaps during the impending battle with Avan. He wants to be careful not to give the slightest sign that there might be anything between us, she thought. And he wants to make certain neither his father nor I suspect that he is planning anything. She smiled to herself and thought, how obvious he is! It was as if she could actually read his mind. And it suddenly dawned on her that she *could*.

She froze, startled as the realization struck her that she was actually reading his thoughts. It took a moment or two for her to regain her composure, but no one noticed. Derwyn was busy talking with his knights, and Aerin kept his gaze upon his meal, as if locked in his own sullen little world, so no one saw the shocked expression on her face. No one noticed that she had suddenly become completely motionless, sitting as if electrified. Her hands were trembling slightly, and she put them flat upon the table for a moment and took several deep breaths, trying to steady her nerves.

She could read his mind.

Aerin was wondering about a man named Alain—if he would have the courage to go through with it, and if Alain could pull it off. So this Alain was the assassin! Katrina did not know him. The name meant nothing to her. She would have to find out who he was from Angharad. But then an instant later, Katrina had her answer. Aerin was thinking that Alain would do anything in order to regain his spurs, and even more to attain a viscount's coronet. His entire future depended on carrying out the task. If Alain failed, he would have nothing. And he knew it.

So Alain was a knight who had been broken, thought Katrina. But why? And she found that by focusing her attention, by simply calming down and concentrating, she could pick the information right out of Aerin's mind. Alain had been sent to spy on Avan. That was why she didn't know him. He had not been present at Seaharrow during her stay. He had been sending regular reports to Derwyn through clandestine channels on Kier of Avan's preparations for war and, in one of them, he had mentioned that the duke had hired a famous mercenary known as Bran the Blade to command his regiment of free companions. Derwyn had sent word back that this mercenary was to be assassinated before he could report to Avan to assume his duties. Alain had failed. And for his failure, Derwyn summoned him back, and broke him.

Aerin, spying on his father from a secret passageway, had witnessed the event and decided that Alain would be his man. He had sent for the fallen knight and bluntly made the offer. Kill Derwyn and be reinstated, then advanced in rank to viscount. It was a bold approach, but Aerin had been confident of his position. Already in disgrace, Alain would scarcely be believed if he reported Aerin's offer. All Aerin had to do was deny that he had ever made it. And Derwyn, who was convinced that Aerin was a reclusive and studious nonentity, devoted only to his scholarship, would never believe that his own son would plan to murder him. If Alain had tried to betray Aerin, it would be perceived as spite and the knight would succeed only in utterly destroying himself. Whereas, if Alain accepted the mission and completed it, he would not only win back his spurs when Aerin succeeded to the title, but he would gain a title of his own, and the lands that would go with it. Alain, bitterly resentful that he had been broken for something that he felt was no fault of his own, especially since he had risked everything to spy for Derwyn, had needed little prodding. He would march with the army against Avan as a man-at-arms, a disgraced and broken knight. . . . But if he succeeded, he would return a titled noble. Given such incentive, thought Katrina, Alain would be strongly motivated to carry out his mission. Even more so since it would also give him the satisfaction of revenge.

Katrina had to give Aerin his due; it was a bold plan, perfectly arranged, with virtually no risk to Aerin himself. Even if Alain failed to kill Derwyn, that failure would almost certainly mean his death. And if he survived and told the truth, no one would believe him. Everyone would simply assume that he was motivated purely by a desire for revenge, and any attempt on his part to involve Aerin would be seen as mere desperation.

Katrina drank more wine as she contemplated what she'd just learned. And how. There could be only one explanation—the mysterious woman and her odd staff. She was a sorceress. There could be no question of it. Her staff had imbued Katrina with power from the first time she'd touched it. Suddenly, she had gained an understanding of the ebb and flow of power in the world and realized how to take the best advantage of opportunities to tap into it. And now, having felt the power of the staff a second time, she had somehow gained the ability of clairsentience. She could read thoughts at will.

As she sat there, she experimented with her newly discovered power. She focused her attention on Derwyn, concentrated, and suddenly she could read his thoughts as clearly as if he were speaking them out loud. They were not, however, organized as clearly as his speech. They were a jumble, one fragment leading to another, jumping around, giving clear evidence of his anxiety. He was trying to cover every possible contingency, going over everything in his mind even as he spoke and issued orders, trying to determine if there was anything he might have overlooked. He was concerned about the route of the march and what the weather would be like, if it would match the predictions of his soothsayers or if it would prove suddenly uncooperative, unleashing a torrent of unexpected rain that would mire the army in a sea of mud and bring the entire campaign to a soggy halt. He was worried about the problems of supplying his army on the march, concerned if they had planned for enough wagons, if they had taken adequate precautions to protect the line of supply and make sure that neither Avan's forces nor brigands could interfere with it. He was recalling the most recent reports of his other spies, trying to determine how quickly Avan would be made aware of their advance and how soon he would be able to respond. . . .

She blinked and turned her focus away from Derwyn. Trying to follow the torrent of concerns flooding through his mind was giving her a headache. Small wonder he was so overwrought. She turned her attention, instead, to some of the knights around him, focusing first on one, then another, picking up many of the same impressions. . . . They were thinking they'd gone over most of this before, time and time again, and that Derwyn, like an old woman, was worrying everything to death. Most of them were resentful at having their few spare hours taken up with these tiresome and endless conferences. The campaign had not even started yet, and Derwyn was already losing their confidence.

She shifted her attention back to Aerin and suddenly became aware that his thoughts were now on her. And what lurid thoughts they were. While her focus had been elsewhere, his thoughts had drifted from his planned murder of his father to what he would accomplish when he took his place. And his first accomplishment, it seemed, had nothing to do with any political act that he would undertake as Archduke of Boeruine. It had to do with her.

As he sat across from her, outwardly not paying her any mind at all, his thoughts were in a steaming turmoil as he imagined getting her inside his secret room. . . . She quickly turned her focus away from him, mentally recoiling from the perverse and frightening images his fervid mind was conjuring up, one after another. In that brief flash of insight, she had seen more of his secret room than she ever wanted to see. And more of his secret heart than she ever wanted to know. And yet . . . she knew that she would have to give herself to him if his plans came to fruition. Or were they really *her* plans?

Feeling suddenly overwhelmed, she drained her wine goblet and excused herself, pleading faintness. Derwyn gave her only a perfunctory acknowledgment before going back to his conference with his knights. Feeling shaky, Katrina made her way back to her chambers.

Once inside, she shut the door and bolted it, leaning back against it for a moment and breathing deeply, trying to compose herself. Then she remembered Aerin's little peephole and quickly moved to cover it. She wasn't going to be playing to any of his lurid little fantasies tonight. She had previously found the hidden entrance to her room from the secret passage and had the servants block it with a heavy wooden armoire under the pretence that she wanted to rearrange the furniture. She sat on the bed and leaned back against the headboard, putting her feet up, and clutched a pillow to her chest. Things seemed to be happening too fast. She wondered just what she had gotten herself into.

At first, when she had realized what Aerin was planning, she had felt a strange thrill at the thought that he was willing to murder his own father for her. It was a father he had always hated, but it had taken his desire for her to make him embark upon his deadly plan. Now that it was all in place, and she knew for certain that it had been set in motion, the thought of it all frightened her.

What kind of woman am I, she thought, who goads a man to murder? And the victim, his own father, no less? Could I truly be so cold and calculating, so heartless, so devoid of conscience? No, she thought, if she were empty of conscience, she would not be thinking these thoughts, or feeling these feelings. Was it contact with Aerin's mind that had brought it all on? Were her self-doubts only motivated by her fear and revulsion over what he planned to do with her—to her—when he could claim her for his own?

Ever since she had met that sorceress, her life had undergone a transformation. It was not really her own. She had felt, at first, a sense of power, of destiny, a feeling that she was taking control of her own fate, which others sought to determine for her. But had she, really?

Her own mother had spurned her for what she had become. It made her angry that her mother didn't understand, but at the same time, it hurt. What else was she to do? It was a man's world and men had all the power. Derwyn had used that power to demolish the life that she had planned. He had not done so with her purposely in mind, of course; she was merely a victim of the larger scheme of things, again, plotted and determined by powerful men. Men like Derwyn, to whom she was nothing more than a possession. To whom all women were nothing more than possessions. Why then, once she understood the rules of power, should she not use those rules . . . and a man's lust for power . . . to regain what they had taken from her, and be paid back with interest? Why should she feel even a twinge of conscience on Derwyn's behalf? He had killed her father and her brothers and the brave knight to whom she had been betrothed, then made her his whore. Why should she feel any guilt or responsibility for what would happen to him?

And as for Aerin . . .

He was an immoral plunderer of women, seducing and degrading, then discarding them when his appetite grew jaded. She was not the one who had made him hate his father. Derwyn had done that himself. She had merely exploited that hate in an attempt to follow the path of power, the only path that was open to her as a woman. It was not a state of things she had created. She had not engendered Aerin's lust for her. She had merely tried to take advantage of it, accepting the inevitable and trying to turn it to her benefit as best she could . . . the only way she could. It was the flow of power, the tide of which she did not control. She could only swim with it, for to try to swim against it would be to drown.

And yet, it frightened her. The feeling she experienced when the power of that staff flowed through her was revitalizing and intoxicating, irresistible. . . . Yet at the same time, it had changed her.

What have I become? she wondered as she hugged the pillow to her chest.

There was no turning back now. Events had been set in motion. She could not change them even if she wanted to. I was not the one who did all this, she told herself. They have done it all themselves. And they have done it *to* themselves. All I am doing, she thought, is trying to survive. Trying to go with the flow.

But to what end?

She lay there, watching the light reflections of the flames in the fireplace dance upon the wall. As she stared at the flickering interplay of light and shadow, she seemed to see the lines of battle marching in them. She could see how it would go, as clearly as if it were a vision. She felt distressed, but there was also a strange sense of clarity. This was how the power had been meant to flow. Derwyn would march against Kier of Avan. And sometime during the march, or more likely during the battle, Aerin's assassin would slay him. In the midst of a melee, there was an excellent chance that—if Alain timed it properly—no one would even notice who had dealt the killing stroke. Aerin would become Archduke of Boeruine and take her for himself, for his own twisted and demented pleasures. She would become his duchess, both because her humble past would render her pliable to her new husband and because that was how Aerin always managed things. Kill my father for me and I will give you back your spurs and raise you to the rank of viscount. Tit for tat. Cater to my erotic desires and I will lift you from your whoredom and make you a duchess, so that none will ever dare to breathe a whisper about what you once were.

Fair enough, Aerin, thought Katrina grimly. And for the pleasure I shall give you, and the degradation I shall be forced to suffer, you shall give me a son who will ensure my future . . . when you die.

* * * * *

At one time, Kristoph had been one of the most powerful and celebrated adepts in the empire. He had graduated with honors from the College of Sorcerers in the imperial capital of Anuire and had served with distinction on its faculty for twenty years until he had been offered the very lucrative and prestigious position of wizard to the ducal court of Lord Kendrew of Avan, Kier's father. He served the old duke faithfully until the end of Kendrew's life, and then he served Kier. Now Kier was approaching the twilight of his years, and Kristoph was still the wizard of the ducal court of Avan. No one seemed to know for sure how old the wizard was, not even Lord Kier. For that matter, no one seemed to know very much about Kristoph at all, at least in terms of recent times.

His sorcerer's sanctum was located in the north tower of the castle, and he was never known to leave it. His old bones were, apparently, too frail to enable him to negotiate the long and winding stairs. Like an old tomcat that did not want to move from its long-accustomed place, he didn't want to leave the tower, so the duke's servants took all his meals to him, as well as whatever supplies he might require. If Lord Kier wished to confer with his wizard, he had to climb the tower stairs to visit him, and Kier had done this less and less frequently over the years, preferring instead to send word to Kristoph through his servants. As a result, with the exception of those servants who attended Kristoph, no one had seen the old wizard in years.

The servant who conducted them up the dusty stairs lit their way with a torch. It was evening outside, and there was still some daylight, but inside the tower stairwell it was dark except for the intermittent, feeble shafts of light admitted by the narrow embrasures.

"Doesn't anyone sweep these damned stairs anymore?" Dulcain said, sneezing from the dust.

"Oh, we give 'em a sweep every month or so, milord," the servant replied as he led the way, his voice echoing slightly in the stone stairwell.

"Every month or so, eh? It looks as if no one's been through here in a year or more. The dust is at least two inches deep on these steps."

"Well . . . surely it can't have been that long," said the servant, a bit awkwardly.

"Liar. No one's been through here in Haelyn only knows how long. We're liable to get up there and find nothing but his moldering bones."

"Oh, no, milord. He takes his meals every day."

"Is that so? How does he get them? I see no sign of any footprints in the dust except our own."

"Well, we've arranged a rope and pulley lift on the outside of the tower, milord. It's so much easier than climbing up there every day, y'see. And ole Kristoph doesn't seem to mind. That is to say, he ain't never complained. Truth is, he'd just as soon not be bothered by us comin' in. He always resented it whenever servants would go in to clean, or so I'm told, so we just stopped, like."

"You're telling me you *winch* his meals up to him every day? And deliver his supplies in the same manner? Without anyone actually going up there?"

"Oh, aye, milord. It makes things so much easier."

"So then . . . how long has it been since you've seen him?"

"Oh . . . I've never seen 'im, milord."

"Never?" Reese said.

"No, milord."

"And how long have you been here?" asked Dulcain.

The servant paused to calculate. "Oh . . . twenty years or more, I'd say, milord."

The three of them exchanged startled glances. They'd been under the impression that at least some of the servants saw the wizard regularly.

"You mean no one has seen Kristoph in over twenty years?" said Reese with disbelief.

"Oh, I'm sure somebody must've seen 'im, milord," said the servant, though he did not sound sure at all.

"And when the duke sends messages to him, you winch those up as well?" Dulcain said.

"Well . . . it beats climbin' all the way up these bleedin' stairs, don't it . . . milord?"

Dulcain could only shake his head.

"Incredible. He hasn't seen a single soul in twenty or more years," said Reese. He moistened his lips nervously. "The old bastard must've gone soft in the head from all the isolation. If he isn't dead, we're liable to find him up there babbling to himself and drooling on the floor. You know, I'm not so sure this whole thing was a good idea. . . ."

"Reese . . ." said Dulcain.

"All right, all right, I'm coming along, aren't I?"

"Just come along quietly."

"Twenty years without seeing anyone . . ." Reese mumbled under his breath, lagging behind a bit so as not to annoy Dulcain.

"Some Sidhelien sages go much longer without seeing other people," Gannd said.

"It's not the same with humans," said Reese. "Elves are immortal. And as we age, our wits grow addled. There are human hermits, true, but the longer they stay isolated, the crazier they become. I don't relish the thought of confronting a sorcerer who is not in full possession of his faculties. That could be highly dangerous."

Dulcain, walking slightly ahead of them with the servant, had reached the landing at the top of the stairs. A moment later, Gannd and Reese caught up with him. The arched door to the sorcerer's sanctum was made of thick and heavy wood. The bronze fastenings were green with verdigris, and cobwebs hung thick in the stone archway. It was obvious that no one had opened the door in years.

"It's not normal, staying cooped up in a place like this so long," said Reese uneasily.

"Clear away those cobwebs," said Dulcain.

The servant complied, and Dulcain knocked on the door. There was no response. He knocked again, more loudly.

"He does know we're coming, does he not?" he asked the servant.

"I believe he does, milord. We sent word up to 'im earlier this afternoon."

"And how did he respond?"

The servant merely shrugged.

"Maybe he doesn't want to see us," Reese said. "We might as well just go."

"We're not going," said Dulcain firmly. He pounded on the door. There was a metallic scraping sound—the bolt within turning and then being drawn back—then the door slowly opened with a long, protesting groan. Reese shivered visibly. The door seemed to have opened of its own accord.

"Well, I'll just wait for you out here, milord, so as to give you privacy, like, in your meetin'," whispered the servant.

"Maybe I should just wait with him," said Reese. "To make sure he doesn't leave and take the torch."

"Oh, I wouldn't do that, milord," the servant said in an affronted tone.

"Come on, Reese," said Dulcain. "Stop being such an old woman."

Reese made a low, growling sound deep in his throat and grimaced, then followed them inside.

The tower room was dimly lit by candlelight and the last, fading remnants of daylight coming in through the narrow windows, one of which had a small wood scaffolding built into it for the little platform the servants used to winch things up. The cool evening breeze that wafted in kept the room from smelling too musty, but there were other odors, some of which Gannd easily identified as herbs and powders his uncle had used, and there were other smells that he did not recognize. Unlike the ordered clutter of Terrell's emporium, Kristoph's sanctum was a nightmare of sloppy disarray. Things were piled up everywhere they looked. The wooden shelving overflowed with books, scrolls, and various bric-a-brac such as little metal boxes that resembled the small cases ladies used for their jewelry, candles melted into stands, tiny ceramic pots, and small glass beakers filled with mysterious powders or dried . . . something. Loose parchment was scattered everywhere, as were human skulls gone brown with age, bundles of herbs hanging from the ceiling beams, wicker baskets filled with human and animal bones, a heavy wooden desk piled high with books and littered with spilled powders, a large crystal ball in an ornate gold stand, blackened iron braziers, brass censers gone green with corrosion, iron caldrons of various sizes, small logs piled in the corner by the fireplace, ritual daggers, and wands . . . It was a dizzying profusion of paraphernalia scattered helter-skelter all over the place.

Against one wall, Gannd saw a small wooden bedframe with ancient, dirty bedding, and a chamber pot shoved underneath. And piled atop the bedding was a peculiar assortment of motley rags that suddenly moved and Gannd realized they weren't rags at all, but the sorcerer himself. Kristoph sat up laboriously and gave vent to a wheezing, rheumy cough. He sounded like a bear cub waking from a long hibernation.

He looked like a human hayrick. His white hair, what there was of it, was scraggly and stuck out in all directions like wisps of smoke escaping from his head. His beard hung down below his waist, and he ran his gnarled, skeletal, liver-spotted hands through it as he sat up. His sorcerer's robes were a motley agglomeration of varicolored patches used to mend rips and tears, so many of them that it was impossible to tell what color the robe had originally been. He resembled a patchwork quilt sewn by a blind man.

He was the oldest man Gannd had ever seen. The wizard's skin resembled worn-out leather and even his wrinkles had wrinkles. He had a huge, hooked nose that looked like the blade of a small hatchet sticking out from his face, and his eyes were like little coals, deeply sunken in their sockets. The lower part of his face was almost completely invisible behind his beard, which resembled trailing moss.

"That's the famous Kristoph?" Reese said in a low voice.

"Being famous does not necessarily involve being attractive," the old wizard replied in a voice as wispy as the hair on his head. "And being old does not necessarily involve being deaf."

"Sorry," Reese said awkwardly. "I meant no offense."

The wizard merely grunted and said nothing. He remained seated on the bed, his feet on the floor, his head hanging down as he stared fixedly at the flagstones. The moments stretched uncomfortably.

"Kristoph?" said Dulcain.

The wizard looked up at them with surprise, as if he had forgotten they were there. "Hmmpf?"

"Did you receive our message?"

"I received a message," he replied. "However, considering the intelligence of those subliterate dolts down there, it could have had something or nothing to do with whatever it is you want."

"We would like you to contact another adept for us," said Dulcain.

"Mmm. When?"

"Well . . . now would be nice."

"Ah." The wizard fell silent and stared at the floor again. He remained motionless.

"Will you?" said Dulcain, after a moment.

"Will I what?"

Dulcain glanced at Gannd and Reese. The latter rolled his eyes and sighed. "Contact an adept for us."

"When?"

"Now?"

"Ah."

Silence. The three exchanged glances. Were they going to have to go through it all a third time?

"Who?"

Dulcain looked relieved. "Terrell of Lofton."

Silence once again.

"Terrell of Lofton," Dulcain repeated. "Can you contact him for us?"

"Terrell . . ."

"Of Lofton," Dulcain finished for him.

"I heard you the first time, young man."

Dulcain raised his eyebrows at the idea of anyone calling him a young man. But then, Gannd thought, to Kristoph, Dulcain was young. Silence fell again.

"So . . . will you do it?" said Dulcain.

"Hmmphf? Do what?"

Dulcain cleared his throat and tried again. "Will you contact Terrell of Lofton for us?"

"Terrell . . .'

"Of Lofton, yes."

"You said that."

"Well . . . would you please contact him for us?"

"Certainly. Who is he?"

Reese shook his head with resignation. Dulcain took a deep breath. "He is an adept. In Lofton."

"Ah." Kristoph returned to his contemplation of the floor. Dulcain shut his eyes in silent suffering.

"An adept, you say?"

"Yes, that's right."

"Never heard of him."

"He's young," said Reese. "Only been around some sixty years or so. A mere whippersnapper."

Kristoph looked up at him and met his gaze. Reese suddenly looked uneasy.

"What is your name?" asked Kristoph.

"Duncan Reese."

"Mmm. Someday, Duncan Reese, you too shall be old. But not if you don't learn respect for your elders."

Reese looked away and scratched his head in embarrassment.

The old wizard glanced at Gannd, as if noticing him for the first time. "You are kin to Aurealis."

"Yes, Grandfather, I am," Gannd replied, addressing him with the affectionate honorific elves used for their male elders, whether related by blood or not. "He is my uncle. How did you know?"

"I am the famous Kristoph," the old wizard replied, looking straight at Reese. "And I have not yet lost all of my faculties."

Reese looked down at his feet.

"How fares your uncle?"

"Well, Grandfather."

"Mmm. It is good."

"It was he who recommended that we contact Terrell to aid us with the war effort," said Dulcain.

"Another war? What is it this time?"

"A dispute over the succession."

"The emperor is dead?"

"Uh . . . yes. He died some years ago," Dulcain replied.

"Hmmpf. Nobody tells me anything." The old wizard sighed and scratched himself. "I really should keep up more with current events."

"Well . . . can you help us?" asked Dulcain.

"Do what?"

Dulcain silently counted to ten. "To contact Terrell of Lofton, an adept."

"Ah." Kristoph shifted a bit, as if his bones were aching. "Oh . . . I suppose. . . ."

The old wizard stretched out his hand and a wooden staff standing propped up against the wall flew across the room to his waiting fingers as if someone had tossed it to him. He leaned on it for support, rose slowly to his feet, and hobbled to his desk. He stood looking down at the desktop for a moment, as if searching for something. After a while he said, "What was I looking for?"

Reese moved to stand behind Dulcain and put a hand up to cover his face.

"Something to do with a contact spell, perhaps?" Dulcain replied, trying to be helpful.

"Contact?"

"Yes."

"Who?"

"Terrell. Of Lofton. An adept. You never heard of him. It's about the war. Over succession. Because the emperor is dead."

Kristoph glanced at him with irritation. "I know all that. I was informed. I'm not completely out of touch, you know."

"Oh, we're in a lot of trouble," Reese moaned under his breath.

"Ah, here it is." Kristoph brushed aside some clutter on his desk and held up a goose quill. He squinted at it as he brought it close to his feeble eyes. "Now what did I want this for?"

"To, uh, write something, perhaps?" Dulcain said, trying hard to maintain an even tone.

"Mmm. Yes, you want a contact spell. I remember now. I'm not completely addlepated, you know."

"No, just mostly," Reese whispered under his breath.

"Now then, whom did you wish to . . . contact?"

Dulcain sighed and shut his eyes. "Terrell. Of Lofton. An adept."

"Mmm. Never heard of him."

Reese stifled a snort.

"I shall need something . . ." said the wizard, staring down at his desk.

"A goose quill, by any chance?" Dulcain said.

Kristoph glanced at him. "Yes. Are you an adept, young man?"

"No, actually, I'm not."

"Then how did you know about the goose quill?"

Dulcain cleared his throat. "You're holding it in your right hand."

Kristoph frowned, then stared at the goose quill in his grasp. "Ah. Thank you. I was looking for this."

Reese stepped behind Gannd, leaned on the half-elf's shoulder, put his head down, and made a small whimpering sound.

The old wizard moved over to the center of the room, using his staff to support himself. He took tiny little steps, not really lifting his feet so much as shuffling them. He poked with his staff at the clutter piled up on the floor.

"Is there anything we can do to help, Grandfather?" said Gannd.

"There should be a magic circle drawn on the floor around here somewhere," Kristoph replied, as he continued to poke around.

They all got down on their hands and knees and started pushing aside the books and scrolls and other miscellaneous debris piled up everywhere.

"I think I found it," Dulcain said after a few moments.

"Found what?"

"The circle you're looking for."

"Magic circle," said Gannd.

"Ah. Yes, there should be one around here somewhere. . . ."

"Right here, Grandfather."

"Oh! You found it. Good for you. You're a good lad. Here, have a cookie . . ."

A vanilla macaroon appeared in Gannd's hand.

"Thank you, Grandfather."

"Now then, what can I do for you, lads?"

"I don't know how much longer I can take this." Reese murmured softly.

They patiently went through the entire procedure once again. But at least they were making progress, Gannd thought. Each time, they got one or two steps farther. However, Gannd was beginning to have serious reservations about the spellcasting. Reese certainly had a point. Any wizard who was so absentminded was liable to conjure up just about anything.

They cleared a space on the floor, exposing the magic circle that was drawn on the flagstones with chalk. The lines were very faint, in some places, barely visible. Reese suggested that perhaps it should be redrawn.

"Oh . . . I think not," Kristoph said. "It should be sufficient to the task."

"But with the lines being so faint, will the circle be strong enough to provide adequate containment?"

Kristoph frowned. "For what?"

Reese looked uncomfortable. "For, uh, anything that might happen to appear," he said.

"You mean this Terrell person?"

"Uh . . . well . . . anything."

Kristoph simply stared at him.

"I mean, you never know. . . ."

Kristoph continued to stare at him with a cold gaze.

"Accidents happen," Reese finished lamely.

"Are you implying that I do not know what I am doing?" Kristoph said.

"Well, no . . . that is, I . . ."

"He is merely nervous, Grandfather," Gannd said, coming to his friend's rescue. "Magic frightens him a little."

Kristoph merely grunted. Leaning on his staff, he shuffled over to the circle and stood in the exact center of it. The magic circle was made up of intersecting chalk lines describing a sigil upon the floor, each point touching an edge of the circle that circumscribed it. Both within and without the circle, arcane sigils were drawn upon the floor, but they were now so faint that most of them were barely legible and some had worn off almost completely. Reese glanced at them dubiously.

"I don't know about this," he murmured very quietly.

Kristoph gave him a look of irritation. "If you do not trust me to do it, then do the bloody thing yourself," he grumbled. And with that, he reached out and placed the goose quill in midair, as if he were simply laying it down upon a table. As he released it, the goose quill remained where it was, floating in midair about five feet above the floor, in the exact center of the magic circle.

Kristoph mumbled some sort of spell, of which Gannd caught only a word or two, and then he made a couple of passes at the goose quill, finishing up with a grunt and a dismissive wave at the quill before turning and shuffling back to his bed.

Dulcain, Reese, and Gannd exchanged puzzled glances. "Well . . . now what?" said Dulcain.

"Summon up whatever-his-name-is," groused the wizard as he made his way over to the bed and laboriously lowered himself onto it. "Haelyn's beard, you expect me to do everything for you?"

Dulcain blinked. "But . . . we don't know what to do."

Kristoph sighed as he lay back on the bed. "Write his name," he said.

"How, Grandfather?"

Kristoph gave vent to a long, drawn-out groan. "Use your mind, lad. Concentrate on the quill and visualize him in your mind. Don't they teach you youngsters anything these days?"

"You mean, all we have to do is think of him and he'll appear?" said Reese.

A moment later, the quill began to write invisible letters in the air, as if guided by an unseen hand. A strange mist rose in smoky tendrils from the cracks between the flagstones and roiled about within the confines of the chalk circle, sparking with bright discharges like tiny fireworks going off inside the blue and violet cloud. The outline of a figure started to appear within the mist and, a moment later, it resolved itself into the form of Terrell.

"Who summons me?" He stepped forward out of the mist, encountered some invisible resistance from the magic circle, backed off a step, grimaced, then swept it aside with a casual motion of his hand and stepped out of the circle. He frowned. "Reese?"

"Greetings, Terrell," said Reese.

"You didn't do this, surely. I don't even recognize the spell. Is this a *gate*? Are we on another plane?" Terrell glanced around the room, puzzled. "Who . . . ?"

"It was I who summoned you," Dulcain said. "That is, with the aid of Kristoph, the wizard to the ducal court of Avan."

"Kristoph? Is he still alive?"

"Yes, and trying to get some sleep, damn it," came the grouchy reply from the bed.

"I beg your pardon," said Terrell. He turned back to Dulcain.

"Terrell, allow me to present Sir Bran Dulcain, lord commander of the army of Avanil," said Reese. "And also my good friend."

"And mine," said Gannd.

Terrell nodded. "Sound recommendations," he said to Dulcain. "What can I do for you, milord? I trust it is an important matter, for me to be summoned in such a manner."

"It is," Dulcain replied. "The army of Avanil is going to be at war. Our spies report that Lord Derwyn of Boeruine is preparing to march against us. We are in need of help. You were very highly recommended by Gannd's uncle, Gylvain Aurealis."

"I am extremely flattered," said Terrell. "That is quite a compliment, indeed. However, with all due respect, I regret to say I must decline."

"Would you mind telling me why?" Dulcain asked.

"Because I do not condone the taking of life. I sympathize with your situation, but I cannot help you."

"There is more to this than the matter of our defending ourselves," Dulcain said. "The fate of the empire is at stake here. If Derwyn of Boeruine succeeds in making good his claim on the Iron Throne, it will be by force, and he will have to rule in the same manner. He will not be able to compel the allegiance of all of the nobility. There will be civil war."

"Perhaps all that is true," Terrell replied, "but it still changes nothing. I have made a vow that I shall never use my Art to kill. Only to heal."

"Suppose you were not asked to kill?" Dulcain said.

"And instead, what? Maim? Injure? Strike down with disease?"

"None of those things. Suppose that what I asked of you did not involve your injuring a single soul in any way? Suppose I asked you only to defend us from the spells of any mages that our enemy may employ? If you were to do this for us, would you not still be remaining true to your vow? Not killing or injuring, but protecting."

Terrell stared at him for a moment, thoughtfully. "I would use my art only to defend your troops against any harmful spells, and nothing more?"

"That is all I ask. And you shall have my word on it. My written surety, if you wish. In addition to a payment of fifty thousand gold pieces. You could do quite a bit of good with such a sum. You could help a lot of people."

Terrell glanced at Reese and Gannd. "Is he a man of his word?"

"He is," Reese replied without hesitation.

Gannd nodded. "I know him to be a man of honor."

"In that case, no written surety will be required," said Terrell. "You speak for Kier of Avan, as well?"

"I have his authority," said Dulcain. "And I shall make it very clear to him that if he should ask you to do any more than what we have agreed upon, our contract shall at that moment be considered null and void, and you shall still be entitled to the full sum we agreed upon."

Terrell pursed his lips thoughtfully, considering for a moment. "Give me your hand on it," he said, at last.

They shook.

"Done," said Terrell. "I shall require decent quarters for myself and for my daughter. She is blind, and I could not leave her behind in Lofton."

"It shall be done," Dulcain promised.

"Very well," said Terrell, stepping back into the circle. "Dismiss me, then. But first, give me a token of yourself."

"What sort of token?"

"An object you wear, a lock of hair, anything that bears an essence of yourself."

Dulcain removed a gold bracelet from his wrist. "Will this do?"

"It will suffice to let me find you. Be in the quarters you have set aside for us tomorrow at this time, and we shall come to you. Now let me go. I must prepare."

"Kristoph!" said Dulcain.

"Hmmmpf?" The old wizard bestirred himself. "What? What is it?"

"Terrell wishes to be dismissed."

"Who?"

"Terrell. Of Lofton. The adept. You summoned him."

"I did? What for?"

"Just send him home, Kristoph. Please?"

"Oh. Oh, well, all right." The old wizard mumbled a few words, made a sort of **X** motion with his fingers, waved both hands dismissively and slumped back onto the bed. The mist rose to envelop Terrell and, in a moment, he was gone.

"Thank you, Kristoph," said Dulcain.

"Hmmpf? What? What is it now?"

"Never mind. Good night."

"Mmm. G'night."

The door closed on its own behind them. The servant was still waiting with the torch, sitting on the steps. He scampered up as they came out. "Everything all right then, milord?"

"Everything's fine," Dulcain said. He turned to Reese and Gannd. "I hope your friend Terrell is trustworthy."

"Of course he is," said Reese. "Why? You think he would renege on his agreement after he gave his word?"

"I am less concerned by that than I am about giving Terrell that bracelet," said Dulcain. "As a gesture of my trust, I have just placed myself completely in his power. Until I get it back, he shall be able to conjure me at his pleasure."

"Terrell would never do that," Reese assured him.

"I earnestly hope not. You had better be very sure of your friend."

"I am. I'd stake my life on it," said Reese.

Dulcain merely looked at him. "You already have."

chapter five

The entire city of Seasedge turned out to watch the army leave on their glorious campaign. The troops formed up on the drill fields just outside the encampment. Early in the morning, the camp had quickly stirred itself into a bustle of activity as teams of horses were hitched up to the wagons and the drivers made last-minute checks to make sure everything was loaded up properly and all the tack was adjusted and in good working order. Then, while the troops packed up their gear, the wagons formed up on the far end of the drill fields, facing the road leading into town.

By the time the sun had risen in the sky, the area around the fields had taken on a festival atmosphere. Peddlers with their carts had come out to serve food and drinks to the onlookers, and people had spread rough woolen blankets on the ground and disposed themselves for picnic lunches. Jugglers, mimes, and bards entertained the audience, passing their hats among the crowd, and children with toy wooden swords and inverted buckets on their heads with holes cut in them for visors staged mock battles as the army formed up for the march.

By noon, the entire army was assembled and prepared to leave. A trumpet fanfare sounded on the field, echoed by another fanfare in the distance, from the heights on which Seaharrow stood. The castle gates were opened, and Derwyn came riding out at the head of the procession of his knight commanders, all in full armor and plumed helmets, carrying their shields and lances with the multicolored, swallowtail pennants fluttering in the breeze. They made an impressive sight as they wound their way on horseback, followed by their squires, down the serpentine road that led from the summit of the rock on which the castle stood down to the fields below. The sunlight gleamed off their polished armor, and the crowd held its collective breath as it watched the knights approach.

Those among the crowd who were old enough to recall the old campaigns—when Derwyn's father had made his unsuccessful bid for the Iron Throne against the youthful Emperor Michael, whom he had denounced as a pretender—remembered how Lord Arwyn would always ride down from the castle with his knights to the accompaniment of drummers who preceded the formation, marching in perfect unison to the low and dramatic beat of *Tum . . . tum . . . tum . . . ta-tum . . . tum . . . tum . . . tum . . . ta-tum . . .*

No such theatrics for Derwyn. He and his knights rode down from the castle in silence, the only sounds were the hoofbeats of their mounts and the jingling of their tack as they approached.

In the past, when Arwyn reached the field, he had his knights fan out behind him in a line; then he approached the troops while the drummers kept up their steady, measured beat. Then, as Arwyn signaled by raising his right hand, the drums would all fall silent as one, and Arwyn would sit astride his mount, staring out at the troops in silence. That silence would stretch for long, anxious moments until the archduke finally started to address them. He would greet the knights and compliment them on their turnout, then state the reasons for the campaign on which they were departing. Gradually, he would build up the momentum of his speech, using his voice like a masterful musician, whipping the troops into a frenzy of excitement. When he finished, the men would erupt into cheers that would reverberate across the fields and meadows, a mighty chorus of "Huzzahs!" that could be heard all the way to the far end of the city. And then Arwyn would draw his blade and hold it aloft, give the command as he brought it down—pointing with it toward their objective—and the drummers would once more start their beat as the army marched off to war. It was always quite a show.

Derwyn, on the other hand, lacked his father's flair for the dramatic. As he rode down to the fields, no drummers played a martial beat. As he approached the troops, his knights remained behind him in a column of twos. And as he rode along the front ranks of his troops, looking them over, he did not pause before them to deliver an oration. He merely took his place at the head of the troops and waited, his mount pawing nervously at the ground, until his knight commanders rode out to their troops, made sure everyone was ready, and then once more formed up behind him. The whole thing was done methodically, without any pomp or ceremony, lending an air of grim anticipation to the entire proceedings. The drummers and the trumpeters were all formed up together at the extreme edge of the field, waiting for their lord to give the word. And when he gave it, he merely raised his arm and brought it down and forward.

The trumpeters gave out a fanfare, and the drummers launched into a steady marching beat as they swung out in formation at the head of the army and moved off down the road to town. Derwyn gave them about a twenty yard head start, then moved off at a walk to follow, with his knights behind him. The crowd broke out into cheers as the army moved off across the field and swung out onto the road, regiment by regiment, the foot soldiers marching in columns of fours.

As Katrina watched from atop the castle walls, the massed body of men resembled a serpent slowly uncoiling and writhing off across the field, down the road to Seasedge. The crowd followed along with them, moving on the army's flanks until they reached the city. The main road through Seasedge was lined on both sides with spectators who had turned out to watch the march. These were their fathers and their brothers and their sons, their uncles and their grandfathers, their cousins and their nephews and their friends, their husbands and their lovers, marching off to war. And whether they met with victory or defeat, many would not return.

Derwyn would be among those who did not come back. Katrina knew it with the certainty of inevitable fate. As she watched him ride across the field at the head of his columns of troops, turn down the road, and disappear into the distance, she knew she would never see him alive again. Somewhere out there, in the darkness of a night encampment, on the march, or in the pitched, chaotic frenzy of battle, an assassin's blade would strike, and the archduke would fall. And as he fell, so would her fate . . . straight into Aerin's waiting hands.

But she would become the mistress of that fate. She would follow the ebb and flow of power, recognize her opportunities and take advantage of them. She would survive.

Aerin had come out to watch his father lead the army off to battle. As Katrina stood atop the castle wall, she glanced over her shoulder and spotted him standing on the balcony outside his chambers, watching. For a moment, it seemed, their eyes met, but at that distance she could not be sure. She turned back to watch the procession once again, and when she looked back, Aerin was gone.

She wondered how he felt right now. She was not close enough to read his thoughts, but she could well imagine that he might be feeling some sense of relief that things were finally under way. But it would not be complete relief. Not yet. Not until word had reached the castle that the archduke was dead. Then, and only then, would Aerin's sense of tense anticipation be abated.

She wondered what it was like to hate your own father so much you wanted to see him dead. Not only wanted to see him dead, but were willing and even eager to hasten his demise. She had loved her father, admired and looked up to him. He was not a very important man, but to her, when she was a little girl, he seemed like a god. All that was so very long ago now it was almost as if it had been another life, as if it had all happened to someone else. That all began to change the first time she had gone with him to the duke's castle. That was when she experienced the rude shock of realizing her father's true place in the scheme of things. That was when she received her first real glimpse of true power.

As she watched the army moving off into the distance and the sound of the drums beating out their cadence grew faint, Katrina began to hear another sound—in her imagination—one that slowly rose in volume until it drowned out all else. Gone were the sounds of the drums beating and feet tramping, wagon wheels creaking, tack jingling, teamsters swearing, people cheering. Everything was overwhelmed by the sound of the incessant buzzing of flies.

It all came back to her again . . . the sight of all those broken, torn, and bloody bodies littering the field. Sword hilts jutting up from corpses, pennants fluttering lazily from lances stuck at crazy angles into the ground, riderless horses wandering aimlessly across the battlefield, gingerly stepping over corpses as they searched for a bare patch of grass to nibble on, buzzards wheeling overhead in ever-descending spirals until they stooped upon their grisly meals . . . and the flies. The horrid, endless buzzing of the flies. Katrina turned away. She didn't want to think about it anymore. So many would die before too long, and all for just one man's ambition, one man who, even in late middle age, was still trying desperately to measure up to his long-dead father. No, she could not feel sorry for Derwyn. His arrogance and insecurities were leading many of those men to their deaths. His ambition knew no pity for their wives or children, just as he'd had no pity for her when he found her wandering the battlefield. He merely took her as his due, a prize of war. A prize willing to be taken, but out of desperation, not desire. It was a man's world. So how was it so few of them were truly men?

She descended the steps leading down from the wall and made her way across the courtyard to the castle. A castle which seemed very empty now, for all that it was still populated with servants and ministers, guards and footmen, all still watching from the walls as the army marched away. She felt tired. All she wanted now was to return to her chambers and sit by the fire to banish the dampness of the late afternoon and evening, just sit there on the fur rug with her shoes off and drink wine and watch the flames dance on the hearth until night fell and it was time to go to sleep.

She entered her chambers and shut the door behind her, bolting it so that she wouldn't be disturbed. Her gaze immediately went to the fireplace. Yes, the servants had lit the fire; enough logs were piled up to burn all through the evening and into the night. A decanter of wine and a goblet had been placed on a small table by the fireside, the way she liked it. She sighed and removed her slippers, then her clothing, and went to her bed, where the servants always laid out her robe . . . and froze as she saw Aerin lying there beneath the canopy, fully dressed, his booted feet stretched out and casually crossed at the ankles. He smiled slightly as he gazed at her. She hadn't even noticed him there when she came in.

"Very nice," he said. "It's almost as if you read my mind."

She could read it now and she did not like the thoughts she saw there.

"What are you doing here?" she said, trying to muster up some forceful indignation. "Get out."

He raised his eyebrows. "What are you going to do, call for my father? I don't really think he can hear you just now."

She stood there, naked, not covering up, not willing to give him the satisfaction of seeing her cowering before him. If she ran, perhaps there was a chance that she could reach the door before he could, but then what would she do, run naked out into the corridor, screaming for help? There would be no help forthcoming. Perhaps she could run, but she wouldn't. That was what he wanted. She could see it in his mind.

"So," she said deliberately, "I see your ardor has been bolstered and your courage spurred by your father's absence. But what will you do when he returns?"

Derwyn wasn't going to return. She knew that. But she wanted to make Aerin admit that he knew it too. He wanted to. He almost did. It was right on the very tip of his tongue. She could see him thinking it. He won't be coming back, he thought. He won't ever be coming back. He is as good as dead already. And I'm the one who killed him. For you, Katrina. All for you.

But he would not say it. It doesn't matter, she thought, I know. I know you, Aerin. I know you for what you are. For the moment, the power flows to you. But only for the moment.

"The question is, what will *you* do when he returns?" said Aerin. "Will you tell him?"

"What do you think?"

"I think not," Aerin replied. "You have toyed with me long enough. The time for games is past. At least, the sort of games you have been playing. I am going to teach you a few new ones. And I think you will find them fascinating."

She saw what he was thinking and her gaze involuntarily went to the armoire which she had used to block the secret passage. Only now she saw it had been moved.

He got up from the bed in one smooth motion and took her by the wrist. "Come," he said. "I have something to show you."

"Let go of me."

She tried to pull away, but he yanked her to him sharply and she stumbled against his chest. She felt his arms go around her as he brought his face to hers and kissed her hard, his tongue forcing its way between her lips as she gasped, his hands running down her sides. She pushed herself away from him and slapped him hard across the face. The stinging blow he returned to her came so quickly it caught her completely by surprise. It rocked her and she fell, stunned, bleeding from her lip where his ring had cut her. He reached down and jerked her to her feet, pulling her to the secret panel.

He pressed a hidden stud and the panel opened with just the softest scraping sound, barely audible, and he pulled her into the darkness beyond. The panel closed behind them, and she felt the goosebumps on her flesh from the damp chill behind the walls. The stone floor felt cold beneath her bare feet as he pulled her along through the darkness. She knew where they were going.

It was pointless to resist. He was stronger and the power was his now. For it to flow back to her, there would be a price to pay. With a numbness, she resigned herself to paying it.

He pulled her through the dark and narrow corridors that ran behind the castle walls, around corners and down several flights of stone steps until she lost all sense of direction. He was on familiar ground. This was where he often lurked, like a lizard in the darkness under a rock, and she was like an insect he had snared and pulled into his lair. She trotted along behind him as he pulled her, moving quickly in his impatience. Another flight of steps descended, then another, and another, until finally they came to a short corridor that ended with a heavy wooden door. He pulled it open and the well-oiled hinges did not protest. He pulled her inside and closed the door behind them.

She felt cold. The light from several torches set in iron sconces cast their shadows on the damp stone walls. Katrina closed her eyes tightly at the sight of the evil devices placed carefully around the floor.

"I call this my game room," Aerin said. He pulled her over to the two wooden supports and manacled one wrist, then seized the other. "I think you will find this a stimulating, new experience."

In seconds she was helpless. Scarcely able to move. He stood back and she could hear him speaking from behind her, his voice echoing through the room.

"Now, isn't that a pretty sight?" he said.

She felt his fingers trail softly down her spine, and she shuddered.

He came around to stand in front of her.

"Now we have time to play," he said, loosening his belt. "We have all night, and there won't be any interruptions. And we don't even have to worry about keeping quiet. We can make as much noise as we like and no one shall hear us. No one."

She shut her eyes. I will get through this, she thought. Somehow, I will get through this. And I shall not forget. Not ever.

Throughout the long, long night, she thought morning would never come.

* * * * *

The spies they'd sent to Seasedge had all sent word that the army of Boeruine was on the move. Lord Kier knew it was coming, though he had not known exactly when. Derwyn had kept the departure date a closely guarded secret, known only to himself and a few of his most trusted knight commanders. Nevertheless, an army could not get on the march without significant preparation, so Kier knew when the final preparations had started to get under way and issued orders that his own army was to be kept in a state of constant readiness. Dulcain did not disappoint him.

Gannd saw the dramatic changes Dulcain had brought about in the duke of Avan's army. The morale of the troops had improved significantly, and the constant drills and unrelenting discipline had sharpened their skills to a fine edge. Dulcain knew how to handle soldiers. He managed to hold himself just enough above the knights that they never lost the sense that he was their lord commander, but he always made it a point to be among them every day, taking time to speak with them, and to crack the whip when need be. Still, he would always take the time to discuss their personal lives as well. In this way, they came to feel that he cared about them, was one of them, and though he was their commander, they all marched to-gether, bound by a common enterprise, and their loyalty to Kier of Avan.

With the troops, Dulcain took a slightly different approach. Though a bit more deliberate and theatrical, it was quite effective. He would assemble a group of knights for a mounted tour of the encampment and send a rider on ahead to gallop through and alert the men that he was coming. "Here comes the Lord Commander, boys! Three cheers for Bran the Blade!" And as the men would cheer, Dulcain would come thundering up at the head of the small procession, waving to the men and calling out to them, every now and then pausing to rein in and speak with some of them in a friendly and encouraging manner.

"How goes it, boys? You ready to teach Derwyn and his troops a lesson they won't soon forget?"

And he would grin at their response and call out, "That's the spirit! I'll be with you, right there in the thick of it. Together, we'll send those blackguards running with their tails between their legs! We'll give 'em what for, won't we?"

And as the troops shouted their assent, Dulcain would grin and wave and tell them he was proud of them, then set spurs and ride off at a gallop with his knights behind him. The men felt privileged that he'd taken the time to stop and speak with them while en route upon some important errand when, in fact, they were the sole pur-pose for the exercise. Dulcain kept them on their toes, rarely allow-ing idle moments, but he had personally seen to it that they received good food, that the camp was kept immaculate, and sanitation was improved. He made certain they lacked for nothing, and in a short time, he won their respect and admiration to the point that they all simply idolized him. They were being led by Bran the Blade, the greatest fighter the empire had ever known, and he had forged them into a fighting force the likes of which had not been seen since the Emperor Michael led the mighty army of Anuire.

Gannd, on the other hand, did not have such an easy time of it. Dulcain had made Reese commander of the mercenary regiment and Reese, in turn, had made Gannd his lieutenant. From the very start, the half-elf questioned the decision, but while Reese had un-derstood his reservations, he insisted that he needed someone he could trust, and that the best way for Gannd to win acceptance with the free companions was to be highly visible and prove himself their equal.

"With that lot, there's only one way you're going to do it," Reese had said. "They're going to put you to the test. They'll push you to see how far you can be pushed. They'll probably pick one man to do it, and he'll be the toughest among them. He'll pick his time and try to take you down a peg or two. And it'll be when I'm not around. When he comes at you with his challenge, you'll have to meet him on his terms. They'll make sure of that. They will be right there, watching to find out what you're made of. You'll have to show them. Do it right the first time, and there will be no second."

"But how far must I go?" asked Gannd.

"As far as necessary," Reese replied. "You will have to be the judge of that. Whatever happens, I'll back you up. But whatever you do, and however you do it, make sure it is *decisive.*"

It had not taken long. Gannd made it easy for them. In part because he wanted to get it over with, and in part because he wasn't going to change simply to suit the circumstances. He was who he was, and the fear of leaving himself vulnerable could not be allowed to overcome his basic needs.

Each night, ever since he'd left the Aelvinnwode, he took time to make a small ritual of prayer. While traveling with Reese he had waited until the mercenary was asleep, so as not to disturb him or have himself be bothered with any explanations. Not that he thought Reese would take exception to it. But his prayer was a private thing, and he liked to be alone to do it. In the encampment, that was difficult. There were always people about, there was always something going on, and there were always distractions. But a mile or so beyond the camp, in the field outside the perimeter guarded by the pickets, there was a patch of woods. It was little more than a thick stand of trees, like a small island of forest in the sea of meadow grass.

It posed no great difficulty for him to sneak past the pickets late at night and make his way out to the stand of trees. Most humans were not really aware of just how quickly, and how silently, elves could move. He would slip past the guards and, blending with the darkness, run out to the trees where he would kneel on the ground in a small clearing under overhanging branches and say his prayers to the Lady. But one night, as he was finishing his prayers, he heard the soft snapping of a dry twig underfoot and realized he had been followed. He stood and turned in the direction of the sound, waiting, already knowing who it would be.

"Well, look who we have here," the mercenary said, stepping out into the small clearing from the trees. He was not alone. There were about a dozen others with him, including a couple of the guards Gannd had slipped past. The man who'd spoken was a burly mercenary by the name of Xandor, a veteran of many hard-fought campaigns. He claimed to have served with the Skirmishers, an elite outrider patrol that guarded the narrow strip of land in the province of Elinie between the swamps that marked the border with—and the only land route from—the wilds of Coeranys. Six feet tall and massively built, with shoulder-length blond hair and a full beard, Xandor was easily the most physically intimidating of the free companions recruited into the service of the Duke of Avan.

"It looks like we've caught ourselves a spy," said Xandor to the others as they encircled Gannd. "A breed spy."

"I am not a spy," said Gannd. "I was merely praying."

"Most people go to the temple to pray," said Xandor.

Gannd indicated their surroundings. "This is my temple."

"Oh, that's right, I forgot. You're a heathen elf. And elves don't pray to the gods. They pray to some mythical woman of the forest. The lady goddess who protected them so well she allowed them to be driven from their lands to live in the woods like the animals they are."

Gannd simply stood there, saying nothing.

"What's the matter, Breed? Do you have so little regard for your goddess that you will not defend her from an insult?"

"You do not insult the Lady," Gannd replied. "You only insult yourself, by revealing your ignorance and stupidity."

"Well now, those are what I call fighting words," said Xandor, drawing his sword. "I would not take that from any man, much less half a man."

"I do not wish to fight," said Gannd. "But if you are determined to prove yourself superior to me, I will meet you at your pleasure on the practice field."

"You'll meet me at my pleasure now," Xandor replied, "and with steel, not wooden swords. They say the blood of elves is green. I think I'd like to spill some to find out."

"My blood is as red as yours. But you shall have to take my word for it."

"The word of a breed elf?" Xandor sneered with contempt. "I'd rather find out for myself." The mercenary raised his sword and it seemed to come alive as he slashed at the air in a fast series of flourishing strokes. "I'm going to wear your ears for a necklace. Draw your blade, Breed. "

"I ask you one last time to put up yours," said Gannd in an even tone.

"I'm through talking," Xandor said, and came at him.

Before he had taken two steps, two daggers suddenly sprouted from each of the big mercenary's shoulders, high in the chest, just below the collarbone on each side. Gannd had drawn them from the cross belts beneath his cloak and thrown them so quickly the others barely saw him move. Xandor cried out, as much with surprise as pain, and dropped his sword, his arms going across his chest reflexively as his hands moved to the daggers buried in his flesh. He doubled over and went down to his knees.

"Anyone else?" said Gannd.

The others exchanged glances, but remained silent.

"Get back to the camp," said Gannd. "Now. Leave Xandor to me."

"Now wait a moment . . ." one of the others said, uneasily, clearly not anxious to leave his friend behind in a vulnerable position.

"I said *now*," repeated Gannd. "And I shall not say it again."

The men departed slowly, with nervous backward glances, but they did as they were told. Left alone with Xandor, Gannd crouched beside the wounded mercenary. Xandor was kneeling, bent over, clutching at the dagger hilts protruding from his shoulders as if he meant to pull them out—which his instincts told him to do—but he didn't. Regardless of his instincts, his intellect told him that if he did pull them out, he might bleed to death in moments.

"Lie back," Gannd told him. "Get down on the ground."

He helped the mercenary down. "Go on then," Xandor gasped. "Cut my throat and finish it. But make it quick."

"Close your eyes," said Gannd.

The mercenary continued to stare up at him for a moment, then squeezed his eyes shut in anticipation of the killing stroke. Gannd concentrated, then carefully grasped the hilts of both daggers and abruptly pulled them out. The mercenary gasped as the blood started to flow. Gannd dropped the daggers and pressed his hands gently against the deep wounds. Xandor felt a strange warmth passing through the half-elf's hands, a warmth that gradually grew into a searing heat that cauterized the wounds and made the blood stop flowing. He felt, to his amazement, the damaged blood vessels and muscles start to knit as the heat continued to flow through him. Moments later the wounds themselves had closed, leaving behind no indication—save for the blood staining the mercenary's chest—that there had ever been any injuries at all.

Gannd removed his hands and sat back on his heels, breathing laboriously, sweat beaded on his brow. The mercenary stared at him in disbelief.

"You healed me! By Haelyn's beard, you're blooded!"

"That is the part of me that is only half a man," said Gannd, with a faint smile.

"You could have killed me just now."

"Yes."

"Why didn't you?"

"Because it would have proved nothing except that I could kill you. And because Duncan Reese has need of good fighters in his regiment."

"But I was going to kill you."

"I know."

The mercenary shook his head. "I don't understand."

"The truth may be perceived in many ways," said Gannd. "One way you can look upon it is that you now owe your life to a hated breed. To an inferior creature who is neither elf nor man, but something in between, something to be despised. And that which you despise has saved you.

"Or, you can choose to look upon it as your having made a mistake in judgment, and then learned from it. I leave you to choose which interpretation you prefer."

The half-elf got up and started walking back to the camp, leaving Xandor sitting on the ground behind him, staring at his back.

The mercenary did not return to camp that night, but came back shortly after dawn, much to the surprise of his comrades. They saw him approaching as they formed up for morning drill. He came straight up to Gannd and stood before the half-elf as Reese stood back and watched.

"I prefer to think that I'm a man who learns from his mistakes," said Xandor. And he held out his hand.

Gannd reached out and shook it. "Form up with the others," he said.

Xandor gave Gannd the mercenary salute, thumping the left side of his chest with his right fist. The significance of the gesture was not lost on any of the others. The man took his place in the formation. Reese glanced at Gannd, smiled faintly, and nodded. After that, there was only one time that anyone referred to Gannd as "Breed." It was one of the farriers, a coarse and surly mountain of a man with arms like tree trunks and a chest like a cask of wine.

The mercenaries beat him senseless.

Now Gannd was one of them. And every man-at-arms in the entire army knew that if anyone showed any prejudice, disdain, or bigotry toward a half-elf by the name of Gannd, they would have the entire mercenary regiment to answer to. It made for a formidable deterrent. Like Dulcain, Gannd had found a way to make the men accept him.

Gannd thought back to the stories his mother used tell him of her days in the emperor's campaigns, when she and his father had fallen in love. In a way, it was as if things had come full circle. This was the part of his heritage he had come to discover. Perhaps some would think it strange, he thought, the idea of looking forward to a war, but it was more than just a path that he had chosen for himself before he was even old enough to understand the choice. He had been raised and trained in the way of the warrior, and now he was going to find out what all that training would amount to. However, that was only a part of what he wanted to discover, and try to understand.

He knew that what his mother had gone through when she left the Aelvinnwode on the orders of Prince Fhileraene to represent the interests of Tuarhievel in the emperor's campaigns had been the defining experience of her life. And it had been responsible for his. The campaigns had drawn his mother and his father closer, despite their cultural differences, and the times she spent in battle had provided her with emotional experiences so intense that she would vividly recall them for the rest of her life. And elves could live forever. When she spoke about those days, her voice and manner changed, as if she were reliving them, and it was clear that even years after the fact, those memories had a profound effect. Gannd wanted to know what that was like.

In battle, his mother told him, men—and those few women who fight alongside them—often discover who they really are, what they're made of. "There is no time in a pitched battle," she had said, with a distant look in her eyes, "for the lies we tell ourselves. It is the most primal of experiences, direct confrontation with the question of survival. And for a Sidhelien, with mortality. We, unlike the humans, often take for granted that we shall live forever, but a Sidhelien can be killed. We are immortal, but not invulnerable. Of course, I always understood that with my intellect, but in battle, I came to understand it here." She tapped her chest. "I could feel that understanding grow as the pressure in my chest grew. But I could not think about it, for in battle, you have very little time to think. You can only act. And how you act can tell you more about yourself than you could discover in any other way.

"In the midst of battle, I have seen men who had spent their lives training to be soldiers, and who believed, deep down in their bones, that they were good, brave soldiers, suddenly discover fear. A fear so overwhelming that it defied all reason as it seized them in its unrelenting grip. And I have seen men who did not define themselves as soldiers—common men who worked at trades or farmed the land, who suddenly found themselves caught up in a battle—discover courage they never dreamed they could possess.

"For those who felt the fear," she had continued, "those who had survived, their lives would never be the same. For the remainder of their days, they would have to live with what they had learned about themselves. Some would never fight again. They could lie to others, but never to themselves, because they had discovered who they really were. Others who'd shared the same experience would ever after seek to replicate it in the hope that they could somehow overcome that fear and be what they thought they were. They would become slaves to their fear. In their quest to overcome it, they would live with it each day, and always be subject to its ravages—fearing it—afraid of being afraid. Sometimes, the fortunate ones could find a way to overcome it. But it was always at great cost."

"And what about those who did not fear?" he'd asked her. "The ones who discovered they had courage?"

His mother had smiled. "They were the ones who discovered the true meaning of courage. It is often thought that the brave man has no fear. But that is merely foolishness, sung by bards who know nothing of battle. The brave man makes the most interesting discovery of all. He learns that courage is the ability to act despite your fear. A man who truly fears nothing is not brave, but stupid. A brave man acknowledges his fear, and does what must be done in spite of it. Or, perhaps, because of it."

"I would not like to be so afraid," Gannd had said.

"No one would. But fear is not the worst thing you can feel. The worst thing you can feel is fear *of* fear. Because then you will always be afraid."

As Gannd stood out on the drill field with the mercenary regiment, he recalled his mother's words and tried to take a careful inventory of how he truly felt. He was not afraid. At least, not yet. He had confronted the question of survival before, and his response had been to fight, not flee, but he had never been in battle before. Would it make a difference? He tried, as honestly as he knew how, to ask himself if he was afraid of being afraid. He did not think so. He knew there was no shame in fear. It was how he would react to it that mattered. And that was something he had yet to learn.

The regiments had all formed up on the field, prepared to march. Armor gleamed in the early morning sunlight. Pennants fluttered in the breeze. Horses, sensing the anxiety in the air, snorted nervously, and pawed at the ground impatiently. Everything and everyone was as prepared as it was possible for them to be. They stood and waited in tense anticipation. A crowd of onlookers had gathered from the city to stand at the edges of the field. When the fanfare sounded, soldier and spectator alike fell silent . . . except the little children. Because they knew no better, they continued playing at their games, attacking one another with little wooden swords, crying out, and clutching at their chests, "dying" very heroically. The children had no way of understanding the irony of their staging such a spectacle before the men they emulated, men who watched them somberly and thought their own private thoughts.

The sound of rapidly approaching hoofbeats signaled the arrival of the duke and his retinue of knights. Lord Kier came thundering up to the head of the procession, mounted on a snow-white charger. He was in full armor, his crest emblazoned on his tabard, and flowing red plumes fluttering from his helm. Behind him rode his squire, carrying the duke's lance and shield, and beside the squire rode his standard-bearer, the ducal chamberlain, carrying the battle standard of the House of Avan, a double dragon rampant on a field of scarlet. And behind him rode Dulcain, the lord commander, newly invested as Baron of Daulton and for the first time wearing his new device upon his tabard, a broadsword on a field of azure. The other knight vassals and commanders rode behind Dulcain in a column of twos. The army raised a spontaneous cheer as the knights passed, then reigned in at the center of the field, facing the troops. As their cheers continued, Kier rode out before them and raised his gauntleted hand for silence.

"Men of Avanil!" he called out to them as his horse pranced skittishly. "Today we embark together on a noble enterprise! Derwyn of Boeruine has set his sights upon the Iron Throne and once more takes the field against us. We, who hold the regent's right inviolate, who believe in government by law and not by sword, who uphold the honorable principles upon which our mighty empire was founded, have sworn to defend it, and the throne, against all would-be usurpers!"

The old man's voice rang out powerfully across the field, belying his age. He sat erect and proud in the saddle as he addressed them. There was utter silence as he paused. Even the children had stopped playing their games to hang upon his every word.

"We met the army of Boeruine in battle once before," continued Kier. "Many of you were with us on that day when we fought them to a standstill and sent them back to lick their wounds. But Derwyn's ambition knows no bounds, so now it is up to us to stop him, once and for all! As we stand here this day, the spirit of our noble Emperor Michael stands beside us, urging us on to victory! We have the might, and right is on our side! By the grace of Haelyn, we shall prevail, and the enemy shall be destroyed! And in the days to come, the bards shall sing of our victory, and you shall tell your children, and your grandchildren, that you were here and took a part when the empire of Anuire was saved from tyranny! Raise your blades for Avan! And for victory!"

The army raised their blades and gave three mighty cheers while the onlookers joined in, the children raising their toy wooden swords in imitation of the soldiers. Kier gave the signal and the drummers launched into their march. As the populace cheered them wildly the regiments swung, one by one, out across the field in the wake of Kier of Avan and his knights, heading out on the road west, toward the Seamist Mountains and the plains of Avanil spreading out before them, where they would meet the army of Boeruine.

As he rode side by side with Reese at the head of the mercenary regiment, Gannd wondered what his friend was thinking. This was his first command. They had come a long way from their meeting in the highlands of Mhoried. Reese had been intent on coming south to join the army of Avan in the hopes of taking advantage of the opportunities a war could offer. In that regard, he had already come further than he had expected. Reese had hoped merely to enlist in the mercenary regiment and now, through a chance meeting with Dulcain, he was commanding it.

And what must Dulcain be thinking, having journeyed to Avanil to accept a post as commander of the mercenary regiment, on what would probably be his last campaign, only to find himself elevated to knighthood, then barony, and in command of the entire army? Nominally, of course, Lord Kier was in command, but despite his stirring speech before the troops, the duke was tired. He was still very fit for a man of his years, but the strain of his position had left its mark on him, as was obvious to anyone who spent any time around him.

Kier of Avan did not want this war. Nor did he want the Iron Throne. But if he succeeded in his goal of stopping Derwyn, the throne would probably fall to him by default. He and Derwyn were the most likely candidates for the succession. One man wanted it, and would do anything to get it. The other did not desire the throne, but would accept the crown if it was offered. Not for his own sake, but to preserve the empire.

The question was, could it be preserved? The unity that had

existed under the line of the Roeles was no more. By the time Michael had ascended to the throne, the empire was already disintegrating. Michael Roele had been forced to fight for what was his by right, and throughout most of his reign, he had waged one campaign after another to keep the empire together. For a while, it had looked as if the Empire of Anuire would once again return to the glory days of old. But then, in the most foolish decision of his life, Michael had waged war upon the Gorgon, taking the battle to the dreaded awnshegh's own ground. There, Michael Roele fell to the Gorgon's blade. And the empire fell with him.

It did not happen overnight. For a long time, Gannd knew, his father had managed to hold things together as regent. But each year, as the regent grew older and the empire became less and less stable, the task must have grown increasingly difficult. When a ruler died without leaving an heir, and a regent could only be a regent, merely holding the throne in custody for a rightfully chosen successor and unable to ascend to it himself, the field became wide open to ambitious aspirants like Derwyn. And Derwyn was not the only one.

The empire of old was gone. What there was of it hung by a thread. The provinces had split into conflicting factions. Knight made war on viscount, viscount made war on baron, baron waged war on earl . . . all throughout Cerilia, the nobility jockeyed for position, intriguing, murdering, plotting, and campaigning, each trying to take advantage of another's weakness and attempting to seize as much power as he could. And those not strong enough to seize more power for themselves lent their support to whoever they believed stood the best chance of coming out ahead.

What this all meant for the Sidhelien, it was still impossible to tell. By and large, whatever happened, the elven kingdoms would remain well out of it. Their heavily forested domains were unsuitable ground for campaigning. The human armies would all pass them by. And while they were intent on battling one another, there would be little time or opportunity for them to pay much attention to the elves. And that, in turn, could lead to opportunities for the elven kingdoms to win back some of what they'd lost.

Sidhelien rulers like Prince Fhileraene realized and understood this and were patiently biding their time. And then there was the wild card, the outlaw Rhuobhe Manslayer and his renegade tribe of

Sidhelien who had never given up the *gheallie Sidhe*, the Hunt of the Elves which the humans had feared so when it was in full sway. The battle they were now en route to would take place within sight of Rhuobhe's borders, that thickly forested and mountainous southeastern section of the Aelvinnwode that abutted the boundaries of the human provinces of Avanil and Boeruine. The Manslayer would probably be able to watch the battle from the summit of one of the foothills in his domain, perhaps hoping the two human armies decimated one another so severely that he would be able to sweep down with his raiders and butcher the survivors, or at the very least kill all the stragglers and attack the supply lines.

And that, of course, raised another possibility. If this war was not decisive and neither Avan nor Boeruine emerged as the clear victor, or even if one of them did, but was weakened so severely by the outcome that he was left vulnerable to attack by one of the many alliances that were forming in the outer provinces, waiting for just such an opportunity, the result would mean civil war and the thread by which the empire hung would snap. And doubtless, that was exactly what the elven rulers were hoping for. Nor would they be the only ones.

Far to the north, beyond the borders of the empire, lay the grim mountain stronghold of the Gorgon, who commanded the allegiance of the traitorous Vos tribe, as well as goblins, gnolls, and renegade mercenaries so debased that they would fight against their own kind for the awnshegh. The Gorgon's army had been strong enough to turn back the Emperor Michael's army of Anuire, the mightiest force the empire had ever seen. And the Black Prince Raesene, seduced by the lure of bloodtheft and transformed by his corrupt enchantments into the immortal Gorgon, had lusted for the Iron Throne ever since the battle of Mount Deismaar. No doubt, he had his spies watching for the outcome. And if, when the provinces of the disintegrated empire had grown weak from battling one another, the Gorgon chose to sweep south with his army, there would be no stopping him. He would destroy everything in his path, human and elven domains alike. All those things hinged on the outcome of this war between Boeruine and Avanil. This would be the last chance for the empire to survive intact.

Gannd thought about his half-brother, Davan, whom he had

never met. The regent had remained conspicuous by his silence. He didn't dare openly support one side or the other. Gannd imagined that his half-brother's private sympathies most probably lay with Avan, who—if Kier emerged the victor—would interfere with the regent the least. If Lord Kier succeeded to the Iron Throne, he would likely be content to rule largely in name only, leaving the actual task of governing the empire in Davan's hands until his son, young Veladan Avan, was old enough to succeed him. And as Veladan was still a boy, the only male child in a household full of daughters, Davan's position would remain essentially secure for many years to come.

On the other hand, if Derwyn were to emerge victorious, he would then march upon the imperial capital of Anuire and force Davan to formally recognize him as the rightful ruler. Then, the moment he donned the emperor's crown, Derwyn would either select his own high chamberlain or else relegate Davan to a subservient position intended only to preserve some semblance of continuity with the line of the Roeles. Either way, Davan's role would be diminished to a point of insignificance. Nevertheless, Davan surely realized that if he made any gesture of support toward Avan, he would lose all hope of retaining his position if Derwyn were to win. And he would almost certainly face retribution.

Gannd tried to imagine what he might have done if he were in his half-brother's place. He found that he could not, because no matter how he looked at it, he could not perceive himself having allowed things to come to such a pass. Though he was still a relative newcomer to human society, Gannd had learned enough of imperial politics to know that the only logical course for the regent to have followed would have been to throw all of his support behind Kier of Avan and prevail upon the rulers of the other provinces to convene in a meeting of the imperial estates to confirm Avan as the emperor. Derwyn, of course, would have dissented, but if the regent could have mustered the majority support of the imperial estates, Derwyn of Boeruine would have been effectively neutralized. He would, perhaps, have been able to prevail upon the rulers of Brosengae, Taeghas, and Talinie to support him, as they had supported his father in the past, but then they would find themselves in conflict with the rest of the provinces that made up the imperial estates. Instead of facing Avan alone, Derwyn would have faced them all. And from what Gannd had heard, Arwyn may not have backed down from such united opposition, but Derwyn certainly lacked the mettle to confront it.

Instead, Davan had dithered, afraid to commit himself and make the wrong move. Perhaps he lacked confidence in his ability to muster significant support among the imperial estates, or maybe he had tried to do so unofficially, to test the waters, and had failed. Either way, he had sown the seeds for what he would now reap. If Derwyn won, Davan would either lose his post or be reduced to nothing more than a figurehead.

Gannd looked within himself for sympathy for his half-brother and could find none. In part, because he didn't know him and had never even met him, but also in part because Davan had brought all of this upon himself. And not only upon himself, but upon the entire empire as well. Had Davan acted differently, this war might have been averted. And a lot of lives might have already been saved.

"You're being very quiet," Reese said, as they rode together at the head of the mercenary column. "Thinking of the coming battle?"

"Strangely enough, no," said Gannd. "I was thinking of my brother."

"Davan? Why?"

"He could have stopped this."

For a few moments Reese did not reply. Finally he said, "Yes, I suppose he could have. But could have, would have, and should have don't count for much in the scheme of things, when all is said and done. What counts is what you do. Or don't do."

"It is probably just as well I've never met him," Gannd said. "Knowing what I know now, it would have been extremely difficult for me to justify what he has done. Or, more to the point, not done."

Reese grunted in assent.

"I was watching the crowd as we rode past," said Gannd.

Reese smiled. "Nothing like a cheering throng to give you a proper send-off on the way to battle."

"Not all of them were cheering. I saw many women looking on with somber faces. And not a few were weeping."

Reese's smile faded. "I did not notice."

"Truly?"

"Perhaps I did not care to notice. I prefer to listen to the cheers."

"I do not envy them. I think that it is easier to go off to war than to remain at home and wait, not knowing if your loved one will return."

For a few moments more, they rode in silence. The cheers of the crowd were far behind them now. As were the tears.

"I've had many women in my time," said Reese, after a while. He paused. "But I do not think I've ever had one weep for me."

For a short while longer, they rode on without speaking. Then Reese said, "Did you see Mariel?"

"No. When?"

"As we were riding past the castle."

"No. Was she there?"

Reese nodded. "She was standing on the battlements with several other women. Even at a distance, I could recognize her. She was the smallest one. And the only one not waving."

"I wonder why she came to watch," said Gannd. "I mean, how could she watch? She cannot see."

"But she can hear," said Reese. "I think if anyone will weep for me, if I fail to return, it will be Mariel."

Gannd glanced at him sharply. "Did she . . . tell you anything?"

Reese shook his head. "No. She would not see me. She refused."

"You think she had a vision?"

Reese shook his head again. "No, I do not think so. That is why she refused to see me. If she had, then she may have experienced a premonition. She did not want to know."

"Did you?"

Silence. Only the sound of marching feet, the steady clip-clop of hoofbeats, and the jingling of the tack.

"I don't know."

"But you tried to see her."

Reese nodded. "Because it may have been my last chance."

"You care for her a great deal."

"Yes. She is the little sister I never had. She and Terrell are like my family. My only family. Well . . . and you."

Gannd raised his eyebrows. "Me?"

Reese didn't look at him. "I never had a brother, either. I suppose you are the closest thing."

For a moment, Gannd said nothing. Then he turned to Reese and said, "Give me your hand."

Thinking Gannd was going to shake it, Reese complied. Instead, Gannd drew a dagger and sliced open the mercenary's calloused palm.

"Ow!" Reese jerked his hand back in surprise, staring at the blood. "What in Haelyn's name . . . ?"

Gannd sliced open his own palm, then reached out to Reese. "Take my hand."

Reese gazed at him uncertainly, then leaned over and took Gannd's bleeding hand in his own as their mounts rode side by side.

Gannd met his gaze and said, "Repeat these words . . . By seed and root, by bud and stem, by leaf and flower, by sun and moon, by life and love, by blood commingled, by Lady blessed, by name of kin."

Reese repeated the words, frowning faintly with puzzlement, then asked, "Have we just made an oath?"

"Of a sort," said Gannd, releasing his hand. "Now you have a brother."

Reese stared at him, then smiled. "Well, I'll be damned." He raised his bloody palm before him and gazed at it in silence.

"My mother, Sylvanna, is now your mother," Gannd said. "And my uncle, Gylvain, is now your uncle. You are Sidhelien now. And you have a family."

In a low voice, Reese repeated, "I'll be damned."

chapter six

The first time the two armies fought, Kier had received little advance warning, and Derwyn marched his troops almost all the way to Daulton before Kier was prepared to meet him. This time, spies sent word as soon as the army of Boeruine was on the move, and Kier had time to mobilize. As a result, Kier would pick the battleground. Derwyn had a greater distance to travel to reach Avanil than Kier did to reach his own border at the Seamist Mountains.

"We shall send parties of scouts on ahead to determine which of the mountain passes Derwyn will use," Dulcain said. He stood over a large map with Lord Kier and his commanders.

"Derwyn has only three options," Dulcain continued, "the northern, the southern, or the central pass. There are other small passes through the mountains here and there, but he can't march an army through them. His first option is to bring them through right here— at Nentril—near the border that we share with Rhuobhe. It would be his closest route, which he could reach either of two ways, by marching around the forest located at the eastern edge of his borders, south of the Aelvinnwode, or going through the forest itself.

"We know Boeruine has marked out trails through the forest, but we don't know exactly where they are. Still, it doesn't really matter. If he cuts through the forest he may save himself some distance, but he won't save any time. It would take longer to march an army through the forest than on open roads. Since he wouldn't be saving any time that way I believe he'll choose the open roads, heading south through Taeghas. Either way, he would reach the northern pass first and come through at Nentril.

"However, the northern pass is also the narrowest of the three. He can still march his columns through, but he would have no real room to maneuver. And there are two further disadvantages. It brings him perilously close to the territory controlled by the Manslayer, and there are several tribes of ogres that live up in the mountain heights. They might attack him as he comes through, or they may shy from taking on so large a force, but still, it is a risk.

"His second option would be the central pass, right here. He would march a little farther south and swing through Taeghas at the Gate of Brosengae. There is a large break in the mountains right here that leads into Brosengae, where he would turn northeast, following the border which runs straight through the pass, and come out at Vanilen. That's the way he came last time, if I understand correctly. It brings him within fifty miles of Daulton. And the central pass is also wider, and essentially a straight shot through. Strategically, it has much to recommend it.

"His third option is the southern pass, which brings him right up to the city gates, but it involves a considerably longer march by a more circuitous route. He would pass through the Gate of Brosengae, then continue south through Brosengae toward Bindier, where he'd come to the end of the Seamist Mountains and turn here, at the Arnienbae, keeping the mountains on his left flank until he reached the southern pass at Coere. It's the shortest pass, and also the widest, and it brings him out within only a few miles of the city. But it's by far the longest march.

"If it were me, that's how I would go. It would bring me within a bowshot of Daulton and easy striking distance of Anuire. And I would then be able to use ships to support my invasion of the capital. However, I do not believe that Derwyn has the patience for such a march, and our spies report that he has no ships. He has put all his resources into his land troops. So my bet is that he'll take the central route to Vanilen.

"We'll send out parties of scouts, together with mercenary out-riders, to find out for sure which way he's coming. One party will cover the pass at Nentril. If Derwyn does not do what I believe he will, and comes that way, we'll swing north for a few miles and meet him. The other scout party will go through the central pass and watch the Gate of Brosengae. If Derwyn comes through and turns their way, then I'm right, and he'll take the central pass. If he continues south, which I believe unlikely, then we'll know he's making for the southern pass and we can parallel his course on our side of the mountains, and meet him at Coere where he will have the mountains on his left flank and the Arnienbae on his right. The advantage of terrain and position will be ours.

"There remains one more possibility," Dulcain continued. "A re-ally bold commander might choose to split his forces, taking half the army through the northern pass at Nentril and half through the central, at Vanilen. It would be extremely risky, but if executed properly, and timed just right, it could give him the opportunity to catch us squarely in the middle, caught between the hammer and the anvil. However, unless it were timed with absolute perfection, such a strategy could easily turn against you, giving your opponent the chance to take on each half of your force one at a time, with su-perior odds. He'd destroy your army in detail. I think we can safely eliminate that possibility. From everything I know of Derwyn, he won't have the guts to try it. I'm not sure even I would. But by hav-ing scout parties cover both the northern and central passes, we can still guard against that eventuality, just in case Derwyn's got him-self a general who's a gambler.

"So there you have it. If it all goes the way I think it will, Derwyn will bring his entire army through the central pass. We'll take up our position here, just west of Vanilen, where we can cover the mouth of the pass. If we can get there before Derwyn—and we should be able to do so even if he's force-marching his troops—we can station archers in the rocks above the entrance to the pass and catch him as he's coming out. The pass is wide enough to allow for a full-scale battle, but if we can keep him bottled up inside it, he won't have much room to maneuver. It would be impossible for him to flank us. We should maintain our position at the mouth of the pass and make him try to force his way through. If he does break through our lines it will have to be at the center, and we'll have him flanked. If he fails, we keep him bottled up until he's weakened to the point that he's forced to retreat. And then we can pursue him through the pass, forcing him to fight a rear guard action and pressing him so hard that he'll have no time to deploy once he reaches the other side. At that point, our situations will be reversed, but he will have no time to take advantage of it. We should be able to force our way through and finish him off at the Gate of Brosengae."

Lord Kier nodded. "Excellent. You have justified my faith in you, Dulcain. You seem to have accounted for every possible eventuality."

"Well, no one can do that, milord. But I have done the best I can."

"This time, let's finish it," said Kier looking around at his commanders. "I do not know if I have it in me to go through this all again without having anything resolved. Inform the troops that I shall personally give ten thousand gold pieces and a laurel to whoever brings me the head of Derwyn of Boeruine."

* * * * *

"I am with child," said Katrina. "Your child."

Aerin raised his eyebrows. "Indeed? How can you be sure?"

"I can feel it. And I have had confirmation from the midwife."

"That old witch is never wrong," said Aerin. "What does she say it will be?"

"A boy."

Aerin smiled. "So . . . I shall have a son."

"Not the first, from what I've heard."

"No, but the first I shall openly acknowledge."

"Why? I could say it was your father's. No one would question it. Not even your father would suspect."

"My father will not be in a position to question anything before too long."

"What do you mean?"

"I mean that I am done with waiting for him to decide when I can start living my life," said Aerin smugly. "It begins now. I am taking you to wife, Katrina."

She had expected this, but had thought he would at least wait until his father's death had been announced, followed by a suitable period of mourning during which it could be made to appear that they had comforted one another and fallen in love. Perhaps some eyebrows would be raised that way, but not too many. Stranger things had happened. But to marry her now, with his father having gone to war, and before his death had even been announced. . . . Suddenly, she saw it all. She stared at him with abrupt realization, and he mistook her response, not knowing she already knew he had embarked upon his father's murder.

"What will my father say, you wonder, when he returns to find his mistress stolen—and impregnated—by his own son? There will be very little he can say, for you shall already be my wife, the marriage sworn and consecrated. Not to mention consummated, if somewhat prematurely. I shall have it announced this very day, so that when it becomes clear to everyone that you are carrying a child, there will be no doubt that it is mine and that it was conceived following the marriage. A small white lie, but I am anxious to preserve your reputation," he added with a smirk.

"So I see now," she replied. "You want to cuckold your father and publicly humiliate him; prove that you were man enough to father a child with me when he could not, never mind that he took special pains to prevent me from conceiving one."

And, she thought, in order to achieve the most impact from this move, Aerin would have to do it while his father was still alive . . . or at least believed to be alive. It would be a great show of open defiance, as if he risked his father's wrath and was unafraid when, in fact, he risked no such thing because he knew Derwyn would not be coming back. Everyone would assume that Aerin was defying his father openly, unafraid of Derwyn's response. Then, afterward, when Derwyn's tragic death on the battlefield was announced, Aerin would inherit the title, and the power that went with it, having already established himself by this silly little show as a man who was not afraid to take what he wanted.

"The announcement shall be made today, and the wedding shall take place the day after tomorrow in the temple. A bit hasty, perhaps, but then we are very much in love and our ardor will not be denied. We shall invite the populace to witness our great moment of joy and affirmation."

"Suppose I were to refuse."

"But you will not, Katrina. For you see, my father never would have married you and, sooner or later, you would have been discarded. And then what would you do? Especially now that you are carrying a child? No, Katrina, you are far too canny to throw your life away like that on some vague principle. You, my dear intended, are a survivor. And you shall not pass up the chance to become the Duchess of Boeruine, with all the powers and privileges that would attend your elevation to the high ranks of the nobility. And in your personal life, so long as you fulfill your role and satisfy my needs, you will be free to do whatever you desire. So long as you remain discreet. It is as much freedom, power, and prestige as a woman could ever hope to achieve. And you shall not refuse it."

"No."

"There, you see how well we understand each other? Now come, give me a kiss to celebrate our betrothal."

She went to him and he pulled her down onto his lap, kissing her deeply while his hands roamed greedily over her body. He was feeling very satisfied and pleased with himself, thinking that he would now have everything he ever wanted. Very soon now, he was thinking, word would come from the campaign that his father had fallen on the field of battle and that he was now the archduke, master of Seaharrow, and free to do whatever he wished, with a duchess who was not only giving him an heir, but would remain pliable to his desires and overlook his appetite for other women. Life, Aerin was thinking, was going to be good.

And as she felt his tongue within her mouth and returned his kiss with a passion she did not feel, Katrina thought, yes, Aerin, and it will be short, too. . . .

* * * * *

Vanilen.

The army of Avanil was deployed and ready. The scouts had ridden back and reported that, as Dulcain had predicted, Derwyn was taking his army through the central pass. They had met Derwyn's scouts and, together with mercenary outriders, had engaged and slain them all just inside the pass. Derwyn's scouts would not be riding back to report on the disposition of Kier's army. Derwyn would assume his scouts had ridden through the pass, found the way clear, and had ridden on to scout the territory beyond for signs of Avan's army. There would be no warning. Derwyn would reach the mouth of the central pass and, with his forces still in columns for the march, would run straight into Avan's army, already deployed for battle. He was on his way.

The archers had gone up into the rocks at the mouth of the pass and taken up position. There—the moment the archers received their signal—they could rain arrows down on Derwyn's army as the troops came through. The signal, three shrill blasts of a trumpet, would also be the signal for the all-out attack.

Gannd waited beside Reese at the head of the mercenary regiment, which was divided into cavalry and foot troops. Over to their right somewhere was Dulcain, with his mounted knights. The knight commanders had taken up their posts at the heads of their regiments, which were disposed in a semicircle around the mouth of the pass. Terrell stood upon a nearby hilltop with a squad of squires to attend him as he watched to see what spells Derwyn's adepts might deploy, and try to counter them. All was in readiness.

The troops stood utterly silent, the only sound was the occasional nervous snorting of the horses. The tension in the air was so palpable that Gannd almost felt as if he could reach out and take hold of it. Everything was so very still. Not even the birds were singing. It was as if they knew what was about to happen.

As he gazed out to either side of him, Gannd could see row upon row of men dressed for battle, their spears and lances sticking up into the air like a forest of saplings. They shifted in place from time to time, putting their weight from one foot to the other, but for the most part, they remained still and motionless, each man with his own thoughts.

How many of them were afraid? How many were simply filled with iron resolve, focused intently on the task at hand? How many were filled with hate for Derwyn's troops, whose aggression had taken them away from their homes and families? And how many were filled, as Reese seemed to be, with a curious exultation?

Duncan Reese, who had become Gannd's brother, and closest friend, was a man of many contradictions. Reese had chosen the path of the mercenary soldier, yet he avoided conflict when he could, such as that night when they were pursued in the streets of Lofton. He was always after some measure of security, and ways to advance himself, such as when he took service with McMurtrie's highlanders. Yet he threw it all away by becoming involved with the chieftain's daughter, knowing full well what the risks were. He was afraid of magic, yet one of his closest friends, the man Gannd realized Reese regarded as a substitute for the father he had never known, was an adept. He was unabashedly lecherous toward women, yet treated Mariel with a respect and tender affection that bordered on reverence. He was often reckless and headstrong, but had thus far proved himself an able commander, fair, patient, and disciplined, able to win the respect and admiration of his men. And now Duncan Reese sat astride his mount, gazing intently at the mouth of the pass, and the air around him seemed to vibrate.

Reese's eyes were alight, and every muscle fiber in his body seemed to hum with tension. His lips were slightly parted, and he kept moistening them with his tongue. His powerful chest rose and fell as he took deep and steady breaths. He kept shifting his grip on the reins of his mount and the horse danced from side to side slightly, forcing him to keep it under a short rein as the animal responded to his tension.

He saw Gannd watching him curiously and gave the half-elf a slight, self-deprecating smile. "Nervous?"

Gannd shook his head.

"Really?"

Gannd took stock of himself for a moment, pausing to examine how he truly felt. "I feel . . . strangely calm."

Reese nodded. "It affects some people that way. Don't worry. You'll do fine."

"I am not worried. Are you?"

Reese looked off toward the pass. "No. I'm anxious. I want it to begin."

"You are eager."

"Yes. It's a funny thing. I'm not normally so eager to fight. You know that. But war is different, somehow. I don't really know why. It makes me feel . . . alive."

"My mother said much the same thing."

Reese nodded. "She understood, then. I don't know, it must be some primal thing. Thrilling. Terrible. Cleansing, in a strange way. At the same time, there is a clarity of purpose, a simplicity of aim, an absence of complexity. . . ." Reese shook his head, searching for a way to put his feelings into the proper words. "Yet, that does not describe it adequately. It's more like a . . . a purity of self-awareness. I can actually feel my blood coursing through my veins."

"The sense of confrontation with your own mortality?"

"Yes, that's it, exactly! It makes me feel like nothing else. Vibrant. Thrilled. Terrified. And I love it. I wonder, sometimes, what that makes me."

"Human?" Gannd replied.

The sudden appearance of the scouts as they came galloping out of the pass forestalled any further conversation. By the time they reached Dulcain to make their report, it was already redundant. The entire army knew the appearance of the scouts meant the army of Boeruine was coming. The air seemed to crackle with energy. Every man tensed in anticipation of the signal. And then the lead troops in Boeruine's column appeared at the mouth of the pass.

Gannd had never seen Lord Derwyn, and though he had been shown his crest, so that he would know it on the battlefield, he would not have recognized it at this distance. Nevertheless, he felt sure that Lord Derwyn was one of the riders in the vanguard, for he saw the standard of Boeruine fluttering among the group of mounted knights that first appeared. The sight of Avan's army drawn up before them in battle formation must have been a shock, for they stopped for a moment; no one moved. And then they immediately erupted into a flurry of activity, some of the riders wheeling their horses and spurring off back the way they came, the remainder quickly grouping together to confer and make some very hasty plans. They didn't have much time. Only minutes.

Derwyn knew that if his army was bottled up in the pass, he would be at a severe disadvantage, so he sent riders back to urge the foot troops forward with all due haste. They had to clear the pass before they would have room to deploy. Moments later, the first of the marching columns came into sight at the mouth of the pass, at which point Dulcain gave orders to the trumpeter, and three shrill blasts echoed out across the field. The archers concealed in the rocks above Derwyn's troops let fly their arrows and, at the same time, the army of Avanil surged forward with a mighty battle cry that reverberated through the hills.

There was little Derwyn could do but wait and brace for it. Some of his troops had managed to clear the pass, despite the heavy volleys from the archers, but not enough to effect a countercharge without its being suicidal. There was but one thing for them to do and that was to fan out as much as possible and form a line for the charge to break against while the main body of the army tried to get clear of the pass behind them. But the troops at the front of the formation, those who had not been felled by the volleys from the archers in the rocks, were too few to make much of a line. However, Derwyn had made at least one smart move—he had his wizard with him at the front of the column.

As the army of Avanil charged, rapidly closing the gap with the enemy, a strong wind suddenly kicked up, and a line of flame erupted with a whoosh, blazing up across the field and moving rapidly toward the charging knights, aided by the wind. As the wall of fire came at them, the army of Avanil's momentum broke.

Those in front stopped at the sight of the flames racing at them, and many were knocked down from behind by their own troops. The charge broke up as the men tried to retreat, pushing at those behind them, and their lines quickly became a sea of tangled, churning bodies. Dulcain rode out before his men, trying to rally them, but having little success. Thunder suddenly crashed above the pass with a deafening roar, and a narrow bank of low-flying black clouds appeared as Terrell cast his counterspell.

The roiling clouds dropped from the sky like a huge bird stooping on its prey until they were only about ten feet above the ground, at which point they unleashed a deluge that was as brief as it was intense, dousing the flames, and dissipating without soaking a single man.

Dulcain managed to reform his troops, and they charged once more, but the momentum they'd lost and the time the enemy gained had allowed more of Derwyn's army to get clear of the pass. They came swarming out like ants, holding their shields above their heads as they sought to deflect the arrows raining down on them from the rocks above. Gannd could see Boeruine's adept getting ready to try another spell as he raised his arms high for the casting. For the next few moments, the battle would turn on the actions of the wizards. Each had prepared a number of spells in advance, in anticipation of what the situation might call for, and what the opposing mage might do. In this respect, the adepts had already begun their battle before they had even left on the campaign. It was a deadly game of anticipation and one-upmanship. From the battery of spells they had prepared, each spell could be used but once, and then it would be necessary to learn and prepare the spell afresh before it could be used again. Such was the nature of magic, and it did not come without a cost.

Unlike elven mages, who called upon the natural powers of earth and water, fire and air, human adepts could employ priestly magic, which called down the power of the gods and had a minimal deleterious effect on the adept. But an effect there was, nevertheless. One could not channel the power of the gods without feeling the effects of that power, and it was wearing on both the body and the soul. An adept who called not upon the gods, but upon his own life-force for the power suffered still more greatly. Without adequate time to recover, the length of time depending on the amount of energy expended, the adept would age rapidly and die. Magic could greatly extend a sorcerer's life, especially if it was coupled with bloodtheft, but copious spellcasting could kill a wizard in a matter of hours.

In this case, Gannd knew that neither of the adepts were priests. The priesthood had wisely stayed well out of this. Therefore, Terrell and Lord Derwyn's wizard had to call upon their own life-forces to empower their spells, which meant they could not keep it up for long without grave risk. Given the nature of the spells they were using, they would soon exhaust themselves. If they tried to continue past that point, they would start to age rapidly. And once the thaumaturgically-induced aging began, there was no reversing it. An adept could age twenty years with one spell, thirty with the next, and certain death would follow.

Boeruine's adept, probably at Lord Derwyn's command, directed his next spell at the archers in the rocks. A mistake, Gannd thought, as he unsheathed Bloodthirst and thundered ahead on his mount with Reese at his side. The mercenaries came charging behind them, followed by the foot troops. Derwyn would have done better to try stalling their charge once more to buy more time for his troops to strengthen their line, but the threat of the archers was closer, and must have seemed more immediate. It was a mistake that could very well cost Derwyn the battle.

Boeruine's adept cast his spell, and the archers in the rocks began to scream. Gannd could hear their cries echoing in the pass. He had no idea what was being done to them, but judging by their frenzied screams, it had to be terrible. Terrell, who could not even see the archers, and had no idea what spell the enemy adept had cast, could do nothing to counter the mysterious spell. Knowing the kindly wizard, Gannd realized how hard it had to be for Terrell to stand helplessly by while the archers died. But now, as Avan's army was almost upon Lord Derwyn's rapidly forming lines, the Boeruinean adept once again turned his attention to them. Gannd tensed as he watched the wizard raise his arms to cast the spell. Boeruine's archers were now coming forward, streaming out of the pass at the run, and taking up position behind the front ranks of the foot troops, nocking arrows for a first volley. There were only about fifty yards separating the two armies now. Then forty . . . thirty . . .

The adept brought his arms down in a hurling gesture, and bright bolts of blue lightning flashed from his splayed fingers. But as Gannd tensed, waiting for the deadly bolts to strike, the lightning seemed to strike some invisible barrier directly in front of the wizard who cast it. The tendrils of deadly force arched back, bursting apart, and spreading around the enemy mage in all directions, outlining a conical shape around the Boeruinean adept and his mount, as if he were trapped inside a huge glass bell jar. The wizard screamed as he was wreathed in the lightning he himself had conjured. There was a brilliant flash followed by a deafening explosion that sent all the horses around him bolting, and both the adept and his mount vanished, totally incinerated. Terrell, timing it perfectly, had cast a spell erecting a containment field around the enemy adept. He had remained true to his commitment not to take any human life. Boeruine's adept had destroyed himself with his own spell.

But now the enemy archers loosed their volley at the charging riders hurtling down at the kneeling front ranks of their troops.

They were only about twenty yards away now, and at that distance, the effect of the volley would be devastating. Gannd held his breath as the arrows flew straight at him, thinking he was going to die at the very outset of the battle, before he had even been able to engage the enemy. But instead of turning him into a pincushion, the flight of arrows arced up, described a wide semicircle in midair and flew straight back at the archers.

Terrell!

The bowmen scattered as their own arrows rained down on them. The mounted mercenaries were plowing into the front ranks of the army of Boeruine, scattering them, and trampling those who could not get out of the way. Gannd saw a lance being thrust up at him and batted it aside with his sword, and then they had broken through. Boeruine's mounted knights were charging at them from the mouth of the pass where they had formed up, and couched their lances for the assault. The spellcasting was done with now. The enemy wizard had been destroyed by his own magic, and Terrell could rest. There was nothing more for him to do now as the charging footmen of Avanil crashed into the ranks of the army of Boeruine, which had been broken by the mounted charge.

Behind him, Gannd heard the clattering of blades and men shouting as steel rang against steel, raising a deafening din. But he had no time to pay any attention to what was going on behind him as the mounted troops of Boeruine came bearing down upon them. Without pausing, Reese cried out and raised his blade high overhead and brought it down, pointing it at the approaching riders. The mercenary cavalry reformed behind him and spurred to meet the charge.

The armies collided roughly forty yards from the mouth of the pass, from which Boeruine's foot soldiers were still streaming out in double time, rushing to join the battle. Gannd found himself surrounded on all sides by riders armed with swords and lances, some from his own regiment, others from Boeruine's. He dropped his reins and blocked a sword stroke with his shield, then slashed a return blow at his attacker, who screamed as the stroke sliced through his helm and split his skull. Gannd felt the impact travel all the way up his arm and into his shoulder. He wrenched his blade loose just in time to deflect a lance that was stabbing at him. He kicked his horse up, meeting the rider and slamming his shield into his enemy, knocking the Boeruinean cavalryman off his mount. Then Gannd was laying about him on all sides, unable to think, only react, as he blocked and parried blows that came at him, and struck back with blows of his own . . . over, and over, and over.

The noise all around him was a cacophony of men shouting and screaming, horses neighing, blades ringing against blades, maces smashing into shields. . . . A sound like a howl rose over the battle-field, the baying of a creature composed of thousands of men yelling and screaming. All the feet and hooves were churning up a cloud of dust as thick as fog as they tore up the ground. Gannd could taste the dirt as he breathed. It mingled with his sweat and caked his skin, but there was no opportunity to dwell on the dis-comfort. He was too busy staying alive.

His years of training took over, and he operated by instinct, fight-ing without even thinking about it, almost as if his body were re-acting on its own. His arm rose and fell repeatedly as he hacked and slashed at the bodies and blades that came at him. As he blocked one blow with his shield and struck back, he felt a jarring impact on his shoulder and realized a blade had struck him from the side and glanced off his armor. He never even saw who struck the blow. He controlled his mount with his legs, moving forward, turning, some-times immobilized by the press of bodies and horses around him.

It was impossible to see which way the battle was going. All he could do was try to distinguish friend from foe in the melee, and try to stay alive. He started to become vaguely aware that his arms were growing tired and that he was breathing harder, but he pushed aside that awareness and redoubled his efforts, concentrating fiercely on trying to kill everyone who came within his reach who wore the colors of Boeruine.

Then, something completely unexpected happened. For an in-stant, it seemed as if his hearing had cut out. There was an incan-descent moment when everything and everyone around him seemed frozen in time and, briefly, the thought flashed through his head that perhaps somehow he had inadvertently triggered the spell of the amulet that took him to the Bridge of Sighs. But as quickly as that thought flashed through his mind, it vanished into a sudden awareness of overpowering rage that flooded through him, energizing him. There was a roaring in his ears, and suddenly, for a fraction of a second, there was a wash of impossibly brilliant white light across his vision, then everything went red, as if tinged with fire or bright, arterial blood. And then the din of battle erupted around him once again, only this time, strangely, it sounded rather hollow, almost muffled, and somehow slowed down.

Gannd perceived a mounted knight in front of him, bearing down, raising his blade for a slashing stroke, but it was as if the knight were moving in slow motion, as if both horse and rider were moving through water. Gannd could suddenly make out incredible detail. The narrow, dark slit in the knight's visor became an opening through which Gannd could clearly see the man's eyes . . . they were blue, wide and staring, the pupils dilated. Everything seemed to stand out abruptly in hard-edged, sharp relief: the wide, flaring nostrils of the horse, its rolling eyes, the nicks and scratches and dents on the knight's armor, the individual links of his chain mail. . . .

A frenzied sound came bursting out of Gannd's throat, and he exploded into movement. He caught a brief glimpse of the knight's staring, frightened eyes as he saw death coming, and then Bloodthirst drank deeply and he fell slowly from his horse, almost as if he were drifting to the ground.

In a white heat, and screaming like a banshee, Gannd erupted into a frenzy of killing rage, smashing into another horse and rider and knocking both to the ground. He engaged another knight, who started to raise his shield, but only felt the half-elf's blade cleave through his armor and bite deep into his shoulder, slicing through flesh, muscle, and bone. Another one down, another coming, and Gannd attacked, slashing and chopping like a demented woodsman. It was as if all his opponents were moving sluggishly, unable to react in time. His muscles sang with vibrant energy, heat welled up in his body, and he cut his way through the mounted knights and burst out into the open, confronting a mass of foot soldiers who were rushing to join the fray as they came out of the pass.

Gannd set spurs and, screaming hoarsely, charged them all, plowing into them and laying about with his blade, cutting through the shafts of spears that were thrust up at him, slicing through bodies, chopping through helms, and splitting skulls, plunging through them like a juggernaut of death that could not be stopped.

He cut his way through their ranks like a plowman making a furrow, leaving a trail of corpses behind him. Then he saw the crest of Derwyn of Boeruine on the tabard of a mounted knight a short distance away. With a cry, Gannd charged.

The standard-bearer saw him coming, and moved to interpose himself between his lord and the berserk half-elf, but Gannd rode right into him, smashing into his horse so hard the animal went down and he was unhorsed. Gannd's own mount stumbled, almost fell, somehow regained its footing, snorted, and responded as its rider spurred it forward toward his intended target. Another knight came rushing at the half-elf at the gallop, blade raised, but Gannd's sword struck him first as he passed the Boeruinean without even slowing down, catching him with a vicious chop across the front of his helm. The knight went over backward, his sword spinning from his grasp, and his riderless horse went on without him. Now there was only Derwyn and another knight beside him. As Gannd came toward them, Derwyn raised his blade . . . and suddenly the knight beside him thrust his sword deep into Derwyn's side.

As Derwyn fell, the knight wheeled his horse and spurred away from Gannd, back toward the pass.

As Gannd rode up to the motionless form of Derwyn, lying on the ground, the rage seemed to ebb from him and, for a moment, he felt dizzy and disoriented. The shock of what had just happened . . . Derwyn of Boeruine had been slain by one of his own knights!

Gannd blinked several times, staring down at the fallen nobleman, and whatever strange fit had come upon him passed. He felt exhausted, filled with a deep and profound weariness. He slumped in his saddle as he sat there, breathing heavily, and his arms and legs felt as if they were on fire. The Archduke of Boeruine was dead. Killed by one of his own men. Why?

"Haelyn's beard, you killed him!"

Gannd jerked, startled, and raised his blade, which suddenly seemed impossibly heavy, but the voice was not that of an enemy. It was Xandor.

"The archduke is dead!" Xandor cried out, at the top of lungs. "Derwyn is slain!"

In a moment, the cry was taken up by others. "Derwyn is dead! Derwyn is dead!"

Slowly, as if coming out of a fugue state, Gannd realized where he was. He was within only a few yards of a steep, rocky slope at the mouth of the pass. There were still troops that had not come through, but they were headed in the opposite direction now, back the way they had come, and Gannd heard their shouts echoing through the pass as they took up the cry, "Derwyn is dead!" Farther down the pass, Gannd could see abandoned wagons just sitting there as their drivers left them and took off on foot after the retreating troops.

He turned and saw that the battle was still going on behind him, but it was slowly winding down as the news of Derwyn's death spread, and his troops either turned and ran back to the pass, or simply surrendered and lay down their arms. Little by little, the din of battle faded away and the dust slowly began to settle. It was over.

Reese came riding up to him. He reined in and looked down at Derwyn's body. "By the gods, you've done it!" he said. "You've won the day!"

Gannd shook his head. "I didn't kill him."

Reese glanced at Xandor. The mercenary shook his head. "No, it was Gannd. I saw!"

"No, you did not," said Gannd. "He was run through by one of his own knights before I could reach him."

"One of his own knights?" said Reese with disbelief.

Gannd shook his head. "I do not know why. It was a treacherous blow from the side. The man struck, and then turned his horse and rode away, back down the pass."

"One of Kier's spies, perhaps," said Xandor.

"But then, why did he go back?" asked Gannd.

"I don't know," said Reese. He glanced at Gannd. "Are you all right?"

"I can barely move," said Gannd. "It is all I can do just to remain in the saddle. I don't know . . . something came over me. . . ."

"I know, I saw you," Reese said, nodding. "And I wasn't about to come anywhere near you til it passed. If I had, you would have killed me."

Gannd just stared at him, uncomprehending. "What? Killed you?"

Reese grinned. "You don't even know what it was, do you?"

Gannd could only shake his head.

"I've seen it once or twice before," said Reese, "but never like that. It was incredible. You were caught in the grip of divine rage."

"Divine rage?"

"He's blooded," Xandor said with the confidence of one who had felt Gannd's power once before.

"Of the bloodline of Anduiras, no less," Reese replied. "His human father was the Emperor Michael's lord high chamberlain."

"Truly?" Xandor said. "But I thought only the Roeles manifested the blood power of divine rage."

Reese shook his head. "It can be manifested by any branch of the bloodline of Anduiras. It is rare, however. It can appear only once in several generations, or not at all. Gannd has it."

"I have never experienced anything like it," Gannd said. He felt profoundly weary, as if he could go to bed and sleep for days.

"We'd better get you to one of the wagons so you can lie down and rest," said Reese. "When a man is in the grip of divine rage, he becomes a berserker and will slay friend and foe alike. It is the ultimate manifestation of the survival instinct. Your strength is increased a thousandfold, you feel no pain, your reaction time speeds up incredibly, and your body is using every last ounce of energy it possesses. I have seen men collapse after it has passed. The fact that you haven't is doubtless due to your Sidhelien blood and greater stamina. But you need to rest now, before you fall out of your saddle."

Gannd slumped forward over his mount. He felt utterly drained. He could not even comprehend what he had just been through. He heard what Reese said and his words made sense, but they did not quite seem to penetrate the haze. He had just been through his first major battle, but he could not even think about it now. All he wanted was to close his eyes and go to sleep. The need was overpowering.

"Here, take it easy," Reese said, riding up next to him. "Give me your reins."

Gannd felt Reese take the reins of his mount and dropped them without protest. Surely, Reese must be at least as tired as I, he thought. They'd both just been through a battle. But although Reese looked dirty and worn out and there was blood on him—probably someone else's, Gannd thought, because he'd said nothing about being wounded and did not act as if he were in pain—there was nevertheless an alert vitality about him, almost a glow. He was speaking in an animated manner, as if charged with energy. He had been through a battle and he had survived. He'd had his confrontation with his own mortality, and he met the challenge and lived through it. Gannd wished he knew what it felt like, but right now, he could feel nothing. He was simply numb with exhaustion. He could barely keep his eyes open.

Reese turned his mount and, holding Gannd's reins, led his friend's horse back to the wagons at the rear of their lines while Gannd sat slumped over in his saddle, just trying to hold on. Now that it was over, the exhaustion was welling up inside him, and every muscle in his body tingled with soreness. He couldn't even raise his arms. He had sheathed Bloodthirst and even that simple motion had taken an immense effort.

As Reese led his horse, Gannd glanced around him at the field of battle. What he saw seemed to mirror what he felt. The ground was strewn with bodies, some moving sluggishly and moaning or crying out in pain, some stilled forever. Men moved about the bodies in a seemingly aimless manner, trying to figure out where they should go now that it was over. Many of them looked dazed; some looked as Reese did, charged up and filled with nervous energy. Groups of men-at-arms were leading prisoners back toward the rear of Avanil's lines, but some did not even bother to take prisoners. They were merely satisfied to stop fighting and walked away while they watched their former antagonists wander back to the pass.

The dust from the conflict was still settling, coating the corpses with a fine brown patina. Gannd stared at their upturned faces as he passed. Their eyes were open and staring sightlessly up at the sky. Mouths were agape in screams that were cut off and forever silenced. Limbs lay twisted every which way, some lay severed from their bodies in pools of coagulating blood. Many of the bodies were draped over one another, former antagonists now embracing in death. This was the aftermath of war. No glory, merely broken bodies and the stench of death.

The roaring din of battle had now been replaced by an ominous silence, occasionally broken by the murmuring of men, the moans or cries of the wounded and the dying, the whickering and snorting of horses without riders, then a new sound that had not been there before. A sound that Gannd did not notice at first until it gradually and subtly impinged upon his consciousness. A low, unpleasant humming sound, a buzzing . . . the buzzing of the flies.

They reached the wagons. Men who had survived the battle without injury were helping the wounded into the wagons for the return trip to Daulton. The physics were hard at work, bandaging, cauterizing with hot pokers—a sizzling, hissing sound of hot iron scorching flesh, accompanied by a frenzied scream—and then they would move on. Some were busy amputating limbs damaged beyond all hope of recovery. Men were holding down their comrades as the physics sawed away, having administered drafts of belladonna for the pain, which would at least dull some of the agony, providing it did not poison the patient first. . . . Moans, screams, pitiable whimpering, more screams. . . .

They reached an enclosed wagon and Reese helped Gannd get down off his horse. Gannd's legs would not support him. He could not help it. He tried to stand, but he collapsed against Reese, who held him up.

"Easy, there," said Reese. "I've got you."

He helped him up into the wagon. It was dark inside. There was a straw mattress laid out on the floor of the wagon. Someone was stretched out upon it.

"Reese?" a voice said, weakly. "Is that you?"

"It's me, Terrell. I'm all right."

"The gods be praised. And Gannd?"

"He's right here. I've brought him to keep you company."

Terrell struggled up to a sitting position, suddenly concerned. "Is he . . . ?"

"He's all right," said Reese. "Just suffering from the aftereffects of a touch of divine rage."

"Divine rage!" Terrell said.

"It was a surprise to him, too," said Reese, helping Gannd lie down on the mattress beside the wizard. "He didn't know he had it. It's one of the strongest blood abilities. Makes me wonder what others he may have that he does not yet know about. Here you go, brother, rest easy now."

"Thank you," Gannd said thickly.

"Brother," Reese repeated. He grinned. "I like saying that."

Gannd turned to see Terrell gazing down at him anxiously. The wizard looked as if he'd aged at least ten years. And suddenly, Gannd realized he had.

"Terrell . . ."

"I am fine," the wizard replied. "A little worse for wear, but I shall recover."

"You saved the day," Reese told him.

"But I could not save the archers."

"Such is war," said Reese. "If not for you, a lot more men would have died. You saved a great many lives, my friend."

Terrell sighed wearily. "I am much too old for this sort of thing."

There was the sound of hoofbeats outside the wagon, followed by the snorting of a horse as a rider galloped up and reined in. A moment later, the curtains at the back of the wagon were yanked aside and Dulcain stuck his head in. "Reese?"

"Right here."

"Praise be to Haelyn. Is that Gannd with you?"

"I'm here, Bran."

"I heard you killed Boeruine. Well done. You won the battle for us."

Gannd was too tired to argue.

"Is Terrell all right?"

"I am well," the adept replied. "How are the men?"

"We sustained some heavy losses, but it could have been worse. It wasn't, thanks to you." He paused. "Dravan is dead. And Lord Kier is badly wounded."

"How badly?" asked Reese.

Dulcain shook his head and sighed. "It's bad. The physics are with him now."

Gannd tried to sit up. "Take me to him."

"Forget it," Reese said, urging him back down gently. "You'd be no use to him now. You're in no shape to heal anyone. You have no strength left."

"I must try."

Dulcain shook his head. "I don't think it would do any good," he said. "He took a lance thrust under his cuirass. And when he fell, he broke his back. Even if he lives, he will never walk again.

And that's no life for—"

A mournful trumpet sounded a long and wailing dirge that echoed across the battlefield. For a moment, none of them spoke.

Dulcain removed his helm and bowed his head. "The duke is dead," he said. "Haelyn rest his soul. Long live Duke Veladan."

"Long live Duke Veladan," Reese echoed softly.

And that was the last thing Gannd remembered before sleep and exhaustion overcame him.

chapter seven

The army of Boeruine returned to Seasedge about a week after the wedding of Aerin and Katrina. It did not return en masse. They dribbled in as a disorganized trail of groups that came trudging back to the city weary and dejected. Many of them didn't even return to the encampment on the fields outside Seaharrow, but broke off and went home to the outlying farms and villages. With the first ones who came back—men who had been at the very rear of the marching columns and had not even participated in the combat— came the news that Derwyn had been slain. The war was over, and Avanil had won.

Assuming, of course, that Aerin was not going to pick up where his father had left off. In that case, it would all start once more. However, Aerin showed no desire to continue in his father's quest to secure the Iron Throne. At least, not for the present. His immediate concern was to secure his own position as Archduke of Boeruine, and make sure that Kier of Avan would not regroup and invade, pressing his advantage and making certain he destroyed Boeruine's ability to wage war for many years to come. It was, however, uncertain how things stood.

The assassin himself brought the news that Derwyn had been slain to the castle. Alain looked very somber and grief stricken when he made his report to Derwyn's ministers—now Aerin's ministers, assuming he intended to keep them on and not replace them with men more to his liking. They were all well aware that their positions were suddenly very insecure, and made all due obeisance to Aerin, falling all over themselves in their fawning attempts to ingratiate themselves with him.

In his first act as archduke of Boeruine, a title which he had now inherited, but in which he was not yet formally confirmed, Aerin elevated Alain to a baronetcy, conveniently ignoring the fact that Alain had been broken from his knighthood, and thus nullifying his father's act by pretending it had never happened. Since there was no emperor to confirm Aerin's claim to his father's title, the official recognition of his status in the empire would have to come from the regent. Lord Davan was so anxious not to antagonize anyone that he was certain to do it. It was merely a matter of formality. As baron, Alain would head up the delegation that would be sent to Avanil to sue for peace. Aerin had heard the rumors that Lord Kier had fallen on the battlefield, but there was no confirmation, and he did not wish to take any chances by appearing tardy in affirming Avan's victory. If Kier had survived, he was likely to be better disposed toward an enemy who acknowledged defeat promptly and sued for terms. If Kier was dead, Veladan would become the Duke of Avanil and a speedy negotiation of a peace treaty with an inexperienced young duke could net more advantageous terms.

Katrina couldn't fault her new husband in his thinking. In his place, she would have done the same. And, in fact, she had.

When Alain returned from Daulton to report the terms that Avanil was demanding, it was the duchess who would be responding, not the duke. Katrina's plan was already in place. And she intended to move quickly, before it could occur to Aerin that in making her his duchess, he had placed her in a position where she did not need him anymore.

Several times since their marriage, Katrina had been taken back to Aerin's secret room, where Aerin consummated their relationship in his own twisted and sadistic way. She knew now how to find it on her own. And she had returned there several times, with

Angharad, to make the necessary preparations.

Aerin liked the night. Like a bat, that was when his appetites seemed strongest. Despite being married to him, Katrina did not share his bed. Aerin liked his privacy. He kept her in her accustomed quarters and came to her when he pleased, usually just before the hour of midnight, and always through the secret passageway, even though, as her husband, he had no reason not to come straight through her door. Coming to her through the secret panel, like a thief in the night, seemed to titillate him. And he liked her to act as if he hadn't been expected.

He did not always come on the same nights, but he always came just before the midnight hour. And so Katrina had arranged with Angharad to go to the secret room each night and wait to see if they would come. If they did not arrive within an hour after midnight, Angharad was to return to her own chambers and go to bed. But if they did arrive . . .

Once the plan was set, Angharad had to spend only two fruitless nights waiting for them in the secret room. On the third night, Aerin once again succumbed to his familiar cravings. Katrina was in bed, lying tensely awake and wondering—as she had for the previous two nights—if Aerin would come. And then she heard the soft, scraping sound of the secret panel swinging open and a curious thrill ran through her. She felt both relief and fear, then a stab of anxiety so sharp it sent pain lancing through her chest. Would Angharad be ready and waiting? Was she up to it? Would it work? Or would they fail and be exposed to Aerin's wrath? Katrina didn't want to think about that, but she couldn't help it. One way or another, it would end tonight.

Unless Angharad lost her nerve.

What if she wasn't there? Katrina closed her eyes as she listened to the soft sounds of Aerin approaching. He was creeping up on her, thinking she was asleep. If Angharad failed her . . . Katrina did not think she could stand another night in that horrid room. She would go mad.

She felt her bedcovers suddenly jerked back, and then Aerin was on top of her, pressing her down as he seized her wrists, and brutally crushed his mouth to hers. As Katrina squeezed her eyes shut, she wondered how any man could possibly find pleasure in such a kiss. It wasn't even a kiss. There was no gentleness to it, no affection, just a painful pressure of his mouth against hers, as if he were trying to suck the life out of her. She whimpered in pain and heard his grunt of satisfaction.

He got up and yanked her sharply to her feet, then pulled her through the secret panel. As before, he moved quickly, forcing her to run to keep up as he dragged her along into the darkness behind the castle walls.

No more, Katrina thought, as Aerin moved quickly, silently, and ominously ahead of her, dragging her along with one hand, and with the other holding a torch he had lifted from a sconce beside the panel. No more . . . It has to end tonight. She decided she would sooner die than suffer through another session of Aerin's twisted pleasures. If Angharad was not there to help her, she would fight him on her own, and he would have to kill her. But she would not allow herself to be so cruelly used again. As he dragged her down one flight of steps after another, into the increasing dampness of the lower sections of the castle, her anxiety increased to a point where her heart was beating so hard it felt like a wild thing trying to claw its way out of her chest.

Aerin didn't say a word as he pulled her along, almost running himself. He was eager to get on with it. She could see in his thoughts what he had planned for her tonight, and she mentally recoiled from the lurid images he was entertaining. She felt suddenly nauseated; the taste of bile was in her throat. Angharad, she thought in desperation, please, please be there, please. . . .

They reached the door. Aerin never locked it. There was no need. He was the only one who came here. Or so he thought. He threw the door open and pulled her inside, giving her arm a sharp yank so that she stumbled, and fell sprawling to the cold stone floor. He turned to light the braziers with his torch and as he did so, Angharad came running out of hiding behind one of the racks and with both hands brought a mace down on his head.

He heard the noise of her approach behind him and started to turn at the last second, and she struck him only a glancing blow. He grunted with pain as the mace grazed the side of his head and struck him in the shoulder, then stumbled back against the wall, nearly upsetting the burning brazier. The torch fell sputtering to the stone floor. As Angharad raised the mace for another blow, Aerin lunged forward, swinging, and struck her in the face with a closed fist. Angharad cried out and dropped the mace, staggered, and fell, still conscious, but stunned.

Aerin picked up the mace she dropped. There was murder in his eyes. "Traitorous bitch!" he said, as blood dripped down the side of his face. He raised the mace for the killing blow. "I'll show you what—"

The whip whistled through the air and cracked loudly against the side of his face. Startled, Aerin dropped the mace, his hands reflexively going up to protect himself as Katrina struck again, her face twisted into a mask of fury.

"No!" she cried out. "No! No! No! No! No!"

Again and again the whip cracked as Aerin hunched over and tried to dodge the lash, covering himself and backing away. Katrina pursued him, striking out again, and again, and again.

"No more! No more! No more!" she cried out with every crack of the lash, and then Aerin managed to catch the whip and, with a deft twist, wrapped the end around his wrist. Katrina tried to pull it back, but he took up the tension and yanked her forward.

"So . . . you ladies want to play, is that it?" he said through gritted teeth, his eyes lit up insanely as blood dripped from the welts on his face and hands. "All right, let's play!"

Katrina leaned back and tried to dig her heels in, but her feet could find no purchase on the dank stone floor as Aerin steadily reeled her in. She could not let go of the whip. She knew only too well what he would do with it. Gritting her teeth, she whimpered as she pulled against him desperately, to no avail. He was too strong.

And then Angharad struck him from behind with the mace.

Aerin grunted and went down to his knees, blood flowing copiously from the split in his skull. As he released the whip, Katrina fell back and Angharad struck again, remembering the times she herself had been his plaything in this room.

"Bastard!" she screamed, bringing the mace down with both hands. She raised it again and brought it down once more. "Bastard!" And a third time.

Katrina caught her arms as she raised the mace for a fourth blow. "Angharad! Angharad, enough! He's dead!"

Angharad's lip was bleeding from where he'd struck her. She had a glazed look in her eyes.

"He's dead, Angharad." Katrina repeated softly, taking the heavy mace from her and dropping it to the floor. It made a very loud sound as it fell. For a while, it was the only sound in the room. And then Angharad whimpered and began to cry.

Katrina put her arms around her and held her as she sobbed, trying to comfort her. "It's all right," she said. "It's all right. It's over, Angharad. He'll never hurt anyone again."

"What will become of us? What will they do?"

"Nothing," Katrina said firmly. "No one will do anything. You were only protecting me. And I am the duchess who carries the only legitimate heir to the dukedom. I won't let anyone do anything to you, Angharad, I swear on my father's soul."

She didn't want to look at Aerin's body. Instead, she guided Angharad to the door. "You saved my life," she said. "You saved both our lives. You are blameless in this matter. You must believe that. Now come on, get hold of yourself. Take a breath. There, fine, now another . . . Good. Wipe your eyes. Then go and get the chamberlain and have him meet me here, alone, at once. Bring him down yourself, then go back to your room and go to bed. I'll send the physic to you with a sleeping draft and have him see to your cut. Everything will be all right. I promise."

Angharad looked up at her, eyes wide, and nodded.

"Good. Now go do as I said. Hurry."

Angharad ran out of the room. Katrina listened to the echoing sound of her receding footsteps, then turned and forced herself to look at Aerin's body, lying in a spreading pool of blood. She felt weak and leaned back against the wall for support, taking several deep breaths, trying to calm herself.

"And so now the power flows to you," a low female voice said from the doorway.

Katrina started.

The Wizard came into the room, carrying her staff. She pulled back the hood of her cloak and her long, ash blond hair came spilling out. She gazed down at Aerin's body speculatively, as if it were no more than a mild curiosity. She prodded it with her staff.

"Well done," she said. Then she turned to Katrina with a smile and added, "Duchess."

"Who are you? What do you want from me?" Katrina said.

"I have told you before, what truly matters is what *you* want. Especially now that you are the duchess and sole ruler of Boeruine. That was quite a battle they had. I was there. I watched. Of course, they never saw me. They were too intent on killing one another. And they did it with considerable enthusiasm." She glanced back at Aerin's body. "Men," she said contemptuously.

"Leave me alone," Katrina said. "I'm tired of being your cat's-paw. You have brought me only pain and anguish."

"Why, Katrina . . . how very ungrateful of you. You disappoint me. I have brought you everything you ever wanted. I have brought you a new life, a far better one than you ever had before, better than you could have ever hoped to have. And I have brought you vengeance. The man who destroyed your family, your life, is dead. His son, whose selfish, twisted lust for you has brought him to his just desserts, is also dead. And now the power flows to you. To you, the Duchess of Boeruine. Look how far you've come. True, there was a small price to pay, but then, there always is."

"You are as bad as he was," said Katrina, glancing at Aerin's body.

"Well, you needn't be insulting. I shall not take offense, however. You have been through a trying time. Soon, you shall come to see that it was all worth it, after all. You are merely tired now. You have been under a great strain. But I have the remedy for that. . . ."

She held out her staff.

Katrina caught her breath. It looked like nothing more than a simple, unadorned wooden staff, like the kind any peasant might use for walking in the fields. Even the ones the peasants used were often more elaborate, decorated with carvings of faces or animal heads, stained various shades . . . but there was something extraordinary about this staff. Just the sight of it evoked a sudden hunger in Katrina. She knew what it could do. The memory of the power flooding through her returned with crystal clarity and engendered a driving, overpowering need for more. She wanted it. She craved it. She lusted after it.

She was just like Aerin.

The thought sobered her as abruptly as if she had been slapped in the face. She caught herself in the act of reaching for it and realized that she had actually begun to salivate in anticipation of the rush of seductive, erotic energy the staff provided. Power. The sensual lure of it was powerful in itself. Powerful, but perverse.

She thought of Aerin and the things he'd done to her in this very room in which she stood, suddenly caught in the same grip of obsessive hunger as he was when he had debased her here. As he had debased so many other women who had been unable to protest. Unable because they had been powerless. He had the power. By virtue of his gender and station, by virtue of his strength, by virtue of his utter lack of virtue.

Or had the power actually possessed him?

Katrina hesitated, her hand still outstretched toward the staff, inches away.

"Go on," the Wizard said in a husky voice. "You know you want it."

A chill ran through Katrina, making her shudder. Those had been the very words Aerin used as he did unspeakable things to her.

"No," said Katrina. She moistened her lips, swallowed hard, and averted her gaze. "No. Take it away."

"You recall what happened last time?" asked the Wizard. "The gift you received? This time, there will be so much more. . . "

"I said take it away."

"Look at me, Katrina."

The voice had a commanding tone to it that Katrina could not resist. She sought to probe the Wizard's thoughts, then recoiled suddenly as if she had been stung.

"Foolish girl! The gift was mine to give. You think to use it on me? You are arrogant in your presumption." Her tone softened and she smiled. "I think that's one of the things I like about you." She stretched out the staff once more. "Go on, Katrina. Take it. Take hold of it and feel the power flow."

Katrina squeezed her eyes shut. "No!"

"Milady?" It was Angharad's voice echoing down the corridor outside. "Milady, are you all right? Hold on, we're coming!"

Katrina opened her eyes. The Wizard was gone.

The chamberlain came rushing in with Angharad. "Milady, what is it? What in Haelyn's name are you doing in—" His gaze fell on Aerin's battered body, lying in a large pool of dark blood. "Merciful gods! What villainy is this?" His shocked gaze traveled around the room. Slowly, it came around and rested on Katrina. "What is this place?"

"Leave us, Angharad," Katrina said.

"Yes, milady."

Angharad needed no further encouragement. Her running footsteps faded away down the dark corridor.

"Behold my marriage bed, Lord Ogbert," said Katrina. "The chamber where my wedding vows were consummated, where Aerin made a cuckold of his father with his unwilling mistress and where he deflowered virgins, tarnished wives, and debased more women than it is possible to count these past many years. Look around you, Ogbert, and see the true nature of your lord."

Ogbert paled as his gaze roamed the contents of the room. He shut his eyes and shook his head. "Oh, gods. What monstrous corruption! Oh, my poor, sweet lady!"

"Save your pity, Ogbert, and steel your resolve to the task at hand," Katrina said. "The people must never know of this. No one must know. I carry Aerin's child, the future archduke. And he must not labor under the burden of his father's deeds."

Ogbert immediately nodded. "Of course, my lady. What do you want me to do?"

"You must help me carry Aerin's body back up to his chambers. We shall wrap it in a heavy shroud and sew it up so that no one can see the nature of his wounds. The physic must be ordered to announce that he has died of a seizure of the heart, brought on by inconsolable grief over his father's death upon the battlefield. And if the physic ever breathes aught else, he must know that I shall have him put to death."

"It shall be done, my lady."

"And I want this room sealed up with stone and mortar, and the passageway that leads to it, as well."

"I shall see that it is done, my lady," said Ogbert. "And by men whose honor and loyalty are beyond question or reproach. I shall swear them to secrecy on pain of death."

"There is more," Katrina said.

"By the look upon your face, I dread to hear it."

"Aerin had confessed to me that he had his father treacherously murdered on the battlefield so that he might marry me and take his place as archduke."

"Oh, horror!"

"This fact must never be revealed. The province of Boeruine has seen tragedy enough. But the assassin is known to me. He is the newly elevated Baron Alain, our ambassador of peace to Avanil." She spat out the final words. "His investiture was his reward for his foul deed, done for profit and to revenge himself on Derwyn for stripping him of knighthood. Alain must be punished for his despicable crime. I do not care how it is done. I leave that to you. And I shall trust to your discretion in the matter."

"You may rely on me, my lady."

"I shall rely on you, Ogbert. I shall need you to guide me in what must be done. The province of Boeruine has been dealt a severe blow by the recent defeat at the Duke of Avan's hands. We must do more than merely sue for peace. We must regain our strength and rebuild our resources. We must plan for the future. We must overcome our differences with Avanil and find a way to forge an alliance with the House of Avan."

Ogbert nodded. "A wise plan, my lady. United, Boeruine and Avanil will make a formidable power in the heartlands, and the western coast. I shall put my mind to it and seek a way to have the task accomplished."

"Allow me to offer a suggestion, Ogbert, and tell me if you find merit in it. The fate of Lord Kier is uncertain, but either way, his son succeeds him. Veladan is young, but he shall marry and have children before long."

"Indeed, my lady, I understand that his marriage has already been arranged."

"Alliances by marriage have always been the soundest," said Katrina. "We could negotiate with Avanil for a betrothal between my unborn son and the first daughter Veladan shall sire, thus cementing the union of our houses. What would you say to that?"

"I say that your presence of mind and your acuity astound me," Ogbert said. He glanced back at Aerin's body once again, and then quickly looked away. "Especially given the attendant circumstances."

"I do not have the time for such delicacies as swooning or weeping with hysterics, Ogbert," said Katrina. "I must subdue my feelings and master my distress, for all our sakes. Later, after we have done what must be done, I shall arrange a time to give vent to my emotions, and it shall be done in private. What the people need now is a strong hand to guide and secure their fate. And I need you, Ogbert, to help make my hand an able one. I pray that I may count on you."

"It shall be my privilege to serve your ladyship."

"Then please accept my apologies that your service should begin with so grisly a task as this," Katrina said. "But it must be done and much as it fills me with dread and horror, we had best get about it quickly."

As they went about their work in silence, Katrina noted that Ogbert never asked her the details of what had happened. Considering the circumstances, thought Katrina, his sense of tact was very admirable. He would make an excellent minister. She would have to see to it that his abilities were suitably rewarded.

* * * * *

When Alain returned to Seaharrow to report that Lord Kier had indeed succumbed to his wounds and that young Veladan, on the advice of his ministers, was more than amenable to open negotiations for a lasting peace, he expected to find a grateful Aerin who would reward him with a bonus for the work he had done. Instead, he was hastily conducted to the chambers of Lord Ogbert and told to make his report to the ducal chamberlain.

Irritated at this slight, the newly invested baron complied, then informed the chamberlain that he had expected to meet with the archduke and that he had some matters of importance to convey to him that were of such gravity that they were for Aerin's ears alone.

At that point, Ogbert calmly informed him that Lord Aerin had passed on to his just reward, and that Alain was about to receive his. Alain was seized abruptly, bound and gagged with efficient dispatch, and dragged from the room to a secret panel in the archduke's chambers. As he struggled, they half-dragged, half-carried him down a series of dark corridors as they lit their way with torches, down several flights of dank stone steps and to a corridor that ended in a room from which the door had been removed. Kicking, thrashing, and shouting uselessly into his gag, he was dragged into the room and shackled to a wall. A torch was set into a sconce on the wall beside him so that he could watch in horror, pulling on his chains until his wrists bled, screaming wildly into his gag, as they walled up the entrance to the secret room with him inside it.

Eventually, the torch went out.

* * * * *

Word of Aerin's death reached Avanil by a special courier who informed the young Lord Veladan and his advisors that the Duchess Katrina was en route to Daulton with her train to personally conclude the peace negotiations. No one seemed to know anything about the duchess other than that she had married Aerin of Boeruine shortly before his untimely death. The spies who had reported on the activities of the army of Boeruine in their encampment prior to the battle knew little, if anything, of what went on in Seaharrow. They could provide no information concerning the new duchess. Consequently, there was a great deal of interest in her impending arrival, and Veladan ordered that the most comfortable quarters in the castle be set aside and prepared for her use while she was in Daulton, and that a staff of servants be assigned to see to her every need.

Gannd, Reese, and Dulcain were all on hand to witness her arrival at the castle. She came in an enclosed carriage bearing the crest of the House of Boeruine, escorted by two dozen mounted knights, her lady-in-waiting, Lady Angharad, and her minister, Viscount Lord Ogbert. Veladan received them in the great hall of the castle, with all proper ceremony and his entire ducal court in attendance. As the chamberlain stepped into the hall and rapped his staff of office on the flagstones, silence fell, and all eyes turned toward the large, heavy double doors.

"Her Esteemed Ladyship, the Duchess Katrina of Boeruine, and her minister plenipotentiary, Viscount Lord Ogbert Torvald!"

She made do without the accustomed string of family names and titles, Gannd noted as the doors were opened and the duchess, together with her minister, Lord Ogbert, made her entrance. She also made do without an entourage, having left her lady-in-waiting and knights out of the official proceedings. She entered attired simply in a black cloak and gown devoid of any ornamentation save for a thin girdle of gold chain around her waist and her coronet. But then, she was obviously in mourning for her late husband.

She was, Gannd thought, a stunningly beautiful woman, with long red hair and green eyes, skin so fair it looked like porcelain and a figure that every woman in the court undoubtedly envied. He saw Dulcain staring at her and turned to see that Reese was wide-eyed and slack-jawed as he gazed at her. A soft murmuring rose in the great hall as she walked up to the dais on which Veladan sat, flanked by his ministers, and curtsied deeply, bowing her head respectfully, even though she was senior to him in years and of equal rank.

"You honor us with your presence, my lady," Veladan said, trying—not quite successfully—to make his boyish voice suitable to the occasion.

"I thank you for receiving me, my lord."

"Please accept our deepest sympathies on the recent passing of your husband, the Archduke Aerin. We did not know him, but we share your loss."

"I am grateful for your sentiments, my lord. And I, in turn, wish to express my sympathies for your own loss in the passing of your father. The people of Boeruine have sustained many losses of late, as indeed have the people of Avanil, and it is on their behalf that I have come, in the hope of arranging a lasting peace between our houses."

"Those are hopes we share in all sincerity," said Veladan. "We have seen quite enough of war."

"Regretfully, my lord, I fear we shall see more." An undertone of murmuring broke out at her remark and Veladan raised his hand for silence. She continued.

"These battles between us have weakened both Boeruine and Avanil severely. We have lost many brave and noble warriors,

which has undermined our strength. We have depleted our trea-
suries, which limits our resources. Other provinces throughout the
empire have not been ignorant of this. Many have formed alliances
behind their own aspirants to the Iron Throne, and our conflict, un-
wisely begun by my late husband's grandfather, Lord Arwyn, has
rendered both our houses vulnerable."

"The Army of Avanil is strong and stands ready to repel any attack," said Veladan a touch too quickly, and too pridefully, prompting Lord Moivar, his minister of state, to softly place a cautionary
hand on his shoulder.

"I would not gainsay your lordship," Katrina replied. "We have
had ample demonstration of your army's strength. However, the
fact remains that both our army and yours have sustained losses
that are far from insignificant, and our conflict has imposed much
strain and hardship on our peoples. The empire is crumbling, and
the current regent is not strong enough to hold it together. He seeks
to appease everyone and, in so doing, fails to serve the greater interests of us all. He cannot prevent alliances from forming because
he cannot control the imperial estates and guide them in a choice of
a worthy successor to the emperor. And he cannot prevent these
new alliances from campaigning against one another to increase
their holdings and advance the cause of their own candidates for
ascension. The regent has become a figurehead and nothing more."

Veladan looked puzzled, uncertain how to respond. He looked to
Lord Moivar for guidance.

"Perhaps Her Ladyship could clarify her point for the further ed-
ification of us all," the minister said. "It does not seem exactly clear
what Her Ladyship's criticism of the regent has to do with the question at hand."

Katrina glanced at Ogbert, who stepped forward to reply. He
bowed and said, "The issue goes beyond the matter of negotiating
a peace between Boeruine and Avanil, my lord. That is, of course,
the prime purpose of our visit, but we must also look to the fore-
seeable future. The empire that we all knew under the glorious rule
of the Roeles is gone. To speak of it otherwise is to blind ourselves
to the reality. Anuire cannot defend itself, and armies are on the
march even as we speak. Weakened by our conflict as we both are—
and we must, for our own good, set aside our pride and admit to the

truth of the situation—we have been rendered vulnerable to these new alliances.

"An alliance between Boeruine and Avanil will unite the two strongest houses in an empire that we still hope will return to its former strength and glory. There will be civil war. It has already begun. The House of Boeruine bears its own share of the blame for that, and we shall not try to deny it. What is past is past, however. We wish to sue for peace and make amends. But beyond that, we both need to think about regaining our strength, and not only protecting ourselves, but doing everything within our power to restore law and order to the empire. And a formal alliance between our houses would be an important first step in that process."

Now they would be getting down to business, Gannd thought. The discussion would proceed between the ministers. Veladan was certainly not up to it, and though the duchess certainly appeared quite capable, she could not conduct negotiations directly with the duke's subordinates. Proper protocol had to be observed. Gannd was curious to see what they would propose.

Lord Moivar's next words echoed Gannd's thoughts. "You have a formal proposal to make, Lord Ogbert?"

"We do," Ogbert replied. "We wish to negotiate a lasting peace between our houses, which an alliance would ensure, and at the same time, our union would make us both much stronger and more secure. However, as I have pointed out, that would be only a first step in attempting to restore order to our land. The regent is ineffectual. No one can seriously argue that point. Of all the noble houses in the empire, those of Boeruine and Avan can make the strongest claims to the succession by virtue of common descent from the line of Anduiras, which gave us the dynasty of the Roeles. We propose a formal alliance between both our houses by a marriage of our children. The Lady Katrina is with child. Since the duchess's midwives have ascertained that the child will be a male heir, and Lord Veladan is formally betrothed, we propose a betrothal of marriage between my lady's unborn son and the first daughter born to Lord Veladan. Thus, our two houses shall provide the future emperor and empress. To assure their mutual ascension, the current regent shall be removed from office and, in his place, the Lady Katrina and Lord Veladan shall rule as regents until such time as the children are of age."

An excited undertone of conversation broke out at the audacity of this proposal. Reese swore softly under his breath. Dulcain gave a low whistle. "She comes defeated, hat in hand, to sue for peace, and winds up negotiating for the throne. Now that's what I call a proposal," he said with admiration.

"That's what I call a woman," Reese added without taking his eyes off her.

Lord Moivar was completely taken aback. He seemed speechless. Veladan glanced up at him, wanting to know what he should say, or if he should say anything at all, but Moivar wasn't even looking at him. He was staring at Katrina with astonishment. Everyone in the hall was talking at once. Katrina simply stood there calmly, glancing around her to observe the reaction to her proposal. Her gaze fell on them and stopped.

Reese stood up a bit straighter and puffed up his chest. "You see that?" he said to Gannd. "She's looking right at me."

Gannd followed her gaze. "No, I do not think so," he said. "She's looking straight at Bran."

Dulcain met her gaze steadily. "She must know I am the man who led the army that brought Boeruine to defeat," he said softly. "Lord Ogbert must have described my crest to her. I'm not sure I'd like to know just what she's thinking right now."

What Katrina was thinking was quite unlike anything Dulcain might have expected. Gazing around at the members of the ducal court with interest, to see how her proposal was received, she tried to maintain an impression of composure and calm self-assurance. These people had brought Derwyn to defeat. They had fought the father, and then they had fought the son, and now the grandson's widow stood before them as a supplicant, come humbly to sue for peace. Except she had not come humbly. She had acknowledged their victory and her defeat—for she was Boeruine now—but her pose was not that of a supplicant, and her posture was not meek. She came not to plead for lenient treatment, but to propose an alliance and plan the future of the empire with herself and young Veladan as regents.

Veladan, of course, would act as regent in name only until he became older and gained more experience. For the next few years, if they accepted her proposal, he would have to be guided by Lord Moivar, who would, in effect, control the regency together with Katrina. Moivar knew that of course, and part of his astonishment was not only at the sheer audacity of her proposal, but at the possibility that he could go from first minister of a ducal court to lord high chamberlain, which would not only give him more power than he had ever imagined, but would ensure the continuity of the post within his line. Katrina knew exactly how he must be feeling at this moment—the same way she herself had felt when the Wizard last offered her the staff.

She concentrated and extended her awareness into Moivar's thoughts. She was not surprised at what she found. Astonishment. Shocked disbelief. Admiration for her beauty, her boldness, and audacity. Respect for her comportment. Dismay at being caught off guard. A feeling of anxiety and urgency, the need to marshal his thoughts and make a proper reply so that he would seem in control of the situation. And sudden comprehension of what accepting her proposal would mean to himself and to his family. They would have to unite their forces, march on the imperial capital, depose the regent, and seize the throne. And in the process, defend themselves against all other alliances throughout the crumbling empire. It would involve great risk, but it would mean wealth and power, control of the imperial treasury . . . and power. . . .

She saw the spark of desire alight within his mind and she felt the beginnings of the hunger for it grow. She smiled inwardly, glancing away from him so that he would not see the certainty and satisfaction that she felt written on her face. Yes, think about it, my lord, she told herself. You thought I came here a defeated enemy to beg unabashedly for any terms you might condescend to offer, and instead I offer you the empire. And you are going to accept. Because you know you want it.

As her gaze swept the room, she observed the reactions of the people all around her. Outrage. Shock. Disbelief. Stunned surprise. None of them had expected anything like this. And then her gaze fell on a group of men who stood slightly apart from all the others, below the dais, to the left of the ducal seat. One was a big and brawny, puffed-up blond mercenary who stood with his chest thrown out like a rooster on a fence about to crow; another was a thoughtful-looking young half-elf, the first she had ever seen, with dark auburn hair that was heavily streaked with bands of silver; and the third was an older man who wore a baron's coronet. Upon his white livery was a coat of arms which consisted of an azure shield charged with a broadsword proper, inverted.

Seeing the device, which had been described to her, she realized who he was. She was looking at Baron Bran Dulcain, better known as Bran the Blade, the legendary mercenary who was said to be one of the greatest fighters the empire had ever seen, the commoner who rose to the ranks of the nobility and became the lord commander of the army of Avanil . . . the man at whose hands Boeruine had suffered a crushing defeat.

He stood just under six feet tall and was not a particularly handsome-looking man, nor a young one, though he seemed extremely fit. His chest looked thick and muscular, his hair was gray and shoulder-length, and his light blue eyes were deeply sunken in a weather-beaten, square-jawed face adorned with a neatly trimmed moustache and goatee. His nose appeared to have been broken several times, and his shoulders were broad, with thick, powerful-looking arms. At first glance, he would have looked unremarkable, an old soldier who was still extremely fit for his age and who still bore himself with a straight, military posture. But he had a presence that made him stand out from every other man within the chamber and drew her gaze to him as a moth flies to a beacon. The man exuded vitality and strength. In any group or situation, he would lead. There was a sense of calm authority about him, a self-possession and assurance that clearly said this was a man with nothing left to prove. He had a magnetism that was compelling, and as he gazed steadily back at her, she felt something stir within her and thought, this is the one.

She suddenly felt as if someone had pulled the floor out from under her. She blinked several times and looked away, down at the floor, to hide the startled expression on her face. She swallowed hard and took several quick, shallow breaths through parted lips. The realization shook her to the core. He was the one.

She struggled to regain her composure, hoping desperately that no one would notice her dismay. He was old enough to be her father. But he was easily twice the man that Derwyn had been and

more man than Aerin could have ever hoped to be. When he un-
flinchingly returned her gaze, unawed by her beauty or her station,
she felt as if he had seen clear through to her soul. Her knees went
weak. He was the one.

How could it be? When the thought came to her, unbidden, it
caught her completely unprepared and threw her for a loop. How
was it possible? How could she know with such a sense of certainty,
at just a glance? But as she stared, blinking at the floor, desperately
trying to get herself back under control, she knew beyond a shadow
of a doubt that this was the man she had been destined for. She
would be with him. It was inevitable.

Moivar's voice rang out through the hall and, with an effort, she
composed herself. She brought her features back under control,
took a deep breath, and looked up at the Duke of Avan's minister.

"My lords and ladies . . . please attend!"

Silence fell on the great hall and, as all eyes turned toward him,
Moivar glanced down at the young duke and patted him lightly on
the shoulder in a reassuring manner, letting him know he would
take care of this. Veladan nodded gratefully and looked back at
Katrina.

"My lady," Moivar said, "what you propose bears great significance for both our houses, as well as for our people and the people
of the empire. A matter of such gravity must be given due consideration and not settled out of hand. We therefore ask for your in-
dulgence while we discuss the merits of your most intriguing offer
and weigh it carefully."

Katrina inclined her head slightly, saying nothing. It was taken by
the onlookers as remarkable self-possession, but in fact, she was
afraid that if she tried to speak, her voice would tremble and betray
her.

"We shall await His Lordship's pleasure," Ogbert said with a
slight bow.

Moivar glanced at Veladan and nodded.

"You have our permission to withdraw, my lady," the young
duke said. "Quarters have been set aside for you and your party.
Please accept our hospitality, and the freedom of the castle, for the
duration of your stay. Do not hesitate to ask for anything you may
require. In the meanwhile, we shall give urgent consideration to

your proposal, and send word to you as soon as a decision has been reached."

"I thank Your Lordship on Her Ladyship's behalf," said Ogbert with a bow.

"Court is dismissed," said Veladan, rising and leaving the dais.

Katrina bowed, then turned and walked away with a firm and purposeful stride. She could feel Dulcain's gaze on her. And much as she wanted to, she dared not look back.

chapter eight

Dulcain knocked at the door, and it was opened by a strikingly pretty, dark-haired girl whom he recognized as the duchess's lady-in-waiting. He ransacked his mind to recall her name, then struck upon it. He inclined his head slightly. "Good evening to you, Lady Angharad. My name is Bran Dulcain. I was informed that the duchess wished to see me, and I came as soon as I could."

Angharad smiled, pleased that he remembered her name, and gave him a curtsy. "Yes, my lord, you are expected. Please, come in."

He entered the sitting room of the comfortable and well-appointed chambers, hung with rich tapestries that had once belonged to the young duke of Avan's late mother. Logs were burning brightly in the cavernous fireplace, casting a welcome, warm glow to the room. The window was admitting a cool evening breeze and, outside, beyond the castle walls, night was falling over the city of Daulton.

The Lady Angharad excused herself and went through the door into the bedchamber, shutting it behind her. Dulcain waited. A few moments later, the door opened once again, and the duchess came out alone into the room and closed the door.

Dulcain was struck by her beauty, which he had noticed before, as had everyone in attendance at the great hall, but now that he was closer, he was in a better position to appreciate it. She wore no cloak now, only a clinging, simple black gown with a circlet of gold chain as a girdle round her narrow waist. The color accentuated her fair skin and long red hair, which she wore loose down below her shoulders, without her coronet. He noticed that, save for the gold chain around her waist, she wore no jewelry, nor did she need to. It would have been like gilding a lily. Her hands were soft and graceful, and she moved with a natural, fluid grace that he found most becoming. The firelight made her skin seem to glow, and caught gleaming highlights in her long, lustrous red hair. Her green eyes were luminous as they regarded him softly with a steady, direct, appraising gaze.

"My lord Dulcain," she said, approaching him and holding out her hand, "I am so glad you came. Thank you for indulging me."

"I am honored, Your Ladyship," he replied, bending over her hand and brushing it lightly with his lips. "How may I be of service?"

Katrina felt suddenly flustered. He was a gruff-looking man, yet his charm utterly disarmed her. He was just a simple soldier. How could he have such an effect on her? For a moment, she felt disoriented. She was uncertain what to say now that he was here.

"I wanted to meet you," she replied after a moment. "And speak with you."

He nodded once. "Yes. I regret, my lady, the circumstances attending our acquaintance. Would that they were different, and I had not been the man who brought you so much grief."

She smiled. "You only did your duty. And you did not bring me grief. I feel sorrow for those of my people who were deprived of loved ones in the battle, and my sympathies are with them, but for my own part, it was not grief that you brought me with your victory, but freedom."

Dulcain frowned. "Freedom, Your Ladyship?"

She moistened her lips nervously as she returned his puzzled gaze. "Would you be so kind as to indulge me and call me by name? It is Katrina."

"It would be hardly proper for me to—"

"Please," she said. "We are alone and I think we may dispense with the formalities. Besides, my beginnings were as humble as your own. In many respects, more humble still, in ways I fear you may find far from proper."

"As you wish . . . Katrina," Dulcain replied, a bit confused. This was not quite what he had expected. "My friends call me Bran."

"Yes, I know . . . Bran. Bran the Blade."

He winced slightly.

She raised her eyebrows. "You do not care for it?"

"When I was younger, it was a name that pleased me greatly," he replied. "And I was proud to bear it. I admit, it filled me with a sense of self-importance. But as the years passed, I came to discover that I did not bear the name so much as it bore me. And I found it wearisome always having to live up to it."

"I think I understand. It made people see the reputation, not the man."

Dulcain was mildly surprised. "You do understand," he said. "Not many people do. But then, if I may be permitted the presumption, you strike me as a woman of uncommon gifts."

"Do I strike you as a whore?" she said softly, staring straight into his eyes.

Startled, Dulcain wasn't sure he'd heard right. "What?"

"A whore, Bran," she said distinctly. "Do I strike you as a whore?"

He stared at her with astonishment and disbelief, shaking his head slightly. What in Haelyn's name? "What kind of a question is that?" he said.

"A simple one. And it requires but a simple answer."

"No. Of course not."

"And yet that is precisely what I am," she replied. She turned away and stood facing the fire. The light from the flames flickered across her features. "My own mother said so."

"Your mother?"

"She is here, in Daulton, somewhere—if she still lives—working as a common serving woman. She has disowned me for bringing disgrace upon her, and my father's memory. She wants nothing more to do with me."

Dulcain shook his head. "But . . . why? What could you possibly have done?"

"I was born Katrina of Tremayne, daughter to a feudal vassal of Lord Kier of Avan. My father was far from an important man. Though we could call ourselves aristocrats, it was the most tenuous of claims, and we lived very simply on a small piece of land, as the common people do. I had two older brothers whom I loved as dearly as I loved my father and my mother. It was a good life. A happy one. I had been to court here. That great hall where I stood before is a familiar one to me. I danced in it with my handsome young knight, to whom I was betrothed. Everything seemed settled, and the future was clear and bright. And then Derwyn of Boeruine invaded Avanil.

"Both of my brothers, and my betrothed, were killed in battle," she continued. "My father was brought home mortally wounded. I should have remained with my mother at his bedside and tried to offer him some comfort in his final moments, but instead, some strange urge drove me to ride out to the battlefield and seek my brothers." She shook her head slowly. "I never found them. I had never before seen the aftermath of war, and it filled me with a horror that was inexpressible. I became numb with it. I wandered through the battlefield, among the corpses, seeing many that I knew . . . I found my young knight, slain. Suddenly, everything was gone. My father, both my brothers, my future husband . . . all gone. My family destroyed, and my future along with it."

Her voice was very low as she stared into the flames. Dulcain stood motionless, listening intently to her story.

"As night fell, there appeared to me upon the battlefield a woman dressed all in black. A sorceress, though I did not suspect it at the time. At least, I do not think I did. We spoke, and she bid me take hold of her staff, which is called Calamity."

Dulcain stiffened.

"I did as she told me, and as soon as my hand came in contact with the staff, I felt a . . . flow. A powerful energy that seemed to rise up out of the ground, pass through the staff, and into me. It was a rapturous sensation that I cannot even begin to describe. And with that flow of power came an understanding. And an acceptance. For the first time, it seemed, I realized the nature of true power, how it ebbed and flowed, like tides. And I knew that the only way to survive in this world, and use that power, was to recognize the ebb and flow, perceive the opportunities, and move with them. Not struggle uselessly against the current, but ride with it, following the paths of power, rising with it.

"Moments later," said Katrina, "I saw riders approaching, and when I turned back, the sorceress had disappeared. The riders then saw me, and accosted me. It was Derwyn of Boeruine, come riding out with some of his knights to view the aftermath of what he had wrought. And I saw that the power flowed to him. I had but little, contained within the happiness I'd known in the bosom of my family. In his greed and ambition, Derwyn had seized even that. I had nothing left. He had it all.

"The power flowed to him," she said again, "and I realized that I must follow it, or have nothing. My father and brothers were all dead, the knight I was to wed was slain. My mother was a widow, and no longer young. I knew I had to think of my survival. And hers. So I offered myself to Derwyn and became his concubine. His whore. Which was what my mother called me when I sent for her to come to Seaharrow. She refused, disowning me, preferring to scrub floors on her hands and knees rather than share in her daughter's degradation. And so I had truly nothing left.

"I saw that my future welfare depended entirely on Derwyn. So long as I pleased him, he would maintain the arrangement, and I would be taken care of. But I also saw that my future was entirely dependent on his whim, and that he could, and doubtless would, eventually grow tired of me. I would be discarded, left with nothing but what he might see fit to grant me, in his charity. I did not want that.

"In time," Katrina went on, "the sorceress appeared to me again, in the gardens at Seaharrow, and I once more felt the power of her staff. The power of Calamity. It was seductive . . . sensual . . . erotic . . . and disastrous.

"Derwyn had a son, named Aerin, only a few years my senior. Derwyn kept Aerin cloistered in the castle, protected as his only heir to the dynasty he wished to found, and Aerin was schooled daily by his tutors in the knowledge Derwyn thought his son would need to become emperor. But Derwyn saw his son merely as his heir, a means to a hoped-for end, and felt no love for him. And Aerin had grown to despise his father with an abiding hatred that he nursed within his breast. It was the power of that hate which had corrupted him. He had no love, and so he knew nothing of love. But Aerin was a depraved seducer, one who used his power to debase nearly every girl and woman who came within his reach. Innocent maiden or faithful wife, it made no difference to him. When he grew jaded in his appetite for virgins, he turned his attentions to the wives of other men, finding satisfaction in corrupting and using them. And when his appetite for adultery had grown jaded, he set his sights on a still more forbidden goal . . . his father's mistress."

Dulcain held his breath as he listened raptly. He did not know why she was telling him all this, but he could not interrupt to ask. He felt spellbound by her tale.

"I knew what he wanted," said Katrina, still gazing into the flames, "and I saw which way the power would flow. I withheld myself from him, but at the same time, in subtle ways, I encouraged him. I discovered that he had a secret. There was a hidden room within the castle, reached by secret passageways behind the walls, where Aerin . . . sported . . . with the women he took there. He wanted to take me to that room, not only to satisfy his perverse desires, but to make a cuckold of his father out of spite and hatred. I resisted and, in time, Aerin saw fit to modify his goal. His plan would allow him to get everything he ever wanted, the dukedom, me, revenge upon his father . . . and power.

"So he set out to murder his own father and marry his father's mistress, who would overlook his depravities because she was really nothing but a whore. Which was how Aerin truly saw all women. He employed an assassin to accomplish the task while Derwyn was on the battlefield, and no sooner had the army left on the campaign than he announced our impending marriage, as if to show that he was unafraid of what his father might do on his return . . . because he knew Derwyn would not return."

Katrina closed her eyes, paused a moment, then continued with her story. "So I became his wife. And I became his plaything. In his secret room."

She took a deep breath and went on. "I shall spare you the lurid details of what went on there. Suffice it to say that I had indignities visited upon my body, and upon my very soul, that I would not wish on my worst enemy. I am sure that even common street whores are treated with more respect and tenderness. Aerin was very careful, and very knowledgeable, and did not leave any scars . . . at least, none that are visible to the eye.

"The battle was fought, meanwhile, and Derwyn was slain. And Aerin planned to make overtures of peace while he secretly prepared to wage another war. By then, I knew that I was pregnant with his child. And it would be a son. Not Aerin's first, but the first he would acknowledge as his heir. Delivered by his father's whore. There was something in that which appealed to him. I had followed the flow of power and suffered for it, and now I was Duchess of Boeruine. I was carrying the heir to the dukedom in my womb. And I determined that my son would not be born to such a father. I had paid the price, and it was time. The power would now flow to me."

She turned to face him. "I killed him. It may not have been my hand which struck the mortal blow, but I planned it. I, and another of his many victims brought his vicious depravity to an end in that very room in which he practiced and indulged it. He would never again hurt another woman. He would never again hurt me, and he would never hurt my unborn son.

"I had it given out that Aerin died from a seizure of the heart brought on by grief over his father's death—the final irony—and then I set about trying to make things right. For me, and for my people. For my son, and for the empire."

Dulcain shook his head. "Oh, my lady . . ."

"There is one thing more," she said. "Well . . . two things that you must know. After Aerin's death, the sorceress again appeared to me. And once again, she offered me the power of her staff. I refused her. There is more to life than power, as I think my mother always knew. I am a duchess now, and will soon be a regent, because Lord Moivar will accept my offer. He would be foolish not to. But for all that, my mother, a common scrubwoman, has more power than I shall ever have. The only kind of power that truly matters. And now, the other thing . . .

"You wonder why I have told you all this," she said, gazing at him. "Why I have revealed myself for what I truly am. It is because something happened back there in the great hall. Something wonderful . . . and frightening. You may think me mad, but the moment

I laid eyes on you, I knew that no matter what happens from now on, you would be the only man for me. In that instant when our eyes met I knew it, and it took my breath away. I somehow perceived in you everything I ever wanted in a man and never thought I'd have. It is not something that I can explain . . . but I just had to tell you. In that one moment, without volition on my part, I fell in love with you."

Dulcain held his breath. He could not move.

"And so," she said, "I had to tell you all about myself. Before I told you that. Because I would not have you thinking that you have won a duchess when, sadly, you have really only won a whore." She smiled wanly. "And now, I have surrendered all my power. To you, Bran Dulcain. Do with it what you will."

She stood before him, feeling nearly as vulnerable as she had with Aerin, and she wondered what he thought of her, what he would say. As he gazed at her, she sought to probe his thoughts, and found that she could not. The ability was gone. She had, indeed, surrendered all her power. And despite whatever happened now, she was glad of it. Now she was truly free.

For his part, Dulcain could not find words to express the way he felt. He had never in his life met a woman capable of such searing, self-effacing honesty. She had laid her soul bare to him. Risking all: his judgment, her position, and her honor. Everything. She had spoken to him from the heart, with an honesty and a forthrightness that touched him very deeply. And she had told him that she loved him. Told him outright, because she knew, and had no doubts. And as he saw her gazing at him, directly, waiting, unafraid, suddenly neither did he.

She swallowed hard, losing some of her composure, and a flicker of anxiety came into her eyes. "Please . . ." she said. "Say something."

Dulcain felt a powerful emotion welling up within his chest. "I am a fortunate, undeserving man," he said. "I have won neither a duchess nor a whore. But it seems I have somehow won a queen."

He went down to one knee, took her hand, and bowed his head to it.

"For Haelyn's sake, get up," she said, her voice breaking, "and kiss me."

And though his arms were strong, they were gentle as they embraced her, and his kiss was soft and tender, as a kiss should be.

* * * * *

He stood upon the Bridge of Sighs, feeling the cold wind blowing through his cloak and billowing it out away from him. The mists were undulating all around him in the desolate gray haze that floated over the abyss between two worlds. Silence. Only the sighing of the wind, rising and falling, rising and falling, like a distant storm.

Gannd just stood there for a while, alone with his thoughts. Alone in time. Precious time to think.

A great deal had happened since he'd left the Aelvinnwode. He had made a friend in Duncan Reese, and now he had a brother. A brother who was bound to him by blood, one who was closer to him than the half-brother he had never even met. The half-brother whom Boeruine and Avanil were now planning to depose. He did not know how he felt about that. Davan was nothing to him but a name. Still, there was a tie of some sort. A bond that was not a bond.

He came to discover his human heritage. He had lived all of his life up to this point as a Sidhelien. And he would always be that, deep down inside. They were his people, and he was one of them. But he was part human, too, in ways he was only beginning to discover. There had yet to be a resolution of some sort. And he did not know what that would be.

He closed his eyes and thought, "Uncle . . . I need you."

"I am here, Gannd."

The mists parted and Gylvain Aurealis appeared standing on the bridge, his midnight blue robes billowing around him.

"Thank you for coming, Uncle."

"Is all well with you, my lad?"

"Yes, Uncle. All is well."

"But you have not yet found whatever it is you seek."

Gannd smiled. "You have always known my thoughts better than I know them myself."

"But you have seen war."

"Yes. I have."

331

"I could tell. There is something different about you now. An innocence has been lost."

"It was not what I thought it would be."

"It never is."

"I am not sure what I expected. I expected to feel . . . something. I don't know. But while I was in the midst of it, there was no time to feel anything. There was time only to act, and react, and survive. And then . . . then there was something else."

His uncle stood and waited for him to go on as the wind rose and fell around them, sending tendrils of mist curling around their feet and bodies.

"I found out that I am blooded, Uncle."

"I thought you might be, but there was no way to know for certain. It was something that would be discovered only with time, and was nothing you could be prepared for."

"I understand that now. I have the ability to heal, as you know. I used it to save the life of my friend, Duncan Reese, who is now my oath brother."

"So? I have another nephew then, and your mother has another son. I trust Duncan Reese understands, appreciates, and is worthy of this honor."

"He does, Uncle. And he is. You will meet him one day and find out for yourself."

"I shall look forward to it."

"But there is more, Uncle. You know that I have discovered in myself the ability to heal. Well, there is also the power to destroy. A fearsome power. I discovered it in the midst of battle, when it manifested without warning. The humans call it divine rage."

Gylvain nodded somberly. "The Emperor Michael had that blood ability. I saw it manifested. And it is, indeed, a fearsome thing. How does the knowledge that you have it make you feel?"

"I am not really sure. A bit afraid, I think, knowing that such rage lies within me, waiting to be unleashed, and beyond control when I am in the grip of it."

"It is a weighty responsibility." Gylvain nodded. "A serious threat to your survival will unleash it. But it is also something that can be unleashed at will. Or manifested at the wrong time, if your will is not strong enough to govern your emotions."

"Yes, I understand that now. As I understand that there is still much that I must learn. I am told that the presence of divine rage within me means that I most likely have other blood abilities I have not yet discovered, powers that are just as strong. I need to find out what they are, and then I must make certain I am able to control them."

"I agree. And that, of course, means you are not yet ready to return to your people in Tuarhievel."

Gannd shook his head. "No, I cannot return yet. And though I miss my people, the humans are my people too. I have found that there are things about them to dislike, to despise even, but there are also things about them to admire. I am only now beginning to learn more about them, and about myself."

"Your mother will be saddened to learn that you are not yet coming home. But she will understand."

"There are things unfolding where I am that will affect us all profoundly," Gannd said. "Boeruine and Avanil are forging an alliance, with an aim to taking control of the regency. There are many who will not wish to see that come to pass. The empire is disintegrating, and I am not sure it can be saved. It will take a long time for it to fall, if it should fall. In that time, there will be war. Many wars. Many will die. Alliances will form to stand against Boeruine and Avanil. The balance of power will shift, and shift again. And it may take many years before it is all resolved, one way or another."

"And you feel that you have become a part of that?" his uncle said.

"We are all a part of it, whether we like it or not, Sidhelien and human alike," said Gannd. "The coming conflict will affect us all. And there are other powers, such as the awnsheghlien, who wait to see how it will all unfold, and bide their time to make their move. For now, perhaps, the Sidhelien can remain aloof from all of that, but they shall not be able to remain so for long. Sooner or later, the events that are being set in motion now shall involve us all."

"You may be right," said Gylvain. "Fhileraene believes the humans will eventually destroy one another, and then our time shall come again, and we shall regain what has been lost these many years. But if the awnsheghlien rise, and the world begins to fall around our ears, we shall not be able to remain passive observers.

We learned that lesson once before, at Deismaar. And it may be time for us to learn it once again."

"When the times comes, we must all be ready for it," Gannd said. "And I am still a long way from being ready. It may be a long time before I shall be coming home."

Gylvain nodded. "Do what you believe you must. Your mother and I will always support you, and our prayers to the Lady shall always be for you."

Gylvain began to fade away. "My time grows short here. I must return now."

"Farewell, Uncle."

"Farewell, Gannd. My love goes with you."

"And mine with you."

Gannd again stood alone upon the Bridge of Sighs, contemplating all he had learned. And he realized that no matter how much time he had to think about it, he would never fully understand it all. Perhaps that was all life truly was, an endless search for meaning. Knowledge gained only brought awareness of more ignorance. It was a never-ending cycle.

He grasped the amulet and closed his eyes to visualize the hawk. In that moment, over the sighing sound of the wind, he heard a horse whickering behind him. Except it did not sound like a normal horse. There was something strange about that sound, a hollow echoing that was somehow insubstantial . . . and malevolent.

He turned and stared into the mists. For a moment, they continued to swirl thickly around him, and then, briefly, they parted. The Cold Rider sat astride his shadowy mount, which appeared to be a part of him—or it—a unified, dark outline of a man and beast, without feature or definition, a roiling darkness that seemed to throb with an ominous presence.

The Cold Rider had no eyes, or at least none that Gannd could see. He had no face. He was just roiling darkness that shifted form from one instant to the next, flowing within itself obscenely. The Cold Rider remained in place. Either by choice, or by the cosmic laws of time and space. He had not yet found a way to cross the bridge. But Gannd sensed his desire and shuddered.

He took hold of his amulet once more and concentrated, imagining the hawk in flight, and as the bird took wing, its screeching cry echoed through the bottomless abyss like a mournful wail. Gannd felt himself hurtling through time and space, back to the world of light, back to his physical body, back to his chambers in the castle. He blinked and waited for his eyes to focus once again, waited for his body to respond to his animating presence, for the echo of the hawk to die away.

He stood and went over to the window that gave a view of the castle courtyard and the entrance to the gardens. Night had fallen. The torches were all lit. The guards stood at the gate. And beyond the walls, the windows of the city glowed with the flickering of candlelight and fires on the hearth. All was quiet and still. Peaceful. For at least one night.

Out of the corner of his eye, Gannd caught a flash of movement. He looked down into the courtyard, by the entrance to the gardens. He caught a glimpse of a figure wearing a long, dark, hooded cloak and carrying a wooden staff, heading toward the garden. As he gazed down, the figure stopped abruptly, turned, and looked straight up at him. He saw long, ash blond hair framing a woman's face, a face he had seen before, in camp one night, before he left the Aelvinnwode and came into the human world.

The Wizard gazed up at him for a moment, then gave him a nod in silent greeting.

"Not tonight, Wizard," Gannd said softly. "Not tonight, nor any other night."

And, as if she heard him—perhaps, somehow, she had—she turned abruptly, and disappeared through the archway leading to the garden. There was a torch set into the archway, lighting the flagstone path, and Gannd could see for a short distance through the archway as the path wound into the gardens. But as she passed through that arch, she did not reappear on the path beyond. Gone. Disappeared into thin air. But somehow, he knew he would be seeing her again.

Gannd wondered what it meant.

Epilogue

It was a day of celebration for the people of Daulton. That morning it had been announced—by criers who went through the city to every square and plaza—that Boeruine and Avanil had agreed upon a treaty of peace and mutual alliance, bound by the betrothal of the firstborn son of Katrina, the Duchess of Boeruine and the firstborn daughter of young Veladan, the Duke of Avanil. Katrina's son had not even been born yet and Veladan's daughter was not quite a gleam in her future father's eye, but such alliances were not unheard of, and a bond by marriage between two noble houses was as strong a bond as there could be.

Weary of war and the hardships it had imposed on everyone, the people of the city celebrated as the temple bells rang out, and dispatch riders were sent throughout both provinces to spread the word. For the time being, no one thought of how the other alliances would respond. No one stopped to consider how the regent would react. Everyone was happy. And no one thought of war.

Gaily beribboned maypoles had been set up in the city squares, and people danced around them with bells tied to their ankles as bards strummed on their instruments and sang happy ballads.

Jugglers, mimes, and acrobats performed for the people in the streets, not even bothering to pass their hats. Almost everyone wore masks and motley, and even the thieves and cutpurses took the day off. There were no strangers anywhere. A festival atmosphere prevailed, one that the city sorely needed after the grim times it had gone through.

For Katrina, it was an opportunity once more to see the city she hadn't seen since she'd come to the ducal court with her father to take part in the ball, and dance at her friend's birthday celebration with the young knight she was going to marry. *So much has changed,* she thought, *and yet the city still looks the same.*

As she walked through the crowded streets with Dulcain, Reese, and Gannd, whom she had gotten to know over the last week, and whose company helped lift her spirits, no one recognized her. The Duchess of Boeruine was not yet known by sight in Daulton, and masked and dressed in motley as she was, along with all the others, she basked in the anonymity which she enjoyed, never having thought that there would come a day when she would be glad to simply blend in with a crowd where no one had the slightest idea who she was.

Dulcain held her right arm, Reese her left, and Gannd walked beside Reese, wearing a short hooded cloak that concealed his silver-streaked hair and pointed ears, which by now had become known to many people in the city. They were just part of the crowd, out for a promenade, and Katrina felt deliriously happy.

Since the night she had declared her love for Bran Dulcain, they had been together almost every hour of every day, save for when she needed to confer with Ogbert over the ongoing negotiations of the treaty, which was comprised of complexities best left to ministers to haggle over, and when Dulcain had duties of his own to attend to. But every night they had spent together, not sharing a bed, but sharing conversation that often lasted into the early hours of the morning.

Most other men, Katrina thought, on having a beautiful woman declare her love to them, would not have hesitated to act upon the situation and take full advantage of it, even if they had the best intentions. Why wait, after all? But Bran Dulcain was different. He had acknowledged her feelings for him, and his for her, but at the same time, unlike Aerin, Derwyn, or any other man she'd ever known, he had not pressed for consummation.

She would have been quite willing. On that first night, she would have surrendered to him gladly. But Bran was not a young man, ruled by passion. He had passion, plenty of it, but he governed it wisely and maturely. They had strong feelings for each other, powerful feelings that came from a recognition that they were meant for one another, but Bran wanted to take the time to let those feelings grow and blossom into something based not on passion alone, or a sense that they were fated for each other, but also on mutual affection and respect that was based on friendship. He wanted to know everything about her. Not just the things that were significant, but little things, inconsequential things, the sum of which, she realized, made up a great part of who and what she was. And each day, as they grew to know one another better, she came to love him more and more.

Though it had not been long at all, the dark days at Seaharrow seemed somehow very distant now, and she was not anxious to return. And now that the alliance had been formalized, there was no real reason why she should. Eventually, she knew, she would have to go back. She was the Duchess of Boeruine, and she had responsibilities to the people of her province. But when that time came, she would go back with Bran Dulcain. At least, she hoped she would.

That was something they had not discussed as yet. She was the ruler of Boeruine, and he was the Baron of Daulton and lord commander of the army of Avanil. If he were to return to Seaharrow with her as her consort, he would not have to give up his title, but in all likelihood, he would have to give up the command of the army, which he had come to love. And the men, in turn, loved their commander, Bran the Blade. But if she chose to remain in Daulton with him, then she would have to make arrangements to ensure that Boeruine would be well governed in her absence, since for the sake of her son and the future plans of the alliance, she could not give up her title, though she knew that if Bran asked her to, she would probably throw everything else aside and do it.

Ogbert could govern the province in her absence. She could elevate him to the rank of baron and appoint him as a sort of ducal regent. He would be more than up to the task and would perform it far better than she ever could. And from time to time, she could return to visit Seaharrow, perhaps much like the emperor used to do during the days of the summer court. That seemed like the best solution, though she had not yet discussed it with Bran. Either way, it didn't really matter. They would solve whatever difficulties they would face together. For today, at least, she was not Katrina, Duchess of Boeruine. She was just Katrina Tremayne, a woman she had almost lost and forgotten, a woman in love.

"Damn, I'm thirsty," Bran said. "I need an ale to wet my whistle. Reese, you're buying."

"Me? Why am I buying?"

"Because it is your turn."

"It was my turn last time! It's Gannd's turn."

"I think not," said Gannd.

"Oh, yes it is!"

"Well, is it or isn't it?" asked Bran.

"I tell you, I paid last time!" Reese insisted. "It seems to me Gannd missed his turn the last two times! He can bloody well pay his share!"

"Oh, I see," said Gannd. "All the times I've saved your life and you begrudge me the small price of a drink?"

"Oh, that's low!" said Reese. "What about all those bloody daggers I bought you that cost a prince's ransom, eh?"

"Well, I suppose if your life is merely worth the price of a few daggers, then I can scarcely argue," Gannd replied.

"Enough!" Katrina said, laughing. "I am going to buy drinks for everyone."

"You?" said Bran. "Since when does a woman pay?"

"And what is wrong with a woman paying?"

"Bran, don't be a fool," said Reese. "A beautiful woman willing to pay her own way? How often does a man find such incredible good fortune?"

"We'll settle this inside," said Bran, stopping at the entrance to a tavern. "This looks like as good a place as any."

"After you, my lord commander," Reese said, opening the door.

Laughing, they all entered the tavern. It was empty. The windows were shuttered and the benches all piled up on the tables.

"The place is closed," said Gannd. "The celebration . . ."

"Nonsense," said Dulcain. "The door was open."

"Halloo!" cried Reese. "Is anybody here? Come on then, you have thirsty customers!"

A woman raised her graying head up from behind the bar. "We're closed," she said. "The festival. You can buy your drinks out on the street today."

Katrina froze. She knew that voice! "Haelyn help me," she said. She came forward and removed her mask. "Mother?"

The woman gasped and held on to the bar to steady herself. "It cannot be!" she said. "Katrina?"

She glanced back at the others. Dulcain just stood there, grinning. So were Reese and Gannd.

"Katrina, is that really you?"

"Oh, Mother!" She ran to her and the two women embraced, both sobbing.

"I'll drink to that," said Reese, clapping Dulcain on the back, and nodding with satisfaction.

Gannd smiled. "I'll buy."